Go Ask Malice: Murder at Woodstock

The Rock & Roll Murders: A Rennie Stride Mystery

Also by Patricia Kennealy Morrison

The Keltiad

The Copper Crown
The Throne of Scone
The Silver Branch
The Hawk's Gray Feather
The Oak Above the Kings
The Hedge of Mist
Blackmantle
The Deer's Cry

Strange Days: My Life With and Without Jim Morrison

Son of the Northern Star (2013)

The Rock & Roll Murders: The Rennie Stride Mysteries

Ungrateful Dead: Murder at the Fillmore
California Screamin': Murder at Monterey Pop
Love Him Madly: Murder at the Whisky
A Hard Slay's Night: Murder at the Royal Albert Hall
Go Ask Malice: Murder at Woodstock

Scareway to Heaven: Murder at the Fillmore East (2013)

Go Ask Malice
Murder at Woodstock

PATRICIA MORRISON

Lizard Queen Press

This book is a work of fiction. Although certain real locations, events and public figures are mentioned, all names, characters, places and events described herein are the product of the author's imagination or are used fictitiously. Any resemblance to actual events, places or persons (living or dead) is purely coincidental.

GO ASK MALICE: Murder at Woodstock

 For further information, contact: Lizard Queen Press, 151 1st Avenue, Ste. 120, New York, NY 10003.

On the Web:
www.facebook.com/patriciakmorrison
pkmorrison.livejournal.com
mojohotel.blogspot.com
myspace.com/hermajestythelizardqueen

Jacket art and design by Andrew Przybyszewski
Interior book design by the author
Production by Lorrieann Russell

Acknowledgments

In the forty-three years since Woodstock, the event itself has taken on mythic proportions. Indeed, it did so almost as soon as the last riff sounded, before so much as a single piece of rubbish had been cleared away from the field.

Therefore, memories of those who were there—memories perhaps never all that reliable to begin with, having been formed in the first instance under the influence of various substances both lawful and un-, or later, as a result of retconning or selective recall—offer up wildly differing accounts. Everybody seems to recollect a different sequence of events: even the artists themselves often do not remember when they played, and the many books and web pages only perpetuate the discrepancies.

I was there, of course, with guest status and a performer's pass (I still have it), even though I was naught but a humble rock critic and editor of a national magazine; and although uninfluenced by anything stronger than a few glasses of champagne and, yeah, okay, perhaps a contact high or two, or four, I too have an occasional bit of difficulty recalling the exact chronology.

Where personal recollections close to my heart are concerned, my memory is word-perfect and crystal-clear. Here, I have simply done my best to be as true to life as I can, based on not only memory but much, *much* research, and the fictional elements are all based on true experiences—my own, both at Woodstock and elsewhere, with members of the rockerverse in general, as journalist, observer, rock consort and record-company exec. Except for the murders, naturally.

Of course, there was a seething volcano of politics, power plays, social subtext, finance and high drama (especially high…) underpinning all this. I don't have the space, time or indeed inclination to get into that here, so have tried to merely suggest it—a sketch, not a portrait. There are many, many excellent books for that intensive, detailed sort of thing, if that's what you're looking for.

In the end, this is a novel, not a Woodstock history text. But it's nice to get things right, or at least as right as one can. Even in fiction, truth must be served…and vice versa.

Oh, and as usual there are geographical shenanigans: such things as restaurants and motels and fabulous East Village brownstones may be unrecognizable to those familiar with the real-life locations, or even invented to suit my purposes. But you knew that.

Thanks as always to Jesse V. Coffey, Susan Harwood Kaczmarczik, Carole McNall, Michael Rosenthal and Lorrieann Russell, the benefit of whose eagle eyes and wonderfully discerning judgments I am most grateful to have;

to Andrew Przybyszewski for another fabulous piece of cover art;

and to Liz Williams for letting me put her into the story.

With deepest admiration and heartfelt thanks to all the great and now-legendary performers who did their best to bring us their best; to all the crew and staff and organizers who worked so hard to make it happen; and to all the fans who held the line for valor in the field. I was lucky to have been there, and I will never forget it.

For, and in memoriam:

Susan P. Donoghue, who accompanied me there;
Pauline Rivelli, who sent me there;
and David G. Walley, who wasn't there but who really should have been.

Lady of the Lake

Do you hear my lady
in the garden singing?
Do you see my lady
in the sunset ringing?

She is gold and she is silver
She is pearl and diamond light
She knows dawn and she knows darkness
She's a palace in the night

She's the new Scheherazadeh
She's the queen of heart and soul
She's the key to my survival
She's my lady rock and roll

Do you know my lady
like the panther springing?
To and fro my lady
like the falcon winging

She will feed you with her stories
You will laugh and you will learn
She will lead you on to glories
You will bleed and you will burn

'Cause she's the new Scheherazadeh
Like a glowing ember'd coal
She's the key to your survival
She's my lady rock and roll

[bridge]

Did you meet my lady
in the tempest walking
Oh so fleet my lady
like a lioness stalking

Listen to her when she tells you
what you really need to know
Pay attention if she warns you
where to run and how to go

She may beckon and beguile you
She may push you straight away
She may wreck and reconcile you
But you'll always get to stay

'Cause she's the new Scheherazadeh
And she'll always take her toll
She's the means of our revival
She's my lady rock and roll

She can fill the world's desire
(Do you see my lady like the moonfire glowing)
She can calm the raging wave
(Do you flee my lady like the night-tide going)
She can dance upon the fire
(Do you hear my lady in the temple chanting)
She can kill and she can save
(Do you fear my lady in the shadows haunting)

Yeah, she's the new Scheherazadeh
She was born to save our souls
She's our witness and our rival
She's my lady rock and roll

She's the new Scheherazadeh
She's the one who keeps it whole
She's the key to my survival
She's my lady rock and roll

[hook out to fade]

~Turk Wayland

Hmmm, something other than the usual is going on here.

– David Crosby,
commenting on Woodstock

Prologue

New York City / Upstate New York: August 1969

A lovely green-grassed hollow under a summer sky like thick blue cream: a vast bowl of a lush, gently sloping alfalfa meadow like a natural amphitheater, surrounded by trees full and heavy in August leaf, rolling hills all around, several tranquil ponds and lakes not too far distant.

Down at the bottom of the slope, workers are busily building a behemoth of a tall stage and its assorted support buildings, erecting something a few dozen yards away that looks like a giant oversized Mongolian yurt with angled treetrunk pillars and open sides.

A bridge is being tossed up over a farm road, connecting at one end to the rising stage, at the other to the vicinity of the yurt. Elsewhere among the cornfields, trailers are parked and tents and stalls are going up; signposts are being nailed to the trunks of trees in the bordering woods. Cows watch placidly from neighboring pastures, wondering what it could all possibly have to do with them.

A pleasant-faced, shirtless young man with wildly curling hair and a buckskin vest rides around the field on a motorcycle or a borrowed horse, giving orders, receiving assurances that it's all groovy and it's all going to happen; vans and trailers deliver huge loads of assorted electronic equipment; other workers are raising tall towers like skeletal metal Christmas trees to carry lighting and sound, laying cables and wires across the grassy fields, building roads, digging water wells. All preparing for Sullivan County's unlikely date with the history books.

A hundred miles to the southeast, in New York City, people are packing their bags and their tape recorders and their guitar cases, getting ready to make the trip. As are their counterparts in San Francisco, Los Angeles, London and all points between. This is one occasion that even the most blasé and jaded of citizens of the rockerverse do not want to miss. The heaviest of heavy groups have been invited, the entire rock and counterculture press corps, mainstream press as well, the officer class of every record label going.

And also, it seems, every person in the world under thirty, and many over, who ever listened to a note of rock and roll music in their lives, plan on being there. And quite a few, as it turns out, will be.

But no one yet imagines that it will be not just a concert but a watershed moment, something to define and delineate an era: that years from now, decades even, people will speak of a thing called Woodstock and wonder at its enduring and historic power. "Were you there?" they will ask—eagerly, wistfully, enviously, as if it had been Runnymede or Waterloo. "Were you! What was it like? Tell us about it. We wish we could have been there too, you are so lucky"...

And the campfire tales will go on.

~1~

"AN OUTDOOR ROCK CONCERT? In a Catskills cow pasture? Can't I just drink some hemlock and die the easy way?"

Rennie Stride *really* didn't want to go to this thing called Woodstock. But Oliver Fingal Flaherty Fitzroy, first Baron Holywoode—gazillionaire publisher, *literal* British press lord and past master of manipulation, universally known as Fitz, Rennie's supreme boss of bosses, and also, oddly, her friend—simply sat back and sipped his tea and gazed contentedly around his luxurious fortieth-floor, midtown-Manhattan office, and after a while Rennie closed her eyes and heaved a sigh of capitulation.

"You do this every time, Rennie darling," Fitz pointed out, quite correctly. "Whenever I give you a splendidly plummish assignment—a huge important cover story, something that any other reporter I know would be giving me great big fat wet kisses for—you piss and moan for a while and then you give in. You know it, I know it, why do we always have to do the same little dance, charming though it is?"

"It wouldn't be as much fun if we didn't," said Rennie, grinning. "And that would be *so* disappointing. So? What else can you offer me? To sweeten the, as it were, pot. And why are you even here in New York anyway?"

Fitz grinned back. "I've relocated for a bit, actually; didn't I tell you? Of course I did; you've simply forgotten. Must be all those drugs you do…just kidding, I know you're most judicious about expanding your already considerable consciousness. In any case, it's all by way of a refreshing change from London, for a year or two. My business interests are moving more to the States lately, and it seems like a good idea to be where they are. Not unlike your own reasons for moving here from L.A., if I may say so. But getting back to this Woodstock thing: if it's any inducement, or even a workable bribe, I'll fly you in and out on my own personal helicopter, or one of the smaller private planes."

Rennie inspected the thin bone-china teacup—she had a passion for pretty dishware—and decided she liked it, but liked her own patterns better.

"I love that you have your own air force…do you have a private navy too? No? New York being an island, I'm sure you'll get around to that. Just a matter of time. I can see you in the tastefully understated uniform of an Admiral of the Fleet… Well, it's a tempting offer, but I'm already set for transport. I live with this guitar player, remember? And he's got this band? And they're really, really famous? They're kicking off this year's big tour actually *at* 'this Woodstock thing'. Sort of a pre-tour warm-up, really; the road trip doesn't start till two weeks later. So I'm going up there with him. With Prax too; her band is playing there too."

"My fond regards to Lord Saltire and Miss McKenna, of course; they've both been very, very good for me. Though of course you've been even better. What a clever lad I was to hire you. But haven't I heard that the reviews aren't so good for Lionheart's new album?"

Rennie went immediately all defensive and protective. "And only a bitch would say so. But no, you're right, they haven't been. But that's not Lionheart's fault. Or Turk's either."

"I never said it was! Christ, you're so touchy on his behalf. It's rather sweet, really. But what's the problem?"

"Besides stupid critics and stupider fans? Oh, not much." Looking aggrieved, Rennie poured herself some more tea. "The tour is their big and only one for this year; it's huge, goes from Labor Day to the sixth of December. With time off for good behavior, here and there. All in support of this album, *Cities of the Plain*, which was released on the first of the month, and which as you so kindly point out is doing not particularly superstarrily. Possibly there will be a greatest-hits Christmas release, Turk says, if this one continues to underwhelm the charts."

"I actually listened to the copy you were good enough to send me. It's rather *different* from their usual thing, isn't it, all that symphonic, orchestrated stuff, backup singers. But I quite liked it, truly I did."

"Sadly, you seem to stand almost alone in your opinion," she bitterly informed him. "It's been blasted by critics and seriously unbought by fans. This is the first time Lionheart has ever been ripped up by the press like that," she added, after brooding for a few moments. "It's like Lionheart's *Satanic Majesties* or *Soft Parade*: yet another hugely famous, excessively idolized, ridiculously good band humbly trying to change up their chops, do something artistically new and different, something to stretch themselves and make their audiences reach a bit. And, not unadjacently, to hopefully stop the critics harping that they keep on making the same damn album under different titles. So when they finally do try something new, they get savagely bushwhacked for trying. By the same people who, if they'd made yet another spectacular blues-rock album, would now be bitching equally savagely that the band wasn't stretching *enough*."

Fitz offered a sympathetic face. "Damned if they do, damned if they don't. How are they feeling about it?"

"Pretty shocked and very rattled. They've had bad reviews before, of course, every band has, but nothing like these. I've spanked bands myself—in the critical sense only, so don't leer like that—but I've never trashed *anyone* for *anything* the way Lionheart's being trashed for this. And especially the way Turk's being personally trashed. They'd cut him more slack if he'd barbecued a puppy."

"How's the house coming on?" asked Fitz diplomatically, after a rather fraught silence.

Back in early spring, following their formal engagement at his family's country seat in England, superstar Turk Wayland and super-reporter Rennie Stride, who'd lived together in Los Angeles for a year and a half now, had decided to change their lives altogether and move back to Rennie's hometown, New York, though they were still keeping Turk's sprawling eyrie high in the Hollywood Hills, and Rennie had come east to look for a place. She'd found a lovely old brownstone in the East Village; Turk, upon seeing it, had been likewise charmed, but had also decided it wasn't big enough, and had proceeded to buy not only it but the two adjoining ones, and to slap them all together. Which is the sort of thing you can do when you're one of the most famous and successful rock stars in the world, and, oh, incidentally, when you're the Earl of Saltire and your grandfather is the second-richest duke in England (recently up from third).

"Three houses, actually. They're smallish, and his lordship didn't think one would be spacious enough to accommodate all our needs. His needs, mostly: a studio and rehearsal space for him and enough bedrooms for the band to crash in. My own needs are rather humbler: more like having separate dressing rooms and separate bathrooms and a nice sitting-room off our own bedroom, because that way domestic bliss lies. And a cozy little den where I can write in peace."

"Not too much to ask for."

"Right? Plus when you're used to living in a castle... well, you know how *that* is. So he bought these houses on East Tenth and Stuyvesant Streets, a few blocks from the Fillmore East. They're in the final stages of being combined into one, by minions who are of a sufficiency to have raised the Pyramids. When you're Pharaoh, nothing is unpossible. Just harness up ten thousand slaves, problem solved. So let it be written, so let it be done."

"Yes, but you said Pharaoh will be out of town and on the road for the next three months."

"That's right, and in his absence, the minions will of course be commanded by his loving Pharaohessa, who will whip them into serving with rigor if she has to. Or, more likely, bribe, cajole and sweet-talk them into it. Whatever it takes to get the job done."

"I don't doubt it for a moment." Fitz offered Rennie more tea, which she politely declined. "How's his grandfather the Duke doing? I read in one of my own papers that he'd had some health difficulties recently."

Rennie snorted. "That outrageous old man. Do you know, he actually quizzed me about my reproductive capabilities when Turk and I were over there back in February getting engaged? Yes! He did! Was wondering if I'd be up to producing the heir and the spare. Which of course I assured him I was; hey, he wants fertile, *I'll* give him fertile! Am I not a terrifically creative person in all fields of endeavor? Damn right I am! I'll plop out baby Tarrants till the cows come home...with Turk's cooperation, natch. Well, getting back to your question, he seems to be doing better, the Duke does, thank you for asking. But though I'd never say this to Turk, I've got a feeling I'd better start looking for a suitable black dress."

"Oh dear. Will Turk be terribly upset, do you think?"

"Hard to say. They love each other, I'm sure, in that strange British way you strange top-drawer British have, but they aren't exactly on the warmest and fuzziest of terms, no, His Grace of Locksley being the one who all but blotted him from the family Bible when he went into rock and roll seven years ago. Still, he is the Duke, and he is also Granddad, so yeah, Turk is down about it, though he tries to hide it and we don't discuss it amongst ourselves. In spite of everything, I rather like him myself, the Guv'nor, as Turk calls him; we got on pretty groovily, even given that fertility issue. So there's a sort of low-grade bummer in the atmosphere, though it's not generally acknowledged. And then of course there was Brian... So not exactly a festive aura going around at the moment, no. And this prospective festival doesn't really improve the festive mood. At least for me it doesn't."

Brian Jones, guitarist and founder of the Rolling Stones, had been, along with Keith Richards, a longtime friend of Turk's, ever since their early starving-artist days scrabbling in dank London blues cellars, and his sudden and mysterious death by drowning a month ago had been a huge shock to everyone in the music scene. There had been some dark murmurs of foul play, but the coroner's inquest had put it down to a chronic asthma condition and being overcome by an attack in his swimming pool alone late at night at his country estate, without access to his inhalers.

Most people seemed to buy the official story, though the rumors of murder and payoff and cover-up continued to bubble darkly; the truth would probably not be known for years, maybe never. Rennie, in her not-so-secret identity as Murder Chick, had typically eyed the whole thing with deep suspicion, though, rather atypically, she had withheld public judgment. For his part, Turk had merely expressed relief that they hadn't been in England when Brian died, or else she would have felt duty-bound to look into it. Which she hadn't denied.

The Stones had already been scheduled that week for a massive open-air free concert in London's Hyde Park, and it had hastily been converted into something of an ad hoc memorial for Brian, with Mick Jagger reciting from Shelley's gorgeously elegiac ode "Adonais" and thousands of white butterflies being released from the stage, in apparent metaphorical token of setting free Brian's soul, or absolution from guilt, or something. Rennie, who with Turk had gone over for the concert and to pay respects at the funeral—and also for a prestigious Lionheart gig at the Royal Opera House attended by royalty, and attended by Turk's family too, which was *much* scarier—had scoffed at the ill-conceived and typically rock-star gesture. The poor farm-raised creatures had all died within moments of being given their freedom—of the heat, of stress, of being crushed like, well, bugs—and their little corpses had dropped like, well, stones, all over the stage and the crowd. How very symbolic.

Butterfly Brian had done the same, and not even metaphorically: for many months he had seemed bereft of purpose, his springs of action dry, his drug use off the chart; and once Mick and Keith had finally cut him loose from the Stones a couple of weeks before, the writing was on the wall for those who cared to read it. Only two of the band had attended his funeral, neither of them those particular two; he'd been laid to rest in an ornate bronze casket rumored to have been supplied by Bob Dylan, in a cemetery in the same little Cotswold village where he had been born twenty-seven years before.

And then of course there *had* been a murder at the concert, yeah right what a surprise, which of course Rennie *had* been obliged, as Murder Chick, to look into, which of course *had* involved yet another encounter with Detective Chief Inspector Gordon Dakers of the Metropolitan Police and his loyal assistant, the pink and shiny Sergeant Plum...

She came back to the moment, listening to Fitz prattle on about his own newly purchased abode a block uptown from Jackie Kennedy Onassis on Fifth Avenue, and the great views of Central Park and how much his wife enjoyed living in New York in a nice place that wasn't rented and was really theirs. Especially since Fitz was expanding his New York media holdings and wanted a permanent base of operations that could also be a solid tax deduction for business, even if it was only a co-op, however duplexed and spacious and palatial, and not three historic brownstones being tastefully smushed into a mini-mansion...

"How's your fair Lady Alexandra getting on? All settled in? You didn't bring the kids with you?"

"We did, but they're only here for the summer hols. Back they all go in termtime, which starts up presently. Sebastian is headed for his first year at Cambridge, having been offered a place at my own old college of Magdalene, which is of course delightful. Jamie is still at Wellington and pointed for Oxford, Christ Church being his first choice; and young Sophie will be starting at Roedean, so pleasing. We're hoping for Oxbridge for her too, naturally, when the time comes, though at the moment I believe she would like nothing better than to be a horse. No, no, that's right, not to *have* a horse, to *be* a horse; she's a strange child. Alix and I discussed transplanting her and Jamie and entering them at equivalent institutions here, of which I'm told there are many and quite excellent ones too, but they wept so bitterly at having to leave their sticky little friends that we decided to let them stay. It works out better for everyone, as who knows how long we'll be based here, and they're at school almost all the year in any case so it really makes no difference. Both sets of grandparents are delighted to keep an eye on them for us; we'll go back between terms to be at home with them, of course, and on odd weekends, and next long vacs they'll come here again. Alix has always loved New York, so she's glad of the prolonged stay; you and Lord Saltire must come to dinner at our place some night."

"And Lord and Lady Holywoode to ours. Once we actually have a functioning dining room. I'll even break out the Wedgwood and Waterford for you, since I'll be the only commoner at the table and will need to demonstrate my gentility. Hey, it's true! Turk and Alix were born noble, and you earned your nobility through the sweat of your brow, but I, alas, am but a humble peasant."

Fitz tried valiantly, but could not control the explosion

of mirth that issued forth upon that straight-faced statement. "Excuse me, but anyone *less* humble or peasanty I cannot *possibly* imagine. No matter the circumstances of your birth, impeccably middle-class as I'm sure they were, you were *born* a duchess, indeed you are more duchessal than all the duchesses I've ever met put together—and I mean that in the nicest possible sense. I'm sure Turk is only delighted he can finally legitimize you, as it were. Because it will not be all that long until you too are ennobled," he added, with a certain archness. "And by the power of love, which is the best ennobling there is. Not that you aren't noble by nature, of course, as I've always said."

"Thank you. And I feel sometimes that I too will have earned it," she added darkly.

"Oh?"

"You needn't give me that ever so significant 'Oh?', thanks ever so much. No, nothing's wrong between us, in fact things couldn't be better. It's just that sometimes it all gets a bit...much. And by no means is it always about his peerage-osity. I was thinking the other day about how rock and roll has catapulted totally unprepared people into social strata they might never have reached otherwise. And that is not meant in a snobby way, so you can take that look off your face right now, Skepticus Maximus."

"Sorry. But what then?"

"What indeed! Instant world-wide fame. Instant hugeous riches. Instant access to any member of the opposite sex, or the same sex, who catches their eye. Instant social clout and public influence and adulation by millions. People hanging on their every word and imitating their every deed. Success beyond their parents' wildest upwardly mobile dreams and aspirations. All at a preposterously young age. And I don't begrudge any of it to any of them, not for a heartbeat. But so many of them are not equipped in the smallest way, shape or form to handle it effectively. Or at all. People who grew up as normal human beings—middle class, working class. People without a handle on this kind of thing, or, indeed, a handle to their names. So we see the ridiculous nouveau-riche spending sprees and the inane public pronouncements and the epic sluttery and the legions of parasite hangers-on and the self-medication with powerful illegal substances. Uncontrolled acting-out spoiled-brat behaviors, sure, but also in many cases desperate psychological coping mechanisms for something we've never seen the like of and have no experience dealing with. Yet I have to say, I don't think I could cope any better with it myself."

"Oh, I don't know about that last," objected Fitz. "But yes, you're dead right about all the rest of it. Still, how does that affect Miss Stride and Mr. Wayland? Both of whom," he added, "seem to me to be firmly grounded in reality."

"Too kind… Well, it's the double whammy for us, or at least it is for me. I didn't set out to be internationally notorious, you know. I only wanted to be a competent journalist, with a bit of the old flair: do good work, write about what I liked or loathed or was outraged by, maybe get nominated for a Pulitzer one day, maybe even win one. A not immodest, realistically achievable goal, as I think you as my employer will agree? Yes… But people *will* persist in getting themselves knocked off in my presence, in increasing numbers and increasingly dramatic ways, thus precipitating me right into the middle of sensational public notice."

"Not your fault."

"No indeed. And then, also through no fault of my own, I fell in love. With Himself: Turk Wayland, superstar guitar stud, *and* Richard Tarrant, present Earl of Saltire, imminent Marquess of Raxton and future Duke of Locksley. Which upcoming loving marital attachment to whom is going to precipitate me right into the middle of the English ruling classes. To the top of the heap, pretty much. Only rung higher than the Tarrants of Locksley is royalty."

She looked him right in the eye. "But you know all about it. You came of poor but honest stock. You had the proverbial fire in the belly, and you worked hard to get what you wanted. And you got it—the First at Cambridge, the media empire, the London headquarters palace in the Strand, the Georgian country estate and Belgravia townhouse and Scottish hunting lodge, the pretty children in the best schools, even the title. And also by reason of your own loving marital attachment to a spouse of nobility, you were precipitated even further up the ranks. You worked for it, and you earned it. It's been the same for you, or near enough, anyway."

Fitz leaned back complacently in his big leather chair. "Near enough... But why are we going through all this now, dear girl? You told me back in London, after your betrothal and before you returned here, that you and Turk and Richard had sorted all that out."

"And so we have. At least to our own satisfaction. No, I was really sort of riffing on what an amazing force for change rock is. On so many levels. Change you don't think you're paying for, but you are, oh yes you are, and you do, and you will. On so many levels. You think you're just playing your music and that's all you ever wanted. But it isn't. Or even if it is, you don't realize what else comes with the dinner, things that you don't want and never ordered. You can have all the fame and money in the world, but you're still not going to be able to pay up when that bill comes to the table. And so you end up making other people pay for it instead."

"I guarantee you that not one rocker in ten thousand thinks that way, ducks," said Fitz gently. "Not one in a million people. And if they do, it's purely because it's something they've decided they want for themselves and they don't care a toss about the consequences. So don't torture yourself. Write a book about it, if it will ease your mind. Or at least a lovely big Sunday magazine think-piece for me. But the only thing you should be bothering your clever pretty little head about is Turk, and from what I've seen he's got it dead to rights, and has from the start. Nailed down, hogtied, mussed and sussed. So does Prax, for that matter. And your friends the Graham Sonnets and the Ned Ravens and quite a few others. All strong, smart people, like you. As for the rest of them, it is indeed tiresome, but they're not really your problem, are they?"

Rennie looked levelly at him for a few silent moments. "They are when they end up dead. That's pretty tiresome too."

~2~

RENNIE BROODED ABOUT it all the way home, as her cab fought through rush-hour traffic on Broadway, heading downtown to the East Village. Fitz was right, of course. It really wasn't anything she should be concerning herself with. Her sole object of concern should be Turk, and as she had told Fitz, they were fine. And they were, they truly were: that wasn't just bright-siding, or denial, or anything else along those lines. They were joyful in their lives and delighted they had made the move to New York from L.A. No, they just had a very particular set of circumstances with which to deal, and they were dealing when and as they had to, and it was all as it should be. And the love was paramount. Again as it should be.

With an effort, she regained control of the mental wheel. This Woodstock thing, now that was something to be *correctly* brooding about, and preparing for, and she only had about a week to do so. It had started off as the East Coast's answer to the Monterey Pop Festival of two years back, and it had quickly spiraled into a big giant rock nebula. Woodstock's organizers, however disorganized they may have appeared, and indeed in truth often were, had nonetheless done a masterful job of pulling the thing together after early and severe setbacks. Chiefest among them: not being able to actually hold the big dance *at* Woodstock.

A small, laid-back, upstate Catskill mountain community in the Hudson River Valley, half artsy-craftsy, half plain country folks, Woodstock had always been hip, in an undertoned sort of way, but had garnered some significant cachet in recent years. Bob Dylan lived there, and indeed had almost died there, in the famous motorcycle accident that had changed not only his life but his music; he was hardly the only local luminary, though perhaps arguably the brightest. So the people who wanted to put on this big exciting blowout festival had naturally thought that Woodstock, as the nearest Monterey equivalent, would be the perfect place to hold it.

But the people who actually *lived* in Woodstock had said no. In fact, they'd said hell no, grimly citing the hordes, the mess, the noise, the traffic, the mess, the hordes, and they had a point, or three or four, and the festival was bounced. And so the site got shifted a few miles away to another pretty mountain town called Saugerties. Then the Saugertisians too declined the honor, necessitating a second move to yet a third Catskill village, Wallkill, a bit further down the Hudson Valley—all the time steadily migrating south and west away from Woodstock itself, but keeping the prestigious Woodstock name for cachet and branding purposes. For a while there, Rennie reflected, it had looked as if it were really going to happen in Wallkill. Posters and tickets were even printed up. But Wallkill, after some hard thinking, had likewise closed its gates, its ranks and its territory against the barbarians.

So, again, it all fell through, and messengers were sent forth in haste across the land, or at least across that region of New York State, to try to scare up a new place for the festival to lay its weary little head. Frustrated and getting a bit desperate at the manifold turndowns, festival organizers and guiding creative lights Artie Kornfeld and Michael Lang had gone west, young men, finally finding the frontier of their dreams in a quiet and verdant corner of the Sullivan County Catskills. The area had been known to New York City residents for decades as the Borscht Belt, a predominantly Jewish family-oriented vacationland, and the names of the resorts bore it out: Grossinger's, Kutsher's, the Nevele, the Concord and many more.

But by the mid-60's the Borscht Belt was already becoming unbuckled: Route 17, the local and scenic, if narrow, artery that ran across the Southern Tier of New York State all the way west, ran past far too many abandoned and deteriorating hotels, camps and resorts on the downslope of their prime. No surprise: for the same money, families were finding that they could fly to destinations like Europe, the Caribbean, even Hawaii, so that a summer sojourn in a little cabin colony or resort in the Jewish Alps, as the hills were affectionately known, quickly lost, for many, its folksy appeal.

But what had always been so good about the region was still good: pastoral green landscapes, convenient highway access from pretty much anywhere, proximity to New York, Philadelphia, Boston and other major cities of the Northeast. So when Woodstock Ventures, the corporation formed by Kornfeld, Lang and their money-man partners

Joel Rosenman and John Roberts, all in their middle twenties, ventured up Route 17 and then hung a left to the tiny, quiet hamlet of Bethel, and came upon Max Yasgur's six-hundred-acre dairy farm, they looked upon it and saw that it too was good, and better than good. And there it was that they planted their flag. Nobody at the time realized that they were effectively founding a nation.

Or so at least it would seem in retrospect. Hindsight is always 20-20 on eyecharts that regular vision blurs out in the actual moment: right now, nobody was planning on anything more than a groovy good time. Monterey Pop had been a music watershed; the plan for Woodstock was more like a music Niagara. The initial publicity had been for "A Weekend in the Country", then it became "Three Days of Peace and Music", and that was what was being prepared for. Licenses and contracts had been obtained, deposits paid, workers hired to build the stage, set up the lighting and sound systems, arrange food and sanitation facilities. And now, on Yasgur's farm, the music, and even some peace, was about to start happening.

In the meantime, Lang and Kornfeld had not been idle. Far from letting a mere trifle like no actual festival site stop them, they had been signing up artists from London to Los Angeles, just as artists had been signed up for Monterey two summers ago. But this time the acts were not naïve unknown minstrels but powerhouses of rock: acts like Jefferson Airplane, the Grateful Dead, the Who, Jimi Hendrix, Janis Joplin. Acts that had begun at Monterey as cheerful little chirping birds had now fledged into rocs, phoenixes, mighty eagles whose plumes blazed in the sun, the thunder of whose wings rent the air, whose barbaric and exceedingly musical yawps were heard from one side of the world to the other.

Such a lineup as had never before been seen on any stage anywhere. And such a lineup as wouldn't come cheap, either. But that was okay too. There was real money in rock these days, big huge money, though not so huge by far as there would be in years to come. At least the artists would be getting paid, and paid well, not like Monterey, where they hadn't been paid at all. And this time, also not like Monterey, there were real film people with real deals up front, to capture the music magic for posterity. Not a Danny Marron in the bunch, thank God.

By the time Rennie got to Danny Marron of infamous memory, who as far as she knew was still in a Northern California slammer, and rightly so, the taxi had turned into East Tenth Street and was stopping in front of the house. As she counted out the fare, she resigned herself to her fate and her doom. It seemed likely that she was not alone in her reluctance to trek upstate and sit in a field for three days, no matter who got up onstage to entertain her. Probably not even the Archangel Gabriel could blow his horn with sufficient chops to inspire her with real enthusiasm for the enterprise, and on balance it was pretty unlikely that he'd show up for the gig.

But Fitz had commanded her attendance, and Fitz was to be obeyed; and in any case Turk would be there, and she could get through anything with him by her side, and Prax, and a bunch more of her real friends. And in the meantime there was other rockerverse action that needed to be attended to, so she'd suck it up and get on with the job. There was nothing else she could do; and besides, it might even prove to be a ton of fun. A warm, sunny summer weekend in the country, in a beautiful location, for free, with the friends and bands she knew and loved best: how bad could it be?

Turk wasn't home, so she went upstairs to their bedroom and considered her dressing-room closet. There was a press bash in an hour at the Bitter End for a new Columbia Records act, and she'd promised their publicist she would show up. And she would, at least long enough to hear a few songs and toss down a few drinks and grab something from the buffet. Since the club was directly across town from the house, over on Bleecker Street in the West Village, she wouldn't even have to go back above Fourteenth Street. Which, as far as she was concerned, was always a plus.

It was an early party, so she wrote a brief note for Turk to come and join her if he got home in time and if he felt like it. He probably wouldn't: he didn't generally go in for that sort of thing, for very specific reasons—Rennie always had to remind herself that he was just about as famous as it was humanly possible to be, and his presence at such events might be construed as endorsement by the flacks and label suits and even by the acts themselves. But this was a progressive kind of group and he might reasonably be interested in hearing them, so she decided to give him the choice. He wouldn't be on the list, but hey, nobody manning any club door anywhere was going to turn away Turk Wayland...

She decided to go with the Mary Quant number she'd picked up last week at Bloomingdale's—flippy little brown rayon minidress, long pointy white collar and cuffs, knife-pleated skirt about six inches long hanging off a hip-yoke—and the block-heeled ribbon-tied tan patent-leather Capezio tap shoes that showed off her legs to such advantage. It seemed hardly worthwhile to get all gussied up, since she was only going to be there for a couple of hours, but it was nice to look nice, and you never knew who was going to be there that you absolutely hated and wanted to look nicer than…

Leaving the note where Turk would be sure to find it, she changed her brown leather shoulderbag for a little wooden-beaded purse and was out the door, waving her arm for another cab.

Forty minutes later, Rennie was turning away from the crowded and noisy Bitter End bar, with a tray of assorted drinks for herself and anyone else at her table who wanted one, when she ran into Kaiser Frizelle. Kaiser, né Joel, was a lank-haired, dour, Ichabod Crane of a guy, who came to press parties chiefly to feed himself, as every person who'd ever written on rock had done, and as many were still doing—no shame in that, it was an acknowledged perk of the profession, like free records and free tickets. He was not her favorite person in the world by any means, but he wrote a breathtakingly accurate astrology column for a local underground paper, the East Village Khaos, and she was deeply addicted to it.

"Heil there, Kaiser!" she saluted him. "What's your prediction for Woodstock, then? Fiesta or fester? Hellhole or rocknroll heaven?"

Kaiser smiled with distant hauteur. "Since I know you're a faithful follower of the stars, Rennie, I'll tip you this much—Mercury, ruler of communication, is adversely aspected for an Aries like yourself, so you might want to take special care with your stories."

"Always do, Kaiser dear, always do."

"Nevertheless. Well, I see only good things, strange to say. Leo is ruling the eighth house, which is host to conjunctions of Pluto and the Moon, Mercury and the Sun. And there are other auspicious aspects I don't really expect a civilian like you to understand."

"Sounds delightful." She couldn't resist a parting shot. "I wonder what our Annadawn will say to that..." And gleefully watched Kaiser begin to seethe.

Oooh, burn, Frizelle! Annadawn, real name Lexie Kagan, was Kaiser's bitter rival in the field of rock astrologers. A pleasant-faced, short brunette whom Rennie had met on numerous occasions and liked on all of them, Lexie was smart and funny and had a regular column in the Village Voice and important magazines like Eye and Teen Angels and Tiger Beat. Kaiser, on the other hand, who fancied himself a much superior interpreter of the stars, and possibly even was, had his column only in the rather meagerly distributed Khaos and a couple of other deep-underground outlets, and he felt the disparity keenly. Not to mention the sheer injustice.

"Now *she* has predicted that there will be all kinds of trouble and woe," Rennie continued heartlessly, "and apparently she doesn't mean bad trips."

But Kaiser was both untroubled and unimpressed, or at least he was doing a good job of appearing so. "Dear Lexie says a lot of things she seems to think the planets tell her. Too bad she's pretty much incompetent to interpret their high and noble speech."

Uh-HUH. There may be honor among thieves, but clearly there's none among astrologers...

Excusing herself from Kaiser after a few more pleasantries, she headed back to her table, where a group of people she knew and liked were now reassembled after hitting the rather good buffet, waiting on the arrival of the alcohol. Record companies might be horrible soulless corporate monsters, and dens of sleazoid iniquity dedicated to ripping off artists every chance they got, but one thing about them, they all knew how to throw a good party. Resuming her seat, she smiled round the table: fellow Fitzian writing property Belinda Melbourne, a close friend since Monterey and now an East Village neighbor; Belinda's on-again, off-again boyfriend Hacker Bennett, a political reporter for several underground papers, currently off again, and forever this time, they both swore it; various visitors in from London and L.A.; Gerry Langhans, known to Rennie since their infancy, now East Coast head of a&r for Turk's record label, Centaur—the usual suspects. But all were fellow lovers of the music, writing about it with passion and care, working for the mainstream press, for the big record-biz trade journals—Billboard and Cash Box and Record World—and for the hip consumer mags like Creem and Crawdaddy and Jazz & Pop.

Also at the table was someone Rennie didn't know, an elegant-looking brunette who smiled as Rennie parceled out the drinks, happily accepting a frosty gin and tonic. Belinda hastened to introduce them.

"Rennie, this is Liz Williams, from across the Pond. She writes for Queen Anne's Fan and Melody Maker and that hippie fashion magazine you like, Sumptuary, and a few other posh British rags."

Rennie reached across the table to shake hands. "How nice to meet you at last. I've read your stuff, and enjoyed it very much. Do you live in London?"

"Sometimes, but mostly I'm way out in the country,

not terribly far from your fiancé's family's stately pile in Wiltshire. Or from my good friends the Sonnets. I live in a rather less stately pile than both, I'm afraid. Still, it counts as a castle."

"Castles are where it's at... But Gray and Prue, those sweeties! Can't wait to see them here." Rennie beamed; if this person was friends with the hugely famous and just as hugely friend-selective Graham Sonnet and Prunella Vye, she was definitely okay. "Prax McKenna and I spent last Christmas with them at Pacings."

Liz smiled back. "So they've told me. I was in Brittany for the holidays, so I missed the Christmas Eve ball, unfortunately. And all the rest of the excitement. Quite the time you had yourself: breaking up an international theft ring in your off moments, catching a murderer or two. *Loved* the Hyde Park hunt, by the way. You really should have been blooded. Did Gray at least put you up for the Pommerel Vale?"

They discussed Rennie's adventures in England for a bit, compared mutual friends and favorite places ("Glastonbury..." "Oxford..." "Lyme Regis..." "Tintagel..."), then rejoined the general table conversation. Probably to Columbia's annoyance, had the label been eavesdropping, the chat was not about the act they were supposedly there to see but all about the imminent Woodstock: how everyone was getting there, where they were staying, what musicians they were planning to interview.

On the festival itself, opinion was sharply divided: those who thought it was all ever so groovy and would be a gentle celebration of peace and music, as it was being hopefully billed by its organizers, and those who—and

Rennie was among them—were hoping for the best but confidently preparing for the worst. Maybe even expecting it. Maybe even looking forward to it.

As it turned out, all of them would be right. But of course none of them knew that. Not yet.

~3~

TURK WAYLAND REACHED for another cheeseburger off the big Talavera platter in the center of the table. It was almost eleven at night, and the Wayland-Strides were having supper in the newly finished kitchen of their otherwise still slightly unfinished brownstone. When he had arrived home earlier, he had gotten her note, but decided not to show up for the press party, and instead had merely lazily, and hungrily, awaited her return.

It was Rennie's night to cook, though her culinary repertoire was a rather limited one. Unlike Turk's own: he had been tutored in cookery by his grandmother the Duchess's chefs, and pretty much no dish was beyond his capabilities. Still, Rennie did make great burgers and dynamite home fries, so he was always glad to eat up whenever they were on the menu. While cooking, she'd filled him in on all the press-party gossip he'd missed, and had just cheerfully informed him of Kaiser's and Lexie's dire and somewhat conflicting Woodstock predictions, which hadn't affected his appetite in the least.

"Pretty safe observations, I'd say. Especially that part about bewaring the storm. Have you looked at the weather forecast? You're going to get drenched."

"What's with this dissociative 'you', Ampman? You guys are playing there, last I heard. So equal drenching for all, yes?"

"We're hoping to get on and off before the rains come—we asked if we could close Friday night, and after Freddy Bellasca leaned on them a bit with all his record-company-president weight the organizers said yes. Even though they didn't really want to let us: Friday is supposed to be the folkie day and they were set on having Joan Baez to close, with the heavy mob set for Saturday and the Airplane last up, and a bit of a mix on Sunday, with Jimi taking everyone off."

Rennie glanced at him. "You seem well conversant with the program. Perhaps suspiciously so?"

"Not really. I charmed it out of Freddy's secretary Sherri a couple of weeks ago. I didn't care for us to be part of the basher brigade on Saturday; and because there was no other place to put them, Sunny Silver, Bluesnroyals and Tenwynter were also slotted in for Friday. So the ever so pure folk menu was already tainted with rockers, and it doesn't matter now that we're there too. And Sunday was much too long to be hanging around up there. In any case, I really hoped on having the weekend free for other purposes. Or as much of it as I can get, anyway."

"Oh? You mean you're not staying up there with me?"

Turk looked guilty. "I will, of course, if you want me to. Or come back up, if you just wanted to have a quiet couple of days in the country afterwards. But the festival sort of thing really isn't madly me, any more than it's madly you, so I thought the band and I might come straight back Saturday morning and get in a couple of rehearsals for the road before we scatter to the winds again before the tour.

Since, as you will doubtless recall, we're going out on the road at the end of the month. Also we need to start working on some new songs. For the next album."

"Which since *Cities* isn't exactly what we'd call tearing up the charts, you're thinking you might push out a little sooner than usual." Rennie's observation was that of a cynical rock journalist, but her tone was that of a sympathetic rock consort.

"Well, yes, that is indeed what I was thinking. Centaur, meaning of course chiefly the idiot Freddy, were wittering on about releasing a greatest-hits album for Christmas, which would be cheap and easy, and as you and I have discussed, we only ever had that one almost five years ago on Glisten and it's long past time we had another."

"And since you have had a fair few more hits since then."

"And especially since *Cities* does indeed look like tanking. Relatively speaking, of course. But those greatest-hits things are really naught but filler, and they don't count in the official LP tally—they're marketing, not creativity."

Rennie took a big bite of her burger, washed it down with milk. "What would you put on it? I can think of a whole side or two right off the bat. You guys have got so much great stuff by now that it really needs a double album."

"Thank you. Though if we do kick a greatest-hits one out there, I intend to hand-pick the tracks and sequencing myself, and not leave the choice to Bellasca's dubious sensibilities. He may be the label chief, but he has a solid-lead ear for how to put an album together. Anyway, I thought if I got started now, we could have a *real* new album out late next spring, with a summer tour to tie into. Rardi and I have got a bunch of things we kept off *Cities*, as they didn't fit the vibe, so we won't be starting from scratch. Things much more in the traditional Lionheart line, so the fans can just shut their faces whingeing," he added, a little crossly.

"Oh, come on, you knew you were taking a chance with all that orchestral stuff! I know why you went that way, and I for one loved it, but you see how it was generally received." She slid the last cheeseburger onto his plate; he still looked hungry, and he was far too well mannered to take it for himself. "But as I recall, you were planning your long-delayed first solo album for next year. Won't that interfere with the timing of a new Lionheart LP, or cut into its sales if they come out close together? I know in the early days all you Britbands were rolling out two albums a year, and amazing ones too, but these days that's a lot."

"It might do—interfere, I mean—but Freddy seems to think it will work and says he's all for it. Because I really, really want to get it out, the solo one. So maybe that for next spring instead, say. And the new Lionheart release around October, even a double LP as you suggest. A live album too, at some point; we've never had one of those either, except, again, way back in the Glisten days."

"And that bootleg one of your assorted test pressings and club recordings, what was it called again? Oh yes, *Young Turk*. Great title."

He gave her a look. "Yes, well, the less said about that little piece of illegal rubbish the better. But if the tour goes well, and especially if the Madison Square Garden show goes well, that should do us admirably for a live LP. As I said, those greatest-hits ones don't count. Except to the marketing staff, of course. Keeps the name out there and maybe pulls in a few more new fans. Especially if you throw in a new song or two as an extra added bonus track."

"No, that seems a good separation," said Rennie judicially. "Though that's a lot of output for one year; maybe just the two records. Also it would make better sense to switch it around: do a spring-summer tour in support of a spring Lionheart album, and make that the double album, or a double with one studio disc, one live. Then get off the road and concentrate on your solo album for fall of next year. Since you wouldn't be going out for that in any case, and you and I have other plans for that fall already."

"Oh, that *is* better. And yes, we do indeed have plans. But to tell you the truth," said Turk, with the air of a man placing a bomb in a crowded restaurant, "I was thinking of taking the band off the road altogether next year. Or the year after, at the latest."

Rennie put down her glass of milk. "Seriously?"

"It's nothing new, you know," he said, a little defensively. "You've heard me talk about it before… I'm just very, very tired of having to go out twice a year, get exhausted on tour, then come home and try to slam out some new songs and get them recorded with no time to think about any of it. If you recall, I've been floating the possible tour sabbatical for at least four years now, from long before we met. Even the Beatles saw the wisdom of retiring from touring, and that was three years ago. Though their road leave is permanent; ours wouldn't be, we like performing live too much."

"What does the band say?"

"They're pretty much with me, except maybe for Niles. We've been a touring band for seven solid years. I think we could all use a year to kick back and take some time off and pursue other projects. Personal *and* creative. And we'd have the prospective albums to keep our names out there." Turk looked blandly innocent. "Plus, as you mentioned, isn't there some wedding or other coming up next autumn that we'll have to be at? Unless I'm much mistaken?"

Rennie laughed. "Oh, is *that* what our respective mothers have long-distancely been putting their heads together about? Oh, darn! Who'd have thought it?"

"It's all on them," said Turk, grinning. "I'm not getting involved. Though it still seems a long time to wait before you're mine in the sight of God and man—another whole year."

"I've always been yours. And you reciprocally mine. Well, we want a fall wedding, and there wasn't enough lead time to make it this one. You have the tour, Stephen and I still have to finalize the annulment, and we couldn't expect your godmum to clear her schedule on short notice for us anyway. She has a lot of stuff on her plate, years in advance. I know that you as a card-carrying male are not expected to be aware of such social refinements, but as card-carrying females all know, a whole year would barely be enough even if we were regular people having a regular old wedding like other regular people's weddings, which, you know, we're not. Good news? We don't have to book a hall, or a church, or a band—you come with all that laid on."

Rennie's long-separated husband Stephen Lacing still being her legal spouse, and Turk's godmother being the reigning Queen of Great Britain, Northern Ireland and the Commonwealth, the points were valid ones, and Turk nodded placidly.

"True enough… In any case, we'll have bags of time to plan out all the details. Though I only care about what music we'll have."

"And I what threads we'll wear."

"Not forgetting the Saltire tiara," said Turk, smiling.

"It's rather impressive, as those things go. You'll look good in it. Or under it, I should say."

Rennie smiled back. "I'm counting on looking even better under Lord Saltire."

As the days passed, the New York rockerverse was increasingly abuzz about Woodstock approaching, as Rennie discovered when she ventured out, over the course of that final run-up week, to a few more press bashes and interviews with some of the prospective participants. At one launch party for a new group just signed to the very prestigious Sovereign Records, held at the Pierre Hotel—typical for Sovereign, whose president Leeds Sheffield ran a tight, classy and very upscale ship indeed—Rennie ran into, probably not coincidentally, Lexie Kagan, and allowed as to how their meeting must have been written in the stars.

"Yes, my darling," Lexie bubbled, giving Rennie a hug, "as everything is, of course. Sovereign actually hired me to cast the horoscope of this momentous occasion."

"Woodstock? I'm confused: I thought you had already 'scoped it, I read the column in the Village Voice..."

"Oh, indeed I did, and I stand by my stars. The ones in the heavens, not the ones onstage. But those too. No, I meant this delightful little lunch. Leeds asked me to do a reading for this new band we're all assembled here to fête—Megatherium, did you ever *hear* a more ridiculous name for a group? All twiddly-twee skippity-sparkly little ditties, gag gag gag. I did them a proper chart, though, and I have a feeling they won't be rilly-dilly-jingle-o for much longer—big creative changes are coming for them. I foresee a name change as well...Leeds was quite right to sign them, they're going to be huge. Anyway, I'm here today to do speedreads, as I like to call them, for the people at the party, little quickie charts, just off sunsigns and ascendants. Fun for the uninitiated. I'd do yours but I can see it already: happily ever after with Lord Right in your castle of dreams. So wonderful."

"It *is* wonderful," Rennie confided. "And I do plan on calling upon Annadawn professionally, to cast a horoscope for the wedding date next year. We've tentatively picked one, a nice number in mid-Libra, but I want to be sure the aspects are favorable. And after all, you *are* the best."

Lexie nodded graciously, accepting the compliment as no more than Annadawn's right and proper due. "Of course, any day would be good for you and Turk, but I'm not going to lie: some are definitely better than others. We'll find the best one for you two—he's a Libra himself, isn't he? I'd be delighted to scan the heavens for you and his rock lordship. People think horoscopes are silly superstitions, but that's because they've never had a proper chart done and have only ever read the ones in newspapers. The more detailed the chart, the more accurate the 'scope. Plus of course I get things psychically, not only off what I see set down in the Houses."

"I know you can't disclose names, but have you done charts for many rockers?" Rennie asked, curious. "With a few well-publicized and ornery exceptions, Turk included, they seem to be deeply interested and invested in this sort of thing."

`Lexie offered Rennie a cup of tea from the pot she'd had one of the bar staff brew and bring her. "I've done lots," she said confidingly. "Every name you've ever heard of and even more you haven't. No matter how big they already are, all they want to hear is what huge famous rich superstars they'll be and how many groupies they're going to score. They don't get it that horoscopes are all about growing and becoming, not necessarily about having and being."

"And what about straight-ahead bad stuff? Like, don't set foot out of the house next Monday because a bus is coming along with your name on it, kind of thing? This tea is delicious, by the way."

"Thank you. Special blend from a little shop in Pasadena. I never go out without it." Lexie's mobile little face, usually so cheerful, was crossed by momentary shadows, then cleared again. "You know, that stuff is always tricky. It very seldom is as specific or clear-cut as your incredibly morbid example, more like an overall vibe. What you see in the Houses is little strings and threads of being and becomingness, as it were, coming to an end or newly starting off. Could be getting slammed by a bus, could be losing a job, could be any number of things. It's all down to interpretation to figure out which of the unpleasant alternatives it actually might be. I do believe in warning people, though, which many astrologers don't, for fear of upsetting them."

"They'd be a lot more upset if that bus came along and you *hadn't* warned them, I would think. At least so they'd have on clean underwear that day, the way their mothers always told them."

"There's that. And of course people change their futures all the time by what they do, knowingly and unknowingly."

Rennie toyed with some giant chocolate-dipped strawberries and a bowl of whipped cream. "Yes," she said musingly. "Yes, I've seen that myself. But you don't read good things for this Woodstock weekend? Kaiser Frizelle certainly did, as you may have noticed in his Khaos column."

Lexie didn't reply right away, and Rennie's journalistic

ears perked up. Then: "Naturally, he'd *say* that, if only to disagree with me. *Dear* Kaiser. But I have to admit that yes, there are some big seriously shadowy areas. Most likely it won't be a riot or massacre or anything—more like frustrations and blocks, maybe things going missing, accidents. And more than anything, and I do agree with Kaiser here, no one should dismiss the power of the storm."

"Hey, it's August in upstate New York, big storms happen. And they're not to be sneezed at, believe me. But do you foresee any, well, really dark things on tap? Like, oh, I don't know, Saturn planet of death squatting in a House of ill repute?"

Lexie's face grew unexpectedly serious as Annadawn took the wheel. "Saturn isn't in the greatest aspect, I'll say that much. It's in the eighth House, and that house is packed full of squares, which set forth energies working at cross purposes. It's not only Woodstock and this weekend, though it might manifest there most clearly. Look around and see how things are tending in the world. Don't discount the dark strength of Saturn, Rennie. You can never tell upon whom it might descend. It hides below the horizon, to strike when you least expect it. And Saturn, as you mentioned, means death. As Murder Chick should know."

They were silent for a few moments, Rennie feeling oddly unsettled, and heartily wishing she'd never mentioned the whole subject in the first place.

Then Lexie, shrugging: "That's the thing with predictions: they don't always reflect the whole picture. Sure, there could be deaths at Woodstock. In fact, there probably will be; I'd be very surprised if there weren't. At a large outdoor festival a lot can go wrong, and accidents do happen. I can see that in the charts, and I'm sure Kaiser can too. He's just being uncharacteristically positive about it. Perverse little weirdo."

"So what's Annadawn's best advice, then?"

Lexie smiled. "The same advice it always is. Watch the heavens, Strider. And watch your back, too."

~4~

When Rennie arrived home, she could hear, or, more accurately, feel, a faint throb of music coming up from underfoot. Turk must be down in the cellar, testing out the acoustics of the new studio that was still under construction. Still not perfectly soundproof, apparently, judging by the vibrations; she would have to tell him. The studio was a new and expensive addition: he also had one in the Los Angeles house and another at Cleargrove, his family's ancestral country seat in southwest England. God only knew how many more he had stashed away. But though it was costly, it was far from being either a rock star's self-indulgence or a rich man's toy: in fact, very much to the contrary. A fully equipped home studio, where a band could record on a professional-quality level, was pure practicality, and saved Lionheart many thousands of dollars that would otherwise go to feed the greedy corporate maw of Centaur Records. And as Turk happily pointed out, swiping bread out of the mouth of Freddy Bellasca never got old.

She tossed her shoulderbag and light shawl and broad-brimmed summer hat on a small refectory table in the living room, and headed down to the kitchen. This part of the house had seen all the construction it was going to, and she had had a few pieces of the newly purchased furniture moved in, so they didn't have to employ sleeping bags or sit on the floor: a leather sofa and armchairs and a couple of tables in the living room; in the kitchen, a round lion-footed oak table and matching chairs that she'd picked up at a neighborhood antique shop; upstairs, their big antique fourposter, and a few more beds in case they had company needing to crash.

Of course, most of it still had to be painted and wallpapered, and the floors waxed and polished, and the vast remainder of the furniture had yet to be delivered. It would be months, probably Thanksgiving, by the time everything was fully in order, and even there would still be rooms and floors to fill; but the heavy work was all done, and soon the real fun could start. By which she meant, first, actually living in the place with Turk—even though she was already doing that, it still felt more like camping out—and then, filling in at her leisure and pleasure with little bits and bobs, to make the place truly their home, hers and his.

And so it would be: the Hollywood Hills house was spectacularly beautiful, and she loved it, and was so happy Turk had decided to keep it, but even though it had become theirs, bottom line it was really *his* house. He'd bought it before he met her, furnished it according to his tastes, and though all that was fine as far as she was concerned, and though she'd contributed things she liked to the household and he was delighted that she did so, this was the first house to be really completely theirs. Maybe the only one they'd *ever* have that would be so: the numerous assorted castles and villas and stately homes they'd come into later, as duke and duchess, wouldn't really belong to them in the same way as this one did—they'd be caretakers, not possessors, inheritors from previous generations and stewards for future ones. And that too was fine. But she rather thought they would hang on to this house, and the L.A. one as well, no matter how many palaces fell to their future lot. For now, New York was the place for them; they would be headed to England on a permanent basis soon enough.

She was drinking a glass of chocolate milk in front of the open refrigerator when Niles Clay came up the stairs from the cellar, and Rennie was so startled to see him that she almost dropped her glass. For his part, he didn't look terribly pleased to see her either.

"Niles! I didn't know you were here?"

"Why would you? I understood that you were out," he said in flat, clipped tones, barely short of rudeness, which no one hearing would ever have taken for the instantly recognizable voice of Lionheart's lead singer. "Actually, Turk and I were messing about downstairs with a couple of tracks he asked me over to hear." He glanced over at the big new Aga stove that Turk had had shipped from England at fabulous expense, where a stainless-steel kettle was bubbling merrily away. "And we thought we might care for some tea; it seems to be about that time."

"No problem. Please. Sit. I'll get it for you."

Going to the cupboard, she took down a green-and-gold ceramic Harrods Food Halls jar containing the tea Turk liked, and lifted two hefty stoneware mugs from a wooden rack near the stove; the teapot they favored for daily use stood waiting on the counter. Niles said nothing more, just seated himself at the table, but she felt him watching her as she moved around the kitchen, and she used the tea-making ritual to buy herself some time for thought, and, not incidentally, to master her already mushrooming annoyance: measuring out the tea with a generous hand, putting it into the pot, pouring the boiling water over the leaves and setting the lid on to let the tea steep.

She kept her back turned as much as she decently could, because, frankly, she just didn't want to have to look at him. They did not have a good relationship, she and Niles, and hadn't from the start. He was spiteful, snarky in a not-good-snark way, touchy and very often plain out-and-out bitchy. She generally ignored it, for Turk's sake, though sometimes she snapped back; neither tactic ever really had any effect. To anyone with a basic knowledge of group dynamics, Psych 101, it was pretty obvious what was going on: Niles was jealous of her—of her influence with Turk, of the attention he paid her and the trust he placed in her, of the part she played in his life that Niles could never fill.

And Rennie in her turn was jealous of Niles, for his longer knowledge of and closeness with her mate, all the good and bad times they'd been through together that she'd missed out on, everything they'd shared before Turk had even met her. Oh, it wasn't a gay thing, or even latently so, Niles's possessiveness, she knew she didn't have to worry about that: it was merely that het-guy grudgingness, the passive-aggressive, jealous resentment that some men often bear toward their close friends' significant others. Turk, for his part, appeared completely ignorant of it all, though Rennie sometimes wondered if he really was.

It was only Niles who had the problem with Rennie, though. The other guys in the band were genuinely glad to see Turk happily settled down with a mate they deemed worthy of him, besides being grateful for all the nice press coverage she'd given them in the past. They liked her honesty, her no-prisoners attitude and her fierce loyalty to and intelligent protectiveness of Turk, and the band as well; they respected her smarts and admired her looks, and she reciprocated admiration, liking and respect. But Rennie and Niles had always been spiky and prickly and antagonistic, metaphorically circling each other like alley cats before a hissing scratching fight, and that didn't seem likely to change anytime soon. If ever.

That tea had steeped long enough. She filled the two mugs from the pot, putting in milk and sugar to Turk's liking, then set the pot and everything else relevant on a nice old wooden tray lined with a crocheted doily. Quite an elegant production, this daily ritual: silver creamer and sugar bowl and strainer, silver teaspoons, small plates with some scones and little raisin biscuits, a dish each of strawberry jam and clotted cream. The only nontraditional bit was the stoneware mugs, not the Wedgwood cups Rennie herself preferred. But that was the way Turk liked his tea, and she enjoyed making sure he had it just so.

Niles made no move to fix his own mug, much less carry everything back downstairs. "Turk tells me he wants to pull the band off the road for a while," he said without preamble. "Maybe for all of next year. He says he's tired of touring and that the rest of us are too, that we need a rest to figure out where the band needs to go next."

"Yes, he's told me that, too. Well, he *is* tired. I would think all of you are. After seven years of Lionheart he feels that he deserves some serious time off, and so do the rest of you. I take it you don't agree with his assessment."

"Is that what you call it—time off?" He looked up at her, and she recoiled a little at the venom in his eyes. "He never had any thought of any of that before *you* came swanning into his life!"

Rennie seated herself across from Niles and took another sip of her chocolate milk, clamping a lid over her temper as she'd clamped the one over the teapot. She was beginning to feel anger rising inside her like a red tide invading a peaceful bay, and for Turk's sake she wasn't going to give in to it until she had no other choice.

"You think?" she asked pleasantly. "May I remind you of an interview he did with Theo Lintern of Melody Maker back around the time of your fourth album, and one with Ralph Gleason after Monterey, and another with Jay Rosevalley for Jazz & Pop, and yet another with... Obviously you don't read your own band's publicity, because in dozens of happy little chatfests he has eagerly discussed his plans to eventually take a break at some point and musically regroup. And he's been talking specifically about getting out of touring, or at least majorly cutting down on it, for at *least* the past three years. Long before I met him, Niles. Long before I slept with him. I'm just glad I can help him make it happen."

She leaned back in her chair, studying Niles' face as if it had been a weather map of springtime tornado country, searching for the line of the front, where the twistiest twisters were likely to form. Yeah, this conversation, or confrontation, was *long* overdue, and she was going to take it however she could get it.

"Besides," she went on, in her best conciliatory tone, "it's not as if he's pulling the band off the road forever, the way the Beatles did. He only wants a year—I think quite reasonably—a year where he doesn't have to worry about touring. A year to rest up, write in peace and unpressured by deadlines, a year to figure out where Lionheart is musically going next. Quite apart from all that, to do the solo album he's been hoping to do for a very long time. And, oh yeah, get married. Listen, you've been on the road since 1962, you've never had a real break. I know for a fact that the other guys think the same as Turk does. They'd like to spend a nice solid twelve months at home with the old ladies and the kids and the dogs, take some real time and care to do the next studio LP, not rush one out in between road trips the way you've been doing. Oh, they've been *great* records, don't get me wrong. But it might be nice if Lionheart had the chance to do something a bit more, uh, considered. It wouldn't be that the band's never going to tour again ever."

Niles made an impatient move. "You don't understand how it is with us. How could you? You're just a—"

With great effort, Rennie controlled her own anger and impatience. *Let's keep this civil, quick and above all quiet, I do* not *want Turk coming upstairs and walking into the crossfire. But Mr. Niles Clay has finally stepped over the line, and for once we're going to have it out...*

"Just a what, pray? Listen, I understand just fine, Niles. For starters, I understand that you're a spiteful little dog in the manger who can't admit how much you owe Turk and who can't deal with how sick with envy you are because he's Richard Lionheart and you're not. You thought when you joined the band that you would be the big hot sexy frontman lead singer, because you see all these other bands out there where the lead singer *is* the big hot sexy frontman, and you're pissed off that because of Turk it isn't really like that for you. Because when people think of Lionheart, the man they think of is Turk Wayland, not Niles Clay. Like when fans say 'the Stones'—some people think of Keith, sure, but pretty much the whole world thinks first of Mick. Probably Keith is just as cross about it with Mick as you are with Turk. But that's the way it is. You can always leave, of course, but really you can't *ever* leave, any more than Keef can, because it'll never be as good for you anywhere else. And oh yeah, right, almost forgot, you've been jealous of *me* from the very first night Turk and I got together, and you've made me a nice convenient scapegoat rather than face up to your own problems. Or could it be more simple than that? Is it that I get to go to bed with him and you can't?"

Niles' face was sneerish, but his eyes showed that she'd hit the big main central nerve: Turk first, Niles second, world-class envy straight down the line. For an instant she wondered if Turk really did know all about it, and had kept it from her to spare her just such an unpleasant little encounter as this...

"That is such a load of bollocks—"

"*Is* it."

"You're nothing but a groupie scrubber," he snarled, and now the hidden toxicity was spread out like an oil slick. "Yeah, you're a bit more well-connected than most, a bit brighter than most, but you're really nothing special, just another stroppy cow trying to get anything she can out of him. I've seen them come and go for years, love, and you're no different and certainly no better."

Amazingly, surprising even herself, Rennie did not blast him through the kitchen wall and right out into the street, but leaned back in her chair and smiled.

"*Am* I. Oh, I think I'm quite a bit better and more different than that. Besides, you know and I know that Turk has never been with a groupie in his life. *He's* better than that, and he prefers women who are better than that. And I'm certainly not your love. I'm *his* love."

She casually draped her left hand on the table, wrist arched and fingers spread—thank *you*, childhood ballet lessons!—so that the enormous heart-shaped ruby Turk had set there back in February shot red fire in the light from the hanging Tiffany lamp, and watched Niles' eyes flick to it. *Check and mate, sucker!* He scowled, but he had absolutely nothing he could possibly come back against that with, and they both knew it.

Rennie let him think about it for a few moments. Oopsie, then. He had foolishly laid all his hate cards out, and she had trumped him unanswerably and forever. She had the winning hand, and all the chips belonged to her. She was, at the bare minimum, Rennie Stride, notorious journalist, a position which carried a certain amount of power, and as such she could certainly make life unpleasant for him should she so choose. As well she might, had it not also meant making life unpleasant for Turk and the other guys, and thus for herself also.

But beyond that, she was going to be Mrs. Turk Wayland, not to mention her progressively ascending identities as Countess of Saltire, Marchioness of Raxton and Her Grace the Duchess of Locksley, which positions carried even more power, and of a different sort. Not only would she forevermore be part of the Tarrant picture, she would also be part of the Lionheart picture, for as long as Turk himself was, which was likewise forever; and as such she could produce even *more* misery for Niles should she so choose. No, Nilesy had fatally and rather stupidly overreached himself, had gone straight over that tempting, looming, self-important cliff. And if she should decide to pass all his septic comments along to Turk, which of course she would never do but Niles didn't know that…hey there, sailor, miscalculation's a bitch!

But the hurt had vanished, and, surprisingly, so had the anger, and the calm clarity she felt now would have served her well with a dueling pistol in her hand.

"Oh, I know you don't lust after Turk in the physical sense, though I could certainly understand it if you did—he's lustworthy to the nth, take my word for it. It's a lot deeper and more complex, isn't it. Yes… Well, fine, you sniveling little pig, if you want to blame me, knock yourself out. But you're not doing anything that's going to hurt Turk. I swear to God I will hurt *you* first—and I mean *seriously* hurt you, break-your-arms-and-legs-and-rip-your-kidneys-out-through-your-nose hurt you—before I'd ever let that happen. And you know I'm good for it. So you see."

"Are you going to tell Turk what I said?" Niles demanded bluntly, no hint of apology or reconciliation in his voice. And no fear either, she noted with interest, meaning he knew the kind of power he himself held, as Lionheart's pretty much irreplaceable lead singer. Well, he was right about that, unfortunately.

"I don't know. What would you do?"

"You're the one with all the answers." He stared at her, and she met his hostile glance with equanimity. "What do you suggest?"

Rennie smiled again, brightly. "Oh, I could *suggest* quite a few things. But, for the moment, I suggest you bring Turk his tea. It's getting cold."

Up in the bedroom later, sitting on the edge of the fourposter and trying to decide what, if anything, she wanted to do that night, she heard the front door slam behind Niles and then Turk's footsteps coming upstairs. There was an ornate Victorian lift that the contractors had recently revived to functionality, but they both usually preferred to climb the sweeping flight of stairs, with its original, glorious golden oak banisters and Carrara marble treads, to their rooms on the second floor, right on the point of the prow. She looked up as he came in, and smiled as he dropped a kiss on the top of her head.

"Have a good day?" he asked, and toppled her over backwards onto the bed, collapsing right next to her.

"It had its moments."

"M'hm?"

Wild tyrannosaurs weren't going to drag out of her the tiniest mention of her little sparring session with Niles; she'd do whatever she could to spare Turk any extra melodrama before the band went out for the big tour—it was hard enough on him as it was. But this thing between Niles and her was going to come back to bite them all, sooner or later… had to happen. Still, it wasn't going to happen tonight.

"I was at a rather upscale press luncheon, actually," she elaborated. "Or perhaps bruncheon. Tossed by Sovereign at the Pierre for their new signing, Megatherium. I remember the Megs when they were a ragtag bunch of folkie tambourine-bangers from the Haight; unfortunately, their music has stayed pretty twinkly. Though it's been suggested that they're on the cusp of big and innovative change, which I wouldn't mind seeing. Still, the party was nice: crustless sandwiches and teacakes and all manner of brunchy foodstuffs, quiche and eggs Benedict and suchlike, oooh la. I hate to sound like a snob—"

"No, you don't."

"No, of *course* I don't, I *love* it, but it was big fun to see all our freaky friends trying to negotiate finger bowls. There were many covert glances to spy out what one's neighbors were doing with these little water-and-lemon-slice traps for the uncouth—highly entertaining. Most of them seemed to treat it like a landmine of some sort. Though that crazy kid Hipshot McGowan, who writes for Creem, actually *drank* his, apparently thinking—well, I have no idea what he was thinking. Do-it-yourself lemonade, perhaps. But we were all very polite about it and nobody mocked him. At least not right there where he could see it. He's only sixteen. He'll learn."

Turk laughed. "I'm sure he will. Sounds good, though; Leeds Sheffield certainly knows how to push the boat out. Pity Freddy can't manage to take a leaf from his book. In so many ways. We must do something classy like that ourselves. For the next album, of course, as it's too late for this one. And of course the Pierre is quite nice. You remember, we stayed there last year when we came here on tour. Because we didn't have a house yet."

She nodded, sitting up to pull his sneakers off, then her strappy little shoes, so as not to mess up the bedspread; they invariably preferred to go barefoot indoors, but the state of construction and the amount of debris lying around still precluded that.

"I do remember, and it was very nice indeed—especially the room service. I still wake up weeping from vain tormenting dreams of their chocolate-raspberry pie. Perhaps you've noticed. Though you've never offered to make me a cover version, as it were…gross negligence on your part, you really must do something about that. Oh, I had a talk with Lexie Kagan, in her professional capacity as Annadawn. She was there to do little minicharts for the lunch guests, and we discussed Woodstock's astrological possibilities as she saw them, as opposed to Kaiser Frizelle's personal take."

He put his arms behind his head and relaxed into the huge heap of pillows. "You know I'm not a believer, but, purely out of curiosity, what did they both predict?"

She pulled herself up beside him and cuddled her cheek against his shoulder. "Sunshine and rain, my love. Just sunshine and rain."

~5~

Thursday morning, August 14

A BEAUTIFUL, HOT, CLEAR summer day: deep blue skies, bright sun, puffy white cottonball clouds—the day before the Woodstock Festival of Music and Art's official opening. Nine a.m., and Rennie was out in front of the house in the shiny dark-blue Mustang she'd just picked up from the car rental place around the corner. She was waiting for Turk and Prax, and had double-parked under the leafy old oaks and sycamores that lined their surprisingly Londonesque street: the prettiest block in the East Village—East Tenth just west of Second Avenue, where it met Stuyvesant Street across from the lovely and historic St. Mark's-in-the-Bouwerie Church.

Their equally lovely and historic brownstone sat on the point of the two streets where they came angling together, right in front of the church. The building was like the prow of a ship, and behind it were spread out along both street frontages more beautiful old landmarked brownstones, making a triangular block called the Renwick Triangle, after its Victorian architect. The block was shaped rather like an ocean liner, so naturally they had christened the place the prow house.

Rennie had found it back in March, and when Turk saw it for the first time he fell in love with it on the spot. But then, as she'd told Fitz, there was that problem of it being too small for their needs. So Turk had bought the other two buildings, and handsomely bribed all the tenants to relocate. The workers had been given time off, with pay, while Turk and Rennie were away at the festival...some of them had gone up to Woodstock themselves...maybe they'd run into them there...

She tooted the horn again, longer and more impatiently this time, and Turk and Prax came down the front steps like fighter pilots scrambling, each with the one piece of luggage she'd permitted them to bring in the car. Hey, they were rock stars, they had roadies and quippies and vans; as much stuff as they wanted had already been schlepped upstate by the professional help, including the stage clothes Rennie had made for them both to wear for this hugely important gig.

Turk beat Prax to the car door. "Shotgun!"

"Oh damn, *that's* what I forgot to pack..."

Rennie motioned Prax—who'd flown in last night from L.A. with her band, Evenor—to stuff her soft-sided leather suitcase in the trunk, next to Turk's battered old Gladstone and her own Vuitton duffel and the ice chest she'd insisted on bringing, and climb into the back seat, where the six-foot-three-inch Turk wouldn't have fit anyway, whether he'd called shotgun or not.

Once everything and everyone was comfortably stowed, she made a right-hand turn into Second Avenue, hung another right on Ninth Street and headed over to the West Side Highway—she'd timed their departure to miss the worst of rush hour, and they'd be going in the favorable traffic-flow direction anyway. From there, she'd take the Henry Hudson and the Saw Mill parkways to the Tappan Zee Bridge across the river, pick up a bit of the New York State Thruway and then get onto Route 17 at Harriman—the old tried and true route upstate.

Rennie had driven back and forth that way for years, from her family's Riverdale home to Cornell, her alma mater in Ithaca, so she knew the road blindfolded—any downstate kid who went to college in upstate New York did. Running northwest from the New Jersey border, Route 17 hung a sharp left at Delaware County, for a straight shot all the way west across the rural Southern Tier of the state, and despite stretches of commercial tackiness as it went through the occasional small, shabby cities, it was really kind of magical. For its entire length it threaded rolling high hills and farmlands and ran beside clean rivers, a countryside full of places with classical names: tiny villages like Ovid, Marathon, Romulus, college towns like Ithaca and Syracuse and Vestal. Passing below the glacier-gouged Finger Lakes, as the names began to speak musically of ancient tribelands—Tioga, Chenango, Canisteo, Cattaraugus—it headed into the higher, colder, sparsely settled mountains of the far southwestern part of the state, the northern fringe of Appalachia, the empty and beautiful thick-forested oil country and snow country that bordered on Pennsylvania, and so on through the flatter lands nearing Lake Erie, to Ohio and the near Midwest.

Not that she'd ever *drive* it blindfolded. In spite of the fact that Route 17's official name was the Quickway, it wasn't all that quick. Too many milk tankers crawling along at fifteen miles an hour so the milk wouldn't churn into butter by the time it reached its destination. The narrow Quickway was full of them blocking the traffic flow, especially in the foggy hours of early morning, heading down from dairy farms way back in the hills and deer-haunted valleys off to each side of the road. But her familiarity with the route meant that she also knew all the good places to hit for eats: on the pre-Binghamton leg, that meant Kaplan's, the famed and fabulous kosher deli in Monticello (pronounced Montisello, not Montichello like Jefferson's Virginia home, for which it had been named), where every student traveling between the city and every upstate college to the west and north stopped whenever they could afford to, or when their parents were driving and would pick up the tab.

They weren't going much beyond Monticello on this trip, though. If they could get to it: there were some alarming reports on the car radio of traffic jams already beginning to form on 17 and on the New York State Thruway and roads leading thereto, even the day before the festival's official opening, though as yet they hadn't encountered any as they sailed along. But they were hungry long before that, so it was the equally famed and fabulous Red Apple Rest in Tuxedo, venerable mother of all roadside hash joints, with its eponymous and jaunty giant Delicious atop the roof, for a late and lavish breakfast.

"I must say that was interesting," remarked Turk as they walked out an hour later, all of them crammed full of waffles and bacon. "Having the entire restaurant turn around and pause, with laden forks halfway to their slack, gaping mouths, to stare at us as we came in. We would have gotten less attention had we entered riding on dragons."

"Oh please! You're a rock star!" scoffed Rennie. "Both of you. Should be used to that sort of thing by now. *I'm* the one who legitimately found it creepy and unsettling."

"I suppose we should consider ourselves lucky they didn't greet us with the traditional pitchforks and torches. Still, of course, that could always come later."

"Well, we probably have the longest hair anyone there ever saw on a human being," said Prax, as they packed themselves back into the Mustang for the last bit of the trip. "And you and I, petunia, have the tightest jeans and the most unfettered tits, ditto. So I'm not surprised they were bugging their eyes out on stalks like little blue crabs. Though they'll be seeing a lot more of this sort of thing in these here parts as the weekend—and the beat—goes on. So they had better get used to it."

"Or we had," said Turk philosophically.

The traffic jam they'd been hearing about on the car radio kicked in soon thereafter, and Rennie whipped them off Route 17 barely in time to avoid it. Even though it spanned the entire width of a valley and disappeared over the brow of a hill, it still didn't look all that bad—a mere minor slowdown compared to the vast parking lot that the highway would become only twenty-four hours later—but she didn't want to take the chance of getting trapped.

Slewing her way out the nearest exit like a rally driver, Rennie grinned as she noticed a familiar big white sign high atop a distant hill, a sign she'd seen for years driving past and which made her laugh every time she saw it.

"Look, Praxie! 'Jesus Is The Answer'!"

Prax never even opened her eyes. "But what's the question?"

What indeed. With great élan and confidence, Rennie continued a big detouring scenic swingaround via country roads known to her from days of yore, past tiny settlements called improbable things like Kiamesha and Wanaksink, and insisted on stopping in Monticello to brave Kaplan's, where she loaded up, despite her companions' mockery, on gigantic sandwiches and tubs of salad and big containers of soup ("We don't know what the food situation will be like, we might not able to drive out all that easily, motel supplies might run out, better be prepared, see, I *knew* that ice chest would come in handy, oh, and that little hotplate I brought too, yes, yes, you're laughing at me now but you'll be thanking me later!").

Once provisioned to her satisfaction—enough food to feed several entire bands, not merely a guitarist, a singer and a writer—they continued, still on back roads, to the small town of Liberty a few miles farther on, and the rather utilitarian hostelry where Lionheart and Evenor and their support teams had been lucky enough to snag rooms.

That motel and the one directly across the road were barracks and homebase headquarters for everyone playing at the festival—and for everyone else who could manage to score a room there, or even space to crash on the floor of someone who had. It was already filling up with bands and other denizens of the rockerverse: in the short stroll between the check-in desk and their rooms, they ran into members of the Airplane, the Who, the Band, the Dead, Crosby, Stills and Nash their very own selves, and about a dozen other groups beside, plus all manner of industry types well known to them.

As they walked through the motel corridors, increasingly bizarre announcements came squawking over the P.A. system: "John Lennon, pay your bar bill...Bob Dylan, you left your harmonica at the front desk...Keith Richards, call your mother...Ringo Starr, come to the housekeeping office..." They were both laughing as the pages kept on coming: it was all a put-on, of course, hijinks from assorted rock pranksters, as none of the luminaries being paged were even at the festival to begin with. Even so, they felt sorry for the poor receptionists who had to take it all seriously. Rennie instantly flashed on the Highlands Inn at Monterey two summers ago, though that had been a far more elegant place than this. Still, she felt strangely comforted to see all the familiar faces: whatever else the weekend would bring, at least the music would be a given. And they would be among friends, which counted for a *lot*.

Their accommodations were clean and comfortable, with all the usual conveniences, though the furniture was less than inspired and the carpeting needed to be taken out behind the barn and shot. Turk, looking around with an eye honed by seven years of touring, sleeping wherever the road took him, cheerfully opined that he and the band had been billeted in much, *much* worse places over the course of their career, and Rennie believed him. Evenor had rooms on the second floor front, while Lionheart's were on the ground floor rear, facing a pleasant mountain view on one side and a graveled parking lot on the other. Still, at least it would be convenient to get away quickly if a speedy getaway should be required.

They stowed the bags, planning to unpack later—all Turk's equipment and the rest of his luggage was already there in the room, brought by the roadies—and put the food away in the little fridge. Then, after a quick drink with Prax at the already crowded bar, it was back into the Mustang and down along the narrow county road that led to Bethel, festival site of destination and of destiny, past little cabin-fringed lakes—Swan, White, Kauneonga—whose names Rennie recalled seeing on desolate lighted green highway signs as she'd barreled by in mountain mist at three in the morning, on a deserted Route 17 on her way to school, or friends' schools, or the city. The helicopter shuttle service being provided for performers and other VIPs wasn't yet up and running, so people were being ferried to the festival field in vans and station wagons. But Rennie liked the idea of having wheels on the ground, to be able to flee whenever they felt like it, or needed to, so, against advice, she planned to drive in and out as she, or Turk or Prax, pleased.

Once they came off the side road and onto Route 17B, which led directly to the site and was hardly any wider, and infinitely more jammed-up, they began to pass cars parked all askew on the roadsides, abandoned along the march like dead camels in the Taklamakan, their occupants apparently having decided to give up and walk to the festival—a day later, even Bob Weir of the Grateful Dead would have to truck in on his own two feets when *his* car broke down. But perhaps the god of festivals was with her, as a bit of karmic reward for what she had endured at Monterey, for Rennie had no trouble whatever driving in, and it was with a feeling of proud accomplishment that she turned off 17B at last onto a farm lane called Hurd Road, which led through woodland and fields to the festival site itself.

We're here! And I got us all here safe and sound! Yay for me! Let the games begin!

They had been steadily passing festivalgoers walking along the dusty verges, and now, here on the final approach, the lane was thick with them: fancifully dressed people who seemed to be going to a beggars' convention or a Silk Road bazaar—people who, hearing an approaching car, tried to hitch a ride with hopeful, or cynical, V-signs, and when Rennie shook her head apologetically, removed one finger from their salutes. Tsk. How very ungroovy of them. But the car *was* full, and more importantly, it was full of rock stars, and Rennie wasn't about to risk Turk's and Prax's privacy or indeed safety by picking up a weary stoned urchin or two. Besides, the exercise would do the little brats good—though when some of them leaped onto the hood of the car, thinking to ride in triumph into the site as if perched on a Mardi Gras float, she heartlessly sped up a bit and then braked, unceremoniously dislodging them. Crude, but effective, and no one got hurt.

The festival had already become a free one, sometime earlier that week. No one had anticipated the hordes of ticketless fans, or thought to have installed something more substantial than the flimsy wire fencing that went down at the first serious incursion. But though the festival itself was now free to fans, the bands still expected to be paid for their weekend's labor, and that would prove a bit more problematic. Still, at the moment nobody was thinking along those lines. Though they really should have been.

The woods-bordered lane emerged into a vast open sunlit space of many acres: cornfields on one side, parking on the other. Their performers' car sticker got them a prime spot, and they eagerly tumbled out of the Mustang to survey the scene, drawing in deep breaths of the clean, deliciously hay-scented air. It was all rounded, rolling hills in that part of the Catskills, thick with trees around the edges of meadows that normally held no more than a herd or two of dairy cows. But the vast field in front of them was populated now by way more than a few grazing Guernseys, and was getting even more so as they watched.

It was already staggering, Rennie thought, with a surge of excitement not unmixed with pride. The three of them paused on the crest of the slope to stare out over the landscape and marvel, their hair blowing theatrically in the strong, warm breeze. *It's like a Persian carpet of freaks! Monterey was a lunar wasteland compared to this...* From where they stood and running all the way down to the stage, it was nothing but colorfully clad creatures lounging in the grass: it looked vaguely Biblical, like an outdoor long shot for some giant costume epic movie starring Charlton Heston. It was indeed impressive, Rennie allowed, impressed in spite of herself.

Longhairs and hippies and heads, oh my! Not a straight in the bunch. As far as the eye can see, nothing but people like us. People like me! *For once we're not the minority, not the odd ones out, though some of us are pretty odd, to be sure. But we all have long hair and we all dress amazingly and we all oppose that evil damn Moloch war that's eating up so many of us who aren't as fortunate as we here are, grinding them up in iron jaws, despite our best efforts to get them home...this is for them, the ones who can't be here, as much as it's for us...*

Down at the bottom of the meadow amphitheater, the tall wooden stage rose up like a child's castle; a little wood-and-cable footbridge, arching up and down across the wire-fenced farm lane running through the property, linked the stage to the backstage—the performers' pavilion and the secured area surrounding it. Someone had put a sign on it: "Bridge of Sighs." Someone else, or perhaps the same someone, had also decorated the homemade structure with strings of Christmas lights, which was either charming or eye-rolling, according as to how stoned or how cynical you were, but which was no doubt really intended to keep people from falling off as they staggered from here to there, in the dark and under the influence of illegal substances. "Bridge of Highs", more like it. Yeah, good luck with that.

"They've done an amazing job, putting it up so fast," remarked Prax when Rennie spoke her thought aloud. "Chip Monck and all his merry men and women…just *look* at those speakers, I bet people will hear us all the way back in Liberty."

"Oooh! I could stay in the motel room and listen, and write everything from there…"

"Doesn't work that way, sweetheart," said Turk, laughing. "Besides, if I have to be here then so do you. It's only fair."

"I guess… Well, Annadawn and Kaiser have already gone on the prediction record; what do you two think? Do you get a vibe of awesome musicality about to unfold? Disaster on the wing? Either/or?"

"More like both/and," said Prax darkly. Turk shrugged.

After their first initial visual orientation, they split up. Turk went off in search of his band, who according to the messages left for him at the motel were supposed to be around somewhere at the field, while Rennie and Prax headed to the trailer that was serving as festival headquarters. Turk and Prax had performers' passes, of course, but Rennie had been given a press pass, which counted for pretty much nothing, as it wouldn't get her either backstage or onstage, which, for her job, was where she needed to be. However, it was nothing that couldn't be fixed. So she went for the gold—an upgrade to "Performer"—and after a few minutes of affable conversation, and dropping Turk's and Fitz's names at least half a dozen times apiece, she got it.

"What?" asked Prax, having given her friend a keen glance as they left the trailer and trudged up the dusty road. "You look more frazzled than victorious in your quest for pass top-of-the-heapness; what's up?"

Rennie smiled, a little ruefully. "It's just that worlds seem to be colliding here—for me, anyway. My collegiate and vacation pasts were spent in this area or nearby locales very similar—as you know, I went to school not far away, and my whole family came up here for summers when I was a kid, over by Deposit, we had a huge old house right on the river, aunts and uncles and cousins and all. So, my past, and now my whole new rockerverse present. Not to mention my very Turk-specific future. One on top of the other on top of the next. It's making me feel a little giddy and off-center, is all." She gestured out at the billowing throngs overspreading the pasture. "And *that*...doesn't help."

"But that's what we came for, isn't it?"

"Is it?" Rennie looked around her again at the sprawling canvas before her, and gave a little shrug, like a horse flicking off a troublesome fly, and tried to deny prescience. "Let's hope."

~6~

"DID YOU HEAR about what happened to Cory Rivkin? And Sunny Silver?"

Rennie looked with sudden alarm at Belinda Melbourne, her East Village friend, neighbor and press colleague, who'd materialized in the road ahead of them, having just been dispensed from a convoy arriving from the motels. The vehicular procession had consisted of half a dozen vans and cars, escorted by state police, delivering a fine mixed bag of musicians from several different bands, a few media types and several of Rennie's favorite people—Belinda herself, photographer Francie Nolting, wildman gonzo writer Luther Dials, newly arrived from Ann Arbor, Rennie's new London friend Liz Williams and old San Francisco friend Marishka Erzog, amicably split from Clarion reporter Stan Hirsch and newly ecstatic with love-of-her-life Bill Looking, also here present, a photographer for the rival Chronicle, though Rennie didn't hold that against him.

"Cory and Sunny? Uh, no, I haven't?"

She tried to keep fear out of her voice: tall, beautiful, cocoa-skinned Sunny was the queen of rock-jazz vocalists and a good friend, and had been directly contributory to kicking off Rennie's career as a crime-solving, or at least crime-contiguous, rock reporter, back in San Francisco, and Rennie was extremely fond of her. Cory she didn't know except by name, but he was the drummer for Owl Tuesday, a solid second-rank L.A. band to whom Rennie had given a few bits of good press in days gone by. The group was also a client of former Lionheart publicist Rose Noble, who'd had a big giant crush on Turk and whom Rennie had once suspected of being the multiple murderer and even bigger Turk-crusher-onner that Rose's business partner had turned out to be instead. Rose would be someone else to carefully avoid here, now that she thought of it...but, again, big field.

"Sunny's okay!" Belinda hastened to assure her, putting one arm around her and the other around Prax, and scooting them both up toward the performers' pavilion. "But she might not have been... She was out back behind the stage when they were loading in and an amp fell while it was being carried past her. Fell right on top of her, actually."

"Oh my God! But you say she's okay."

Belinda nodded. "The amp whacked her on the arm and they think it's broken. Her arm, not the amp. The amp's broken too. But otherwise she's fine, just pissed off at the roadies she claims were responsible. Which they claim right back equally pissed-offedly they had everything secured just fine and someone must have messed with it. She's going on tomorrow anyway. Wearing a sling too, how dramatic is that. Too bad you didn't think to bring that fringed leather one that little groupie made you last year when you got shot, she could borrow it."

"I can't remember *everything*... So, about Cory Rivkin? Another broken arm? Broken leg? Black eye?"

At the suddenly somber, closed look on Belinda's face, Rennie closed her eyes briefly and shook her head and stopped in the road where she stood. *And so it begins...* "Oh God—tell me it isn't true."

"I can't tell you that."

"So what *can* you tell me?"

"That's it." Belinda looked even unhappier than she already did. "Nobody has any idea. He was apparently out roaming around the festival, happy as a clam, picked up a cute little groupie—no one anyone knows, and she hasn't been seen since, in case you were wondering—and he was sitting in the pavilion alternately talking to some people from his label and making out with the chick when all of a sudden he fell over dead."

Prax let out an incredulous disbelieving half-laugh, half-scoff. "But surely—"

"Nope." The three started to walk up the hill again, more slowly this time. "Some people from the medical tent came running right over, of course. They couldn't do anything; he was gone before he hit the ground. They said it didn't appear up front to be drugs, but they couldn't say what it *might* be—heart attack, stroke, allergic reaction—nobody knows. They flew his body out an hour ago on one of the choppers, to the county morgue. I would think there'll be some sort of autopsy. But they're keeping both incidents and especially the death as quiet as they can, so the fans don't flip out before this thing even gets going." Belinda looked sideways at her friend. "Do you think it's an omen?"

An omen. What was it Lexie Kagan had said, something about Saturn was not to be trusted? Sounded as if the prediction was going to be right on the money. But she wasn't about to admit *that* out loud. Much as Rennie liked her, Lexie, or rather Annadawn, had an slightly overinflated sense of her abilities as it was. And now the festival hadn't even started yet and already someone was hurt and someone else was dead. Rennie found to her surprise that she was shivering, and not with cold.

"I wouldn't like to speculate. But it is obviously something. And having the suspicious minds we all have—"

"Or have developed over the years," Prax put in.

"As you say… Let us consider this. But not now."

They flashed their passes to the smiling mustached freak standing guard at the pavilion entrance. Through the grace and clout of her betrothed, Rennie had scored not merely a performer's pass but a performer's pass as an actual member of Lionheart—which did not make glad the heart of Niles Clay when he heard *that,* though he couldn't do a damn thing about it in any case, as Turk himself had suggested it, to give Rennie the maximum possible access—and now as she entered the pavilion, she resumed the conversation.

"About Sunny, then? Are we thinking accidentally for real, or are we thinking nastier thoughts?"

"You're the one who can best judge that sort of thing, I'd say," said Belinda, deferring to experience. "But purely offhand? I'd say accidentally on purpose. Just a feeling."

"And Cory? That's *really* all you know?"

"Yes, it *is,* Strider, I swear. You know I'd tell you if there were any more to tell. My journalistic rival, nay, my admitted superior, though you may be," Belinda added with a smile that said You know I really think no such thing, I'm only putting you on because you're my friend. "Even if there happened to be a scoop involved."

"How gracious of you to say so. Well, okay. Okay. For

now." With an effort and a deep breath, Rennie pushed the fear and misgivings away. "Would you *look* at this place! It's like a big huge circus tent. Or a teepee without the tee. Hopefully also without the pee."

The spacious performers' pavilion, open to the air on all sides, was surrealistically pillared with huge wooden rough-barked telephone poles arranged in a modified teepee or giant campfire formation, as Rennie had noted; floored with wood chips and roofed with canvas, it was a landbound galleon, heading for the Gates of Eden. And its long metal tables accoutered with white linen cloths and wooden chairs were beginning to fill up with a fine crew of pirates, all sporting official Woodstock badges. Though many of them had faces sufficiently universally known as to make such identifiers purely superfluous. Looking around, Rennie felt another surge of excitement. This was going to be good. Or, if not, then at least interesting.

Hungry again, she and Belinda made a beeline for the caterers' table, already set up, while Prax scouted out a good place for them to sit. Loading up plates with cold shrimp, cheese chunks, homemade bread, chopped salad and sliced fruit, they headed over to a long table already occupied by members of the Dead, the Airplane, Prax's band Evenor and a few rock writers—all people they liked—where Prax had secured three of the folding wooden chairs.

Rennie accepted a glass of Moët from the chilled bottle that Pigpen of the Grateful Dead had just opened. Which was living dangerously, since that band and their minions liked to merrily spike the drinks of the unsuspecting with acid, and Owsley the LSD king had of course supplied the festival with his best. In fact, some Dead roadies had already tossed some of that primo acid into a big bowl of innocent-looking punch over on a side table: Rennie watched Daily Pillar columnist Alvy Larrable, one of her least favorite people on the planet and forty years older than just about everybody there, gulp an enthusiastic mouthful before someone leaned over and obviously warned him, for he instantly spat it out and flung the remainder angrily onto the ground.

Huh. With any luck, maybe he'd swallowed enough to start him tripping like a hobo riding the psychedelic rails, the septic creep; could be fun to watch, especially if he started hallucinating that he was turning into a taxicab, or a potato chip. She couldn't really complain from the moral high ground, though: she'd done as much to guests of her vile mother-in-law Marjorie, at a society tea party in San Francisco, right after she'd left Stephen to live on her own in the Haight. It had been a stuck-up assemblage of San Francisco's upper-crustiest dragonesses, and Rennie, full-on pissed off at pretty much every single thing about it, including the hot-pink Chanel suit she'd been forced to wear, had treated them to a little touch of Strider in the night—orange sunshine tossed into the tea samovar. It had turned out to be an interesting party, to say the least, once the acid had kicked in, even though much diluted... Still, she needed *something* to drink, and the bubbly was the only thing cold and going at the moment. And as she'd seen Pig actually uncork the bottle, with no funny business apparent, she'd take her chances.

After a while Belinda drifted off to go sit with some other people they knew, and Rennie and Prax were alone. By mutual unspoken agreement, they intended to say nothing about Sunny or Cory to anyone but Turk and Prax's main squeeze Ares Sakura, who was expected later that day. But apparently the news was already common knowledge, and a shocked buzz was running around the pavilion. Rennie was aware of covert glances being cast her way—*oh yeah, sure, Murder Chick will know all about it, right? Probably already solved it, even, right?*—and was deeply annoyed. And even more deeply determined not to play into it. Still, she wasn't too proud to listen to the waves of unsound speculation sloshing up and down the tables, though nothing seemed to throw any more light on events than Belinda had: Sunny, stacks, broken arm; Cory, happy one minute, dead the next. Big help.

Diego Hidalgo, the tall, dark and tiresome lead singer of the superhot L.A. band Cold Fire, came ambling past, nodding and smiling vaguely at them in greeting, and Rennie looked speculatively after him for a little longer than perhaps was strictly necessary. Prax caught the look.

"Yes? You want to tell me—what?"

Rennie grinned. "Oh, I may have mentioned it a while back. A little spot of matchmaking I have in mind."

"I remember you saying something of the sort, but you never gave out any specifics. So who *do* you have in mind?"

"Diego, of course."

She'd been expecting Prax to choke on her champagne, but instead her friend gave her a serious and considering glance. "Not a bad idea. He's completely bonkers, as we all know, but lately, like a few other people on his level, he's been getting more grown-up and interesting, and he'd probably be a lot of fun. He's certainly cute enough. Obviously you're not in the market yourself, nor am I. But I thought he was involved again, or still, or again again, with that platinum-blond bimbo we can't stand. Portia Paradise!" she chortled. "Now there's a nice traditional hooker name for you! What the hell were her parents thinking? Does the name make the woman, or vice versa?"

Rennie was struggling to keep a straight face. "She came into the hotel room once when I was interviewing Diego for the Clarion and introduced herself." She affected a wispy helium singsong. " 'Hi Rennie, I'm Portia, Diego's wife'." She resumed her own voice. "Diego rolled his eyes and shook his head quite definitely, behind her back where she couldn't see him doing it. Naturally, I politely commended her parents' choice of name as being doubly Shakespearean: *Merchant of Venice* Portia, quality of mercy is not strained, and *Julius Caesar* Portia, noble wife of Brutus, right? She looked at me as if I'd suddenly sprouted another head and squeaked, 'What are you *talking* about? They named me for a *car*!'"

When they'd stopped screaming with laughter and picked themselves up off the ground, Prax shook her own head, marveling. "Sweet Mother of God and all the little angels! What do you suppose a guy like him sees in someone like her? He's not stupid, after all. It can't just be the sex. Or can it?"

"They don't have sex," said Rennie, pouring out some more Moët. "Not with each other, anyway. They both told me. I've been trying to bleach it from my memory ever since."

"Then what's the deal?

"She's his Cheeto, of course."

"His *what*?"

"His Cheeto." Rennie's eyes sparkled with malice. "Cheap, artificially colored junk food that guys go for when they're stupid and drunk and stoned. As we all know, Diego's often drunk and frequently stoned, and so he's kept her around, wondering all the time why he's not happy. But as you said, he's not stupid, and in those ever-increasing moments when he's sober and serious, he realizes he's allowed himself to settle for a shallow, shrieking, vapid, uneducated, parasitical, heroin-shooting gold-digging bleach-blonded over-tanned harridan, with the intellect of a flounder, the attention span of a flea and, in time, the complexion of a saddle, whose only real redeeming virtue, at least in Diego's eyes, is that she gives him permission to behave like a jackass."

"Wow, I didn't know you liked her so much!"

"Not finished, my sarcastic little pumpkin... Naturally, it makes him miserable to think that of himself, so then he goes out looking for a woman of substance and spirit and sexiness and brains. Problem is, any woman like that knows all about the Cheeto. And not only does such a woman want nothing to do with any man who'd keep a Cheeto around, however fine-looking and talented he might be, but such a woman won't put up with his jackassery the way the Cheeto does. Our Diego knows he can, in a sick, twisted sort of way, rely on said Cheeto to always be there for him."

"And being the sort of creature she is, she's not about to kiss off her meal ticket, at least not without another equally good one lined up—she's stupid, but not *that* stupid."

"Zackly! So, sadly, he ends up back with her as the course of least resistance. But hopefully not forever. As we've noticed, he's been changing. He's getting tired of behaving like the king of the jackasses: he's cutting out the drinking and the drugs and the assholic behavior—our little boy is growing up, Mother! I think he's ready to get serious for real, and when he is, I intend to fix him up for real."

"Do you have a candidate?"

Rennie smiled mysteriously. "Oh yes, you bet I do. She doesn't know yet, of course, and neither does he. But it will be the best thing that ever happened to either of them. It probably won't last, but while it does it will be fantastic."

In the meantime, there was lunch. As they worked their way through the salad and shrimp and fruit, Rennie was only half-listening to the nearby biz-heavy conversation, then something caught her ear and she turned to the speaker.

"Wait, wait, you're telling me RCA won't let you guys print 'fuck' or 'fucking' or 'motherfucker' on the liner notes, but you can *sing* any or indeed all of those in the songs?"

Spencer Dryden, Jefferson Airplane's impressively mustached drummer, nodded a mournful shaggy head. "Yeah, and not even mixed down. Weird, isn't it? They said we can sing it as much as we please, so apparently it doesn't offend human ears, or at least some human ears, but we have to use a substitute word fit for human sight in the liner notes and on the jacket. That's their idea of free speech. Whose ears, we wanted to know? Whose sight? What humans? What do you mean, 'fit'? After a few rounds we gave up and said we'd write it out as 'fred'."

Rennie knocked back the remainder of her champagne. "Hey, fred that, brother! I don't know about the rest of the world, but I'm going to strive my damnedest to keep the verb 'to fuck' and all its possible conjugations and variations safe from motherfucking dodo-like extinction. And, indeed, from dodos. Who's with me?"

General agreement and toasts of approval from those at the table—yeah, they'd drink to that, all right, the champagne sure hadn't taken very long to kick in. Nor had that first bottle lasted long: emboldened, Rennie grabbed another from the ice-water tub it and its fellows stood in.

She struggled briefly with the wire cage holding the cork, and succeeded only in breaking off the twisty bit that unwound the cage. Looking around for something to give her leverage, she saw Dian Cazadora, short blond head of publicity for Sovereign Records, watching her critically. Not to mention unhelpfully.

"I'm trying to get this bottle open..." Rennie explained, nursing a scratched and bleeding finger—the sharp little wire point had gotten her good.

Dian frowned, and spoke with, to Rennie's ear, more than a touch of condescension. "Why don't you ask one of the cats to do it for you?"

Well, up yours, bitch! But that kind of attitude's only what I'd expect from someone who's secretly bonking a Delta blues legend twice her age – and a married one at that...

"Oh, *I* like to be independent every chance I get," Rennie said sweetly, and with one final rotation of her uninjured forefinger and thumb succeeded in popping the cork. "Care for a drink?" But Dian thought not.

Feeling comfortable and at ease now that she was sure she wasn't tripping, Rennie sipped her self-procured glass of fizz and looked around her. This wasn't half bad, no, it wasn't. It was already like the world's biggest press party, and normally she didn't enjoy such things, or at least not too many of them, but the vibe was mellow and the weather was warm and the champagne was cold, and without even turning her head she could see at least several dozen people she knew and most of whom she liked.

A cast of hundreds of thousands out front, mere hundreds backstage. All the top echelons of the rockerverse were already well represented. There were musicians, publicists—including Lionheart's and Evenor's flack Pie

Castro, who greeted Rennie and Prax with delight—label executives, photographers, managers, writers, people of all degrees of clout from all levels of media. But the musicians were the ones who held everyone's covert, and not so covert, attention: it wasn't often that you got so many of them assembled in one place, and all so affable and available, not to say vulnerable, even. There would be some good stories to be written from this unprecedented bounty.

Sitting there, she could see future articles popping up like mushrooms after rain. Not merely the old reliable Airplane and Dead, but Jimi Hendrix and Peter Townshend, English guitar sensation Plato Lars, singer-songwriter Romany Rye, Sledger Cairns, the best, and just about only, female lead guitarist in rock—however would she decide? She sat back and happily considered the luxury of choice. Perhaps she would simply toss an acid cube over her bare halter-topped shoulder and see who it hit…

Even famously reclusive Bisk Hastings, founder of that classic California band the Sunset Surfers, had shown up, sitting off at a side table like a large pallid Malibu Buddha, nodding magisterially to her when their glances met. Ah, he hadn't forgotten her, had he, no, he hadn't. She proudly recalled the totally bizarre though amazing interview she'd managed to dredge out of him one hot afternoon last summer, while he floated in his clifftop pool above the Pacific like Moby-Dick and she sat cross-legged at poolside, watchful as Ahab and interrogative as Ishmael, gradually and skillfully harpooning the Whiteness of the Whale—literal as well as figurative.

Fitz had been delighted with the vivid and scooperific piece she had turned in, particularly since Bisk had steadfastly refused to speak to any reporter at all for the past two years and was known to leave his walled Point Dume compound only under cover of darkness. He hadn't spoken to any reporter since, of course, either, and swore he never would again, but Rennie quite reasonably felt that that was hardly *her* fault: he had said what he had said in front of a journalist, presumably because he'd wanted to say it, and that journalist had written it up with perfect honesty and scrupulous fairness. She certainly hadn't put a gun to his head, and he had no business whatsoever complaining of her treatment of him. No, she had done quite right by Mr. Hastings, and she had nobly refrained from making him look like the complete wacko he *so* was. He had done that all by himself.

And now look! Here he was, at this huge and extremely public event, way out of his comfort zone and his geographical preference, looking as if he were enjoying himself, even. So perhaps she had let a little crack of reality daylight shine in on him after all, which would of course only be a great service to rock and roll, and rock and roll should give her a medal. Conspicuous valor under fire. Rock and roll should really have come across with at least a few Purple Hearts for her already, considering what she'd done for it, and suffered for it... So she returned Bisk's nod with equal majesty, one potentate to another, and smiled, and let her gaze drift on.

Well, things seemed off to a reasonably good start. Except for the news about Sunny and Cory, of course, which was neither good nor reasonable. Rennie brooded about that for a while: if already there had been a death and a serious accident, what did it bode, proportionately, for the next three days? And the festival didn't even get going properly until tomorrow anyway—who knew what could, or would, happen? Still, it was absolutely no good worrying about it: what was going to happen *would* happen, no matter what you did or said, and the more you thought about bad things the more you drew the possible badness to you. Even Kaiser and Annadawn would agree there. In the meantime, no doubt she and Turk and their friends would find ways to amuse themselves. There appeared to be ample scope for that.

Once again she felt that shiver of excitement running through her as she looked out at the pavilion and the field, and it had nothing to do with the champagne and it flew right in the face of the bad stuff. In here and out there was what she had gotten into rock for; maybe everyone else had too. *The song of my people! Let it ring out across the land...* One way or another, they were all about to hear it.

~7~

SHE WAS ON her third glassful from the paranoiacally guarded champagne bottle—no one was getting close enough to electrify *this*—and feeding little pieces of shrimp to the tiny Persian kitten a fellow writer had brought along when someone pulled up a chair beside her and grabbed her right breast.

Instead of throwing an instant left cross death blow, as one does, she just grinned. "Ah, I'd know that hand anywhere..."

"Considering it taught you how to fight, I should damn well hope so." Ares Sakura leaned forward to accept the kiss on the cheek and the drink she offered, both at once.

"When did you get here? We thought you wouldn't show up till later tonight. Did you see Praxie? She was around somewhere..." Rennie fluttered vague fingers at the entire festival field.

"Just now. Landed at JFK from L.A. and drove straight up here. Haven't seen anyone yet, not even that girl of mine. I came in with a state police escort from Liberty, shepherding Daltrey and Townshend and some of our other British pals. Including—"

"Gray and Prue! Oh, I *am* glad—when I spoke to them

last week, they said they weren't sure they'd be able to make it."

"They did, and they have." He took a deep swig of champagne. "Argus Guardians has been officially booked to look after them. I'm here in a general overseeing capacity, not really on the job personally—unless a situation arises, of course. But ever since he got shot at the Albert Hall back on New Year's Eve, Gray's been a mite, shall we say, gun-shy."

"We were there. Who can blame him?"

"Indeed. Though it was Prunella herself who insisted on the armed escort on his behalf. So I assigned two of our London staff to come with them, and two more to handle things back at the castle—chiefly to watch over their kiddiewinks. They're becoming my best customers, the Sonnets. Not that I encourage paranoia for the sake of personal profit, you understand, but the fees *are* fat and pleasant even with a friends' discount and we all want to keep those adorable kids safe, so I'm happy to oblige."

"Well, as an ex-Budgie, Gray can certainly afford you, and the former Prue Vye, queen of the top-40 charts, isn't short of brass either. And now they've got Thistlefit. I'd say the wolf is nowhere near their joint marital door. Or portcullis, actually."

Ares nodded agreement. "Rhino Kanaloa's here, too, to be my second, and I brought in half a dozen other reinforcements from San Francisco and New York, to serve on an ad hoc and as-needed basis, roaming around. Though our presence doesn't seem really necessary," he added, automatically checking out the surroundings. "Nobody's violent. So far, anyway."

"Well, it's early days yet, let's not get carried away by optimism. But apparently not able to avoid death and disability. Have you heard what happened to Sunny Silver and Cory Rivkin?"

Ares' face went suddenly somber. "Funny, *I* was going to ask *you*—"

After splitting from Rennie and Prax, and collecting his band, Turk hadn't stayed long at the fair. In fact, he'd herded Lionheart onto helicopters headed back to the motel—the air shuttle had started flying at last, and were busily bringing in not only performers and other VIPs but food and blankets and medical supplies to cover future needs. He'd set up a few small practice amps in one of the roadies' rooms, so that the whole of the band could run through, albeit in rather cramped confines and at greatly reduced volume, the setlist for their performance tomorrow night. There would be no sound check and no chance to rehearse on the actual festival stage—not just for Lionheart, for anyone—so they were doing what they could to get themselves worked up into performance mode.

When Rennie walked by a couple of hours later, fresh from the festival field herself, and peered around the corner of the half-open door to see them still playing, everyone but Turk took her arrival as an immediate signal to punch the clock and knock off work. She looked after them, faintly smiling, as they scurried out of the room before Turk could stop them. Niles kept his face averted from her as he sidled past, and ended up catching his toe in the hideous carpet, almost ending up *on* the carpet, nose first. Rennie watched his ungraceful exit with a certain amount of amusement that for all her efforts, and they weren't that assiduous to begin with, she was unable to keep concealed.

"Goodness! I hope it wasn't something I said?"

Turk laughed, stretching hugely and reaching for her. "No—they were glad of any old excuse to scarper. Right before you came in, they were pissing and moaning that I was working them ever so hard and anybody else would have let everything happen ever so groovily and I was nothing but a horrible taskmaster control freak on a power trip."

"And you, being the person you are—"

"I wasn't doing it for my personal glory. There's no 'I' in 'band', you know," Turk loftily informed her. "Or in 'control freak', either, for that matter."

She put her arms around his neck and kissed the top of his head, massaging his shoulders, where she could feel the tension already knotting up his deltoids like macramé. "No, but there are two in 'nitwit'. Can't you spot them a few hours off? You could use a break yourself, judging by the feel of these muscles," she added. "So let's go to our room to change, and then go get on the outside of some serious chow. I'm so hungry I could eat the *moon*..."

They went out for dinner in the town at a little place they'd noticed as they were driving by earlier and decided they could walk to. They'd glanced in at the motel dining room, wondering if perhaps they should give it a try, but it was crowded and noisy, with Judy Collins presiding over a long table full of top record-company personnel, and other music luminaries doing likewise at other tables, and stars strewn all over in tipsy constellations. The adjoining bar was even worse: dozens of boozy rockers sitting with linked arms and swaying along to the jukebox as they joined in on the chorus of "Hey Jude", which someone had programmed fifty times running. Definitely *not* their sort of scene. They had taken one look at both rooms and withdrawn without a single word spoken, heading out instead into the summery early evening.

By contrast, only a handful of rockfolk were patronizing the cozy village restaurant they had in mind, which was, they saw to their relief, just full enough to be quietly and pleasantly festive. Those of their kind who happened to be present were dining in a sedate and civilized fashion, she was glad to see. Across the main dining room, décor heavy on leather and oak and big stone fireplaces, Del McCluin, lead guitarist of Ned Raven's band Bluesnroyals, raised his arm and waggled his hand to catch their attention, and they went over to join him at his otherwise empty table.

The first thing they asked was where were their dear good friends Ned and his lovely wife Demelza, why were they not dining here too, and Del shook his head, wide-eyed.

"Did no one tell you? Incredible. Ned almost got electrocuted onstage. Well, he *did* get electrocuted, actually."

"*WHAT?*" they said together.

"He was doing a little sound check for the techs, just helping out, and trying to avoid a big puddle onstage where it had rained earlier this morning. He was all up on the mike stand the way he does and didn't notice he had his feet right smack in *another* puddle. His belt buckle touched the stand and grounded, and he went flying across the stage. He was out for about fifteen minutes."

"Christ!" said Turk. "No, nobody told us. But he's all right now?"

"Oh yeah. One of the doctors came dashing over to take a look. Once he came round, he was right as, well, rain. Melza was more freaked than he was."

"She would be, wouldn't she. I'd be a lot more than

freaked, I promise you." Rennie touched Turk's arm, and he put a reassuring hand over hers. "Looks like Annadawn's predictions are right on the mark, for starters anyway."

Del looked puzzled. "How do you mean?"

Though Rennie had briefly filled her consort in on Sunny's accident and Cory Rivkin's mysterious death, back in the motel room, sobering him considerably, Del in his turn had not heard, so she gave them both the whole story, while they all munched on tasty little homemade corn fritters. Del was suitably appalled; Turk less so, since he'd learned about it earlier, but also since his life had come to have Rennie in it he had also learned to expect this sort of thing at more or less regular intervals. Still, it wasn't exactly pleasant dinner-table conversation.

"I knew Cory," offered Turk, when Rennie had finished her account of events. "We did a month as house band at the Troubadour in L.A., with Owl Tuesday as our opening act, the year before Monterey; we were over from England to try to break through, yet again, and yet again unsuccessfully, in the U.S. market. They're a nice little outfit. I was considering asking them to open for us on this tour, but Freddy said no, wants to use us to help him push a new Centaur signing called Sir Topaz, with whom we are now, alas, stuck—at least for parts of the tour. But Cory was a very decent chap. We had some good jams together."

"Nobody knows what he died from?" asked Del, as Rennie herself had earlier, and she shook her head.

"Not yet, anyway."

"I know this is going to sound horrible and heartless," said Turk after a moment, "and I also know that both of you are thinking exactly the same discreditable thought, but what do you think Owl Tuesday will do now for a drummer?"

ꟹ

They discussed that for a while (some band would certainly lend them one for the gig, presuming they still had the heart to play at all, which yeah right of course they would, they weren't about to miss the biggest festival *ever*, were they?, no of course they weren't, show must go on, sort of thing, and no doubt they'd find someone else after the festival), and made short work of the food when it arrived: nothing fancy, just hearty homestyle cooking on a level that they quite snobbishly hadn't thought to find in an upstate eatery—char-grilled steak, roast chicken, bacon-wrapped pork tenderloin, all fresh and all delicious with the taste of local summer produce. Liberty might be a country village, but it was situated in the heart of Catskill vacationland, with food-savvy New Yorkers of various ethnicities filling the surrounding resorts; so there was more decent grub to be had than might have been expected, and this place was something of a local landmark, around for decades.

During the meal Turk and Rennie had naturally inquired about other bands and friends, and Del, whom they'd both known for years, had been happy to fill in such details as he was aware of: Jimi Hendrix would be driving over from his rented house in West Shokan, forty miles away and not far from the real Woodstock, where he'd been woodshedding with his new band; the British acts were arriving by ones and twos; Janis was here with her own new outfit; the Doors had been asked but had declined, claiming they weren't an outdoor band, or Morrison was afraid he'd be assassinated, some psychic he knew had warned him, or something; the Monkees had apparently been deemed not hip enough, even though Hendrix himself had opened for them on their tour the summer before last.

As for their own personal friends, Powderhouse Road had been invited, but they were touring Europe and would miss the whole thing, while Dandiprat, busy recording in London, didn't want to take the time off. Sledger Cairns had just come off a big road trip and was wiped out, preferring to be entertained herself for a change, and Stoneburner apparently couldn't be bothered. Cold Fire, like the Doors, had remained at home in L.A., though both Diego Hidalgo and John Densmore had come to hang out on their own, while Gray and Prue Sonnet were already here with the rest of Thistlefit, scheduled to play on Sunday, and staying at the same motel Lionheart and Evenor and Bluesnroyals were. Though Rennie had missed seeing them at the festival site, they would surely be back at the motel by now, available for cozily catching up on events since all of them had shared the Albert Hall, uh, excitement.

As they discussed the full roster, with Turk and Del judicially commenting on their fellow musicians, Rennie was impressed all over again. The promoters had done an amazing job of securing the cream of the crop; even the lesser names were solid and good, and there was no more than a scant handful of unknowns or possible snoozers and misfits. Some of the biggest acts around had unfortunately ceased to be over the past couple of years, disbanding under various circumstances for various reasons: Cream, Buffalo Springfield, Lovin' Spoonful, the Jeff Beck Group only last week. Even the Mamas and the Papas had broken up, and would not be appearing here or anywhere else.

Others had declined right off the bat: Led Zeppelin felt they would be just another band on the bill and their interests would be better served by playing Asbury Park,

New Jersey that weekend; the Byrds had had a recent bad experience with an outdoor festival and decided to pass on this one; the Moody Blues opted to play a gig in Paris instead and would regret it ever after; Procol Harum was just wrapping up a long tour and Robin Trower wanted to be home for the birth of his child; and Ian Anderson of Jethro Tull had reportedly declared he didn't care to spend a weekend in a field with hundreds of thousands of unwashed and probably naked hippies. Not even standing on one leg.

But despite hopeful rumors that refused to die among the fans, the true giants in the earth would be conspicuous only by their echoing absence. The Beatles and the Rolling Stones had visa drug issues as usual, and too many other issues as well, plus they reportedly had asked to be paid far more than the festival could afford; while Bob Dylan had never planned on getting within fifty miles of the thing to begin with, being already fed up with fans staking out his house in the real Woodstock. He was said to be boarding an ocean liner at the moment, headed to England with his family, to play instead at the Isle of Wight festival two weeks hence...lucky old him, then. And clever old him too.

Walking back to the motel, holding hands and intent on an early bedtime, Turk and Rennie encountered a few others of their tribe, on a quest for a good evening meal; they recommended the place where they'd dined and passed peaceably on. Still, looking around in the blue dusk wrapping the quiet hills, Rennie felt not the serenity she had expected to be feeling but an inexplicable unsettledness rising up from her toes and settling in her middle, making her solar plexus quiver like a trapped sparrow. It communicated itself to Turk, right down along her arm and hand and over to his, and he looked down at her, concerned.

"Problem?"

"Not sure yet."

Which was only the truth. She felt shiveringly excited by the prospect of the music to come, as she had twice earlier that day, but now there was this other, more dreading shivery feeling mixed in with it. The one Prax had christened, with horrible accuracy, slaydar. She had learned, the hard way, to ignore it at her peril.

~8~

"WHAT HO, SUGARBRITCHES!"

Ned Raven, looking only slightly the worse for wear after his exciting encounter earlier that day with the forces of electricity, came up beside Rennie in the crowded motel hallway and threw an affectionate arm around her neck.

"Ah, Reddy Neddy Kilowatt, the Amazing High-Voltage Shockman! Del told us all about it; we ran into him in the town having dinner." She hugged him back, then punched his shoulder. "Why you do things like that, Edmund, why you *do* them, why why why?"

"Not my fault," said Ned promptly. "Blame it on Mother Nature for tossing a whacking big rain puddle right by the mike stand. How was I to know I was standing in a pool of hidden peril waiting to strike me down?"

"Only the heir to the throne of the kingdom of the idiots would say so." Rennie sighed, and hugged him again. "Please. You people have *got* to be more careful. Gray Sonnet gets shot at the Albert Hall back on New Year's Eve. Last month Moggy Barnes ends up stabbed to death in Hyde Park. This morning Sunny Silver gets clipped by a falling amp and Cory Rivkin mysteriously drops dead in the pavilion. Now you and this."

Ned shook his head mournfully. "I heard about Cory and Sunny... Mel is threatening not to let me out at all in public anymore without a bodyguard—I understand Ares Sakura has brought a whole platoon, perhaps I could commandeer a small one he'd never miss. But at least *I* haven't gotten carbon-monoxided to within an inch of my life or shot or beaten up or kidnapped or held hostage. Nooooo, that would be *you* two. And of those two, mostly you. Yes, yes, I keep tabs on all your little adventures, don't try to deny any of it."

Rennie had the grace to look embarrassed. "Never mind that. You *sure* you're feeling okay?"

They were standing outside Airplane manager Bill Thompson's suite, one of the few the motel boasted—Joan Baez, to her amusement, had been assigned the bridal suite, which seemed about right for her queenly status, though, true to her egalitarian nature, she'd given it away to someone and ended up in a regular old room. Thompson's rooms and a connecting one were crammed full of hard-partying people who had overflowed into the corridor, and Turk and Rennie had been fighting their way past to get to the quieter hallway further on where their own room was located. At the moment they were stalled in traffic, so had decided to hang out a bit while trying to eel their way through; it shouldn't take that long, she thought, and they could chat with friends as they tunneled past. Someone had propped a nearby emergency door open, and there was a nice cool breeze blowing through, dispelling some of the heat and pot smoke; Rennie turned her face to it gratefully.

Ned was grinning at her discomfiture. "Never better. No, wait, I tell a lie, I've felt loads better on many occasions.

But you needn't worry, Renners, it's all fine. And we're looking forward to going on tomorrow, as Del surely mentioned."

"He did. You lot and the Lions and Sunny together on one night should be epic. Maybe you and his lordship and Miss Silver can mutually sit in with one another."

"We might do that. Friday was supposed to be all folk-you, but they crammed us heavy mobbers in at the last minute. Speaking of Turk, I take it you and he are still madly in love? No chance for me at all?" He mock-sighed dramatically. "And yet again I am doomed to tragic disappointment! Whatever do you see in him, I wonder? Besides the fact that he is tall, gorgeous, brilliant, titled, came to Earth with powers and abilities far beyond those of mortal men..."

"Oh, not much, really. He's tall, he's gorgeous, he's brilliant, he's titled, he shares my hatred of Jerusalem artichokes, which are as kryptonite to me... Besides, there's Melza to think of. And I know you do. It would never work between us. But we knew that years ago."

"Ah me, a bloke can hope..." He abandoned the teasing and gave her a buoyant smile. "It's all worked out very much for the best all round, I'd say, right? Where is he, by the way? You two are never more than an arm's length apart, you crazy romantic kids."

"He went inside to say hi to Thompson and the band. I saw them all this afternoon, so I didn't feel the need."

"Too bad you didn't feel the need to stay away entirely. We'd all have been happier for it. In fact, we'd be even happier if you just stayed away forever, slag."

Both Rennie and Ned turned in surprise at the waspish voice, which they had recognized at once as Niles Clay's.

He was standing a few feet away, glaring at Rennie through narrowed eyes under his trademark tangle of coal-black curls. He looked like a malevolent cocker spaniel, and he was obviously exceedingly drunk—and in no merry fashion. And he also looked only too willing to continue the little firefight they'd had in the kitchen at the prow house a few days back.

"Slag", eh? Well, tu quoque, *ratbag*... Turk not being around, she'd be happy to return fire, if that's what Nilesy's slimy limey heart was set on...

Ned unobtrusively stepped between them, in case Niles was planning on taking something more substantial than a verbal shot, or, more likely, in case Rennie was, and she opened her mouth to let blasting words have their way. But someone else had heard everything, and got there first.

"Speak to my lady like that again, you sodding little wanker, and I'll punch your face out the back of your head. And then I'll sack you. And I don't care if I have to sing lead vocals in your place for the rest of my life."

Turk, in full-on Lord Saltire mode, looked as if he not only *could* do all that but was only *longing* to do all that, and clearly the knowledge that he needed Niles intact for the next day's performance was the sole thing that stayed his hand.

"You're drunk, Niles," he pronounced then, with a snap to his voice like a breaking icicle. "And you're making a comprehensive arse of yourself. Now shut up and go to your room. We have a gig tomorrow, or had you forgotten?"

The Oxford-modulated baritone had cut sharply through the surrounding chatter. Heads turned and voices were momentarily stilled as eager gossipy note was taken: oooh, Niles Clay insulted Rennie Stride and Turk Wayland is pissed off about it, could be good, let's see what happens next, maybe a brawl if we're lucky, money's on Turk! But when nothing further developed, and when Niles merely smirked at Rennie and then strutted away with a sneer still on his face, everyone disappointedly turned back to their previous conversations.

Turk, who had seen Niles off in silence, glaring after his singer's retreating back to be sure he quitted the vicinity, now stood close in front of his mate, looming protectively between her and the rest of the crush, his arm braced against the wall barring anyone from coming near and a scowl as black as iron still on his face.

"Are you all right, sweetheart? Christ, I'm sorry… He's a nasty buggering tosser when he wants to be, especially when he's drunk. Just give me the word and I'll kick him into the middle of next week."

She smiled and let Turk shepherd her away from the crowd; Ned, with a parting peck on the cheek and a quick hug, drifted away to find his wife.

"No, no, I'm fine. It's not the first time he's been rude to me, as you're well aware. And I daresay it won't be the last either. As *I'm* well aware. But thanks for the chivalrous rescue, Studly Do-Right. We just don't get on, Nilesy and I, and that's all there is to it. Oil and water. Burning oil. Tsunami water."

Turk's mouth tightened. "I know. I wish I could do something to fix it, or at least more to help."

By now they had succeeded in fighting their way out of the party hordes and down the short, quiet corridor where the Lionheart lodgings lay. As they entered their room, Rennie immediately turned on the TV and took off her clothes. She still had no intention of telling him exactly *how* rude Niles had been the other day, in her own house, the house she shared with Turk. That revelation would set off an explosion that would tear Lionheart apart, shattering the group unity when unity was most required, both for the festival performance and the upcoming tour, and that was something she was not prepared to do, no matter the circumstances—there was no way she was going down in rock history as the Yoko Ono of Lionheart. No, they would have to work it out, or shoot it out, between them, she and Niles, as obviously neither one was going away. Until then, she would just have to behave like a lady, since one of them clearly had to and it didn't look as if it was going to be Niles. It was an easy sacrifice to make; and for Turk, and for the band itself, she would.

"All the same," she said generously, "we pardon Niles muchly for the sheer wonder of his voice. And I could even be wrong about him. I have recently eaten pie, and I am both sleepy and forgiving of mood."

Turk made an effort to match her light tone; no reason to let Niles' spite spoil the evening, though he was well aware that Rennie wasn't telling him everything.

"How great is pie!"

"Great indeed, and homemade fresh blueberry pie? Even greater. That was the best thing I ever wrapped my mouth around. Well, second best."

Turk grinned. "How kind of you to say so."

She grinned back "My pleasure. We must go back and have some more. Pie, I mean."

"We could do that. If everyone could have that pie, no one would ever fight again. War would be over. Well, perhaps not, because people would go to war over that pie. But we could buy a country house in this neighborhood and have pie anytime we like. All things should end in pie."

"I feel quite strongly that they should, yes. But we just bought three houses; aren't you a little real-estated out?"

"You ask this of someone whose family, not to boast, or at least not overmuch, owns half of England and a nice chunk of Scotland too? Silly girl." He stripped off his shirt, distracting Rennie as usual with well-muscled bare-chestedness. "And the answer, by the way, is never. One can never have too much land, Katie Scarlett; didn't you read *Gone with the Wind*? It's the principle by which my family got most of what it's got: land acquisition by fair means or foul. Usually we married it, which could be both foul *and* fair, come to think of it, but quite often we simply conquered and grabbed."

"Traditionalists!"

He laughed and stripped off the rest of his clothes, distracting her still further. "Very pretty country up here, though; reminds me of the Cotswolds. Didn't you mention at dinner that this was a rather depressed area? Which is very sad, but I bet property is dead cheap. We could buy a hundred acres with a big old farmhouse and a couple of barns; it would be quite pleasant to have a place to get away to for weekends."

"Nice investment, too. Always thinking ahead, aren't you? I like that..."

Turk was getting that faraway look, of acquisition or conquest. "I could build a studio in one barn, and you could design the other as a guest house. We could hire the place out to bands wanting to record and get away to the country at the same time, and we'd be helping the local economy as well."

"It's a good idea. But there are nicer and higher

mountains farther north or farther west, in more sadly depressed country still. More of a schlep from the city, but maybe a better deal house- and land-wise. Also there's oil to be pumped way west, it's an old petroleum-producing region. The Seneca used it to waterproof their canoes since the beginning of time, and later traded it to the white man, who of course then promptly stole it. Lots of houses have little oil rigs in their yards, thunking away and bringing up high-grade crude; they look like tiny dinosaurs, it's fun to see them. We could be oil magnates; I bet your family would approve of that…we'll have to look around." She lay back on the pillows. "Not for a while, though. I'm not up yet for buying still more antique furniture."

"I find that statement almost impossible to accept, but, if you tell me so." He slid into bed beside her, and lay there quietly for a while, his arm around her and her head on his chest.

"Are you okay?" murmured Rennie presently. "You're not nervous about the gig, are you? I wouldn't blame you: it's the hugest thing ever."

"No…no, I don't believe that I am, actually. I was just thinking how the next few months are going to be so rugged. We'll be on the road until Thanksgiving. That's a long stretch to be out and away from home. And then two weeks off and the big Madison Square Garden show in December."

"You signed off on the tour schedule yourself," she pointed out. "We know how this goes. It's what you do. You've been doing it for seven years. More."

"Yes, but I wasn't leaving you behind then, the way I am now."

"Well, we managed last year, didn't we. It wasn't as big

a road trip as this one, but it was bearable, right? It's not fun, it'll never be fun, but we can manage. We'll be fine. Besides, it won't be as bad as all that. It's not solid touring: Mr. Francher Green, clever manager chap that he is, built little rest breaks into the dates around gigs in places we like. And you guys *need* a big successful tour, to remind people exactly what it is that Lionheart does so well. Which they seem to have forgotten."

He acknowledged the compliment with a gentle pinch on her rear. "Little bit, yeah. And I know we need the tour, you're quite right... I just don't like to leave you with all the slog of getting the house together and then come swanning in to take advantage of your hard work."

"Don't be silly, it's my job. All the big messy dusty macho construction stuff is done, anyway, and it's nothing but batting cleanup from here on in. And then moving in all that stuff I bought. Which is my favorite part. Except for the buying more stuff part. You're the one I worry about, out there flipping between cities and me not there to comfort and defend you against the hazards of the road."

"Very thoughtful of you."

"I live for others. As you know."

"Good intentions?"

"Road to hell?"

"That's more like it." She felt his chest move under her cheek as he took a deep breath. "Among those hazards of the road? There's Niles. I don't want to bring it up again, but it does need to be addressed appropriately, before it all blows up in a much worse way. He makes a surprisingly good fist of things on the road, as can be seen from reviews and public opinion, but on a personal note, he can be a pest of hell and he does throw his toys out of his pram quite a bit. We've all had to get used to the tantrums. Still, he was unspeakably vile to you tonight, and that's just not on."

"Oh love, don't get into it. Don't even worry about it. He was reeking drunk and he's been bitchy to me from the start, it's just one of those things."

"You've never been bitchy back."

She twisted to lie stretched atop him, and he put his arms around her to hold her there. "On account of I have the most perfect manners in the world in space in the universe. When it comes right down to it, though, how do you know how bitchy I've been toward him in my heart? Perhaps the time has not yet presented itself for me to be bitchy to him right out front where he can see it. And I won't be shy about it when it does. But before I start unpacking *that,* I want to say one thing: you showed up in my life with two families, Lionheart and the Tarrants. I'm the new recruit to the ranks of both. And I love them both, because I love *you*. I'd love Lionheart even if I didn't love you, since I loved Lionheart before I ever even met you, but you know what I mean."

"Yes, I should think I do."

"And as in every family, there will be little squabbles and prickles and tensions between the members thereof. Certain individuals you don't like as much as you like certain other individuals. Maybe some of them you even loathe, hate and detest. And nothing that you or they do can change it. It's all quite human and natural. I've seen it to one extent or another in every band I've ever, well, seen. Though they, of course, deny it, dear little lambs. So even if Niles and I go to our graves despising each other, and all indications seem to point that way, it's okay. I'm just the lead guitarist's bit of crumpet, I'm not actually the one in the band with him; you and the other guys are. I could wish it doesn't have to be like that, but it's certainly something I can live with if it is. How he handles it is *his* business. But that's how *I* plan on handling it. Subject to your lordship's approval, of course. So. We okay on that?"

"Perfectly. But you and I are always okay." Shifting under her: "Moving right along, there's how much I'm going to be missing you—like this—whilst we're out."

"I'll be joining you, don't forget, the way we did last summer. And you'll be coming home for those little mercy breaks and off weeks, or we could take them in the Bahamas or someplace. So what's really the problem, Flash? Because I can see damn well there is one."

Turk was silent for so long that she lifted her chin from his chest to see if he'd fallen asleep. But he hadn't.

"For the first time ever, I don't think we have anything good enough to go on with. The album, I mean."

She sat up straight astride him and leaned back, looking him full in his troubled face. "WHAT? Are you *kidding* me? You've *never* had doubts about the work! What is it that prompts you to have these feelings now?"

"It's a famous first, then. I don't have to tell *you*: the new album is very different to what the fans were expecting. They're already making no bones about their displeasure with what they've heard off it, from the radio airplay it's been getting. Or rather the lack thereof. Not to mention the barracking from reviewers. It hasn't exactly been one of our big sellers straight out of the gate, and I have infinitesimally small hopes of it picking up later; that's not been our sales pattern over the years, and I don't foresee that changing now. Besides, Centaur aren't behind it with all their might, and that bodes even worse for its fate. So, though most of the setlist for the festival and the tour is material from previous albums, which will be fine, we still have a goodly amount of new stuff in there, which will not be."

He ran a hand over his beard, impatiently. "It's not that I'm afraid we'll get booed off the stage—Christ, that's happened before, we can cope with that. They won't really jeer and hiss, of course; they'll just applaud in lackluster fashion. We'll do well enough money-wise, even if we don't sell out all along the way, so no worries about you and I being forced to live in the street. No. I'm afraid of finding out, in front of half a million people, that our creative cupboard is bare. I'm afraid of not having anything to bring to the table. Or not enough of the *right* thing."

"Oh, honey..." Rennie's voice ached with love and compassion, and she touched his cheek, gently. "You guys have got so much of the right thing it isn't even *true*. Except it is. You bring *so* much to the table that no other band can even find space to put anything on it and they have to go put their own stuff back in the cupboard. You know this. So I ask again: what is it you're *really* worried about?"

Another long pause. "...I sometimes wonder if we're in tune with the spirit of our times after all. Or at least as much as we should be. You know?"

"No, I don't think I do."

"The way the Airplane are, or the Stones, or Cold Fire, or Dylan, or any number of other artists and bands. More in touch with what's going on. We don't do that. We never have done."

Rennie felt a great wash of relief. "Oh, you mean that political protest crap? Well, no, that's right, you *don't* do that, and I for one give thanks to God that you do not. Honey, that's not your thing! Anybody can write simplistic whiny protest songs; that's easy. You guys are hunting much bigger game. And you don't need me to tell you what it is, because you already know."

She collapsed back down atop him, snuggled close, her mouth against his ear. "But I'm going to tell you anyway. You're hunting truth, and art, and beauty. And deep within those things is the only kind of protest that is really worth making, the only kind that's valid and right: a calling out to the world to bear witness. And if you're worried, don't be. You can count on your pride to bring you through. It's the best virtue you've got. I promise. Didn't you know?"

Turk was silent, but she could sense that her words had deeply touched him. "You seem to know all about it," he said at last.

"I do, I really do. And I'm not saying it because I love you and because here you are in bed with me and I plan on taking full advantage of that delightful fact in about thirty seconds or so. I'm saying it because I love your music, and because it is beyond question the pure and beautiful truth. So what if the fans don't like the album? It was what you guys wanted to do, and you did it, and it's good. If it's too different for them to get their tiny fannish heads into, that's not your fault and too damn bad for them. I don't *ever* want you second-guessing yourself and your art. Or your setlist. Because I'll have to smack you. And if that's really what you believe, which I don't for a *heartbeat* believe myself, then you are called over the line and out. You lose serve, go to your room without your supper, and may God have mercy upon your soul."

Turk smiled, but all at once he felt immeasurably relieved, as if a great weight he hadn't known he was carrying had been suddenly lifted from him. She was right, of course. It didn't do to doubt artistic decisions that couldn't, and wouldn't, be changed: all any artist had to go on was what felt right to him. And, in this case, what felt right to his bandmates as well. They had built Lionheart up together for the past seven years on the trust they shared in what they were doing; even if they went out onstage tomorrow and sucked with a giant sucking noise that could be heard on Mars, in the great cosmic scheme of things it wouldn't matter. It would have no real effect on their work, because it couldn't. It might bruise their egos for a while, sure, but that was a hazard of the profession. Ultimately their confidence would be utterly unshaken. Because it had to be. They were artists, and that was what they did.

He kissed Rennie's hair, then grabbed a fistful of it and rolled them both over together. "How did you get to be such a clever girl?"

She smiled up at him, sensing the change in his mood. "Hard work and inborn superiority, of course. And you're a very clever boy to have picked me."

"Quite right about that."

Woodstock, Friday August 15

Richie Havens
Swami Satchidananda
Sweetwater
Sunny Silver
Bert Sommer
Bluesnroyals
Tim Hardin
Ravi Shankar
Lionheart
Melanie
Tenwynter
Arlo Guthrie
Joan Baez

~9~

"HONEEEEEY, I'm sooo booored. Come on, let's get outside for a while." Rennie tugged on Turk's sleeve, and he agreeably rose to follow her, not averse to moving around and stretching his muscles.

Well, the scene in the performers' pavilion *was* getting a bit—static. It was Friday afternoon by now, a mostly sunny day, and they'd been at the festival site since shortly after a lateish breakfast. They could of course have slept in longer—the music wasn't due to start up until around four p.m.—but Rennie had wanted to find out any new information about anything she could, meaning of course Sunny Silver's and Ned Raven's "accidents" and Cory Rivkin's death, and Turk had been likewise eager to find his road crew and talk about the evening's setup. Lionheart would not have the grace of even a sound check before going on, in their scheduled headliner slot as Friday closing act: but then no other group would, either. Nobody was happy about that, but there was no help for it. It was going to be rough and tumble all the way.

Like the old days, Rennie thought, glancing up at Turk, and was reassured. He may have had misgivings in the night, as who wouldn't, on the verge of so momentous a public performance, but they had dealt with that between them, and now he looked happy and ready for anything.

Nodding to people they knew as they went by, they

slipped out the pavilion entrance, where the heads checking passes cheerfully saluted them, then made their way across the grassy slopes beyond the wire fences, intending a little Haroun al-Rashid action. Today's crowds were colossal: many, *many* thousands more than yesterday's: from the foot of the stage to the crest of the slope, the bowl of the former alfalfa field was now nothing but people, sitting or sprawling, crammed and close. And pretty much universally stoned out of their gourds: so many bodies, so few functioning brain cells. Rennie was concerned at first lest Turk be mobbed—most of the other performers were staying safely put in the pavilion, having that same concern—but she soon realized that people were either too high to realize it was actually Turk Wayland come amongst them or too high to care.

Hand in hand, they strolled up the hill to the bordering woods and the vast campground beyond, looking over to where the Hog Farm commune had set up shelters—though plenty of strangers who had tents were happy to share with those who didn't—and bad-trip tents to ease trippers in off the ledge that acid had put them on; back the other way, the Farmers had a huge free kitchen that over the next two days would feed multitudes with bought, brought and locally donated food. There was also an art area which, sadly, had failed to materialize, and the space had been put to other uses; a playground for the kiddies that many young hippie parents had brought with them to witness music history; a small auxiliary stage where people like Jerry Garcia and Mimi Baez Fariña were jamming; and even a little village built by Native Americans who'd taken the long trail all the way from the Southwest and the Plains to the territories of their Woodland kin.

Past all that, in the thick belt of surrounding woods, was a cluster of craftsman's stalls. Rennie brightened, like a dog who hears the glad cry of "Walkies!" Hooray, *shopping*, now *this* was more like it! Here the vibe was a little different, spurred by commerce and, yeah, okay, consumer greed: one tent after another, showcasing macramé, jewelry, incense, paintings, clothes of a gossamer fineness and a rainbow of colors to deck both body and soul. At a leathercrafter's booth, Rennie managed to buy a small fringed purse and a gold-beaded brown suede belt and Turk a handsome tooled-leather duffel bag before recognition struck and Haroun was busted.

Not in a bad way: the kids were all sweetly polite—thrilled to rap for a bit with their idol and his lady, who as she always did stood tactfully away for Turk to do his public job—and *much* too wiped out for bad behavior. Still, it was a little unnerving—like being surrounded in warm, calm shore waters by a shoal of longhaired, beaded, bearded, face-painted, tie-dyed, gently grinning dolphins. Only probably not as smart.

But that certainly didn't keep them from continuing to shop. Rennie bought a little antler-hafted knife from a local Indian-tribe dealer, and, delighted to see that her favorite jewelry maker from Ojai was there, proudly showed off the heavy little silver peace sign of the jeweler's designing that she was wearing. Turk bought her a strand of gold rutilated quartz chunks strung with freshwater pearls, and at another stall she purchased a chain of turquoise scarabs, to be her luck gift to him for the night's performance, as was her custom whenever Lionheart played big important gigs.

There was a neighboring area a little deeper in the woods; one of the fans had told them helpfully that it was known as Drug Alley, and when they were done encouraging commerce they wandered over to take a look from a prudent distance. Booths and blankets were spread out across a little clearing, and thereupon was likewise spread out for sale an impressive and tasteful array of illicit substances, everything from pot to psilocybin. They had no intention of availing themselves of any of this druggish abundance, of course; on the infrequent occasions when they purchased mind-altering herbs or chemicals, they did so from reputable and impeccable dealers, the same discriminating way they did with wine, and if they felt the need to do so here—as possibly they might—they would seek out someone they knew and trusted, not suburban hippies with wares of dubious provenance and uncertain purity.

"I wonder," said Turk reflectively, as they made their way back down through the trees to the pavilion, "if this is going to be the pattern and template for all festivals hereafter."

"You say that as if you're not sure it's a good thing."

"Now that you mention it, I'm not. I mean, *look* at it." He jerked his chin to indicate the landscape before them. "It couldn't get much bigger than this and still be feasible. Not that this really *is* feasible, come to think of it—it's only working so far because everyone's too happy and too spaced out to make trouble. But if the music doesn't start up soon, and continue in timely fashion..."

Rennie nodded. "We're already only a hair away from Lexie's prediction of riot and rampage. There *would* have been a riot by now, if the organizers hadn't declared the festival a free one—though considering that all the fences have been down since Wednesday I don't see how it could have been otherwise. But suppose the food and water run out? Suppose our bonehead Republican draconic antidrug governor decides to send in the National Guard to bust us all for being high? Suppose something really terrible happens? Like someone getting hurt, or even worse? Three someones we know already have…"

Turk said nothing, though he squeezed her hand comfortingly; but Rennie was not comforted. Be careful what you put out there into the cosmos…

The Woodstock Music & Art Fair: An Aquarian Exposition officially opened on Friday August fifteenth, with some official announcements by Chip Monck, tech genius and unofficial voice of Woodstock. The first official music was heard at 5:07 p.m., as Richie Havens' warm voice and cool guitar rang out over the fantastic sound system, and things were officially under way. Everything was there: stage, audience, huge speakers. Only one thing was missing: musicians. Rock stars to make the rock music that half a million rock fans had come to hear. And for which they were all waiting. Patiently. At least for now.

Many of the scheduled performers, including the opening acts, had gotten trapped in the vast traffic jams, on their way either from the city or from the motels, and hadn't managed to get there yet, which nobody had counted on. The stage managers were frantically running around trying to find emergency fill-ins and the tech guys were equally frantically trying to get the place fully and successfully wired up. Because he was there, and because he was acoustic—needed only his guitar, a mike and two sidemen, one with another axe, one with some conga drums—Richie was asked to open the show, and to stretch his set out as long as he could. He hadn't been expecting to assume the full and historic mantle of First Act at Woodstock, and, as he admitted later, he had run out his setlist and had had to improvise. But that improvisation would come to be known as "Freedom, Freedom"—and it did the job.

Though the ever-growing audience had been delighted with the initial offering—music! Finally!—things weren't so smooth after Havens, his orange kurta soaked with sweat, finally left the stage. A master yogi from New York City known as Swami Satchidananda, with flashing eyes, floating hair and a beard like cotton candy, laid a blessing on the festival and the people, getting everyone to happily chant "Hari Hari Om" and "Rama Rama Rama" with him and his saffron-robed acolytes. Which was great, and good for the energy, but which unfortunately didn't eat up all that much time, and the organizers were desperately casting about for anyone they could fling onstage.

But artists had finally started showing up, much to the organizers' relief; they were unceremoniously put to work as soon as they did, and the festival was off and running, or at least jogging. As darkness began to fall, the acts started to take longer and longer to get on, thus setting up the pattern for the whole rest of the weekend. In the atmosphere of controlled chaos that was inevitably taking hold, the delays, though they hadn't been predicted, were at least understandable. The stagehands and techs did their utmost best to battle through, especially after the rotating stage platform broke down about twenty minutes in and all the gear from then on had to be wrangled by hand.

The performers too made their greatest efforts: Sunny Silver, injured arm dashingly strapped against her chest, her powerful voice and equally powerful presence undiminished; Bluesnroyals, rocking so hard that the stage actually shook; Tim Hardin, who asked for and received if not the first recorded match/candle/lighter-flicking moment in rock history, then certainly the biggest.

Making full use of her performer's pass, Rennie had been bouncing back and forth between the pavilion and the stage all evening, sometimes with Turk or Prax or Belinda, sometimes alone. She had wanted to be up close and personal for her friends' performances—Sunny's and Ned's—to provide moral support. They had needed it: no doubt because of their earlier and unsettling mishaps, they had both turned in rather shaky and nervous sets, and Rennie had felt both sympathetic and relieved once they left the stage. Just Lionheart tonight and Evenor tomorrow to pull for, now...

Her first view from the Woodstock stage, in daylight, had been almost beyond her comprehension: it was like nothing anyone had ever seen. Ever. Well, maybe Moses, or Charlton Heston, had, when he'd finally gotten all the Hebrews, or all the extras, lined up and ready to light out for the Red Sea, but that was it. Now the vast darkness spreading out from the stage apron was an endless shift and murmur and tide of vibes: most of them good and amiable and excited, of course; but, extending her awareness out over the crowd, Rennie sensed something unnerving way down in the mix, as she had earlier, a thin cold hard silvery thread running like a garroting wire through the dual atmospheres of fraternal stonedness and rampant consumerism. Sure, the audience was bringing huge amounts of appreciation and approval and love, and that was always good, and vastly to be preferred to boos and screams and murders, which in her experience was how these things all too often turned out. But really they had come, most of them, simply to devour: vibes, music, veneer and outward show; they hadn't much to offer in return but druggy mindless enthusiasm. Not enough. And still she was edgy, and not all of her uneasiness could be attributed to what had happened yesterday to Cory, Sunny and Ned.

Or maybe her sudden downer uncertainty was because she had seen Annadawn off to one side of the stage during Sunny's set, and the expression on Lexie's face as she gazed out over the crowd had made Rennie very thoughtful. But Lexie had apparently not noticed her in return, and Rennie made her way back to the pavilion without their paths crossing. Kaiser Frizelle was also there, floating about, still predicting super grooviness all round, and Rennie very much preferred to believe his take on what was going on in the stars instead.

An indeterminate while later, when a light mist was veiling the darkened field and Ravi Shankar had sent her running away screaming, just as he had done at Monterey, Rennie was returning to the pavilion from a quick pee stop in the nearby woods, after a vain quest for a porta-potty that wasn't either already occupied or completely disgusting. *From now on I pee only at the motel! Good thing I've got a bladder like a camel's...* In spite of the fact that there were half a million people beyond the trees, or perhaps because of it, she'd gone a bit farther and deeper into the thickets than other people on the same errand. She dodged behind some leafy bushes, attended to business, then adjusted her bellbottoms and looked around. *Right, that way. I think?*

Or maybe not: as she walked, the trees seemed to be getting taller and the underbrush thicker, and the sound of rain on leaves could actually be heard over the distant raga being played. *How could you get lost* here? *There's more people on the other side of that hill than live in* Buffalo, *for pete's sake…* She turned around and was headed back the way she thought she'd come when she heard a sudden scuffle behind her. She started to turn, but not quickly enough: an arm flung itself around her throat and another circled her waist and lifted her from the ground, pushing her front against a tree.

Oh man, haven't I been through this before in London? Well, this time I'm ARMED*!*

She reached into her belt for the little knife she'd been getting dirty looks for wearing, oooh *so* not peaceandlovey what a bringdown, slid it out of the buckskin sheath and struck blindly backward into the leg pinning her to the treetrunk. There was a bellow of pain with many bad words in it, the arms fell away; and then she was running as fast as she could in the direction of the music.

Tearing through the woods, listening for the sound of any pursuit, Rennie suddenly found herself at the signposted intersection of two narrow trackways called, apparently, Groovy Way and Gentle Path, and even in her flight she spared time to be eye-rollingly annoyed at the naïve preciousness demonstrated by the handmade little wooden signs. Or the cynical exploitative commercialism. Whichever it was. Stupid goddamn hippies.

"How did you come to be packing a blade?" asked Prax, aghast, after Rennie had finished telling her the story. "It does not surprise me, of course, though I *am* curious. But, I see you're okay, and first you need to know that—"

They were sitting at an empty table in the pavilion and Rennie had been calmed by yet more champagne and a joint pressed on her by her friend JoAnn Langhans, who was sitting with them and who had also gently cleaned the slight scrapes on Rennie's cheek and arms where she'd been shoved into the rough bark of the tree trunk. JoAnn was there with her husband Gerry, who was sitting at another table with other Centaur Records brass, perhaps a dozen in all—though, surprisingly, not Freddy Bellasca, who had not troubled himself to cut short his Mazatlán vacation and fly up to watch his acts, which was fine with everybody, particularly Turk.

"I wanted to cut a hole in the pass holder so I could wear the pass around my neck, and I needed a leather fringe off my bag to hang it on," said Rennie. Distracted by the strangeness going on around them, and shaken by her woodsy encounter, she didn't notice that Prax clearly had something of importance to tell her. "I didn't have any scissors so I bought this knife at a tent that was selling local tribal handcrafts, look, it's from the Seneca, it's got this cool antler handle and its own little sheath..."

"Good score, then. But listen—"

She didn't. "I did note a lot of contemptuous sniffs from people who thought wearing a knife on my belt—a new belt too, see, isn't it pretty—was soooooo antithetical to the Woodstock Spirit. Whatever that might be. Yeah, eat dirt, hippie morons. Because you know, *all* the campers over in the tent field have knives on *their* belts, to help chop up whatever it is that campers need to chop up, roots and logs and whatever the hell, and you don't see *them* getting sneered at. But it's all okay now, and we can look around for the rest of the weekend to see who's limping or has a little blade-shaped hole in their jeans. Wouldn't it be delicious if it turned out to be Niles? I'd have a great excuse for loathing him the way I do. Great*er*. Don't tell Turk about this, okay?

He'll only freak out and he's got quite enough on his mind right now."

Prax leaned across the table and grabbed Rennie's hands. "More than you know, glitterbug. *Listen* to me. I know you're freaked out yourself, and you did beautifully, but while you were off merrily puncturing people up in Dingly Dell, Lionheart was moved up in the schedule. In fact, they'll be going on as soon as dear Mr. Shankar finishes up, which at this rate could be Tuesday but will probably be momentarily, or at least thereabouts. So you better go find your squeeze and wish him luck. I don't mean to be a downer, but I think the Lions are going to need all the damn luck they can get. I'll let them tell you why."

Instantly diverted from her own difficulty, and thanking Prax for the tip-off, Rennie dashed over the little bridge to the rather crowded stage, where the members of Lionheart were already getting set to play. She ignored the photographers and crew milling about and gave the band a hard once-over. At first glance, they didn't look any different from all the other times she'd seen them tuning up. But there seemed to be something missing...

"Where's Niles?"

She'd addressed her question to Turk, but for the first time ever he ignored her and continued concentrating on his Strat. Rardi Lombardi glanced at his bandmate, then came out from behind his Vox organ and over to Rennie where she stood behind the amps.

"Niles is too stoned to go on," he said in a low voice. "He spent most of the day wandering around happily dropping or smoking or snorting anything anyone handed him, the utter pillock. He's back at the motel, or off in Xanadu, or possibly both. We just sent him out with a state police escort; Rhino Kanaloa said he'd take care of him and put him to bed."

"So that means—"

"So that means Turk has to do lead vocals, yes, and as you see, he is not pleased about it. Also as you see, we're not closing the night. Since other acts got delayed by rain and traffic and we were here and ready to go, they put us on early, and we're *all* not pleased about *that*. Though, the way things are tending, perhaps it's best to just get out there and get it over with. So Lionheart will be playing Woodstock as a five-man group. Not our favorite thing, as you know. But we'll manage."

"Of course you will," said Rennie swiftly.

Rardi smiled at her, with great fondness; he was one of Turk's oldest and closest friends, from their Oxford days, his songwriting partner and a founding member of the band, and he and Rennie had an excellent relationship. As indeed she had with all the members of Lionheart. All except Niles.

"Do you even *want* to be onstage for this? It's going to be rough and it's going to be if not exactly bad then definitely not particularly good. Especially for Turk. I know you want to be in the wings for him as usual, but tonight you might consider steering clear."

"You'd have to put a harpoon in my leg to keep me away." She reflected a moment, said tentatively, and with some hope, "In all the times I've seen you guys play, I've never seen you once give a really bad performance..."

Rardi raised an eyebrow. "I'd say that's about to change."

~10~

HALF AN HOUR later, Rennie, the performer's pass around her neck identifying her as a member of Lionheart—which had done nothing to make Niles Clay a happy man even before he drugged himself out of the lineup—stood on the side of the stage in the muggy darkness, and it took only one look for her to see that Turk, who'd been merely sullen while tuning up, was now full-on furious as the band blasted out the intro to their first song.

Man, I knew *I should have given him something more powerful to wear tonight! That little scarab necklace wasn't ever going to pack enough mojo to get him through something as big as this…though at least it's stopped raining and I don't have to worry about him getting electrocuted like Neddy…*

Still, there was plenty enough else to fret about. Especially the fact that, without Niles, there really might *not* be sufficient mojo. As Rardi had said, Turk would have to sing, and he wasn't pleased about that, not one little bit. Rennie couldn't understand it: he had an amazingly great voice—on most of his songs, for her money he was miles better than Niles, and in her professional opinion he possessed the best male voice in rock and roll. And that wasn't because she got to hear it in her ear late at night, up close and personal: you had only to listen to those early records, the British ones on the tiny Glisten label, where he did the lead singing, besides playing lead guitar and several other instruments—he was incredible. Gorgeous baritone, great phrasing and timbre, all fantastic.

But he simply wasn't into singing anymore, except very seldom and only on certain songs—like the love-song suite he'd written for her that made up the whole second side of the album before the current one. Apart from those rare occasions, once Niles had joined the band Turk had happily turned over the singing chores, and since Richard Lionheart's opinion was the one that counted, Niles Clay's voice had become the one that counted.

Anyway, here they were at Woodstock. They began with three solid hard-rocking hits, "Walking Through the Walls", "Home Before Dark" and "Lady of the Lake", to set the table, as it were, with familiar material; the songs were blissfully received, and Turk sounded great. Then came a couple of tracks off the new album—and the crowd was audibly less blissed. So they went back to earlier albums, and that worked for a while. At last, knowing what their people craved, they held their noses, rolled their eyes and played "Clarity Road". Not that they didn't love it, but they'd felt it didn't fit the vibe here and they hadn't planned on having it in the set; besides, Turk had no piano, only Rardi's electric organ, and mulishly chose to perform the song on the Strat instead.

To Rennie's ear, it sounded—not bad. There were moments of beauty and fire, when the lyric snarl of Turk's guitar curled over the crowd like the whip of art, or his voice touched them as caressingly as a hand—for someone who was angry and resentful about having to sing, he sounded absolutely terrific—or when Rardi's violin took wing and lifted everyone along with it. But for the most part, though they fought like heroes, they still couldn't make it happen, not the way they were accustomed to, the way their audience was accustomed to hearing them. She felt for them, achingly: for some reason, they were off balance, and it just wasn't coming together. Shockingly, they were so *un*together that they even, at one point, turned the beat around, and Jay-Jay needed to flip the backbeat over to keep them on the mark—a mistake to be made by stoned teenage amateurs in garage bands in New Jersey, not by seasoned pros. What made it worse was that nobody in the audience even noticed.

Not having Niles didn't help, of course, and Turk was visibly angry—at least to the eyes of those who knew him well—that he had to sing lead. She watched with nervous concern as Turk and Rardi consulted briefly. Then, in response to the stage managers' desperate appeals—stretch the set out as long as you can, guys, keep on playing until we tell you to stop, we need the time—they changed everything right there.

With Rardi on violin and Mick on a newly acquired melodeon, Turk, on banjo, led them into an instrumental off their first album, "Cat's Squirrel", a rollicking blues standard covered by everybody from Cream to the Budgies to Jethro Tull to Hendrix. Mick took over lead guitar chores while Turk blew harp—which astounded Rennie, she'd never heard him play blues harmonica live, and he was really good—then after a couple of scorching blues numbers Turk got back on the Strat for the closers.

The crowd had suddenly woken up to what was going on and really liked it, starting to dance and clap. But it was hardly the most discriminating audience of all time, was it, no it wasn't, and yes indeed, you *could* blame drugs for that. As you could for so much else.

Lionheart did three more songs: another oldie, another number off their new album—a big fat sucks-to-*you* to anyone who didn't like it—and finished up with "Svaha", the gorgeous epic hard-rock love song Turk had written to get her back after their breakup last year. The audience, by now totally won over, ate it all up and wouldn't let them off the stage. Finally Turk, with a face like thunder, took the band straight into an unplanned encore: a raging staccato fuzz-laden "God Save the Queen", thus neatly setting up to anthemically bookend, though nobody yet knew it, Jimi Hendrix's "Star-Spangled Banner" that was to come on Monday morning. Equal time for Brits: Lionheart ripped through two angry instrumental verses and a screaming improvised hook, closing down with a superchord longer than a python and bigger than a woolly mammoth. Later, people would claim they heard it ten miles away.

As Turk unslung the Strat and flung himself offstage, almost knocking over Joan Baez and Jack Casady as he went, Rennie caught one glimpse of his eyes. And wished she hadn't: she'd seen him angry before, of course, sometimes even with her, but this was different. And completely understandable: no artist likes to give a sub-par performance, especially not before the biggest audience in rock history. He stormed down the wooden stairs and stalked around behind the stage for a while, blowing off steam, talking, or shouting, with the rest of the guys, who looked every bit as pissed off as he was. This was band business: she wasn't going to even approach her mate until she got a clear signal that it was done. And judging by the frequency and fury with which she heard Niles' name pronounced by every single one of his bandfellows, she certainly wouldn't like to be in *his* little handmade snakeskin Beatle boots when they caught up with him.

Finally, twenty minutes later, Turk seemed to have gotten to a place slightly less volcanic—it had been real Krakatoa territory for a while there, bordering on Mount Doom—and he ran a hand through his hair and looked around. When he saw her sitting small and quiet on the backstage steps, chin in hands, he smiled ruefully and came over, pulling her up into his arms.

"Come on, sweetheart, let's blow this dump."

"Fine by me. Back to the motel?"

"Unless you want to go home."

"No, I kind of have to be here for the whole thing, you know. But *you* don't. I know we planned on staying on for a day or two after, but maybe you should just spend the night and then take the car yourself and drive home in the morning. I'll draw you a map of the back roads out, since I hear that 17 is still closed up tight, and I'll hitch a ride down with someone on Monday."

"I might just do that." Again he ran his hand through his hair; realizing he still clutched his Strat in the other hand, he looked at it as if it were some artifact from another planet, or an arcane medieval weapon, and then handed it off to the nervously hovering roadie. "No praise, no pudding, as my dear old nanny used to say. Right, let's head over to the pavilion and get a bite to eat…no, bugger it, let's just split for the motel. We have your supplies, and thanks to your stunning foresight we can eat them in bed and then crash and not have to deal with anyone else until tomorrow."

"I'm so sorry…" she began.

"No, it's fine. Well, it isn't, but we were overdue for a rubbish performance, and of course our *Niles*"—vicious emphasis on the name—"wasn't with us. And we and Bluesnroyals and Sunny and Tenwynter really didn't belong on tonight's roster anyway, in case you hadn't noticed."

"I noticed."

When they finally got back to the motel, it was getting on for midnight. It might as easily have been noon: the hallways were bright, noisy and full of colorfully clad folk who were household names in households around the world. And most of them were stoned on something. Or several somethings.

There were numerous ad hoc parties in progress, as there had been the night before and all day long. There were people dancing in the corridors and people playing poker on the floor and people rolling joints on any flat surface and people playing music with other people in any corner they could find. It was almost too much to deal with. Turk and Rennie fought past the merry spillover and finally gained the safety of their own room, insulated from the madding crowds by a set of double doors and seven other Lionheart rooms—three plus theirs on one side of the hall and the facing four rooms on the other.

"And we were very lucky little punters indeed to get eight whole rooms all to our deserving selves, or even to get rooms at all," said Rennie cheerfully. She was changing clothes after a shower; Turk, calmer and more settled now that he'd had a nice hot shower of his own and two enormous roast beef sandwiches with soup and tea and potato salad, was staring unseeing at the TV. *Clever old me,* I knew *all that food would come in handy, he's always starving after a show, good or bad, and they laughed at me for bringing the hotplate, but see, I could feed him hot chicken soup and tea at this hour of the night, and not have to rely on room service, which shut down hours ago anyway...* It had been a long, long day for them all, but his day had been much worse than hers, so she was determined to raise his spirits, and babbled on resolutely.

"Good thing we planned ahead and reserved early, right? I heard from Dill Miller, you know, Evenor's manager, that every hotel and motel and resort and fishing lodge for thirty miles around is full to the rafters. No room at any inn. People are staying with local friends of friends or long-lost cousins or old college roommates or any random farmer they could persuade to let them sleep in the spare room or the hayloft or the manger. Or camping out in Max Yasgur's spare cornfield. Lots of the really unfortunate have had to double or quadruple up or crash on the motel floor, or even snooze in their cars. Reminds me of Monterey. Let's hope that's the *only* way in which it will remind us of Monterey. Though I guess it's already too late to hope that, isn't it."

"I guess it is. But let's not get into that either." He turned the TV set off with the remote, looking maliciously amused. "Niles and Mick actually do have to bunk together. Two beds, thank God, but still. That cramps their style a bit, to say the least. Or, knowing them, perhaps not. Though I'm told that Niles is still too out of it to get up, or to get anything else up."

"You're 'told'? Didn't you look in on him personally?"

"I don't *trust* myself to look in on him personally, because when I see him I am going to personally tear him into little small pieces and then personally feed him to the geese. And I do feel sorry for Mick, at least, having to share.

But the way I'm feeling about Niles just now, I say it serves the little toerag right and I only wish he *did* have to sleep on the floor. In the open air. Inside a tornado. And as far as accommodations go, the rest of us got here first, and it was *sauve qui peut*."

Rennie sat on the bed to brush out her hair, and as usual, after a few strokes he took over brushing duties from her. "I love it when you talk French, Gomez… "

He nuzzled the back of her neck, through the heavy hair. "Why did we put our clothes on again, Tish? *Couche avec moi, ma belle chérie, tu veux? Baise-moi, donc…*"

She complied, happily. Then: "Nothing I would like more. But there's a party in Elk Bannerman's suite for Amander Evans, and I promised we'd stop by."

"Who?"

"That little New Zealander folkie chick Elk signed to Rainshadow. We met her at the Fillmore East week before last, when we were backstage to say hi to Bosom Serpent before they left for Europe. She was opening at the Bitter End for Leezil Barnes. We had that whole big discussion about how Bosom Serpent got to use the word bosom in their name and yet you weren't allowed to call that prospective album of yours *Cockchafer*. Which is only an insect, after all, and a bosom is, well, a bosom. You remember her."

"Yes, vaguely. But not long, please? I'm tired and cross and I want to go to sleep, or be as one with the universe, whichever comes first, and we have to get up early for breakfast with Francher and Christabel. That roadside diner they plan on taking us to sounds quite nice, and I want to be awake enough to really enjoy it."

"No, no, just hi and bye." She hesitated. "Don't be too upset about how you guys played. Nobody else was at the top of their form either. I know you're used to absolutely pinning your audiences to the deck, but you really didn't do so badly. At all. You opened big and closed hot; it was only the middle that sagged a bit. Yeah, it took them a while to get into it, but you had them long before the set was over. So technically you only played a third of a bad set. The first third and the last third were great, they really were. Besides, I have a feeling the other big-name bands won't be covering themselves with glory either. There's something in the air here, something strange. We're not going to be having another Monterey."

"Doesn't help, but I appreciate your saying so." He smiled, to soften his words. "And yes, I am. Upset. And it doesn't much matter that everybody else might do wretchedly too. 'Didn't do so badly' is not the same thing as 'a really good performance'."

He flopped on the bed next to her, stared up at the acoustic-tiled ceiling, toying with the scarab necklace, Rennie's mojo gift that had fallen so far short. She privately resolved to hide it as soon as he took it off and give it away later, or throw it away; clearly it had nothing but bad fu attached, at least for Turk. Next time she'd make a better choice, or make his gig gift herself as she often did.

"I truly hate it when it's halfway bad like that. I'd rather it was plain outright godawful. When it's sort of there and sort of not—it's like being as hard as you can get and fucking as hard as you can and yet you can't come and you can't make your woman come either."

"I wouldn't know. My old man and I don't have that problem."

"We could make sure of that, if you like."

"Oh, anything to cheer you up..."

ꕤ

Peering through a momentary opening in the press of bodies in the small suite, an hour or so later, Rennie saw Elk Bannerman, president of Rainshadow Records, over on the couch talking encouragingly to Amander Evans. Elk had taken over the helm of Rainshadow two years ago, after the label's former president and founder, Pierce Hill, had been murdered at the Monterey festival and Rennie had been so deeply involved in the case. Frankly, few people had sorrowed to see the egregious Pierce bite the dust, and quite a lot of them had said so right out loud; he had not been much respected nor particularly loved. Not loved at all, really. Everyone in the music biz had unanimously agreed that Elk was a huge, huge improvement, and Rennie was deeply fond of him, for personal as well as professional reasons.

As for his protégée… Amander was a cute little folkie from Auckland—the twee sort of folksinger, unfortunately, not the lyrically protesty sort like Joan Baez or Buffy Sainte-Marie. Chick was a pretty good guitar player, and enjoyed decent success Down Under, but she certainly wasn't up to playing in the Northern Hemisphere big leagues yet. Nice voice, though, and as they all knew, things of wonder could be wrought in the studio with talented New York session musicians and really good producers. Especially when such matters were arranged by Elk.

There were several other guitar-totey floaty-skirt-wearin' super-sensitive singer-songwriter chicks recently arrived on the scene, Rennie reflected: among them a cat-faced, dark-haired New Yorker named Melanie, just Melanie, who had played tonight following Lionheart and who was the owner of a gargling vibrato said by the unkind to cause seasickness on dry land; an alabaster-skinned Irishwoman called, even more annoyingly, Juneau; and a blankly blond Canadian by way of the Village and Laurel Canyon, Joni Mitchell, who had so far bedded half of Crosby Stills Nash & Young and who possessed a loopy falsetto that could crack an egg.

The ironic word going around the pavilion was that Mitchell's manager had persuaded her not to come to the festival, fearing she wouldn't be able to escape in time to make a scheduled appearance on the Dick Cavett Show—which of course, being national television, was deemed a far more important gig than some silly upstate hippie musicfest. And so she'd stayed in her manager's Manhattan pad and enviously watched the coverage on the TV news. But the important thing was that she would write a song right there in that apartment, from that TV experience and from what people who'd been at the festival would later tell her, and it would be a glowing, magical song that would, incredibly and wondrously, for all time encapsulate the spirit of Woodstock if not the actuality, and Crosby and the boys would sing it into glory. And perhaps that was even better than if she'd actually been there herself.

Pushing through the crowd, Rennie headed over to talk to Elk, a reputedly mobbed-up guy who looked like Jimmy Cagney and who had the manners and the dress sensibilities of Beau Nash. He was delighted to see her, as always, for their own personal reasons, reintroducing her to Amander, who looked about ready to cry from stress and jet lag and too many people, and when Turk joined them and smilingly reminded Amander of their previous meeting, all the girl could do was gibber.

But Turk persisted, with his usual friendly courtesy and the charming air of equality, without an atom of condescension, that only *noblesse* can *oblige* with, and very soon Amander was talking animatedly. Though there was a look in her eye as she looked at Turk that Rennie had seen before, a look she rather noted than liked. In fact, it was a look that she liked not at all. Excessive female admiration of her fiancé was something she was slowly learning to live with, but, man, it stung like a bee convention.

Rennie was a hotly possessive person at heart: what was hers was damn well *hers*, and though she knew that her affianced deserved every ounce of the appreciation that came his way, sharing him with the world, and especially with starry-eyed chick devotees, was difficult to get used to. But she knew it wasn't going to change, not now, not soon, not ever. She also knew that Turk wasn't ever going to take advantage of the adoration, so she could reach a reasonable degree of détente with it, chiefly because there was nothing else she could do and Turk would only laugh at her anyway.

Still, there was a vibe that was coming off Amander and aimed squarely at Turk, a kind of taunting, flaunting, calculating groupie vibe that needed to be smacked down more than a bit; observing it coldly, Rennie decided she would let it pass for now, but if it continued, some small sharp correction would have to be arranged. For someone who was as yet an unknown, Amander Evans was radiating an aura of self-importance and entitlement that was way up there on a Jaggerish level, and that wasn't right at all. You needed a *lot* more going on to back up that sort of thing, and by all accounts, Amander didn't have it. Nor was she likely to come by it in the future, however disappointed Elk would be.

Indeed, Rennie had heard from more than a few people so far tonight that Amander really shouldn't have been at Woodstock at all, wasn't ready for a gig like this, might be in a year or two but not now. Her brief Friday afternoon appearance on the auxiliary stage—officially known as the "free stage", though everything was now free and the qualifier had become redundant—had confirmed that judgment beyond a shadow of a doubt. She'd been nervous and shaky to the point of quavering and mis-chording terror, and she hadn't been able to hide it. If she'd been up there on the main stage in front of everybody, where the organizers, desperate for somebody, anybody, to fill the empty Friday space, had seriously though briefly considered putting her, she would have disintegrated like a bitten-into croissant. Maybe she had a high and inflated opinion of herself, both personal and professional, but frankly, her presence on any Woodstock stage at all had been purely a favor to Elk from the festival organizers, and nobody was pretending any different. As it had been with those acts at Monterey Pop who'd been the personal pets of Lou Adler, Paul Simon and the other honchos—who now remembered Beverly, or the Paupers, or The Group With No Name?—nobody'd ever hear much of Amander Evans again after this weekend.

Yeah, right.

~11~

Saturday morning

RAIN. DRUMMING ON the windows, dropping on the lawn. Making a noise like a bell... *Rain rain rain. Oh great, just what we need,* more *rain... But rain doesn't ring like that?*

Climbing her way up to consciousness, Rennie groped for the shrilling telephone and acknowledged the chirpy desk attendant's wakeup greeting. From under weary lids, she saw that the windows were pale sheets of opal: not raining at all, or at least not now, but pearly glowing gray outside, with that unreal, hushed, just-an-illusion stillness of very early morning in the country, the mist low on the hills and the dew sparkling on everything and the birds bellowing in the trees. Groggily replacing the receiver, she looked over at Turk beside her, sprawled on his front, his blond hair disarrayed on the pillow.

God, I never get tired of waking up next to that. Even at ungodly o'clock a.m. Which, in the normal course of our lives, we usually only ever see when we're going to bed...

But he was still deeply asleep. As a rule, he awoke on his own no matter what hour he had to get up: he had this internal alarm clock, resettable and always right on time—he must be really wiped out to be so sacked out. No surprise, after Lionheart's difficult night. She sat up, reached over, shook him gently.

"Wake up, honey—I know we only got about four hours' sleep, but we'll be late to meet Francher and Christabel. It's fifteen miles to Roscoe and it'll probably take us half the day to get there, even though I know some more back roads."

He didn't stir, not even when she shook him harder.

"Turk? TURK!"

Fighting rising panic, she grabbed his bare shoulder and pulled him onto his back, gave him a few quick sharp taps to the cheek. He never opened his eyes. Breathing shallow, skin cool, pulse faint and slow—and not waking up, oh dear God in heaven, *not waking up...*

She leaped out of bed, wearing nothing but her tattoo and the thirteen silver bangles on her right wrist and the eight gold ones on her left—the famous bullet bracelets had been left at home, as not even Rennie had felt she could pull off diamonds in a cow pasture—and was out of the room and down the hall so fast she thought afterwards that she must have teleported. Coming to Francher's room, she pounded frantically and clankingly on the door.

"Francher! Get out here! I can't get Turk to wake up! Damn it, *Francher*! NOW!"

Francher, already dressed for the breakfast for which Turk and Rennie were going to be late, came flying out. One look at her face and he was running back down the hall with her, pounding on a couple of doors himself and yelling for their occupants as he went.

"What did he drop?"

"We didn't drop a damn thing. I woke up and I couldn't

wake him—"

Turk was lying as she had left him; his breathing seemed slower, his skin colder, and fresh terror washed over Rennie. She tore back the bedclothes and grabbed his black pants from the chair where he'd put them, neatly folded, and began to work them onto his lower half. Still standing in the doorway, Francher seemed to have turned to stone.

"Come on, Francher, *move* it, help me get him dressed..."

He came back to himself, ran over, started pulling a t-shirt over Turk's unconscious head as Rennie snapped shut the jeans waistband.

"I know your hair covers more than your skirts do, babe, but you probably should get some clothes on yourself, before the cops or the ambulance get here."

She scooped up yesterday's bells and white gauze blouse and mirrored gold-embroidered velvet vest from the floor where she had tossed them and hastily struggled into them, totally unembarrassed. By now, everybody in the band had seen everybody else and everybody else's old lady in the altogether countless times, so it didn't bother her even a little and Francher didn't spare her bareness even a glance. Besides, she had more important things to worry about.

"I haven't called them. No, don't freak! I don't want anyone knowing it's Turk, and you may have noticed that this motel is full of people, all of whom know us and many of whom are press. We're lucky to be down here at the end of this wing where nobody can see or hear us."

"But—"

She blitzed right through him. "And I am absolutely *not* waiting around for some hick volunteer paramedics to hitch up the mules and mosey on over. Shane, Jay-Jay, Rardi" — they were standing frozen in the doorway, exactly as Francher had, staring horrified at Turk unconscious on the bed — "the emergency exit door's right here. Bring one of the vans up through the parking lot and you guys carry him out. We'll get him to the hospital ourselves. I know exactly where it is, we can get there a lot faster than any ambulance."

When they still didn't move: "Did you *hear* me? Just fucking DO it!" And such was the command in her voice that they leaped to obey.

"Patient's name?" asked the hospital desk nurse.

"T—" began Francher, as behind him Turk, who had been hurriedly placed on a gurney, was being rolled into the ER. They'd come blasting in, after a miraculous tire-screeching drive from the motel with Rennie at the wheel, the guys supporting Turk between them and she running ahead to alert the medical staff.

"Tarrant," said Rennie sharply, cutting across Francher like a terrible swift sword, and watching like a hunting falcon to see where Turk was being taken. "His name is Richard Tarrant."

"Double R-A Tarrant?" asked the nurse, not even looking up, and Rennie nodded, much relieved. Obviously Turk's real name was unknown in these parts: that might buy them some time, or even save them altogether. "Are you his wife, miss? Since he's unconscious, we need a family member to approve his treatment."

"Yes," said Rennie, eyes like emerald lasers, daring Francher to contradict her and die where he stood, and he raised his palms and backed away. "Yes, I'm his wife. I'm

Rennie Tarrant. I approve anything. We can pay. Just help him. Please. Can I go be with him now? When can I be with him?"

"Richard!" said Rennie brightly, entering the curtained ER cubicle three hours later, Francher at her heels. "How are you feeling, honey?"

"Look, your pretty wife's here, and your friend too," said the nurse, smiling.

"So they are," said Turk, smiling himself, though his voice was painfully hoarse, and raised his face to Rennie's kiss. Francher gripped Turk's shoulder, hard, but said nothing; he'd obviously had a very bad few hours worrying about Turk, who had obviously had a far worse few hours himself. Shane, Rardi and Jay-Jay had been left in the waiting room, equally freaked out.

"We have a van outside. We're taking you home," said Rennie. The van was merely interim: Rennie didn't want the nurse to hear Turk's real mode of transport, lest she find out that her patient wasn't just any old hippie overdose case. But at a small airstrip a couple of miles away, the rather grandiosely titled Sullivan County International Airport—yeah, maybe, if the nations involved are Lilliput and Munchkinland—Oliver Fitzroy's personal plane and pilot, hastily scrambled from LaGuardia, had landed fifteen minutes ago, and now stood ready and waiting to convey them all back to Manhattan.

Francher had been unable to arrange chopper transport home, not for love or money or begging or threats, so in desperation Rennie had called Oliver Fitzroy himself, and Fitz had responded nobly and instantly to her plea, thoughtfully dispatching to her aid one of his smaller, lesser aircraft, like some sort of rock and roll Dunkirk. As her publisher he was also hoping for a hot and exclusive front-page story, naturally, as the quid pro quo du jour, but Rennie had told him not a chance, at least not about Turk, or at least not yet, and he'd only laughed. But he'd also sent the plane.

Anyway, Ares Sakura was lurking out in the hall waiting to help get Turk on his feet and drive the getaway vehicle. Prax waited with him, to do what she could to help Rennie, and Francher's wife Christabel had come too. The other three guys would take the van back to the motel, once Turk and his escort were safely airborne, to join Niles, Mick and the roadies; after that, Lionheart would find their own way out of Sullivan County. For them, Woodstock was over.

"Usually it's you sitting here and me sitting there," said Turk with somewhat forced cheer once the nurse had left, his hand clasped numbingly hard by both of Rennie's. "Makes for an interesting change."

He was lucid, but he looked drawn and exhausted. The verdict had been overdose: downers, a lot more than one, and he'd had his stomach pumped. Just in time, apparently, and Rennie had been commended for not waiting for an ambulance. But she didn't want to think about that right now. She was still shaky herself from her confrontation with the doctor right before she'd entered.

"We don't *do* a bunch of downers at a time," Rennie had snarled in answer to the entirely non-judgmental and matter-of-fact medical question. They'd gone toe to toe in the hall outside the ER, and she really had tried to keep her temper, but her fear and anger had dictated otherwise.

Moron upstate cheesehead quack…

"We hardly ever even do *one* downer at a time, and

we certainly didn't do any last night. If what you say is true, *doctor*—it *is* 'doctor' and not 'veterinary'? Because I wonder?—then it was obviously an accident."

Or somebody poisoned him. On purpose. But she wasn't going to say *that* out loud, for fear of getting the police called in. And local country cops, or worse, New York state troopers, were something she absolutely did not want to deal with. At least not before she had Turk safely out of there and home.

The doc had looked both pitying and skeptical, as if her denial problem wasn't *his* problem. But in the end he'd said Turk was very lucky he'd taken on board enough food to absorb the pills' worst effects—score another one for Kaplan's!—or else it might be a very different story this morning. In any case, he was in no danger and simply needed a lot of rest. Though his best medical advice would be for the patient to be admitted for at least a day or two, certainly Turk could be moved if she thought it best, and Rennie had made it very clear that that was exactly what she did think and exactly what she planned on doing.

Now she put her hand on Turk's arm, as much for her own reassurance as his, and he sat up with care, moving his legs off the bed preparatory to trying to stand.

"That's as may be," she told him, with a smile to encourage both Turk and herself. "But right now Francher and I are just trying to keep this away from the local lawmen and my ever so charming press colleagues, who would come down on this hospital like the wolf on the fold if they got so much as a whisper of what's going on. So we'll keep it secret, for as long as we can, anyway; it's bound to come out sooner or later. But not yet. Fitz sent his plane to take us all back to the city, that's where we're going as soon as you can stand up. In your own time, of course. But like the whirlwind of the desert for quickness. What the hell *happened*? I woke up and—and you wouldn't."

"I drank some red wine at Amander's party, as I told the doctors when, much to my surprise, I woke up here," Turk recalled with an effort, pulling on his black jeans with Rennie's help. "I'd heard the fruit punch was electric—somebody said some roadies had put acid in it—so naturally I stayed away from that, and I figured wine would be safe enough."

"Where'd you get it? From a bottle?"

"No, someone handed me a plastic cup. I don't remember who, if I even noticed at all. I thought the wine tasted kind of off—a little metallic and bitter. I figured it was just bad cheap hippie swill, but I was thirsty and it was only a cupful so I drank it. Incredibly stupid, really, when I'd been so careful about the punch, but it was noisy and confusing and I wasn't thinking. I didn't see you around, so I went back to our room by myself, got undressed and fell asleep before you came in. That's all. Then I found myself here."

"So, someone at the party," said Francher inanely. He could be forgiven the inanity; he had never in his life had a moment like the one where he had burst into the motel room and seen Turk lying on the bed unconscious and unmoving, only a little less white than the sheets, and he hoped he never had a moment like it again.

"Yeah, but there were probably two hundred people in and out of those rooms last night. We'll never find out who did it. Which is too bad," added Rennie evenly, "because I plan to kill them when I do find out and I'll have to kill them all if I don't. Here, honey, wear this, it's chilly outside."

Turk had pulled on the thick cotton sweater—nice multicolor earth tones—and was sitting down again, winded, when Prax came in, ashen-faced, and told them that she'd heard on the lobby desk radio that Amander Evans had been found in the meditation yurt earlier that morning. And she wasn't exactly meditating. Mostly because she was dead.

The first words spoken into the shocked silence were Rennie's. "Who killed her?"

The others gave her a strange shared look, and she returned it impatiently. "I *am* Murder Chick, you know, as you all always keep reminding me; it's my default position. Are you saying she *wasn't* murdered, then?"

Prax shook her head. "I have no details, nor did the news story offer any. Only that she was found dead in the tent. And she's not the only one: there was a kid who got run over by a tractor; he was sleeping under it to stay out of the rain and a farmer came along and started it up and… Though I can see *why* you'd ask right off the bat if Amander was murdered, being as Turk was poisoned with downers at her party and you're always looking for connections."

"Hey, pretty nifty deductive reasoning! You've been hanging around with me too long, Miss McKenna…"

But the terrible news only strengthened Rennie's resolve to get Turk out of there before the hospital staff started coming to the same conclusions that Prax had. Fitz was apparently going to get the hot story he hoped for… and more than one, it looked like.

"But even if we split before they find out, can we still keep out of the papers?" asked Francher anxiously. "Amander dead this morning, and Cory Rivkin on Thursday, and Ned and Sunny—that's two artists dead and two hurt in three days, and now an attempt on another. There's going to be cops all over the place, if there aren't already."

"I don't know." Rennie was distraught, watching Turk gather himself together preparatory to standing up, panicked lest they run out of time but unwilling to rush him, looking every second to see police and press rushing in instead.

"Fitz was already making hopeful noises, and now he won't be the only one. Well," she said after some reflection, "none of the hospital staff recognized Turk by sight, or his real name either. Obviously not rock fans; the locals go in for country-and-western up in these parts, thank God. So, right now at least, they think he's just another stupid hippie longhair from the festival who overdosed himself. I used his international driver's license, which is in Richard's name and has the London address, when they asked for his ID. We paid cash, so no insurance trail. So maybe it'll be okay. Besides the doctor and nurses, the only people who know he was here are us. I mean us here now. And Fitz and the pilot."

"And Gray and Prue," said Ares, who had come in to help support Turk on his way to the van. "I called the motel once we knew Turk was going to be okay, to let them know so they don't worry when they find us all disappeared. But that's it."

"Lord, I hope so. I don't even like the rest of the band knowing, really. Shane and Rardi and Jay-Jay will tell the other guys all about it as soon as they get back to the motel, but there's no help for that—" To Turk: "Oh, honey, great, you're ready…let's softly and suddenly vanish away." Her voice had begun to shake. "Let's go home."

ꟈ

Even with help, Turk barely made it up the front steps from the limo that had been waiting for them out on the tarmac at La Guardia—where the plane was on standby to fly Rennie and Prax back upstate again—and Rennie silently blessed the architect for restoring the fancy little brass-and-mahogany elevator, and the contractor for having it operational.

Carefully decanting Turk into the lift, Ares and Francher held him upright for the short haul to the second floor, Rennie dashing ahead of them to open the master bedroom doors. They brought him in, Rennie stripped off his boots and pants and sweater, and Turk fell back on the pillows and slid a million miles into unconsciousness.

Once Rennie had covered him up with the summerweight duvet and was sure he was asleep, they all went down to the kitchen, where Prax and Christabel Green were sitting at the table staring at each other in mute helplessness.

"How is he?" they both asked at once.

Rennie threw herself into a chair and gratefully accepted the mug of hot coffee that Christabel handed her.

"Already asleep. The trip really wiped him out. He hates flying, and I asked the hospital to give him something, which they weren't happy about doing but did. Though they thought it was for a long van trip, not a short plane one."

"Better a half-hour flight and another half-hour in a limo than a van all the way down from Monticello," said Ares sympathetically. "It was a very smooth ride and the plane was very plush, and at least it was over with much,

much quicker. With the roads the way they are, we probably wouldn't have made it here much before suppertime. If that. A chopper would have taken twice as long as the plane and been ten times more uncomfortable, so huzzah for the RAF—Royal Air Fitzrovia—and its gallant and generous Wing Commander. And you wouldn't have wanted Turk hanging around in that hospital any longer than he did."

"No… Francher, I'm not letting him out of bed for a *week*, so any rehearsals for the tour are going to have to wait—"

"Oh, no, no, babe, of course not, no problem."

"—and I'm going right back up there to find out who did this to him," she continued as if he hadn't spoken. "And when I do, with my bare hands I will tear them into such tiny pieces that even the maggots can't find them."

Rennie had said that with all the evident emotion of someone reading a soup can label, but Francher and Ares looked at her apprehensively.

"I know you're upset," said Ares cautiously. "But you can't—"

"I beg your pardon, I think I perfectly well *can*! In case you've forgotten, people died up there. Amander *died*. Cory *died*. And Turk could have died too. So peace and love *that*!" She drained the mug and slammed it down hard on the table, looking with sudden pleading at Francher and Christabel. "Please, could you guys stay here with him for the rest of the weekend? I hate to ask you to miss it all, but Lionheart's done with Woodstock anyway. I called our doctor from Monticello, so he's on standby alert. Just in case! I don't expect anything bad to happen, but better to be safe. And I need to know Turk's safe in all ways, so you too, Ares, please? Again, you know, in case."

They quickly assented, all a little afraid of her at the

moment, even Ares, but even if they hadn't been afraid they would have gladly foregone the rest of Woodstock on Turk's behalf: Ares didn't care about the festival one way or the other, except for missing Prax's performance, and Rhino Kanaloa could easily run Argus' security operation, while Francher's chief concern was his friend's well-being and Christabel's concern was Francher's.

Rennie almost dissolved with sheer relief. "Oh, God, thank you so much. There's plenty of food in the fridge, and your pick of rooms to sleep in. Which means they have beds and clean linens and bathrooms, and no work is going on. I know the place is a mess, but"—her voice had started to falter—"I really need you here. I have to get back up there. And I don't want to leave him alone."

"Of course not," said Prax. "And I still have a gig to play tonight, or Leeds Sheffield will kill me. He *is* my label president and must be obeyed even as Fitz must, so I'm going back up with you. But you have to eat something first or I swear I'll call Lord Holywoode and ground that plane myself. Now go upstairs and kiss your boyfriend to make him better. We'll all have something to eat, then you and I will head back."

Rennie smiled, a bit shakily. "Into the valley of death rode the half million?"

"Plus two, my sunshine. Plus two."

Slipping into the master bedroom again, Rennie quietly closed the door behind her; leaning against it, she started to shiver. She wouldn't let the others see, least of all Turk, but she was whipped, physically and emotionally. It had been a brutal day, and it wasn't over yet; incredible to realize it wasn't even noon.

At least the other bedrooms on this floor were habitable, as she'd told her unexpected guests, and the bathrooms, kitchen and air conditioning were all working. Ares and the Greens would be very comfortable, and quite nearby, so Turk wouldn't be all alone in the house. The construction crews had the week off, so there would be as much peace and quiet as he needed.

She stared at him across the room's sunny width, then went over and sat beside him, cautiously balancing on the edge of the bed so as not to disturb him. He was motionlessly asleep, and still paler than she liked—but it was a restful, real sleep, not that godawful clammy pallid stupor that she'd seen that morning at the motel. No, never mind what Prax and the rest had said, she *would* kill whoever had done this to him. She would kill them lengthily, and painfully, and extremely imaginatively; wait, even better, she would *almost* kill them, for a very long time, and then she would almost kill them some more, and some more, and on like that, until she got bored or felt merciful, which would be never and never.

She gently touched his hand. Now she knew how he felt seeing *her* like this. He was right: it wasn't a fun or pleasant thing. But it seemed worse that it should be him: he was so strong usually, and now suddenly he wasn't—it reminded her much too much of the incident at Prax's cottage last year. But at least they had been in that one together—carbon-monoxided together, in the ambulance together, in the hospital together, recovering at home together—"together" being the important, operative word.

She realized that Turk had opened his eyes and was smiling at her. "Oh God, I'm sorry, did I wake you? How do you feel?"

"Very much better. But very tired still. And no, you didn't wake me. Actually, I'd really like to take a shower. I can stand up by myself. Hungry, too," he added hopefully, after thinking about it. "I could eat something. Nothing complicated. But a lot of it, please."

"Whatever you want."

Despite his assurances of stability in the vertical plane, she commanded him not to set foot out of bed until she got back, then ran down to the kitchen to ask Ares to go up and help him into the shower. With Prax and Christabel assisting, she assembled scrambled eggs with cheese melted in and warm chicken broth with noodles and chocolate pudding and vanilla ice cream and tea with honey—everything easy on a ravaged throat. Taking the tray upstairs in the lift, she hastily put clean sheets on the fourposter, by which time Turk, not nearly so steady on his pins as he had boasted, was with Ares' support out of the shower.

After he'd eaten everything she'd brought him, he fell asleep again, and Rennie, calmer now that she could see he was clean and fed and feeling better, changed her clothes and then went back down to join the others at the kitchen table. Christabel and Prax had fixed grilled ham and cheese sandwiches, and everybody said Rennie wasn't going anywhere until she'd had some.

"I hate to leave," she said, inhaling two sandwiches back to back, surprised to find herself ravenous, "but our housekeeper is available—her number's by the phone—and she can help you guys out if you need anything. Turk will probably be all raring to get up later, but I don't want his little blond noggin leaving those pillows. Ares, you make sure he stays in bed. Otherwise I'll tie him to it."

"I hear that usually goes the other way around."

"Cute. But quite true. Anyway, I've got to get back to the airport, and Praxie still has to play tonight."

"*You* don't really have to go back, you know," countered Christabel. "Turk's fine now, but he needs you here. Let Prax take the plane—Fitz won't mind—and let the cops do their job for a change. Turk's *your* job."

"The festival will be over tomorrow night...more likely Monday, the way things are going. And there are two murders to be solved. Yeah, yeah, I know they're not proved murders yet, but I think we all know better than that. Whoever killed Amander and probably Cory Rivkin and poisoned Turk will get away if the cops don't grab him—or her—before that. And as I don't exactly have a whole lot of trust and faith in Sullivan County law enforcement, I intend to find them first. That's my job, and Turk knows that better than anyone. Plus, whoever poisoned him? I'm going to slit their throat with a boathook and then bathe in a tubful of their hot steaming blood. *That's* my job, too."

"Now, see, that's the part I have the problem with," said Prax carefully. "I know you're just reacting, because you're upset about Turk and who could blame you, and I know you're only venting and you'd never *really* kill anyone, but other people might not know that and they might take it the wrong way if they hear you talking like that. And by 'the wrong way' I mean 'the way you absolutely meant it', and by 'other people' I mean 'law enforcement officers who are not generally known for their grasp of colorful metaphor'. Not that *we'd* rat you out, but you have been known in times past, under similar circumstances, to—oh, how do I put it—perhaps not keep your rhetoric as firmly reined in as you might. Besides, I really think you should tell the fuzz about Turk. Especially since Amander died."

Rennie looked at her. "My plan precisely. Now that he's safe at home, it can't hurt if they know. In fact, they might already know if they've talked to the hospital people. It wouldn't take much investigative talent for even an upstate cop to find out who Richard Tarrant, recent accidental-overdose outpatient, really is... Poor Amander, though. And Cory too."

"We don't know that the same person did for all three of them," Ares pointed out. "Why would there even be a connection? Turk and Cory knew each other from a few years back, but Turk and Amander didn't know each other at all. They only said hello at the party and at the Fillmore a couple of weeks ago."

"That's *exactly* why," said Rennie, rounding on him so sharply that he actually flinched. "Turk was poisoned so I wouldn't start looking into Cory's and Amander's deaths. Someone thought I'd be so freaked out and concerned about Turk that I'd be too busy to meddle the way I usually do, and they didn't care if Turk died, as long as it meant I was kept away from investigating the other two. And let's not forget Ned and Sunny. *All* accidents? Yeah, pull the other one, it's got bells on."

"You can't know for sure, though," said Ares, recovering his cool, and always ready to stick his neck out. "Such an assumption seems paranoid even for you. It's probably not about you or Turk at all. They obviously didn't mean to kill him, or else he'd be dead, right?"

"No, *not* right. And I *don't* know it, but I sure do *feel* it. And if it's about Turk, it's about me. And because they didn't actually *mean* to kill him, that makes it okay? Believe me, that's not going to save them. They asked for it and now they've got it coming, in spades. I'm going to hunt them down and shoot them between the eyes like Old Yeller and leave their lifeless bullet-riddled bodies lying in a ditch. Only, unlike Yeller, it won't be sad at all." She glanced at Prax. "You with me? Good. Let's ride."

Woodstock, Saturday August 16

Quill
Honest Mollusk
John B. Sebastian
The Keef Hartley Band
The Incredible String Band
Santana
Turnstone
Mountain
Canned Heat
Evenor
The Grateful Dead
Creedence Clearwater Revival
Janis Joplin
Sly & The Family Stone
The Who
Jefferson Airplane

~12~

FITZ'S PLANE HAD barely touched down and taken off again, ahead of a nasty oncoming storm front, before Rennie was arranging a helicopter lift to the festival field, intent on coming on with a nasty little storm of her own. Prax followed along sedately, and they both got onto an available chopper that already carried John Entwistle of the Who, whose band would be playing that night, and their friend Chris Sakerhawk, who'd come to observe even though his band wasn't playing there at all. The pilots, all of whom seemed to be young, cheerful, longhaired Vietnam vets, appeared totally unfazed by the meteorological upheaval that was fast approaching, and flew their famous passengers right into it. Not the smoothest flight, certainly, but a quick and confident one.

When they reached the landing area at the field, the two girls parted company, Prax making her way to the pavilion to talk to her band, whom she was hoping to find there not too stoned and ready to go on later, and Rennie heading down the hill, straight for the command-center trailer from which the whole scene was being run.

She spent half an hour informing the organizers of Turk's incident—they were shocked, of course, in a vague, hippie sort of way—then repeated herself to the local county police, who were there on at least two or three separate and unrelated matters, apparently, though no one saw fit to fill her in on what else besides the two deaths. In return, she was hoping to acquire the latest news about Amander.

"Yes, we've heard about you even here in the boondocks of Sullivan County, Miss Stride," said the officer who seemed to be in charge, and who looked and sounded nothing like the hayseed lawman that Rennie had been unfairly characterizing him as in absentia.

On the contrary: he appeared pleasant, educated and smart, and decidedly no redneck; or if he was, he was hiding it well. Stereotypes work both ways, to be sure, and no doubt he had been characterizing her equally baselessly as—what? A pampered rock star's compliant sex kitten? A liberal commie pinko reporter? A godless hippie slut? Who knew? But almost certainly not as the serious, hard-working journalist she really was. *Well, we all make mistakes…*

"How gratifying." Rennie's voice held the chill metallic clink of swords crossing in a meadow at dawn.

If the cop heard it, he ignored it. "In the course of our looking into the deaths of Miss Evans and Mr. Rivkin, we had a nice chat with the staff on duty in the hospital ER, who very helpfully described you and Mr. Wayland."

Uh-oh… "I didn't tell any lies," said Rennie defiantly. "Only the little white one about how I'm his wife, so I could get him the emergency treatment he needed without a timewasting hassle. Anyway, we're engaged and planning the wedding—see, here's the ring. I was just—anticipating."

"My congratulations. But that's not what we're interested in. What more can you tell us about how Mr. Wayland ended up in the hospital in the first place? Since we would really prefer not to bother him as he's recovering, down in the city."

Rennie heard the not-so-veiled warning, which was

basically *Tell us what we want to know or we* will *go and bother him, no matter* what *shape he's in,* and she settled at once into her familiar old police-enlightening mode. Hey, she'd fought Scotland Yard to a draw, twice; wrangling a rube upstate cop should be a pushover. And not even Detective Chief Inspector Gordon Dakers had held a grudge.

"Very kind of you. Okay, Officer...?"

"Sheriff." He touched his hat brim in salute, with a small accompanying nod. "Sheriff Caskie Lawson, ma'am. But you were saying?"

"Of course. Sheriff, then. Well, Lionheart played at the festival last night, and then afterwards Turk and I went back to the motel, where there was this party for Amander Evans in Elk Bannerman's suite, he's the president of Rainshadow Records—"

When she was done detailing finding Turk unwakeable the next morning and getting him to the hospital and the diagnosis and treatment and how she'd conned a person who would remain nameless into sending his private plane, she looked at Lawson, who'd been taking notes as she spoke, and who looked back at her now with an expression of complete neutrality.

"So, there you have it," she said with renewed defiance. "May I ask how you found out about Turk? Who blew the whistle on us?"

Lawson's facial muscles contracted in what was apparently a small, brief smile, and he took off his hat and brushed back his brown hair—surprisingly long for a country cop. Rennie was struck by how young he was, now that she was really looking at him. Not much older than she was; definitely on the near side of thirty, anyway. So did that mean she could trust him? That remained to be seen.

"Just about everyone we asked, ma'am. His manager and three of the members of his band were observed at the motel very early this morning, carrying him to the parking lot and putting him into a van, with you on the scene watching. He was obviously unconscious, and the whole proceedings were equally obviously under your direct supervision. It wasn't hard to put two and two, or five and one, together. The doctor and nurses who treated him at the hospital had no trouble identifying some photos. Smart work to get him away in Mr. Oliver Fitzroy's plane—yes, we know all about that too. I hadn't known you had such impressive resources at your command."

"Oh, I'm full of little surprises like that. Good scouting, by the way. And now what about Amander Evans? I only know what was on the radio. Maybe I could help—"

Lawson gave her a real smile this time. "I surely do know how helpful you've been to police authorities, Miss Stride, and I mean that sincerely. And I'm not saying we wouldn't be grateful to hear if you happened to find something out. All I can tell you right now is that Miss Evans was found dead in what they call the meditation tent, around dawn. There were a few people around, but nobody seems to have seen anything, at least not that they'll admit to. We're trying to find more of them to talk to, but you can imagine how impossible that is. How she got from the motel party where you say you last saw her back to the festival site—no one knows anything about that either. And certainly nobody's saying they know how she ended up dead in that little tent. Or yurt, as the festival people keep calling it, whatever that might mean."

"I have no idea why she might have been killed, in the first place. But if she *was* killed, obviously she was left there in the tent as some sort of sign or boast," mused Rennie, half to herself. "If it was just plain random murder, it would have been much easier and safer to have dumped her body in the woods, or in one of the little lakes. Or even in some remote barn or something that no one would ever look in."

Lawson nodded. "Plenty of woods and lakes and out-of-the-way fields around here. And lots of barns, sheds, stables, even deserted houses way off the beaten track. Every farm in the county has outbuildings that nobody goes into for months on end, especially in the summer when the animals are mostly outdoors. But that would mean the killer would have had to know the countryside hereabouts, and I don't believe for one minute somebody local did this to Miss Evans. I don't *want* to believe it, at least."

"Someone was making a statement by leaving her right there for people to easily find. But what that statement might be, or who could have made it— Oh, by the way, who did find her?"

Lawson went suddenly blank-faced, as if someone had wiped a damp cloth over his sturdy sun-tanned visage. "That's something we're not real comfortable with putting out there yet, ma'am. I'm sure you understand why I really can't tell you right now."

"Oh yes," said Rennie, amused and not troubling to hide it. "Yes, I do understand. More than you might think."

He studied her for a moment, then came to a clear decision. "I *can* tell you this, though: the medical examiner has given us a tentative verdict on cause of death for Cory Rivkin."

"I thought it would take a while for test results to come in; usually autopsies do."

"That's very true, ordinarily, but in this instance we

could tell right off the bat what he almost certainly died of." Lawson was clearly enjoying stretching out, for as long as he could, his little moment of confounding the big-city reporter, and for her part Rennie was content to let him have it—allowing a small triumph now might pay big dividends later. Besides, it never hurt to humor the cops.

"And that would be..."

The sheriff could restrain himself no longer. "Well, Miss Stride, he died of peanut allergy. And the reason we can say so as early as this is that he carried a card in his wallet saying that he was violently allergic to peanuts and peanut products. Only no one found it until after he was brought to the hospital. Someone finally saw the card when searching his person for evidence, and then the diagnosis was made, based on the appearance of the body as well, but I have to say he was dead pretty much on the spot, right there in the pavilion. Long before anyone could have done anything about it, anyway."

Rennie leaned back in the plastic chair, frowning slightly as she processed the admittedly startling information. "But if he knew he was allergic, and even carried a card saying so—"

Sheriff Lawson wore a pleased expression, as if Rennie were a clever pupil who had just figured out a tough math problem in his algebra class. "Then why would he have eaten something with peanuts in, is what you're asking. And that is a very good question. From what people who witnessed his attack had to say, nobody forced peanuts down his throat, and in fact peanuts weren't even served at the pavilion buffet table."

"Could someone else have given him some? Some other person who was at the festival? It's a big crowd, I bet lots of people have peanuts or peanut butter sandwiches and stuff with them."

"Sure, someone could have, but again, why would he have accepted, knowing he was fatally allergic? I very much doubt that anyone put a gun to his head to make him eat them."

"I guess suicide by groundnut is out of the question…"

Lawson looked a little shocked by the flippancy, as most lawmen who had to deal with Rennie were, sooner or later. "I guess it would be!"

"And Miss Evans?"

But Caskie Lawson of Lawson's Farm, Long Eddy, Sullivan County was far too cagey to be caught by Rennie's completely natural, casual tone—the one that had caught so many of the more incautious or dismissive before him, the one that even journalism school hadn't taught her.

"As I said, we can't say yet. Nice try, though," he added, with the first real grin he'd favored her with.

Rennie grinned back. "Worth a shot. So to speak."

"A shot would have been a damn sight easier to figure out," said Lawson a bit unguardedly; Rennie had *that* effect on people too.

"Though that would have created a whole new, and worse, set of problems. Thank God for small favors, right?"

"Thank Him for sure," said Lawson, with genuine piety, and Rennie felt a little ashamed. "If an idea occurs to you, even one that might seem foolish at first sight"—he got to his feet, and Rennie likewise rose to take her leave, as the interview was clearly over—"I'd be quite honestly grateful if you shared it with us. There are plenty of security people around, both public and private, and we're working together on this, but truth be told, probably nobody else here has as much experience with this sort of thing as you do, at least judging by what I've heard. Though I'm sorry to have to remind you. Anyway, this festival has been real peaceful and pleasant so far, which frankly surprises the hell out of me, and I've been enjoying it myself, which also surprises the hell out of me. So you can see where I want to make sure it stays that way. In fact, it's my job to see it does. It's important to Sullivan County, and that means it's important to me."

She gave him her best professional-reporter smile—half strength only, as, much to her own surprise, she was rather liking him. "I have a long history of sharing ideas with peace officers, Sheriff Lawson, not to mention a long history of being, let's say, murder-adjacent. As you've obviously been told. If I find out anything, you'll be the first one I bring it to."

He smiled his best professional-police-officer smile right back at her, and she flattered herself she could discern equal liking in it. "I'm very glad you say so. I may tell you I've heard a little bit otherwise from some of my colleagues out West."

"Ah. Well, don't you believe everything you hear about me. And in return, I won't believe everything I've heard about upstate New York country law enforcement. That's fair enough, don't you think?"

"Got that right."

Having been dismissed with further thanks and the usual cautions, Rennie trudged back up the hill to the pavilion. Prax was off with Evenor somewhere, but Rennie was greeted by numerous friends, who, unavoidably, had heard all about Amander Evans' demise, seeing as it had taken place barely a hundred yards away in the yurt that they had all used to cool out in before going onstage, or to cool out in generally, and who now demanded Rennie fill them in on what had happened.

When she had wrung out every possible detail and they were all sitting there agog, she continued doggedly, "And of course that's bad enough, but now it's gotten even worse, which I wasn't sure was possible." And then she told them about Turk, and they were even more horrified. The news about exactly what had killed Cory Rivkin she kept quiet, at least for now, though she couldn't have said quite why.

But Ned and Melza Raven were looking at her as if they could only too easily believe what they were hearing, while the rest of them at the table—the Sonnets, Ares' lieutenant Rhino Kanaloa, Belinda Melbourne, Gerry Langhans, some Britband and Dead personnel—were blank with shock.

Even Jerry Garcia's usually sunny countenance was looking unusually grim in the watery sunlight. He and Rennie had been friends since her earliest days in the Haight, after she'd left Stephen and before she'd gotten her big break as a reporter with the San Francisco Clarion. They'd never been romantically involved, not even casually, but their paths had first crossed over the Fillmore murders for which Prax had been so wrongfully thrown in jail and from which Rennie had gotten her sprung, and the ones the following summer at the Big Magic and Monterey festivals. Plus they'd gotten together professionally, at Garcia's own plea for help, over another homicide at Airplane House, that band's magnificently weird communal Victorian mansion on Fulton Street, when the Airplane were on the road with the Doors in Europe back last fall.

He shook his head now. "Bad and bad enough. When

you speak to Turk, give him our best. But it's gotten even worse on a humbler scale, though in numbers perhaps not so much humbler at all."

Rennie accepted the joint he passed her. "Oh? How can that possibly be?"

"The festival itself is still all peace and love, which is groovy, but—"

"What did I just *tell* you people?"

"Nobody's making light of it," said Belinda quietly. "Even though hardly anyone knows about Turk yet, thanks to you—and nobody really knows why Amander is dead. But I know what Jerry means. A few festivalgoers were roughed up this morning in Bethel, and another kid got the crap beat out of him when he and his chick tried to walk to White Lake. Plus a few more in Liberty and Monticello. Some local teenage hoods even destroyed one girl's guitar, and her wimpy boyfriend couldn't stop them. Though the Dead were kind enough to give her one to replace it, when they heard." She gave a respectful nod in Jerry's direction, and he nodded back, a little embarrassed. "And all of this was for no offense other than walking around in front of straight, short-haired rustics while being longhaired, citified, stoned and hip."

"Maybe not the best idea to leave the site? Safety in numbers and all that."

Jerry looked indignant. "They were hungry! They weren't hurting anybody. They only wanted to buy something to eat. They weren't going to steal it. That's no crime."

"Of course it isn't. And I doubt it has anything to do with what happened to Turk or Amander. Or Cory, or Sunny, or you either, Neddy. That happened at the festival.

Among *our* people."

"Are you saying—"

Rennie rolled her eyes. "You're a bright boy, Garcia; do the math. Half a million children of the planet? Stands to reason there must be at least a few among them who walk on the dark side."

Rhino stirred uncomfortably; on a man his size, it was like a mountain twitching. "Or people who aren't ours. Sorry, but I have to think that way—Ares taught me to be paranoid. In a positive way, of course."

"Village, town or county denizens, you mean?" asked Rennie. "Or professional troublemakers, even narks maybe, sneaking into the festival to work their evil ways in our muddy midst and make us look bad? Could be. I myself saw signs on grocery stores and little roadside shops that were not exactly shall we say welcoming to our kind. What did we expect from the natives? They're decent sorts for the most part, and they tend to accept people as they find them, but they're not used to people like us or what we represent, and frankly, they don't want to be. I went to school about three counties away, in a hip little town surrounded by country just like this, and I know what these folks are like. They can be the salt of the earth and the nicest souls you ever met, or they can have the reddest necks and uptightest minds you ever saw. And the scary thing is you never know which one you're going to get. Sometimes both at once."

"True enough," said Gerry Langhans. "Just witness all the other stories we've been hearing of farm families and church and synagogue groups supplying the hordes with floods of water and bushels of food, no charge. What a bunch of communal Communists, right? On the way here today from the Holiday Inn I saw farmhouses with picnic tables out front loaded with fruit and baked goods, and water hoses for filling gallon jugs or paper cups, all free for the taking, whoever needed it."

"People have been running food trucks to the Hog Farm field kitchen like guns to the IRA." Rennie smiled. "Max Yasgur, may God set a flower on his head, owner of this here now farm *and* the leading Jewish dairyman in Sullivan County, is selling eggs and bread and his cows' milk for mere pennies, giving it away, even, and filling up empty bottles with water for free. His wife Miriam, bless her heart, has been rallying those local help outfits to buy up all the groceries for miles around and kick in free food. No kids are going to starve on a Jewish mama's watch, not on *her* farm!"

"They've been sending over thousands of sandwiches, jelly and peanut butter and anything else that will stand up in the heat," offered Belinda. "Surprisingly few people are being greed-headed jerks, and the ones who are, are getting smacked for it by their neighbors; the people who started the giveaway are doing it because it's the right thing and they don't want to see anyone go hungry. And between them and the Hog Farmers, no one has."

Prue looked grave. "We've had a welcome we really had no right to expect, and that's absolutely wonderful; but perhaps you're right, Rennie. Perhaps we oughtn't be surprised to now be seeing the other side of it."

"Is Turk all right?" asked Melza, after a thoughtful silence. "You took him home, you said."

"Yeah, he's okay." Rennie ran her hands over her face. "Pretty exhausted and shaken up, though. Having your stomach pumped is no picnic. He's under orders to stay in bed until I get back. Francher and Christabel are staying there with Ares to make sure he does. He'll probably spend most of his time sleeping, which would be a very good thing. Prax and I came back for her to play her set tonight. Woodstock was over for Lionheart, anyway. And more than Woodstock may be over for Niles goddamn Clay, once Rardi and Turk catch up with him." *Or once* I *do…*

"Tell Turk I said they didn't play anywhere near as badly as he thinks," offered Jerry consolingly, into another silence, this one even more uncomfortable.

"How do you know how badly he thinks they played?"

Garcia grinned. "I'm a guitarist too, remember? I know *exactly* how he's thinking. They were a bit mangy, sure, but they got on top of it and they finished off fine. And if they were a little sloppy, so's everyone else. Do you remember how we all said there was magic in the wood of the stage at Monterey? Well, this stage seems to have the anti-magic. Bad fu. It's been putting out iffy energy from the first."

Belinda had an abstracted look on her face. "You could be right. It wasn't even supposed to be happening here, but fifty miles away. They kept the name 'Woodstock' because they thought it sounded cooler than 'Bethel' or 'White Lake' or 'Max Yasgur's Farm.' Which it does, but still. It's a lie up front, false pretenses. It's gnarly karma."

Prue nodded wisely. "No wonder nobody's repeating their Monterey triumphs. No one's played to seriously blow anyone's mind, and I don't think anybody will. We're certainly not expecting to, are we, Gray. Lionheart did just fine under the circs; they had some very nice bits. But that won't make them happy."

"No."

"It's *all* karma, baggage." Ned took another toke on the currently circulating joint. "Witness the fact that quite a few thousand dollars went missing Wednesday from the organizers' lockbox, money meant to pay bands, several of whom have insisted on being paid in cash, and now there's not enough and the banks are all closed for the weekend and those bands might not go on unless they get dosh in fist first. So whose karma is that, then?"

"WHAT?" Rennie gave him a sharp look. "I talked to those guys *and* the local fuzz not half an hour ago, and none of them ever said word one about stolen money. What are they doing about it?"

"They brought in some heavy-duty ex-detective cat; he arrived yesterday, I was told," Jerry informed her, as he got up to leave. "Private muscle from L.A. He's supposed to be into the music, and a head too, in spite of being an ex-cop, and he was at Monterey, so maybe he won't come on so much like a stormtrooper. Hey, you were there with us, you were involved with those murders; maybe you know him."

OhGodohGodnononopleeeeeeasenooooooo..."Uh, his name wouldn't happen to be Marcus Dorner, would it, by any weird and horrible chance?"

Jerry beamed. "I believe it is. So you do know him! Well, if he's *your* friend, he can't be bad."

PLEASEGODPLEASEKILLMEWITHLIGHTNING... "Don't be so sure of that."

Though Rennie looked to see Marcus at every turn, now that he was there and she knew he was there, her personal horizon continued to remain Dorner-free, though she was well aware that that happy state couldn't last indefinitely, especially with her poking into the murders and Turk's poisoning. But with Garcia's revelation, at least she now knew where Sheriff Lawson had gotten his information on her. Well, she'd worry about all that later; right now, she had more important matters to concern her.

Someone at the table had mentioned that the late Cory Rivkin's band, Owl Tuesday, had decided to withdraw from their Sunday afternoon spot on the main roster, which everyone could of course understand. But as a tribute to their late drummer, they had chosen to play a set on the free stage instead, and they were doing it right at that moment. So after a few more casual remarks, Rennie had gotten up with even greater casualness and headed purposefully through the pavilion over in that general direction.

More of a roped-off, low-platform, open-mike area than a proper stage, and intended for anyone who wanted to play or rant or whatever, the free stage was way over by the woods and campgrounds, so situated as to not interfere sonically with any act on the main boards. Good thinking; and the artists who were playing there, just for fun or because they wanted to get in a bit of acoustic warm-up before going on the big stage, were well and happily received.

Picking her way across patches of mud and trodden alfalfa, Rennie went up the hill and past the thick woods, which reminded her of the roughing-up she'd had last night. Could it really have been only last night? Trippy—though the memory reminded her that she still needed to check people out for knife wounds in the right thigh. But that was not the priority of the moment: her present errand was to talk to Cory's bandmates, to see if, wallet warning card notwithstanding, there really had been a potentially fatal peanut allergy, and if so, as seemed likely to be true, how widely known it was outside immediate Owl Tuesday circles. Because clearly *some*body had known all about it.

She got there in time to hear their last five numbers. Turk was right: they really had become a very tidy little outfit. Even with a substitute drummer filling in for the late Cory—oh, look who it is, Jack Paris from Evenor, how nice of him to play this set when Evenor was going on itself later tonight—Owl Tuesday was tight, bright and together. As the drummer, Cory would have been responsible for a lot of that, of course. But Jack was superb, as he always was; he and the rest of Evenor were all musicians several cuts above the Owls, of course, but his playing didn't show them up, it made them strive to match him instead.

The result was possibly the best set Owl Tuesday had ever played in its life—and maybe its also being an ad hoc memorial to their fallen friend had something to do with the excellence. Rennie's mind flashed back to Lionheart playing the Whisky, after Tansy's murder, when Turk had seemed to be taking out his anger and his sorrow in the absolute transcendence of his music. She hoped this band would find it in them to go on with a new drummer, because Owl Tuesday didn't deserve to end any more than Cory had…

When the band filed off the stage, Rennie was waiting. She nodded to Jack, who casually waved back at her and wandered away down the hill, then collared the three surviving Owls and led them over to flop down on a patch of soft grass under some oak trees. They were quite happy to talk to her—she'd given them a couple of nice write-ups in the past and they knew about her and Turk—and they were also eager to go on record regarding Cory.

"He was a really groovy guy, Cory was," said Terry Janoff, the lead vocalist and rhythm guitarist. "We all met at Santa Monica High School, and started playing together six years ago, in Cory's parents' beach house's garage. Then after high school we all went on to Santa Monica Community College, though we surfed and played music more than we actually studied."

"All of us except Fieldsie over there," put in lead guitarist Alec Faldo, and everybody laughed, including bass player Doug Fields. "He's smarter than the rest of us; he went to USC. We all graduated, though. We'd been playing together all along, you know, parties and bar mitzvahs and high school dances and stuff, and then we decided to get into music for real."

Rennie smiled; they were nice boys, and she liked them, and felt desperately sorry for them, and even sorrier for the reason she had to be here bothering them with questions. "No intraband squabbles or anything like that?"

No, they averred wide-eyed, shaking their heads, nothing like that. Apart from the usual bickering over who was going to get to sing lead on which songs—their band structure was modeled on that of their idols the early Beatles, though in all other ways they were far from imitative—they got along really, really great, and in fact they all lived together in a house right on the beach, next to the Santa Monica pier.

"But you know all this, Rennie," said Alec after a few more queries. "What is it you really want to find out?"

She took a deep breath—in, out. "What did you know about Cory personally? Did he have any physical problems that, you know, might have killed him?"

They all looked surprised. "None that he ever told us about," said Doug, after a moment's thought. "Why do you ask?"

"Doing my thing, that's all. You sure?"

Light dawned on Terry's face. "Oh, you mean that

peanut allergy trip? That was nothing. Just meant we couldn't keep anything with peanuts in it around the house. No big deal, none of us like the things anyway."

But Doug was quicker. "Oh my God—you're saying that's what he died of? But how? He would *never* have touched a peanut, not if his life depended on it." He heard himself, and stopped short, staring at Rennie helplessly.

"Which it did," she said with great gentleness. "At least that's what the county fuzz told me a while ago. The medical examiner is ruling that as cause of death."

The Owls sat in stunned silence for a few moments. Then Alec shook his head. "It makes no sense. Like Dougie said, Cory would never have gone *near* a peanut. Never. He knew what it would do to him—he'd had some serious episodes as a kid before they figured out what the problem was. You know, dear sweet teacher Mrs. Blah innocently serves peanut butter and jelly sandwiches for lunch in kindergarten, little Cory ends up in the hospital. His parents were really, really careful about it, and they drummed it, ha, into him. If he'd been starving in a ditch, he wouldn't have laid a finger on a peanut."

The others were nodding, and Rennie nodded back. "You're sure? —No, no, I believe you! I just need to be sure for myself, before I take it to the cops."

But they were absolutely positive, telling her that no one had ever asked them about allergies and that it had never occurred to them to mention it, and sounding totally honest, if perhaps colossally clueless, when they said so—and she had enough experience to know the truth when she heard it. So she moved on to more innocuous questions, telling them she planned to write an obituary piece for Cory as well as for Amander Evans, which happened to be true, and needed to get her facts straight, which also happened to be true; and she sincerely encouraged them to find a new drummer hard as it was to think of right now and to please stick together and don't disband, and they thanked her with equal sincerity and answered whatever she asked.

Okay now, *that* had been interesting, she thought as she headed back down the hill. So the band knew about Cory's allergy and had not been questioned about it. Neither had they volunteered the information, though that proved nothing one way or another. Still, she would take those confirming facts to Sheriff Lawson, as she had promised to do if she found out any. And, much, *much* more importantly, she would also take to Sheriff Lawson the fact that none of Owl Tuesday had picked up on, seemingly: if Cory Rivkin had not fed himself peanuts, someone else clearly had, and in such a manner that he accepted them unquestioningly. So who had that person been, and how had that person known of his allergy? And knowing, did they do it anyway?

Which would, of course, make it something entirely different. It would make it murder.

~13~

IT HARDLY SEEMED possible that it was not yet four in the afternoon. Rennie felt as if she had been up for days, weeks, had never slept in her whole entire life; even her hair was tired. And then she remembered that drugs existed. Oooh.

Maybe a reviving hit of speed would be just the ticket? Or some lovely fluffy white coke? She didn't trust anyone at the festival to supply her with the necessary, but she also remembered that she didn't need to: she had that nice gold Victorian compact Stephen had given her in another life, and she had packed it carefully for the weekend, with as much attention and forethought as she'd given to Turk's and Prax's stage clothes. She'd adapted it long ago, of course, for her present needs: one side contained about two grams of very decent cocaine, in the little spill-proof compartment formerly used for face powder, with the mirror in the compact lid to snort it off, and the requisite tiny spoon and short silver straw fitted very nicely in the attached, and empty, lipstick tube.

The other side was an ad hoc pillbox, and held, besides a sharp new single-edged razor blade to chop the coke, a well-curated selection of assorted caps and tabs: Quaaludes,

Turk's occasional necessity on flights; Valium and Tuinal, for her to get to sleep on; and right there in the middle her own zipper-upper of choice, a couple of black shiny capsules of biphetamine, the gentlest sort of speed—if that wasn't some weird oxymoron—or so at least the obliging prescribing doctor had told her. Neither she nor Turk did a *lot* of unlawful substances: mostly drugs bored them silly, and their supplies, except for the odd bag of pot for parties or a couple of joints for Fillmore East nights, and the occasional equally recreational gram of coke, were strictly and legitimately medicinal in nature. She just believed in being prepared for anything.

Her fingers hesitated over one of the sleek black caps, then with a sigh she firmly shut the compact and put it away again in her shoulderbag. Speed would be a help, sure, and so would coke, but she didn't think she could afford the almighty crash that would follow. And she needed all her wits about her for the rest of the weekend, not merely for the few hours that she'd be flying higher than Pegasus. No, she'd get through this one straight. Cold stone sober. Even if she happened to be the only living soul at Woodstock, and she probably was, who was.

When she got back to the pavilion, thinking to have something to eat to keep her strength up, since she'd bravely decided not to rely on chemicals to get her through, Elk Bannerman was beckoning to her from his seat at a table across the pavilion's width. She nodded and waved, and after she'd gotten herself a plate of food she headed over, with guilty reluctance, to join him.

Reluctance because she thought she knew what he wanted to talk to her about—his late client Amander

Evans—and guilt because, much as she liked him, and she liked him a lot, she really *didn't* want to talk about it. It had been hard enough talking to the guys in Owl Tuesday about Cory; but with Elk, in his capacity as president of Rainshadow Records, there was not only Amander but the ghosts of Baz Potter and Finn Hanley and Pierce Hill and Tansy Belladonna hovering around. Especially Baz and Tansy... Ignoring the usual feathering touch of sorrow at the thought of her dear dead friends, she sat down beside Elk and began to organize her plate. But Elk surprised her.

"Rennie, *ketzeleh*," he said in his unexpectedly cultured voice, greeting her with a hug, and she smiled and hugged back. Most people who didn't know him expected a hood from the depths of Gowanus Brooklyn; instead, he sounded like the yeshiva boy he had started out as and the prep school lad he had later become—until he got into organized crime. Not that the record biz was any different from the crime biz, of course, though mostly no one mentioned *that*, not above a whisper anyway. But both Red Hook and prep school had trained him perfectly for the businessman he had ended up becoming—running the lawful business as well as the other one.

In those long-ago Brooklyn days of rum-running and bank-robbing, crime had been a legitimate family enterprise: Jewish families, Irish families, Italian families. It was all and always about kin and connections: Rennie's own maternal grandmother had in her springtime been courted by Al Capone himself, before he moved to Chicago, and had once been chivalrously protected by Willie Sutton, gun blazing, when she was caught in a street shootout. Her family had known Elkanah Bannerman's family since the last years of the last century, and they had been reassured by the fact that in this weird business their cherished young Ravenna Catherine insisted on getting into, at least she would have someone known to them to look out for her, as guardian and protector, and, if necessary, defender.

Not that Elk had been any of those things to her so far, Rennie had reflected privately as she'd piled food on her plate, every mouthful apparently deeply grudged her by the rather sullen caterers—see, if she'd dropped that speed she wouldn't be hungry at all, what a waste that would have been, though the buffet Nazis would probably have preferred it. Elk hadn't done as much for her as Al or Willie had done for her grandma, certainly, at least not yet. But pretty Vinnie Albini had been no gangster's moll, just a nice blue-eyed girl from Milan who made great spaghetti sauce, and when young Michael Kevin McBridgetts had come calling, it was the talk of the South Slope.

In those days and that milieu, Irish and Italian didn't mingle, and they certainly didn't marry, at least not without much neighborhood censure and even shunning. Indeed, Rennie's mom and aunts had told her that they and their brothers had been treated by their kinfolk on both sides as half-breeds, and actually called so to their faces—her mother had appalling stories of them not being allowed to enter certain relatives' houses, being forced to eat Sunday dinner outside on the porch, even in the winter. It was like "West Side Story", only with Italians and Irish instead of Sharks and Jets. And this despite both sides being Catholic, which you'd think religion would have totally trumped ethnicity. But it didn't.

So when Vincenza and Michael started seriously keeping company, to general local disapproval, Al and his boys had gone along to pleasantly suggest to Michael that, not being part of the tribe, he had better make extra sure he was a damn good husband to their little Vinnie, or else steps might have to be taken... And Grandpa Mike had been the best husband ever married in St. Saviour's church, even after Al had left Brooklyn for Chicago, because you never knew. Not that he wouldn't have been in any case, of course. But steps were steps.

Apart from that, though, that side of the family was totally law-abiding, at least until Rennie had come along. Well, no one had ever actually been *caught* doing anything illegal, including Rennie. If it came down to it, Rennie had done more for Elk, certainly in the matter of Tansy at a bare minimum, than he had done for her, and both of them knew he owed her and would eventually repay her handsomely, and probably even lawfully. But she also knew, and he knew, and even Grandma Vinnie knew, that he *would* guard and protect, and, yes, avenge if he had to. And in a strange sort of way, she found that very reassuring.

"Hi, Elk," she said, sitting down next to him, and he put an arm around her, in the manner of someone who, if things had worked out differently, could have been her uncle. "I'm so sorry about Amander."

He nodded for a long time, slowly. "A strange thing, Rennie, a very strange and terrible thing. And we know all about strange things, don't we, you and I. But how's your young man? I heard about what happened to him, right in my own suite at the party I was giving. My apologies."

"He's much better, thanks. I took him home, and he's resting comfortably. But you know, of course, that none of it is your fault. Were you thinking it might be?" she added, tentatively, so as not to give offense.

"Not so much my fault as the fault of someone who

found fault with me," he said, after another measured silence. "I got to thinking that maybe somebody was trying to get a message to me. Baz, Tansy, now Amander… It does seem like that, a little."

"Well, it shouldn't. Because it almost certainly isn't. And I came back up here to find out whose fault it really *is*, and to do whatever I can about it. I'm kind of hoping it will involve severe physical punishment. Administered by me, of course."

Bannerman laughed loud and long. "If I didn't know better, I'd swear you were old Alphonse's granddaughter after all. I know your *nonna* didn't fool around, but maybe it came down to you by osmosis or something."

Rennie laughed too. "If Grandma had decided to marry dear Mr. Capone instead of my grandfather, I could have been a Mafia princess! Ah, the wasted opportunity… With my brains and my Ivy degree, and a bloodline like that, and my willingness to engage in battle when necessary, I'd have been running the entire show by my fortieth birthday."

"And you would have been damn good," he said approvingly. "Not that I'd know, you understand. But you don't want to even be thinking like that. What you do is plenty enough, *shayna maidel*. You busted up that loony bitch who killed our Tanze, and before that the ones who killed Pierce and Baz, and that wacko fake treehugger in San Francisco. And all the other times you managed to figure out who the bad guys were, long before the cops did. That's what you do. And you'll figure this one out too, I don't doubt it for a second. Your grandma must be so proud of you. Your great-grandma too, she's still around, right? I remember them both so well from the old days. They were good friends to my own family, all *gantze mishpocheh*, and back in those days Catholic and Jewish didn't mix much except to mix it up."

Rennie nodded happily. "*Bisnonna* Giulia. Oh yes, she's still here. And still as sharp as a tack."

"And so's her great-granddaughter." His demeanor altered to one of great seriousness. "Give her and Vinnie my best respects. And you know I'll do whatever I can to help in this."

She laid a hand over his. "I know you will, Elk. I know you will."

It had gradually dawned on Rennie, as she made her way through the afternoon, that not only had the music become increasingly erratic, due to recurrent rain showers, but she'd heard surprisingly little of whatever had been going on in the rain's despite. An unknown band called Quill had started things off around noon, but she had been busy talking to the cops and had missed it, except from a distance.

Possibly as a response to the deaths and other stuff, there was more of a general police presence today than there had been previously, and it wasn't just Rennie's imagination. Sure, much of it was investigative—Caskie Lawson's boys at work, with help from the state troopers—but it was more than that. In fact, a local mounted police patrol came riding into the festival like an old-time posse going after the Hole in the Wall gang. But by the time they'd trotted into the heart of Woodstock Nation, the horses were decked from mane to tail in flowers and beads, and had had more pats on the neck and more apples to eat than they'd ever enjoyed in their whole horsy lives. As for the cops who rode them, they'd become completely entranced by what they saw; watching this remarkable development, one such among many, Rennie grinned. Score: Straights 0, Freaks 500,000.

But then there had been still more lulls, mostly to do with groups not being there yet, having miscalculated the traffic problems, or being too stoned to go on in their assigned running order, or the on-and-off rain, or the complex and expensive rotating stage that wouldn't, but finally it had all started running smoothly, with only minimal delays between sets. Rennie was pleased to catch another unknown, a new Latin-based powerhouse called Santana, a Bill Graham act making their big-stage debut; they didn't even have an album out yet, but here they were knocking everybody out, with a monster percussion section and a dynamite lead guitarist for whom the group was named. As she listened appreciatively, she thought that Turk would be sorry to have missed them; then again, considering how he felt about his own performance, perhaps it was just as well that he had.

A bit later, she crossed over to the stage with Prax to hear their friends Turnstone, another Elk-owned act, play a longish set; their co-lead vocalist, the knockout six-foot-tall Lakota Sioux, Tokalah Broken Bow, had replaced the late Tansy Belladonna a year ago. From what Rennie saw, Tokie and Turnstone leader Bruno Harvey were very much on top of their form this afternoon, and since they were both close friends of hers and Prax's she was honestly glad of their triumph—one of the Woodstock few.

She was sitting in the pavilion again, waiting out more brief showers blowing through, trying to restrain herself from running down to the banks of pay phones and calling home to find out how Turk was, what he was doing, how he was feeling. If there had been a problem, which of course there would *not* be, why should there be, Ares and the Greens were there and could cope; she wouldn't be the least bit helpful bugging them, and would do far better to let Turk rest.

In the meantime, even though she was hours yet from going on, or perhaps because of that, Prax required a bit of careful wrangling, as she generally did before a gig; perhaps tonight more so than usual. It was hard to remember sometimes that Evenor's big giant superstardom, like Lionheart's, like the late Tansy's, was only two years old, born at Monterey and built upon ever since. Though Prax had been singing professionally since the age of sixteen, first with little local groups and later with her first band, Karma Mirror, she was still subject to extreme moodiness when in the throes of the run-up to a big performance.

Lionheart, of course, had been around a lot longer, first as a journeyman band and then as genuine stars; and because of that training, in dank blues cellars in places like Manchester and Birmingham and the seedier parts of London, they were by now better accustomed to the fits and starts of stage nerves. You couldn't really call it stage fright, since none of them were particularly frightened, exactly, not at this late date, but they all had their little calming pre-show rituals and requirements. Even Turk professed to sometimes having feelings of panic, though you'd never know it to look at him. Still, the only thing he seemed to need these days was to know that Rennie was nearby, while the others had demands ranging from a good book to cool out with (Rardi) to a cup of tea (all of them) to assorted light drugs (Mick and Niles).

Few musicians did really heavy drugs before a performance, except of course the Dead, for whom tripping was by now their natural default state. You really couldn't, not if you wanted to be able to play: drop even the smallest hit of acid and your fingers would turn into giant purple tennis racquets and your guitar strings would swell up like bridge cables—not exactly conducive to good onstage work. Sure, some artists did stuff anyway: there were harrowing tales of rockers gobbling acid like Halloween candy, or snorting blizzards of coke, to the point where they should have been hiding under the stage, or under their beds, yet somehow they managed to go on. But that was rare. Most of the performers whom Rennie knew regarded jitters as the necessary kickstart to their jobs, and if they didn't exactly welcome it, at least they knew how to make it work for them.

With a start, she came back to the moment. Not much had happened, it seemed: they were still between sets, though Canned Heat had at last gone over to the stage and was waiting for their cue. To Rennie's everlasting surprise, Prax, seated beside her, had not yet commenced her usual snappishness and fidgets, and instead was looking calm and unnaturally serene for someone, for herself, waiting to go onstage and perform before the most colossal audience ever. Catching Rennie's eye, she smiled with cheerful, not to say even smug, satisfaction.

Rennie raised mocking brows. "Did someone travel back in time and step on a butterfly? Because usually by now you're a surly little rat's nest of moodiness, missy, and I can't explain this strange behavior any other way. Unless it's drugs. Which you don't do before a show."

"No, nothing like that," said her friend, laughing. "For some strange reason I don't happen to be feeling my usual nervous self right about now. I have no idea why this should be so, but I figured I would roll with it and see where it takes me."

"How nice for you," Rennie told her grimly. "Can I come with? Because it seems that that would be a place I wouldn't mind being myself, what with Turk and the murders and Sunny and Ned and everything else."

Prax was instantly contrite. "Then let's talk about it, to make it go away, shall we? Have you come to any conclusions?"

"Nothing we haven't already been over a gazillion times." Rennie drew aimless little patterns on the amber suede of her big oversized shoulderbag. "I don't think once more will make any difference." She sat back in her chair and looked out over the festival field. It seemed like a great amiable conscious beast breathing and stirring in the dark, not hostile, merely expectant. And yet—

"I wonder how they'd react if they knew what's really been going on here," she said then, indicating the audience with a jerk of her head, and Prax shot her a quick glance. "The guys in charge have been falling all over themselves trying to keep the terrible fearful news from the masses, lest there be a riot or something. But the news got out about that kid who was run over by the tractor, not to mention that other kid's heroin overdose, and the heart attack victim, and nobody flipped out. No, it was all Oh wow what a bummer, bad stuff happens, must be karma, man, you know? Nothing like the freakout of epic proportions that the promoters seem to be afraid will manifest if the audience hears about Amander and Cory. And Turk and Sunny and Ned."

"They haven't freaked *because* they haven't heard. You can't seriously believe that two murders and attacks on three of the biggest stars around would be reacted to in the same way as an accident with farm equipment, an OD and a heart attack, all suffered by people no one but their friends have ever heard of."

"That is quite likely true. But I am pretty darn sure I haven't told you I suspect murder," said Rennie, eyes narrowed. "I haven't mentioned that to anyone yet. Except the fuzz, of course."

Prax waved it away impatiently. "Hey, this is me, right? I ought to know by now when Murder Chick's slaydar goes off, and it's been pinging like a son-of-a-bitch since Thursday—it's like a damn metronome in my head. Besides, you did too mention murder, back in New York at the house. What did Elk have to say?" she added, as Rennie started to scowl. "I saw you talking to him earlier. Does he know any more about Amander?"

"Not that he's telling me," her friend said, diverted. "He did suggest, rather delicately, that it might be, how can I say this, some kind of smackback on him for unspecified infractions of the mob code. But of course we know he's not mob at all, don't we, yes we do, so it obviously can't be that. And why would they take it out on Amander anyway? She wasn't even a primo client of his and worth anything yet."

"Of course not, and why would they indeed," agreed Prax. "But back to that murder thing—how do you think it was done? And why?"

"Not sure yet. But I have some ideas. And I will be."

Prax was *finally* getting ready to go on, after yet another rain delay had pushed everybody back yet again. Maybe they should be looking for a likely Ararat among the surrounding hills. It was long past dark now, and Evenor had been scheduled to have wrapped their performance around sunset. But because of the hard rain falling yet again out of the apparently quenchless skies, a halt had been called until the stage could be wrung out and declared safe for a reasonable interval. Nobody wanted a repetition of what had happened to Ned Raven on Thursday. Or worse.

When the harried stage staff finally gave Evenor their get-ready call, Prax summoned Rennie to help her change clothes, and they repaired to the little dressing-room tents and trailers behind the pavilion, where rows of garment racks held stage attire for the performers who'd brought it.

Quite a few artists hadn't bothered to dress up at all, going on instead in garb more suited to the place and weather, things like jeans and t's and workshirts—which, considering the mud and downpours and staggering jungle steaminess that alternated with shivery chill, was probably smart. But most, like Janis Joplin and Roger Daltrey and Grace Slick and Prax herself, had chosen to vest themselves in full rock plumage, peacocking for the audience and the cameras alike in all their leathered, feathered, fringed and tie-dyed glory.

Which occasionally proved to be not the best idea: Grace, who earlier, expecting to go on before midnight, had been immaculate in a white sleeveless-top-and-pants outfit, had become smudged and rumpled as the night wore on. Turk had split the difference, yesterday: he'd worn comfortable black jeans, his black Frye boots and a white cotton pirate shirt, with a studded brown leather doublet of Rennie's creation. He had looked amazing, if she did say so herself. But in his fury he had ripped off the doublet and flung it to the ground as soon as Lionheart left the stage. She didn't mind; it had been hot, he had been angry, she would recycle it.

Now she looked over at her friend, who was still in a suspiciously cheery mood as she riffled through the racks looking for her garment bag. "Just be careful out there, for God's sake, will you, Mary Praxedes? I don't want you ending up like Sunny or Ned or Turk. Or Cory. Or Amander."

"Not my call, lambchop. The universe will dictate."

In spite of her apprehensions, Rennie grinned. "I thought you didn't take dictation."

"Not as a rule, no," said Prax serenely. "But perhaps an exception can be made... It's a weird thing, being a performer," she added almost irrelevantly, pulling on a close-fitting Rennie-made halter top in soft thin blue fringed leather. "There are all these people out there who are in love with you. And no matter how you try, you can't wrap your brain around why they should feel like that. Because they're not in love with *you*. They can't possibly be. They don't even *know* you. They've never met you and they probably never will. They're in love with their fantasy picture of you, projecting it onto you like you're a blank screen; they're relating to you as they need you to be, not to who you really are, you as a person. No wonder so many rock stars have such problems with drugs and booze. It's a way of protecting themselves. But it's such a *bad* way."

"Well, yes, that is all completely true, but by choosing to be a rock star, you kind of asked for it, didn't you."

"*Nobody* asks for *that*," said Prax with a certain grimness, echoing, though she didn't know it, identical sentiments expressed to Rennie by Turk himself, last year on the night of Tansy Belladonna's funeral, a continent away. "All we ever asked for—me, Turk, Janis, Gray, Prue, the Beatles, whoever—was to be able to play our music. Instead, we got this. Rock star... There isn't any other job in the history of the world—okay, maybe Hitler, or Jesus, oops, didn't Lennon get into trouble for saying that?—that pulls so many people into its nutty trip. Right now, there's half a million heads in that field over there waiting for me to go out there and sing to them. That's a hell of a lot of eyetracks, a hell of a lot of attention to be focused on your own little self."

"Don't freak," said Rennie, brushing out Prax's blond hair and slipping a dozen strands of beads over her head, including the ones that Tansy Belladonna had made for her as a thank-you gift, years ago and miles away. "Most of it's loving and appreciative and positive."

"Oh, I know, and I'm not freaking, and I'm not ungrateful either, but it's still overwhelming. It's soul sucking *and* soul overload. Outgo and input at the same time. They're like two-way vampires, draining your energy out and feeding their own in."

"Can't you learn how to work with their energy, use it for your own purposes, instead of getting all flipped out by it?"

"Maybe. Eventually. Right now, nobody I know can really do it, and if they say they can, I say they're lying."

Prax slipped off her bellbottoms, wrapped the matching blue leather microskirt around her slim hips and fastened it on one side. Arranging the halter's deep fringes over it, she looked critically at herself in the full-length mirror, checking to see if it was all going to hold together onstage, spinning round to see how the fringes moved in action and that the glimpse of tanned thigh above the blue suede boots wasn't too revealing, or at least not more revealing than she wanted it to be.

"What do you reckon? That stage is pretty high—will people way down in the front, or in the photographers' pit, be able to see up my skirt? I don't think I feel like giving them *that* much of a cheap thrill. Though I do have knickers on, just in case."

Rennie thought not, and said so. There were tall wooden barriers and camera platforms and ample space in front of the stage; photographers and viewers alike were at such a distance and angle as would prevent indecent exposures. Prax nodded, reassured.

"So, anyway, there you are, out there in the spotlight like a goddamn target," she continued, returning to her point, "and all this high-power stuff is being channeled your way. And it's mostly the media's fault, thanks ever so much."

"Hey! You guys are the ones who are always coming to us asking for press, or hiring flacks to ask on your behalf—stoking the furnace of public notice, doing all manner of fun and interesting things to call attention to yourself. Can't have it both ways, sassyface."

Prax's grin flashed. "Good point. As for the energy, maybe you can't actually see it, but you absolutely can feel it. It's aimed at *you*, you specifically, like a laser cannon. It's got your name on it, and it blasts through your skin, your mind, every sense you've got. If you can't somehow ground it through what you're doing, it'll fry you to a crisp. It's like psychic feedback: you're the guitar, they're the amp. What the hell do they *want* from us?"

"I don't know," said Rennie hesitantly. "Sometimes I think you guys bring the energy and incite the audience, sometimes I think it's the other way around. Either way, though, you have to use it if you hope to survive. It's like they want to either love you to pieces or tear you to pieces. Or both. Eat you or own you. In the long run, maybe there's really no difference."

Prax laughed, and made a final check of her clothes. "There is if I do it to them first. I'm gonna go out there now and mindfuck them until their heads explode."

"That's my girl!"

~14~

For all Prax's fighting words, though, she and Evenor had little more success than Turk and Lionheart had had, or most of the other bands, for that matter, and, in the pavilion afterwards, Rennie had reluctantly brought up Prax's pre-set comments.

"It doesn't matter, whatever," said Evenor's rhythm guitarist, Chet Galvin, with a certain amount of weariness. "The fans are pre-programmed in their heads to hear what they want to hear. They want apocalyptic and mind-altering, so that's what they get. Even if that's not what we play. Even if what we deliver is a sloppy, messy, mediocre set. They need it to be amazing, and so for them it is."

"Autohype," muttered Juha Vasso, the lead guitarist. "We've been seeing it for years, and nothing real is ever going to make them see otherwise. Certainly not a mere off day by a band they're into. They *think* they're hearing something great, they *need* to be hearing something great, so for them they are and they do."

Jack Paris nodded glumly. "And who the hell are we to say they're not? Wait till you read what everyone has to say about this after it's over. I guarantee you they'll be describing this heap of musical second-rateness as the Second Coming,

Mardi Gras, Napoleon's coronation and the birthday of the world, all in one. With the best music that was ever heard in the history of ever. Because *that's* what they want to have spent their weekend at, not a wet, cold, hungry mudbath punctuated at intervals with sloppy, messy, mediocre or even downright godawful music. And that's what they'll tell people, and by God that's what they'll end up believing. You'll see. They'll persuade themselves into it, and they'll persuade everyone else into it too. You can't stop the power of autohype."

They all were sitting around the crowded pavilion, dejected, but glad their set was finally over; for her part, Rennie had been secretly, guiltily, almost glad that Evenor had been less than brilliant, because of how a stellar performance on their part would have made Turk and Lionheart feel—and yes, she was fully aware of what a horrible person that made her. Too bad. At the moment, another long rain delay was in progress, and the performers scheduled to go on next, the Grateful Dead and after them Creedence Clearwater Revival, had been put on hold. They were sitting nearby, looking glum, and consoling themselves with champagne.

"That's a little too existential for me, cutie-pie. But whose fault is that?" asked Rennie. Prax was absent for the moment: coming offstage, she'd headed straight to the trailer to change out of her stage clothes and into something more suitable for the current weather, which Rennie had thoughtfully provided in her garment bag o' tricks. The ongoing rain and gusts of wind had made the night an unseasonably chilly one for August, though she'd warned everyone she knew, beforehand, about the changeability of the upstate climate, with the fatalism of one who had seen snow in September and snow in May—if they hadn't brought a jacket or a sweater, it wasn't her fault. And, of course, a lot of people *had* ignored her good advice, and now were sitting there shivering in the rain-cooled air, while she was warm and dry all over, and so would Prax be too.

Juha laughed. "I hate to say it, but—"

Rennie rolled her eyes. "Oh, sure, blame the press! I admit we spout a lot of wild-eyed guff, but nobody ever said you guys have to *listen* to us. The record companies, are they at fault? You bet. The fans? Likewise. But basically it's you people yourselves who start it all off. You perform your art and indulge in all your little tricks and capers. We just write about it. The fans just dig it. The labels just sell it. Nobody ever expected it to get as big as it has."

"Only going to get bigger," said Bardo, the usually taciturn bass player. "Can't you feel it coming? Pretty soon it's only going to be about the bread, not the music. Bands who used to play for beer and burger money, and thought that was the big time, are now playing for ten or twenty grand a night, and bands like Lionheart are playing for forty. We're all becoming rich people, when all we started out hoping for was to be able to buy a new axe without worrying about how much it cost. And that won't be the end of it. Tickets that used to be three dollars will be ten times that. More. Nobody will play in little clubs, or even the Fillmores, purely for the love of the music—it's all going to be big stadiums and it's all going to be about the bucks. I hate it."

However dismal the sentiment, that was practically a Shakespearean soliloquy for Bardo, who generally communicated in Zen koans or smiling Buddhist silences. They all duly considered, and without a word exchanged all agreed that he was right; and further, that there wasn't a damn thing anybody could do about it and likewise there was not a damn thing more to be *said* about it, depressing thoughts though those were.

Rennie tried by main force to change the topic. "It's so surreal, though, when you think of it: a rock festival here in Borschtland, the heart of the Jewish Catskills. All these young heads, but you can bet your ass that their parents are all big fans of very different musicians indeed. Bing Crosby, not David Crosby."

"True," Evenor manager Dill Miller pointed out, glad to give Rennie a hand shifting the grim scenery. "But don't you remember, the Airplane actually played Grossinger's last year? I hear the kids of the resort's patrons, who were stuck there with their folks, were thrilled to bits. Even their parents didn't entirely hate it. And the Airplane is musically pretty easy to follow, being quite melody-driven. Jorma said his bubbe would have loved it."

Prax had joined them, in a surprisingly cheery mood considering how the set had gone. But she'd had a short chat with Leeds Sheffield as she changed out of her stage clothes, and the Sovereign Records president had managed to soothe her unsettled soul with diplomatic words. Now she had Rhino Kanaloa in tow, and everyone greeted him cheerfully; they hadn't seen much of the huge, amiable Hawaiian who was Ares' longtime second in command, as he'd been busy with security duties, especially so since Ares had gone down to the city to keep an eye on Turk.

Prax flopped down next to Rennie, and grinned at them all. "Not so much Janis or the Dead or the Who being easy to follow, though," she said, thirstily swigging down the hot tea with honey, her usual post-set tipple for a tired throat, which Bernadette, Chet's wife, had had ready for her in a thermos. "Or even maybe Lionheart or us. Those vacationers at Grossinger's might hate our end of rock considerably more."

Rennie grinned; the mental picture and accompanying audio track of Lionheart or Evenor doing their thing for the Grossinger's crowd was just too delicious for words. Even contemplating the Airplane playing for the blue-rinse set was a trip and a half. She flashed on Lionheart at London's Royal Opera House in Covent Garden last month, when the Duke and Duchess of Locksley, with a hair-raising mix of stateliness and familial pride, had occupied their ancestral box, accompanied by Turk's parents, to hear their grandson and his band play for charity with major royals in attendance. It had been quite an occasion, as one would expect—tiaras and all. Turk had been deeply thrilled and very proud to play in front of his family for the first acknowledged time in public; his mum and dad had separately snuck out years before, in secret, to catch Lionheart, and had never told him, or indeed each other. But his grandparents had never seen him play at all, and it was only because of Rennie's bargain with the Duke that they were there—though she had never come right out and 'fessed up to Turk about their deal.

"Even so," said Rhino, "we did see those charming handmade signs on the way in—the ones that said No Hippies Here and Hippies Go Home and Hippies Use Side Entrance."

"Yeah, we saw those too," said Bernadette Galvin. "Gave us quite a feeling of solidarity with the civil rights marchers, or at least as much solidarity as middle-class college-educated white kids *can* feel. Sort of Jim Crow Lite. Instructive."

Bardo snorted. "To say the least."

They were all quiet again for a while. Rennie knew they were waiting for her to tell them something dramatic about Turk, or Cory, or Amander, but she was in no mood to break the mood, and besides, there really wasn't much she could say. She might talk privately to Rhino later, before she went back to the motel, but she really didn't want to hash it over again. What she usually did in situations like this was to go woodshed with it for a while, like a jazz musician: hole up with no distractions and run variations on what she had on her mind. Knowing Turk was safe at home relieved said mind hugely; but by her best reckoning, everyone here was still in possible danger, and she needed to find a way to protect them. As quickly as she could.

Prax ran a hand over her face, wiping away the mist, and provided a diversion, as she knew Rennie was hoping for. "How is Elk coping? Everyone says that Death is *your* groupie, petal, but I tell you, Elk seems to be rapidly gaining on you. Need I remind this company of our late friend Basil Potter? Or the late Pierce Hill? Or the late Finn Hanley? All connected to his label? Not to mention our late darling Tansy, whom I won't mention because if I do we'll all end up crying. And now the late Amander Evans. Quite a score."

"Yeah, but he's supposed to be mob, Elk is," Juha remarked, lowering his voice and glancing around. "Kind of goes with the turf—he trails an aura of cement overshoes everywhere he goes." Looking squarely at Rennie: "*You* have no such excuse. And I saw you talking to Elk this afternoon. So. Spill it."

Cornered, she gave them a brief account of her chat with Elk in the pavilion. They were all much impressed with her hitherto unsuspected familial connections to organized crime, and it was borne in on her that they were all of them, even Rhino, even Prax, a little bit afraid of Elk. And yet if she wanted to, she could call him Uncle, and he would be delighted. Weird.

Just then Janis Joplin wandered over, looking like some brilliant tropical orchid in her tie-dyed velvet and beads, though a rather sad and drunk and disheveled and probably shot-up one right about now, and sat down to join them for a round of drinks. Rennie and Prax knew she would never have admitted it, but Janis was really nervous about going on with her new band—she'd left Big Brother the year before, at her manager Albert Grossman's persuasion—and public reaction to the change had been decidedly underwhelmed. Everybody loved *her*, of course, nothing would ever change that, but they'd adored Big Brother too, and this lineup hadn't yet jelled and set behind her.

Maybe that was the problem, Rennie mused, watching Janis enjoying herself rapping happily with Evenor; the new band was "behind" her. It was good—the musicians were all talented and played capably. But it didn't seem to kindle her or inspire her—it wasn't beside her and around her and together with her the way the loved and lamented Brother had been. People hardly knew the names of these new guys; they might have been gun-for-hire session players. The consensus out along the rock jungle telegraph was that Janis had allowed herself to be seduced and hyped, by Grossman and her own publicity, into a star trip, believing that she was bigger than any band, and this in turn fed into her need to dominate whoever backed her. Or maybe it was all out of her deep vulnerability, her junkie's insecurity. But either way...

Bad move on her part, thought Rennie ruefully. Nobody

was *that* big, and she wondered suddenly exactly how major a role Janis's now-rampant heroin and alcohol abuse played in it. Had the addictive habits caused her to lose her artistic and/or personal judgment? Or had it simply made plain to her, and to everybody else except the fans, that she'd maybe never possessed all that much judgment to begin with? Hard questions: and if Rennie was asking them, who was extremely fond of Janis as both an artist and a person, how much more must others be asking them who didn't care for her at all? And the big unspoken question, worst of all, which everyone was at present avoiding as hard as they could, was how long could even the greatest talent survive under such conditions. Nobody wanted to ask, because nobody wanted to hear the answer.

She had a feeling, too, that Janis envied Prax a little. Not in herself, but because Prax had gathered to her banner a band like Evenor, a band that was not only top-notch but really family and really equals. Bardo and Jack and keyboardist Dainis Hood had been with her from the start, in her original band Karma Mirror; the other guys, Juha and Chet, had come out of the wreck of the Deadly Lampshade, after the murder of their lead singer Tam Linn. Under the leadership of Prax and Juha—who had been romancing each other at the time they were setting up the band, and who still enjoyed the occasional encounter for auld lang syne even though both were solidly ensconced with new partners—Evenor had become a real and organic whole, one of the first-rank four-star American bands, with five stars, or at least four and a half, well in sight. Praxie was a superstar, sure, but Janis was a supernova, sadly without a constellation in which to shine, and her galaxy seemed to more people than Rennie alone to be rapidly becoming a very lonely one indeed. And the fate of supernovas was to flame out spectacularly and swiftly.

As Rennie, suddenly unsettled and unhappy, got up to fetch something to drink, she impulsively dropped a kiss on Janis's head as she passed; it just felt right, and when Janis, surprised for an instant, threw her a spacious grin, acknowledging the support, Rennie knew it *was* right.

Earlier that evening, the folk-rock band Honest Mollusk, whom Rennie knew from the old days in San Francisco, had turned in one of the better Woodstock performances so far. Today was supposed to be hard-rock day, as yesterday had been folkie day, but the Mollusks, like the Incredible String Band, had begged off playing in the rain on Friday, for fear of their acoustic instruments going soggily and quickly out of tune, and so, much to their annoyance, both bands had found themselves playing in the rain on Saturday instead. Resigned to their damp karma, the Mollusks had nonetheless performed admirably, and the highlight of their set had been a stunning rendition of the old and spooky British folk song "The Cutty Wren."

'We'll hunt the cutty wren'... Waiting for some band, *any* band, to go on, for God's sake let *something* happen *soon*, the rain hissing down again like snakes, Rennie sang the eerie little song softly to herself, remembering, inevitably, another wren-hunting, earlier that year in London, and shivered a little in the dark. Her mind flashed again and again to Turk, as it had been doing all day, wondering how he was faring. Hopefully Francher and Christabel and Ares were holding the line on him staying in bed to regain his strength, though she knew he'd be bored to tears by now and trying to charm, pout or command his way downstairs. All she wanted to do

was somehow transport herself instantly back home, beam herself there like something out of "Star Trek"…

" *'We'll hunt the cutty wren',*" she sang again, aloud this time.

"As long as it's still wren, not Ren-*nie,* that they're hunting." She startled violently; she hadn't noticed the person who'd quietly taken the empty chair on her left, listening to her half-whispered song. Now she regarded him for a few moments, then shook her head.

"I was wondering when you were going to turn up," she said, and Marcus Dorner smiled. "Garcia told me you were infesting the premises."

"Oh, I've been out and about. Once I heard about the deaths and everything, I figured I'd run into you sooner or later. How's Turk?"

Rennie's gaze narrowed at the unexpected question. "You know about that?"

He nodded, both sympathy and amusement on his face. "Had a little talk with the county sheriff as well as with the festival security chief. That was impressive work to spirit his lordship away like that."

"Not a bit," said Rennie coolly. "There was no need for us to stick around and have to deal with—whatever. Turk didn't know who gave him the wine and that was all we could tell them."

"All you *wanted* to tell them, you mean. All you thought they *deserved* to be told."

"That is as it may be." She settled back a little in her chair, with the air of a veteran knight couching a lance at the start of a joust: equal parts tension, caution, bloodthirstiness and something rather like enjoyment. "Are you here in an official capacity, may I ask, like Supernark or Junior

G-man or something? Is it *Agent* Dorner now? *Secret* Agent Dorner? I've been told you work with the Feds a lot these days; are you a certified Fed? And if you are, do you plan on certifiably busting half a million people for being stoned out of their gourds?"

Marcus laughed. "No, not really. My original brief was to look after things on a general basis—liaise with the locals and with the hired security help, the way I did at Monterey. Though there I had some lawfully official clout and standing. But now that it's all gotten more serious..."

He trailed off, and Rennie smiled with a certain grimness, noting that he had not answered her question about his possible FBI secret-agentry. Well, no answer was also an answer.

"You really mean, though of course you are much too polite to say, 'as it so often does when you, Rennie Stride, chance to be around.' Am I right?"

"As you so often are...both around and right, I mean. I'm still not *officially* on the case. Though of course if some relevant information turns up, my employers won't kick it in the teeth. They still want to keep Cory Rivkin's and Amander Evans' deaths as quiet as possible, so as not to spook the killer."

"Or not trash the vibe and bring down all the attendees, is more like it. Last thing the festival czars are looking for is half a million tripped-out and panicky people turning on their neighbors thinking a serial killer's on the loose among the hippie lambs. Bad press, bad karma, possible massacre. Or massacree, as our friend Arlo Guthrie would have it."

"Something like that. But you still haven't told me about Turk."

"Still not much to tell. After Lionheart played, we

went back to the motel, which is also the motel where Amander was staying, and after a little rest in our room, we went to the party for Amander, which I had promised Elk Bannerman we would drop in at. And when he was briefly out from under my guardian eagle eye, his idiot lordship drank some wine some anonymous someone handed him. When I couldn't wake him up in the morning, we took him to the local hospital and he had his stomach pumped. That same someone, or perhaps someone else, had ever so thoughtfully put a bunch of downers in the wine. According to the doctors, it was a very near thing."

Marcus was watching her very attentively, and she kept her voice as even as she could. "Then I called Fitz and borrowed one of his planes—a little small sparrow, not the opulent and mighty Fitz Force One—and we took him home. He's there now. He's fine. Ares and the Greens are with him; they'd had enough festival, and even if they hadn't, they were happy to stay and take care of him till I get back. Also I told them I would kill them if they didn't."

"A fine inducement. And very decent of Fitzroy to come to the rescue. So you came back up here, intent on finding the person who did that to him, so you can punish them as they so richly deserve. Oh, don't look so surprised, I know all your little ways… I'm sure you've been snooping around as is your ever so charming wont. Find anything?"

Rennie had regained her professional look. "Not really a lot of places *to* snoop. Or maybe too many: there's rather a lot of people here, as you may have noticed. I'm mostly hoping someone will let something slip. And then I can rip someone's head off—literally—as I so dearly long to do. In the meantime, I had to worry about Prax, who just came off, and Ned Raven, who went on yesterday—Friday, day before now—and who was almost electrocuted the day before that, and Sunny Silver, who was nearly flattened by a falling amp stack that same morning and was lucky to escape with only a broken arm."

"Ah, the usual suspects. I'm glad nothing happened to Prax on your watch...I'm fond of that girl and would be sorry to see her hurt. And the others too. And I know you don't believe me when I say it, but I'm sorry to see Turk hurt like that."

"Thank you for saying so, at least."

Refilling his plastic cup of champagne, Marcus casually scanned the pavilion with a professional eye, like Genghis Khan checking out an assemblage of possibly double-crossing warlords. Rennie regarded him judicially. He was looking pretty good, actually. Even though he was no longer with the LAPD, which he'd joined after leaving the SFPD, he'd kept the longish hair, so useful for undercover work, so he must be doing something similar in his new gig, whatever that might be, and he appeared relaxed and even slightly tanned. No one would ever pick him out as the fuzz by his clothes, either: he was wearing a workshirt and jeans and sneakers and an old Mao jacket, all artfully ragged and muddied by way of camouflage, and looked totally at home sitting elbow to elbow with rock stars.

She hadn't seen or spoken to him for many months, not since the aftermath of her being shot in L.A. in June of last year, when Turk had brought her home from the hospital. Her friends had assembled to celebrate her return and successful solving of the murders, and Marcus had shown up, uninvited, to humbly apologize for his suspicions and arrest of Turk. Which apology, technically, she had still not yet accepted, nor had she forgiven him, really...even if Turk had. At least he *said* he had, and she'd reluctantly taken his word for it.

And so here he was, Marcus Lacing Dorner, Stephen's second cousin and her imediately pre-Turk ex—though really not much of an ex, given as they'd spent perhaps eight weekends together in all before coming to their senses. Or at least Rennie's senses—Marcus had been in love with her, and had continued to hope for a reconciliation right up until, and even after, Rennie had fallen from a great height, and forever, for Turk, and he for her. Yet here he was, looking like a, yes, quite believable head, smiling and nodding at faces he recognized in the pavilion. But if any of those faces, let alone the giant seething mob outside, knew what he was, they might not be all so smiley and peacey and lovey about it…

She clattered hastily on, to avoid an uncomfortable silence. "How's Stephen? And the rest of the dear mummified Lacings? Not that I really care about any of them except Stephen and Eric, and Ling and Petra and Trey and Davina too, of course, and now young Master Tizzy and the new tiny Carly. I'm her godmother, you know, and she's named for me, too," she added boastfully. "Charlotte Rennie. For the founding Lacing whore and the current Lacing bolter. Eric's idea, and Petra was delighted with it. I'm told Marjorie threw eleven blue-tailed fits when she found out, more furious that they were naming the baby after me than after Charlotte, even. Sorry I couldn't be there to watch her throw even one of them; I bet they were well worth seeing. She does that sort of thing so beautifully—she's like a gold medalist in the Outraged Overprivileged Socialite Olympics. But Eric and Petra wanted me to be namesake as well as godparent to their little princess, and their will rightly prevailed over Motherdear's. So, like a good fairy godmother, I gave the bonny wee lassie a suitable string of very nice pearls and a little engraved gold cup, most traditional."

Marcus chuckled. "I can see it now: you all demure and righteous holding the child at the font, and Marjorie on the dear vicar's other side ready to blow like the San Andreas, taking out half of Nob Hill in the process. You're lucky she didn't rip the infant out of your auntly arms, shrieking at you for being the bad fairy at the christening and looking around for spindles. Who's her godfather, by the way?"

"Stephen is, actually. Since Eric's true spouse Trey filled that churchly office for his namesake Thomas three years back. Oh, come on, don't give me the stink-eye, it was all quite civil and pleasant. After the church ceremony, everyone had a fun time at Marjorie's little Hell House reception, very good food, too bad you missed it; as soon as we decently could, we all escaped and went to the Avalon to see Quicksilver. Stephen and Ling too. We even danced together. Didn't bring the sprog, though. There's plenty of time to get her and her brother into rock."

She looked at him. "Where *were* you, by the way? You and the Erics are on good terms; why did you miss the occasion? Nothing to do with me, I trust."

He snorted. "The whole world doesn't revolve around Rennie Stride, you know."

"No! *Really*? You're joking." She passed him another cup of champagne and glanced at him sideways. "I bet you were investigating some super-duper secret spy thingy, with your new Fed pals."

"Could be. Or maybe I simply didn't feel up to yet another Lacing family event."

"Now *that* I can understand."

"So why are you not home with Turk, sitting attentively by his bedside and being all Nancy Nurse for him?"

"Three reasons: I didn't want people to know about Turk being attacked and if I left the festival entirely, questions would definitely be asked; I never imagined there would be two murders; I figured I could figure it all out myself; and I wasn't expecting that you'd be here."

"That's four reasons."

"Well, I thought you'd buy one of the first three, but I could see that you weren't, so I tossed out another."

"Uh-*huh*. So now?"

"We work together? That is how it would be, in a perfect world. I don't know about you, but I seldom get to go places like that."

"And you don't get to go there this time either. The local police told me they'd made that quite clear to you, when they and I were having our little professional-courtesy chat. You know they're really pissed off with you, that you snuck Turk out from under their country noses like that. Impressed, reluctantly, but pissed off."

"Too bad, they can't get at him now," said Rennie, with considerable satisfaction. "I very much doubt that Sullivan County has an extradition treaty with Manhattan. And them not being able to pester him is all I care about. Except him getting better, of course. And me finding the vermin responsible for the poisoning and thrashing the living bejesus out of him. Or her," she added as an afterthought. "Plus I *want* to help, I really do. I could be useful, you know. What about Cory Rivkin? You're up to speed on him, are you, as well as on Amander? I wonder if he could be somehow linked to either Amander's death or the attempt on Turk."

Marcus sighed. "I suppose. But we still don't know why Rivkin's dead. I mean, we know why in the sense of how it was accomplished, or so I've been informed. We just don't know why in the sense of what for. Or by whom. And we absolutely know none of those things yet about Amander's death. Or much else either, at least according to what the cops told me."

"They haven't looked hard enough, the torpid yokels. Now do you see why I had to get Turk home, to a city of *real* cops and *real* hospitals, not to mention *real* doctors who don't have a sideline as cow midwives?"

"You have a point. Several of them, actually. In fact, you're a pointy person all over, aren't you."

"I am just that very thing." She looked balefully down the slope at the stage, which was empty at the moment on account of the rain, and the huddled masses spread out in front of it, who were invisible at the moment on account of the darkness. "And before I'm done I'm going to give this peace and love hippie crap the pointy end of several different sorts of sticks. You wait and see if I don't."

"Well, before you go poking anything with metaphorical sticks, or, knowing you, actual ones, there's a bit of news, and you're not going to like it."

"And what's that, then?"

"Ned Raven was taken into custody a couple of hours ago by the state police. In connection with Amander Evans' death."

Rennie went very still and stared at him. "You have got to be kidding me."

He shook his head, clearly enjoying the effect of his news, though equally clearly not the news itself. "I never kid about things like that. As you know. And I like Ned, so no joy there for me either."

"Can I see him?" asked Rennie, after a rather prolonged silence. "What's the charge?"

"Technically, he hasn't been arrested. Not yet. I believe the correct term for his current condition would be 'assisting the authorities with their inquiries'."

As bad as that, then. Oh deary deary me...

"You can see him in the morning," added Marcus, getting up from the table. "He's in the sheriff's headquarters in Monticello; they decided to offer him their hospitality overnight, though they were at pains to tell him, and me, that he was not under arrest. Yet. But you might want to put a pre-emptive call in to King Bryant, or at least his Manhattan branch office. As for you getting backstage at the cop house, I'll leave your name at the door."

As he went out on that really pretty good exit line, Rennie stared off in the direction of the stage, where the Grateful Dead were in the starting gate and raring to go. Yeah...good to have your name on the list, all right.

For all her anxiety about Ned, she gamely stuck it out in the pavilion. Prax was still drifting about somewhere, but the rest of Evenor had left the grounds, planning on doing nothing more taxing or exciting than getting something to eat and crashing. Apart from Gray and Prue Sonnet, and the Langhans, and a couple of others here and there, there didn't seem to be too many of Rennie's friends on site at the moment. Everyone had cravenly decamped back to the motels, where at least it was warm and dry and merry, and would presumably show up again before the end of the evening, which now looked to be about dawn.

Not so much of that warm and dry and merry here at

the moment, though. Sweeping curtains of rain and cold wind, not to mention equipment trouble, were cutting short the Grateful Dead's really poor and severely truncated set—the worst of any major band's, as it would turn out, which was saying a lot—and delaying Creedence's, and by the time things got moving again, the vibe was pretty flattened. Though Creedence battled gamely, the Dead had come offstage in a foul mood; they immediately jumped into waiting station wagons and roared off into the night. They didn't even stick around to watch their good buddy Janis Joplin perform, perhaps because by now Janis was in a much-dilapidated state and a foul mood of her own, due to smack, booze and a ten-hour wait since her too-early arrival at the field; even her dearest friends thought that her historic Woodstock appearance would not be a pretty sight, and they didn't want to have to see it if they could possibly please-to-be-excused.

None of it was mattering much to Rennie at the moment, because there was a nasty little war going on, inevitably, between her thinking hominid front brain and her instinctive reptile back brain. And it looked to her to be about evens which was going to win.

Oh Neddy…what have *you done, you stupid stupidhead, for them to be entertaining you at the sheriffry, or the troopery, or wherever the hell?*

After a while Marcus came back and sat down again. He was silent for a while, not looking at her, and she felt tiny prickles of dread rising along the back of her neck and shoulders.

"Well, I shouldn't have given you false hope," he said finally. "They seem to have something pretty solid against Ned after all. Because he was the one who found Amander

Evans dead in the tent."

And Rennie felt her front brain and back brain together kick her heart to the ground and stomp all over it.

~15~

SHE CAUGHT A ride back to the motel, as she had left the Mustang parked there from Saturday morning, in its slot outside the room she and Turk occupied. Shivering a little with chill and stress, not to mention hunger, Rennie picked up the phone, desperate to call him, to find out how he was, to hear his voice, then put it down again. No…it was very late, and hopefully he was healingly asleep; no need to disturb him, or indeed the others, merely for her own selfish need for comforting.

She'd called home earlier, anyway, while waiting for Praxie to go on, though she hadn't spoken with Turk himself. There being mile-long queues for the pay phones down the hill, even in the pouring rain, she had asked to borrow the super-duper space-age briefcase spy phone that was never more than a few feet from Elk Bannerman's side, and Elk had been delighted to oblige his honorary niece. The gadget really was like something the Man from U.N.C.L.E. would use, and the bull-necked guardian and bearer of the briefcase looked like someone employed by T.H.R.U.S.H. Rennie had come round the table to approach him, a little nervously, and he hadn't been exactly welcoming.

But Elk had nodded once, a nod to be obeyed, and Mr.

Bullneck had silently unsnapped the handsome leather case and punched in the numbers for Rennie on the gleaming, fitted phone, handing her the receiver. So, feeling like Illya Kuryakin on assignment, or on acid, she'd taken advantage of the opportunity and had phoned not only the prow house, where Ares had answered and eased her mind considerably, but the paper as well, giving the latest information to someone who would pass it along to the appropriate editors, speaking to be heard over the pelting rain still drumming on the pavilion roof. So all that was taken care of, and she'd expressed her gratitude to Elk, who indulgently waved it away. But she still fretted for Turk.

At the moment, she was lying on the wide bed, hugging Turk's pillow and staring up at the ceiling. She'd spoken to the paper again just a few minutes ago, from here, delivering the latest news about Ned and providing updates on the general situation, so her journalistic jobwork was up to speed; but if she called the house now she'd wake everybody up, and she'd only get somebody not-Turk anyway. There was nothing else she could do except maybe eat another sandwich, or some soup—there was still plenty left in the fridge—or have a hot shower to warm up, or a cool one to wake up. She didn't want to take a nap, because she planned to go back to the festival to catch Jefferson Airplane, one of the chief reasons—besides Lionheart and Evenor—that she had come at all. It now looked likely that the Airplane wouldn't be going on much before dawn, so a nap could be dangerous—nod off now and she'd sleep until Monday.

Marcus had said she could talk to Ned in the morning, though not first thing; maybe she *should* try to line up a lawyer for him? High-powered Lacing family lawyer King Bryant's office was a good idea...Neddy wouldn't know anyone in New York legal circles, though his record company would no doubt have counsel available...the memory of Pamina Potter's eerily similar situation at Monterey flitted through her dimming awareness...

MELZA! She shot upright as the thought tore through all levels of consciousness, galvanizing both body and brain much as Ned's electric shock on Thursday must have done to his. Where was Mel, what was she doing, was someone at least with her? Talk about comforting: now *there* was where Rennie could be immediately helpful... She threw her clothes on again and ventured out of the room and out of the quiet, private little Lionheart wing. Into pure pandemonium: the halls were like Times Square on New Year's Eve, the dining room was full of loud roistering drunks from every band that didn't need to be onstage that night and even some that did, open doors invited any passersby in for further partying. But she slipped past all the invitations and propositions and cheerful proffers of drinks and drugs, and headed for the other side of the motel.

She found the Ravens' room without difficulty—especially since one of the Sonnets' Ares-assigned bodyguards was standing loomingly outside, which was a bit of a surprise. Seeing her, he smiled and tapped briskly on the door. After a moment, Graham Sonnet warily opened it a few inches; seeing only Rennie, he pulled her unceremoniously inside with an air of passionate relief, nodding to the guard, who shut the door behind them and resumed his station.

"Christ, I'm glad you're here," said Gray, without preamble. "Prue is doing her best, but she's not had any luck whatsoever. Mel hasn't said a word since the local plod took Ned off; all she does is weep and lie there catatonically, and who can blame her. Still, it doesn't help. Here, have some wine, maybe you can do better..."

He handed her a glass of wine and drew her over to the couch that faced the bed. Despite the luster of the superstar heads that were laying them down to sleep upon its pillows, the motel was generic tourist class, catering to the business or family trade passing by on the Quickway or vacationing in the area, and didn't run to real lavishness. The rooms were mostly rooms, not suites: clean, fairly spacious, just the basics—two wide and rather good beds, a couple of dressers, a couch and two armchairs and a table in a sort of visitors' configuration.

Not exactly the kind of accommodations the current clientele had become used to with their ever-enlarging success, which accommodations these days usually were called things like Plaza or Claridge's or Ritz; it was more a regression to the digs of their first tours, when even staying in a place like this was a very big deal for young and unsophisticated kids who'd never before stayed in any kind of hotel at all. How times had changed. This particular room differed from Turk and Rennie's only in its color scheme, the Ravens having to endure lovely jaundice and dirt tones where the Waylands had been afflicted with screaming turquoise and tangerine.

Prue looked up, smiling with equal relief to see Rennie, and nodded at Melza, who was huddled on the bed nearest the window, seemingly oblivious to her surroundings or the people present. Rennie was shocked to see her: the cover-girl face was blotched with tears, the huge dark eyes reddened and weary. Quickly knocking back the wine, Rennie carefully seated herself on the bed beside her and touched her shoulder.

"Melza? Mel, it's me, sweetie, it's Rennie. *Cariad—Melys-fach—*"

At the Welsh endearments, Melza's head came up and she focused on Rennie's face, then with a wordless moan she made a dive for her friend's lap, sobbing as if her heart would break.

Rennie instinctively put her arms around her, holding her as she would a weeping child, looking helplessly at Gray and Prue as they sat there, Gray sprawled against the back of the sofa, Prue collapsed against his shoulder with tears in her own eyes and her hands to her mouth. She let Melza cry herself out, rocking her gently, stroking the long dark hair, murmuring gentle words, none of which made any sense. Sense wasn't what was required now, just sympathy. Or empathy: Rennie could take all the comforting she wanted to give Turk and give it here where it was immediately needed.

After too many minutes the convulsive sobbing eased, and Rennie transferred Melza to lie across the nest of pillows beside her. She offered a hand, and Melza grabbed on to it as if it were a lifeline, and she about to drown.

"Rennie? It's you? Oh, it *is* you…" She clutched Rennie's hand so hard that their rings were driven into the flesh of their hands. "Now you're here, I know you'll help Neddy, promise me you'll help him. He didn't do it, you know—"

"Of course he didn't, *blodyn*," said Rennie, trying to put as much conviction as possible into her tone, and all too aware that, apart from 'please', 'thank you', 'good day' and 'Is this the road to Harlech?', none of which seemed particularly appropriate at the moment, she was now right out of soothing Welsh vocabulary. "Why would he, the dear daft creature? We'll sort it out in the morning and he'll be back with you by lunchtime. You'll see." She glanced despairingly at the Sonnets, who nodded and smiled in eager unison like demented but encouraging marionettes, yeah yeah you're doing great, keep it up. "Here, take this, there's a good little daffodil..."

She put a ten-milligram Valium in a glass of water, watching alertly while Melza obediently drank it down, and Prue and Gray managed a smile between them.

"It will be fine, Mel darling," said Prue, a shade too heartily. "Not to worry."

Melza darkly murmured something in Welsh that sounded either disbelieving or evil, still clutching Rennie's hand. Then: "Sing me something...please...just sing to me so I can sleep."

Rennie threw another panicked glance at the Sonnets, to whom, she quite reasonably felt, this request should properly have been addressed, they being the professionals in the room. But they shook their heads, with an "Over to *you*" gesture from Prue, and Gray grabbed one of Ned's lesser acoustic guitars from where it had been leaning against the couch and handed it to Rennie.

What to do, what to do...I wish Turk were here...

She settled the axe, a nice Goya dreadnought, into playing position. Melza snuggled down into the pillows with a sad little sound, and after a moment's thought Rennie began to sing. Something she'd learned in college: a folky ballad called "Melora", adapted from an old poem, set to haunting music and sung to a half-strummed, half-picked accompaniment. Rennie had a quite pretty soprano voice, though of course nothing in the same musical universe as Prue's or Prax's, and her guitar playing, next to Turk's or

Gray's, was likewise charmingly amateur, but both suited the song, and the simple words came as soft as the thrum of the nylon strings.

"Love came by from the riversmoke
When the leaves were fresh on the tree
But I cut my heart on the blackjack oak
Before they fell on me.

The leaves were green in the early spring
They are brown as linsey now
I did not ask for a wedding ring
From the wind in the bending bough.

Good girls sleep in their modesty
Bad girls sleep in their shame
But I must sleep in a hollow tree
Till my child can have a name."

She continued even more softly to the end of the song, improvising when the lyrics eluded her—Melza would hardly be criticizing the content. Not the most cheerful ditty in the world, but it had a plaintive minor-key grace that served well to soothe. Melza's eyes fluttered closed as Rennie moved on to the beautiful and famous old Welsh lullaby "Ar Hyd Y Nos", in which she was joined very quietly, and exquisitely, by Prue and Gray humming backup harmony in fifths. The familiar words and tune did the trick: the tense little body relaxed and the ragged breathing became peaceful and even as the music and the Valium both completed their work, and Melza slept.

Ending the last verse, Rennie played on for a few moments longer, watching her sleeping friend, then brushed her fingers across the strings in a gentle upswinging minor chord, sighed and looked at her audience—the two who were still awake.

"You ought to be doing some backup chores on all our albums, me beauty," said Prue, after a small and impressed silence, and Gray nodded vigorously in agreement. "Especially your old man's."

"Not a chance! What am I, Linda McCartney?" Rennie set the guitar carefully aside and moved to one of the armchairs so the three of them could talk without fear of waking the sleeper. "I picked up a bit of guitar hanging out with Powderhouse Road back in college, and then I was led astray by the folksinging crowd, those hoodlums. Don't you *dare* tell Turk," she added. "I'll lose all my critic cred if he finds out I can fret a few chords and do a little Travis picking. I'd die of embarrassment to play in front of him. It would be like filling in a coloring book in front of Michelangelo and having Mike say I stayed inside the lines really well. Hard enough having you two bear witness to my musical shame..."

"Nonsense," said Gray, leaning over to squeeze her shoulder. "It was wonderful. And she wouldn't go to sleep for us at all, so that's down to Ravenna Stride. Well done you! But what now? Have you heard from the cops yet?"

"Oh yes. I guess Mel's told you—it was Ned who found Amander's body, and that's why they brought him in."

Judging from the shocked looks on both Sonnet faces, apparently not. Oh dear.

Prue found her voice first. "I don't think Mel knows that part of it yet," she said carefully, glancing at the sleeping Mrs. Raven. "All she told us was that the county cops showed up at the pavilion tonight and took him away during Mountain's set, and said Mel couldn't come along, and she's been hysterical ever since. We knew about Amander from this morning, remember. When you were all at the hospital with Turk, Prax phoned us to let us know what was going on, and we told Ned and Mel. She said we could," added Prue, a little defensively.

"Oh, sure, of course, of course, why the hell not... Well, it's true," said Rennie morosely. "Ned did find Amander—dead—and now the fuzz want to know all about it. Listen, don't tell our girl yet, if she wakes up. She can hear in the morning, when we go down to the station, hopefully to spring Ned. I can get a lawyer up here from the city, if it turns out he needs one. But I'm sure he won't. I'm sure it's nothing."

From the new and even more apprehensive looks on their faces, it seemed that Gray and Prue did not share her certainty one little bit, and what was more, it seemed that they didn't think she even shared it herself—and they were quite right to think so. But they also seemed happy to follow her lead; after all, she was the pro in these matters.

"So? What would you like us to do now?" asked Gray.

Rennie glanced at Melza, curled up peacefully under the blanket. "I need to get back to the festival. And you two need to get some sleep. Which I do too, at some point. But I don't want to leave her alone, and the Argus guard on the door needs to stay with you two." She thought for a moment. "Tell you what: I'll go see if I can find someone to relieve you and sit with her, and get another of Ares' boys to come and do the guarding so your guy can stay on duty with you. Does that sound good?"

It did, and leaving the Sonnets as minders for the nonce, much relieved on all counts, she went out into the corridors, where in a fine confluence of happenstance and karma she immediately ran into Sunny Silver. After exchanging hugs and greetings, Rennie explained hastily, and though she would never have been so crass as to remind Sunny that Miss Silver owed Miss Stride big-time for that little episode in San Francisco with Ro Savarkin, Sunny knew very well what was right and due, and instantly offered to spend the rest of the night companioning Demelza.

"Happy to," she told Rennie. "I like her and Ned both, and I'd be glad to stay with her." She lifted her casted left arm in its tie-dyed sling, and her face clouded. "I can't do much with this, though, *chica*, if anything's, you know, needed?"

"Don't you worry about that," Rennie told her. "I'll send one of Ares Sakura's not-so-little helpers to stay with you, under orders to let no one in but me or the Sonnets. I've given her some Valium, so she should sleep through till morning. You don't have to stay awake all the time yourself, just be there in the room in case she wakes up; I'll come get her to bring her into town after breakfast. Marcus says not to show up at the police station much before ten or eleven, so maybe we can all cop a few z's. But I actually have to do some work, believe it or not, so I have to go back. What a freakin' bore. Good thing I'm not missing all that much."

She had just gotten Sunny settled comfortably on the other bed in Melza's room, with blankets and pillows of her own, when Car Darch, yet another of Ares' incredibly hulking employees, turned up at the door to relieve the Sonnets' guard. She joyfully appropriated him to watch Demelza, and Gray said they'd make it okay with Rhino Kanaloa, so she shouldn't worry. Leaving Car lurking in an armchair facing the door, his hand rather weaponfully in his jacket pocket, her mind at ease for the moment, Rennie and the other guard escorted Gray and Prue to their own room, then she got in her car and drove back out to the festival. Why she was going back, she had only the vaguest of ideas. The reptile brain was calling the shots now, and it was getting everything all its own way. So she went.

By the time she parked the Mustang in a prime spot, among assorted psychedelic buses and Volkswagen vans with fetching little curtains in the windows, and made it to the pavilion, Sly & The Family Stone, who'd been sulking earlier and pissing off the stage managers, were in the middle of their set, and the Who were getting ready to go on next. In the brightly lit pavilion almost every seat at every table was taken, despite the ungodliness of the hour, but Prax, still there and still wired from her own performance, waved to her from the steps of a small camper-type trailer, over behind the pavilion and off to one side, next to the one that John Sebastian was using to helpfully store instruments and things for his fellow artists.

Rennie joined her, sitting in the open door on the trailer front step, under a little metal canopy and out of the prickly mist, and quickly filled her in on developments. "And so I'll take Melza to see Ned tomorrow, after I tell her what the deal is," she finished. "But I'm supposed to be working, so I really do kind of need to hear some actual music."

Prax drew herself up with mock hauteur. "You heard *us*. Isn't that enough?"

"Ordinarily, more than enough," said her friend, laughing. "But Fitz demands maximum payoff for my paycheck."

"I would have thought you'd paid him off more than amply over the past couple of years," complained Prax, only half in jest. "What with the nearly getting killed at Monterey and Malibu and London, and our own little San Francisco encounter with the forces of evil, and Airplane House, and Golden Gate Park, and the Avalon, and Hyde Park..."

"Yes, well. He's a hard taskmaster, is Lord Holywoode." She glanced sideways to catch Prax's eye, and both of them burst out laughing. "He likes to think he is, anyway. I'm not about to disillusion him. But I'm going to have to come up with something really big to offset the favor of Turk's airlift. Like, you know, solving the whole thing. Plus I have some avenging to take care of."

"I can understand that," said Prax cautiously, "and I do approve. Up to a point, as I've said before. But Ned?"

"Will have to wait till morning. Even if he *did* discover the body, that's a pure circumstantial nothingness...as we all know."

"As we all know," echoed Prax, but her voice, expressive as ever, held the tiniest shade of doubt. In San Francisco, similar circumstantiality had presented her with a very rugged lesson, and she had not for a heartbeat forgotten what it had taught her...

Although she was practically asleep on her feet by now, and heartsick about Ned, Rennie found that Woodstock was rewarding her with several moments she was very glad indeed to be present and awake for, though not so much the actual music, that was still pretty poor—chief among them seeing Pete Townshend give Abbie Hoffman a mighty biff with his guitar for being an insufferable jerk, and oh, how many others, including herself, had dearly longed to do the same, and had cheered to see it—and she even managed to catch a small amount of snooze inside the tiny trailer, while Prax sat watch.

Only when it was full light outside did Prax wake her. They were both running on fumes now, but at last a cloudy dawn had happened behind the eastern hills, seeping over the sleepy thousands in the fields like a slow and sneaky tide. Rennie was more tired than she even knew, but at long last, and only about ten hours late, Jefferson Airplane was getting ready to play Woodstock, and no way was Rennie going to miss that.

A clear, familiar voice came over the P.A. system: "All right, friends, you have seen the heavy groups, now you will see morning maniac music! Believe me, yeah. It's a new dawn!"

Let's hope so, Grace... Rennie grinned, and headed for the stage.

"Right on! That was pretty darn—not entirely terrible. I'm glad I stayed awake for it, even though I practically had to stick toothpicks in my eyelids to keep them open."

Rennie was talking to Belinda Melbourne, who had joined her and Prax onstage for the Airplane's energizing thirteen-song set, longer than any band so far but Lionheart; they had all danced like bacchantes, to keep awake as much as anything else. After the set, Belinda had asked Rennie for a ride back to Liberty, and, more diffidently, for the use of one of Lionheart's vacated motel rooms, since she'd been sleeping three to a bed in a motel fifteen miles away; Rennie had agreed happily to both requests. Prax had decided to hang around and talk to the Airplane, indicating to Rennie that she would get a lift back to the motel with them later, which departure, considering how wiped out everyone was, wouldn't be long delayed. Now the two were in the car, heading north on the back roads to the west of the site, which were still surprisingly undiscovered by the festival hordes, and avoiding Routes 17 and 17B, which were still unsurprisingly parking lots.

Rennie Rock Critic was still opining judicially on the Airplane's set. "Ragged, sloppy, nowhere near what they can really do. What seems to be establishing itself as the Woodstock tradition. I'm babbling. Don't mind me."

"It was considerably off their usual terrificness, yeah. They didn't look at all happy, either, especially Grace. But the guys looked hot, at least; they all have such good rock hair. If I weren't—"

"Yes? If you weren't what?"

"Oh, nothing. Just—nothing. Well. Something." Belinda appeared to come to some great decision. "Could you introduce me to—okay, I really mean could you, or Turk, fix me up with—"

"Who? Speak and be rewarded. If it lies at all within my power, and let me tell you my powers are considerable, I shall make it happen."

"Diego Hidalgo," said Belinda, and wrung her hands and waited.

Rennie grinned, not all privately. *See how occasions do present themselves...* "I told Turk *ages* ago that I was going to fix you up with Diego, when you finally dumped that idiot Hacker and when Diego finally decided he was ready for a real woman and dumped that gold-digging druggie tramp. I was talking about this with Praxie on Thursday, in fact, though I didn't tell her it was you I had in mind. How delightful. Great minds think alike, greatly."

"I've kind of had a crush on him for a while now," said Belinda confidingly. "But is he available? Only, I thought—"

Rennie shook her head and swerved the car to avoid

a deer leaping across the road from the dense woods that pressed in on both sides. "Oh no, he is absolutely up for grabs. One of the Cold Fire groupies told me yesterday that he tossed the tramp out on her bony butt a month ago and hasn't been with anyone since—except for the groupies, of course, but as you know they don't count. He had to seriously pay her off through his lawyers before she'd finally leave, but hey, freedom never comes easy or cheap. You *are* available yourself, then, are you? I'm not going to venture out on so delicate a limb as this for nothing, you know. You swear to me you're really broken up with Hacker for good this time?"

Belinda looked outraged that she would even ask. "He nailed all my shoes to the floor! So I would have to stay with him because I had no shoes to walk out on him in! Is that what a normal person does? No! It isn't! Of *course* we're done! I went out and bought all new shoes, anyway. But really? You would do that for me? Diego *is* stunning, and I've always loved Cold Fire's music, and he really is smart, though he tries hard to hide it. I think it might work."

"I think so too. Can't promise anything, of course, and frankly, I'd rather nail my actual feet to the floor than go out with him myself, even were I free to do so, but you're right: he's cute and he's smart and he makes great music. Perhaps this will be a match for the ages. Or, if nothing else, for the ever so satisfying here and now. I have no doubt whatsoever that the pair of you will melt the bedsprings like lava. I'll handle it when we get back to the city; he's living in town for the next few months, he told me. I'd introduce you here, but the vibe is too weird, and Diego is as easily distracted as a two-year-old. This needs care and attention to be done correctly."

"Speaking of care and attention—" began Belinda.

Rennie looked at her sharply, or as sharply as she could out of bleary, weary eyes that were struggling to stay open wide enough for her to drive, and not land them and the car in a roadside ditch commingled inextricably with another deer.

"Turk's fine, if that's what you're wondering. I talked to Ares at some point, I can't even remember, and apparently his lordship has come to the conclusive conclusion that he has had a narrow, narrow escape and owes me his life. Which of course was mine already, but don't think I'm not going to collect. Anyway, Ares says that reaction has finally hit and the poor thing's a puddle of exhaustion, hardly has the energy to get out of bed except to stagger to the bathroom, and when he isn't stuffing his face like a hog he's been sleeping nonstop, totally wiped out. Which is fine by me."

"Speaking of wiped out—"

Dismissive finger-fluttering. "I had a nice nap waiting for the Who to go on, and again waiting for the Airplane. I'll sleep for a few hours before I drive Melza to the stationhouse. In case you haven't noticed, I'm running out of time, and it only keeps getting more and more complicated."

"For *you*? A cakewalk."

"I don't think it matters how much cake I walk on," remarked Rennie after a thoughtful pause, "and I can see where I may have to tread heavily on several sets of important toes, but I swear by the power of rock and roll that I *am* going to figure it out. All of it. You'll see."

~16~

Sunday morning, August 17

BLACK, BILLOWY STORMCLOUDS had conspiratorially foregathered half a dozen counties to the westward, and now they were racing east, to launch themselves over the hills and come crashing down, with diabolical suddenness, on the unsuspecting little valleys below. They hadn't reached Sullivan County yet, but they were on their way. In those parts, the weather changed with breathtaking speed: you could be sunny and sweating one minute in ninety-plus heat, then dripping and freezing in thunder rain and slashing hail and a forty-degree temperature plunge the next, struggling to stand upright in a wind that could punt you clear to the Atlantic. The upper atmosphere was unsettled to the eye, and the feel of the lower air seemed to promise worse to come.

It was under such a literal cloud that Rennie drove a small and subdued Melza Raven to the police station Sunday morning, accompanied by Rhino Kanaloa; since, despite her nap, Rennie looked exhausted, and since the intermittent early-morning showers, a mere prelude to the oncoming main barometric event, had made the roads slippy, Rhino had insisted on handling the actual driving, and she hadn't refused. Besides, she could use him at the cop shop, for a bit of equalization—she had a feeling she might need backup, and he was bigger than all the officers there. Put together. And they were not exactly little wispy things.

The Sonnets would have come too, for moral support, but they were scheduled to open Sunday's roster with their band, Thistlefit, and had needed to get some rest. The way things were going, Rennie would probably miss their set, and would not have a chance to see them again, either, as they planned on heading straight to New York right after their performance and jumping a plane for London to get back to their kids; she was disappointed, but first things first, and she'd see them play another time.

On her return from the field, she had gone straight to the Ravens' room, where she'd been admitted by a watchful Car Darch and a concerned Sunny. She'd sent Sunny off with warm thanks, then had fallen asleep on the other bed for a few hours, as she'd told Belinda she planned on doing. On waking, more refreshed than she'd expected, she'd ordered room-service breakfast for all of them, and once Melza had woken up and gotten on the outside of some fruit and toast and tea, Rennie had broken the news to her of Ned's arrest—that it was no longer a mere matter of helping the police with their inquiries. Melza, perhaps still under the influence of the Valium she'd been dosed with last night, had received the update on her husband's new status with a kind of bemused resignation. Rennie, wondering but glad of the apparent calm, had bundled her friend into fresh clothes and then, still escorted by Car, they went down to her own room, where she changed and called home and spoke briefly with Christabel Green, as Turk was still, or again, sleeping. Then, Rhino having shown up at the door, the three of them hit the road into town.

Entering the police station, the first person Rennie saw was Marcus Dorner. Oh well, she'd been expecting *him*... But suddenly she was possessed of a splendid fit of bad temper that swept in out of nowhere, like a little personal thunderstorm of her very own, and she stepped protectively in front of Melza, who was still sad and dazed and out of it, and who didn't deserve to be harassed by a proto-Fed at this hour of the day, or indeed any other.

"Don't start with me, Marcus! Do not, or I swear to God I will snap your arm off and beat you to death with it. Do I make myself clear? Let her go in and see Ned in peace. You and I can handle whatever we need to be handling right out here on our own. And you have exactly one minute to tell me about it. Fifty-eight seconds. Go."

Marcus stepped over to her, making sure his back was blocking Melza's view and possible lip-reading skills, and spoke in a low voice. "I think *you* had better go see Raven first, Rennie, I really do. Before his wife goes in. He's made a preliminary statement to the police, which they graciously let me observe, and he said some things you need to hear. And they'd probably fall better on Mrs. Raven's long-suffering ear if they came from you, her friend."

She stared at him, not having expected that. He looked sympathetic and sad for her, and nothing chilled her to the bone more than Marcus Dorner looking at her with that particular expression on his face. He'd done it a few times before, and it never boded well for people Rennie knew and cared about... She drew herself up.

"Okay. Okay. Then I will."

He gave her the merest sketch of a smile. "Good girl. I'll stay with her. We'll wait right here for you, and I'll get her some coffee and make sure no one bothers her. Look"—nodding at the placid, vigilant bulk of Rhino—"we even have our own bodyguard."

Shaking the water droplets from her jacket, trying not to drip too much on the clean, waxed floors, Rennie was escorted back into the depths of the county police headquarters and shown into a small bare room. The only person in it was Ned himself, sitting at a dark-stained oak farmhouse table of Arts and Crafts design and considerable age, which Rennie lusted after as soon as she set eyes on it.

OOOH! I wonder would they sell me that table, it's probably an original one, up here in the boondocks like this, it would look great *in the downstairs hall, they would do so much better with a nice new one, I'll buy them* two *to replace it, I wonder if they have anything else nice lying around that I could take off their hands, maybe a bench or something...*

She pulled herself back to the moment, and gave Ned a sharp raking once-over. He'd obviously gotten into the spirit of the weekend, as he was wearing a tie-dyed t-shirt, faded jeans and patchworked leather sneakers. The footwear sported a sheen of dried festival mud, though a closer look would have seen where he, or perhaps someone else, had tried to brush the mud off in the interests of respectability. The mud not being wet spoke to his having been here at the station all night.

"Hey ho," said Ned, with his usual gallant-desperado smile, though a closer look would have seen it wavering a bit, "who'd have thought it'd come to this, Renners, eh chiz?"

Rennie did not respond to the smile; she knew it of old, and she had long since learned not to let it sway her. "This is *serious*, Neddy. Please try to remember that."

"Hard to forget, really. In all the years I've had the pleasure of knowing Murder Chick, I never thought for the tiniest instant that I would ever stand in need of your professional skills. Which are considerable, as I've often told you."

"Never mind the flattery." She reached across the table for his hand and squeezed it once; she wasn't going to tell him Melza was outside until she had gotten everything she could out of him, because once he'd seen his wife, or even knew she was there, he'd be completely useless for Rennie's purposes.

"Tell me about it. And I mean *all* about it," she added warningly, and took out her little leather-bound notebook and the gold Mark Cross pen that had been a graft gift last Christmas from RCA Records. *All the better to write you down with, my dear. And I know perfectly well that we're being observed through that one-way mirror, and maybe recorded too, if this backwater's budget runs to taping devices, so by all means let's give them something they can really observe...*

Ned sighed and sat back. "It was nothing, truly. It was quite late Friday night, but nobody was ready to go back to the motel for good. Well, I mean, we'd been back there briefly, Melza and I, at some of the room parties, but I was bored, and was hoping maybe there might be some more music. So Mel stayed at the motel and I got a lift back to the field with Plato Lars—we both thought we might like to play a bit. I was wandering around by myself when I saw that little tent over by the woods and was curious, so I asked a passing someone about it."

"Who did you ask?"

"Haven't the foggiest. The world and his wife are out there in that pasture, as you may have noticed. Could have been any of them."

"So? Was it the world or was it his wife?" Ned looked blank. Rennie sighed. "Man or woman, Neddy?"

"Oh. It was a chap. Tallish. I think. Or possibly smallish. Anyway, he said that the tent was the meditation yurt, and it was open to anyone. So I decided to have a squint."

"And what did you see?"

Ned unfocused a bit, recalling. "Not much at first. There was a tent flap covering the entrance, with strings of beads and paper ornaments, and some bells. I pushed them all aside and went in. The bells made a really pretty sound."

"No doubt. And then?"

He shifted in his chair, putting his folded arms on the table, leaning forward, intent on her and his recollection alike. "Right… Lots of fancy cushions—pillows—and a couple of Oriental rugs. Some kind of incense burner. Candles in glass vases. A hookah. There was a ground cover of some sort underneath the rugs, they weren't lying right on the grass or the dirt or whatever. Everything was all rather damp; it gets so clammy here at night, even when it isn't pissing down rain. Anyway, it looked like a harem or something. I reckon all that was in aid of meditation, it being, as you know, the meditation tent."

"You didn't see anyone else?"

His face altered. "Not at first," he said slowly. "Then I saw her. She was over on the far side of the tent, leaning back on some pillows piled up behind her. Her eyes were open, but she didn't say anything, or even seem to know I was there, so I figured she must be rapt in some sort of trance, maybe tripping, or just generally stoned. I didn't want to be arsed talking to her, or rather not talking, so I turned to go out. But then—it seemed weird, yes? So I looked back at her and she hadn't moved at all."

"At all?"

"It was as if she was frozen." Ned clamped his hands together; Rennie noticed they were shaking slightly. And who could blame him? "So I said 'Are you all right, luv?' and she still didn't move. I thought maybe she was having a *really* bad trip, so I went over to her and touched her shoulder. You know, just to touch. And she fell over on her side and didn't even blink. So I could see that she was dead."

Rennie was silent for a moment, remembering a hauntingly similar moment for her and Turk, in the Hollywood Hills house, a year and a half ago, then put her hand over Ned's clasped ones, which were shaking a lot more now. "It's okay. What did you do then?"

"What did I *do*?" he repeated incredulously. "Sod it, what *could* I do? I'd never seen a deader before. I ran screaming the bloody hell out of there and over to the medical tent for help from anyone I could find."

"Who presumably came hot-foot to the rescue?"

"Yes, they were very quick. A doctor and a nurse, I think, at least some kind of medical types. They seemed to know what they were doing. But there was no rescue on, I can tell you that. She was as dead as a doornail. Dead as Marley." He looked up at her. "Funny thing, well, not funny really, but the first thing I thought of was that drummer from Owl Tuesday they found croaked the other day. What is going *on* here, Strider? Is it some sort of death squad against musicians? Secret ninja warrior assassins? And Turk and

Sunny and even me, what about what happened to all of *us*? Who is *doing* all this?"

She sighed. "Honestly, dear man, I don't know. I wish I did. So go on. Did you know her, recognize her?"

"No," said Ned, a shade too promptly, "no, not then. They told me later who it was."

Rennie felt the denial whiz past her ear like a little bee, or possibly a bullet. Well, she'd let it go for the moment…

"And then what? After the doctor showed up?"

"Do you know, baggage, I'm not quite sure. I remember the two medical persons working over her, or working her over, but they didn't seem to be having any success. I don't know anything about first aid, but it seemed to me that she was already gone beyond hope of recall. They laid her down on the cushions, and someone ran out to tell someone on the festival staff. It all becomes rather blurry after that."

"Yes, I can see where it might." Rennie's tone was noncommittal, and it seemed to pierce even Ned's abstraction, for he looked at her with sudden alarm. "Did you talk to the cops?"

He straightened in the wooden chair. "Oh, rather! Both here and at the site, when it all happened. You were back at the motel yourself by then, and then you had other things on your mind, with Turk and all, as I heard later. Anyway, you weren't around," he added candidly. "Or else I'd have run straight to you for help. But the cops only asked me some questions and let me go. It wasn't until last night that they carted me off here."

"And did you feed them the same load of total twaddle you've just fed me? No, no, don't even try! I thought that by now you knew better: you're not a very good liar and you know I always see right straight through you. Now let's have it. Are you, rather, *were* you having it off with Amander Evans, which I *know* you were because I know you and I know your guilty look, and how long had it been going on, and when did you really realize it was she who was dead in the tent?"

Ned was silent for a few long moments, and Rennie let him run out the line as much as he wanted before she planned on pulling him up again; that hook was *set*. But, as it turned out, she didn't have to: the fish had decided to hold up its trembling little fins and surrender.

"Christ, you're good… And so *annoying*. Well. Right. I met Amander in Edinburgh back in February or March," he said then, "when Bluesnroyals were on tour. She was opening for us; an odd pairing, we thought, as we're so bluesy and she's so folky, but the management company that runs us both, the egregious Tontine Bookings, fiefdom of the slimy Ted Tessman, dictated we share the bill for the final U.K. leg of the tour. The equally slimy Jack Holland, president of my own egregious record label Isis, dictated it, actually, even though Amander was on Rainshadow which is a whole different label, but Elk Bannerman, *her* label president, and unslimy as far as I know, had suggested her, and both Holland and Tessman were quite pleased by the idea. I expect you know how *that* goes," he added darkly.

Indeed she did. It was a favorite bit out of every record company's playbook: sure, they'd say, Booker A or Venue Z can get in on the tour and have the big superstar act they're dying to have, but they also have to take the unknown opening act from the same label. Which would usually be green as grass and nervous as hell and, with barely one album or even one single out, no audience to speak of. It wasn't always the record label who insisted on the deals, sometimes it was the management company; but either way, unless you were Elvis or Dylan or the Beatles or the Stones, you weren't going to have any kind of say in the matter. And sometimes not even then.

Almost every band around had suffered from the policy, even Lionheart, though sometimes groups lucked out on both sides: the Doors' tour early last year, the one that had included their one and only Fillmore East gig so far and probably ever, had had an opening act attached called Ars Nova. The name meaning not Arse Hole-a, as certain cruder Britbands would flippantly have it, but being the Latin for "New Art"—they were an absolutely stunning Renaissance-rock band, with innovative medieval brass instrumentation and exquisite vocals.

Both Ars Nova and the Doors were Elektra Records properties: so the Doors would get an interesting opening act that reliably wouldn't overshadow them or compete with them but that also wouldn't bore the audience waiting for the main event, while Ars Nova would get some valuable exposure before a prime target audience who'd come to see the superstars, and Elektra would, hopefully, shift some serious product by each. The plan had worked very nicely—at least until Ars Nova imploded right after the Fillmore gig, before either they or Elektra could capitalize on their initial momentum. Not unanticipated, really, these things happen; most people were only surprised it hadn't been the Doors to screw things up.

Getting back to Ned and Amander: Ted Tessman, the monosyllabic thug who ran Tontine, had probably been severely annoyed when he found out what was going on, especially as it might affect more people than just the two of them, but then he was usually severely annoyed at pretty much everything, and he had a loathing for rock bands that was perhaps a tad bit inconvenient for anyone who dealt with them as heavily as he did. So, it was all about money, as usual; no bolt from the blue there. As for Jack Holland, he made Centaur's Freddy Bellasca look like St. Teresa, Eleanor Roosevelt and the Dalai Lama all rolled into one, and Rennie was glad he hadn't deigned to come to the festival, though he'd sent a few evil minions.

So...Elk's idea, was it? To put Amander right under Bluesnroyals' noses? I may have to talk to him about that...being as he certainly didn't see fit to mention it when we were having our little chat...

"Anyway," Ned went on with a certain dogged despair that stamped his words as truth, "it was Amander's first time in Britain and her first time on a stage bigger than a breadbox. She was a jolly little thing, and the guys were all hitting on her like a cricket wicket. I felt sorry for her, so I sort of stepped in to protect her. I paid her some flirty attention, I admit, but she took it entirely the wrong way, and seriously came on to me when we played our next gig, which was Glasgow. I told her, very nicely, that I was happily married and didn't fool around. Anymore," he added quickly, seeing Rennie's eyebrows go shooting skywards at the speed of light.

"Oh, don't mind me. Then what?"

"She didn't want to hear it, and she kept coming *at* me. She said she'd like me to, you know, mentor her a bit. Take her under my wing, sort of thing."

Ah. Rennie saw where *this* was headed: right straight over several different cliffs. "And I'll bet you just mentored the heck out of her, didn't you, you pinhead. So how far under your, uh, *wing* did you end up taking her, this slutty little Kiwi fledgling? Who was, I have to tell you, no innocent sparrow. She was hunting you like a yellow-headed vulture."

Ned had the grace, or the good sense, to look intensely embarrassed. "Let's just say that, in keeping with the avian metaphor, cocks figured largely in the picture."

"You stupid, *stupid,* STUPID—what the hell is *wrong* with you?" Rennie leaned forward and let the explosion roll. "You risk your marriage to one of the most beautiful women I've ever seen, and one of the nicest, you jeopardize your standing with your own record label, you risk the gossip pages of the noxious British press, and yes I say that last as someone who is a paid wage slave to said noxious press—in the name of God, why the hell you do this, why *why*?"

"Just because you've got Sir Lancelot on your arm, Strider, doesn't mean that the rest of us are cut from the same superior cloth he is." Ned looked up at her, and she was taken aback by the sudden bleakness on his face. "I wish I were. You remember from when we were together..."

"Yeah, the whole, what, four weekends. I'll never forget it. You were a total hound. Not that we were ever in it for more than the momentary bit of fun, or consolation, or whatever the hell. And you *were* terribly cute." She let her expression soften a bit; he looked so wretched, and she really was very fond of him. But fondness wasn't going to cut it if he was busted for murder. "I presume Demelza knew?"

He nodded. "She walked in on us in the dressing room, in Manchester the third week of the tour."

"And? Come on, I'm not trying to embarrass you! Well, not very much. But I need to know all this before I can try to help you."

"She's Welsh." He shrugged. "She threw a few things, as one does, including a guitar I particularly liked. She hit a few things, including me. She broke a few things, including two of my fingers, which I also particularly liked. She moved down to the country place in Devon and she wouldn't let me see the baby for a month."

"I don't blame her, and I think you got off quite lightly, considering." Rennie was silent for a moment or two. "Did she confront Amander about it?"

"Did she not! She blistered the little tart's face like some cheesed-off Druid. In English *and* Welsh. I'd never *heard* some of the words she used, even the English ones."

"And Amander?"

"Seemed to think it all a great joke." He shook his head, spoke candidly. "What I can't understand is, I didn't even *like* her, Amander, and she wasn't very good anyway. She really was a trampy little bint."

"You're a trampy little bint yourself, my friend, and I'm only surprised you and the lads in the band and your ever-lovin' manager and your publicist, who is obviously grossly underpaid for the work he did here, were able to keep all this quiet. But that's neither here nor there. The cops wouldn't have hauled you in if they didn't have some compelling evidence. Did they tell you what they had?"

"No. But I'm the one who found her, as I said, and my fingerprints were in the motel room, and I'd had an affair with her—"

Rennie snorted disdainfully and closed her notebook "Is that the best they've got? I daresay so were Turk's fingerprints there. And mine. And the prints of half the artists at the festival. And Melza's even too, probably. It was a *party*. We were *all* there. And just because you bonked her a bit… No, they have to have more than that. Either that or they're only fishing, because they have *nothing*." That last was said staring directly and challengingly at the one-way mirror.

Ned looked imploring. "Can you find out which?"

"If I can't, I might know somebody who can."

But she didn't have the chance to say who, because at that moment the door of the interrogation room slammed open and Demelza Rhys-Jones Raven, in the finest and blackest Celtic temper Rennie had ever seen, came through it like a North Wales cloudburst, the kind that is powerful enough to crack slate and kill sheep and bring down mountains to bury little villages, and began screaming at anyone who would listen that *she'd* killed Amander Evans herself because the little slut had shagged her husband and they should bloody well leave that husband the bleeding bloody hell alone because he didn't do it.

And Ned Raven leaped to his feet and began screaming even louder that nobody should believe a word out of her mouth, because *he'd* killed Amander Evans, to keep her from telling the tabloids that he'd raped her and that Melza had known all about it.

Five long, *loooong* minutes later, Rennie put her head in her hands and let Mr. and Mrs. Raven continue to whale on each other. How silly, really. No, how *stupid*. It was exactly like Pamina Potter at Monterey, vainly trying to take the blame for her husband Baz's murder, in order to protect her boyfriend, Baz's singing partner Roger Hazlitt. Nobody had bought Pamie's story then, and nobody was buying either Raven's story now. All they were managing to do with their demented sacrificial nobility, if that's what it was, was to muddy things up and take up time that could be spent running down real leads. And annoy the life out of everyone within hearing, which was probably most of Monticello. Starting with Rennie.

And why wasn't Caskie Lawson stepping in to put a stop to it? No, scratch that, she knew *exactly* why: the good sheriff was hoping that one or more of them would say something he could use. Not that any mortal power on the face of the earth could have stopped Melza from flinging herself into the breach…still, he might have tried. Rennie could sense him watching through the glass. Marcus was probably watching too.

She stood up abruptly, and almost laughed out loud as Melza and Ned, as if controlled by a single switch, instantly stopped roaring at each other and turned to look at her with identical outraged expressions, like How *dare* you interrupt us when we're so busy here confessing to murder!

Seeing both their mouths open to start yelling at her instead, Rennie forestalled them with a warning glance like a shot across the bows.

"Shut it, you two. Just *SHUT IT*. You're giving me a headache, and I daresay you're giving this nice sheriff and this nice FBI agent one too." She jerked her head in the direction of the glass. She still wasn't sure if Marcus was legitimately FBI or just a temp hire, but that wouldn't sound nearly so impressive. She couldn't remember if he was known to the Ravens from previous run-ins in L.A. or San Francisco, but it didn't matter either way, because she was going to fold up this little traveling sideshow like an ironing board. Right now.

The Ravens began to squabble in protest again, and she slammed her palms down hard on the table she coveted, one little corner of her mind admiring its original and untampered-with finish and patina and thinking how nice it would look in the entryway with a blue Chinese vase full of hydrangeas on it, even while all the rest was concerned with getting the whip hand over Ned and Mel.

"I *said*, zip it, the pair of you! Not another word, either of you, until I say you can. Don't make me hit you. Because you know I will. —That's better. Now. We're shutting this whole thing down this very minute." She seated herself again. "Right. Demelza. Excuse me, you did nothing of the sort. You were back at the motel and I saw you there myself Friday night, well, Saturday morning, before Turk and I went to bed. And you couldn't have gotten back to the festival site because first, you don't have a car up here, either of you, and second, even if you had one, you don't know how to drive American. Yeah, you could have gotten a lift from someone, but that's unlikely, and besides, no one's come forward to say so. So there's no way you could have been up there in the meditation tent killing Amander Evans, not with the time of death we have. And that's what we're here trying to make sure of. Or we would be, if only you would let us."

She turned a baleful gaze on Ned, who quailed a little under it. *And so he should! Wasting everyone's time like this...*

"As for you, mister, I'm ashamed of you for so many, many reasons. So, you bonked Amander. Deplorable and incomprehensible, but whatever. You did it and it's done. And no jury on the face of the earth is going to believe you killed her to keep her from spilling the beans to your wife. *Or* trying to call it rape, which, again, I don't believe for a heartbeat. I *said* shut *up*! Don't even *think* about saying anything until I'm done talking..." Rennie took a breath and resumed. "Because Mel, who is a smart lady, already knew about Amander long before Friday night and did nothing about it but deservedly smack you around a bit. Am I right? You may indicate yes or no by a nod. A *silent* nod."

Both Ned and Melza gave grudging nods, in unison, but they said nothing, as Rennie had bidden them.

"Good. So why then would either of you bother to kill the young lady here at the festival?" Rennie shook her head in exasperation. "And I don't want to hear that she was going to the London tabloids with rape allegations, either. *Did* you rape her, Edmund? No, of course you didn't. Would she really have lied and claimed you had? I don't know and can't say. Did either of you kill her? No, neither of you did. You give me the pip, you really do. P-I-P pip. And may you be forgiven for it."

She threw another baleful glance toward the mirror, behind which she had no doubt that Marcus, Sheriff Lawson and probably most of the local constabulary were enjoying the show. Well, the hell with the lot of them. She was done here. Let them winkle their own information out of these two clowns, if they could.

"I'm exhausted and I'm cranky and I'm worried sick about Turk," she went on grimly, "and instead I have to deal with you two behaving like complete and utter toads. You should be ashamed of yourselves. Now. I'm going to ask *you*, Melza, to go outside, just for the moment, and I'm going to ask *you*, Ned, to recant your previous statements and revise them into something that more closely resembles the truth."

Raising her voice and turning to the one-way glass: "And I suggest that *you*, Sheriff Lawson, come in and get all this properly taken down. Not that I presume to tell you how to do your job, of course. Wouldn't dream of it. And now I am out of here. You're on your own, and God help you all."

~17~

When Melza, in floods of tears and equal floods of apologies and hugs for Rennie—"I'm so sorry, Strider, you were so good to me last night, calming me down and singing me to sleep and all, and here's how I repay you"—finally withdrew so that Ned could make his statement, Rennie pushed her way past them all and went out to her car alone and sat behind the wheel, staring at the street ahead of her. She couldn't think any more about Ned and Melza and their mutual idiocies without stroking out, so she turned her mind to the scene that met her eyes.

Usually at this time of year, the little villages of western Sullivan County and thereabouts were full of vacationers: pink, happy, shiny families. Or, at the other end of the spectrum, poor pallid weedy worms who'd crawled up from the city to get some sun and mountain air for the weekend, not to mention nice farm-fresh homegrown produce.

But not this weekend. This gray Sunday morning, and ever since last week, the streets were clogged with longhaired kids *in* clogs, and in bellbottoms and little halters and fluttery print minidresses and workshirts and dashikis and fringed buckskin jackets. Most of them looked much the worse for wear; but the strange thing was, no one was out of sorts. Tempers remained sweet, punches were unflung, voices were cheerful and unraised. It was surreal, actually. And everybody was *smiling*, that damn Woodstock Smile, like benign grinning tie-dyed zombies. She put it down to drugs: back at the festival field, you could stand at the intersection of Hurd Road and West Shore Road, the nexus and crossroads of the whole clambake, and actually see floating three feet above your head, like a Big Sur fogbank, a sort of marijuana miasma, visible in sunlight and guaranteed to give a contact high to anyone in breathing range. But somehow that didn't seem to cover it, not entirely.

The overriding outside sentiment, at least in the media, was that the barbarians had come to town and had brought their freak show with them. At least that was what some of the much put-upon locals were calling it—these colorful, longhaired locusts who came swooping down to devour all in their path, untold unclad numbers of whom really *were* doing it in the road, and frightening the Republicans, if not the horses. Probably souring the milk inside the cows and stunting the crops in the fields, too, with their nekkid hippie commie pinko ways. People who were inclined to think that way were going to think that way no matter what, even if every single male festivalgoer had been clad in a suit and tie and every single female one in a Sunday church dress.

Astonishingly, though, that very same media lunacy wasn't the prevailing opinion here at Festival Ground Zero, deep in the heart of Redneckia. Oh, sure, plenty of upright, uptight county burghers hated the whole idea of the festival, and had from the first—despite the fact that they weren't too proud to make money off it. On the other hand, local after local was being heard to publicly sing the praises of the festivalgoers: how polite they were, how well behaved, how honest, how—being nicely brought-up children—they were paying for every mouthful of food they ate and every bottle of Coke they drank. After the festival was over, merchants in Bethel and White Lake and Monticello and Liberty would declare with wonder that not a single check had bounced, local farmers that not a single honor-payment roadside-stand box had been dishonored.

Which was way more than they could claim about grown-up tourists or even their neighbors, and they couldn't say enough good and praiseful things about these nice, nice kids who maybe dressed kinda funny and who could use a haircut, but who were fine and decent young folks, and they were proud to admit they'd been wrong about them and their parents should be proud of them too. Even the bus drivers who had ferried thousands of concertgoers to Monticello were full of compliments, declaring how these kids had completely changed their previous views about the hippie generation and they'd be proud to drive them anywhere anytime. Many of the newly converted had announced these opinions to any media who would listen, and even from the Woodstock stage. Fair enough.

But much less fairly, it was being quite deliberately distorted, and actually lied about, outside the little Bethel bubble. Rennie had seen it first-hand: the stories she'd phoned in to her longtime editor at the Clarion, Burke Kinney, and her new overlords Ken Karper and Kiva Rodman, respectively crime editor and music editor at the New York Sun-Tribune, were of course accurately reflective of what was going on. She would scorn to write otherwise, and they knew she would slice their ears off with a machete if they dared to edit otherwise, presuming to meddle with either her copy or her point of view. Besides, she had Lord Holywoode on her side, which alone was way more than most writers had, and he was especially careful about what appeared in the Sun-Trib, his North American flagship paper of record. Especially what appeared under the Rennie Stride byline, which these days was gilt-edged blue-chip syndicated journalistic stock.

By no means was she writing paeans to the occasion, or even puff pieces; in fact, by now she'd determined that Woodstock was an overblown, overrated heap of hooey and she hated the whole messy, self-congratulatory thing. But thousands of other people were enjoying themselves tremendously, so clearly there was ample scope for difference of opinion. However, the kind of Woodstock reports that were appearing in other papers seemed to have been composed on some other planet, and a much more lunatic one at that. Wild, inflated tales of starving ungovernable hordes living like animals, or peasants out of the Middle Ages, copulating in public, running around naked—well, that was the thing, it was *sort of* true? At least the naked and copulating part. But that was incidental, and it wasn't even close to being the real story. Press colleagues had told her, outraged and horrified, that they'd filed accurate reports, only to find sensationalized fiction and even outright lies published under their Bethel bylines, in place of what they were actually saying. And that was plain wrong, and probably evil. You can't call yourself a legitimate news source if you're ignoring what your own reporters in the field are telling you, choosing instead to make up lies to stroke your anti-kid, anti-rock, anti-antiwar, old, rich, Establishment audience who probably hadn't had sex in, like, ever. At least she knew she could trust her editors to print what she sent them, and her publisher to back her up.

And speaking of lies and idiots—her tangent had brought her back to the original circle—what the *hell* was she going to do about the idiot Ned and the other idiot Demelza? If the cops had real evidence that either of them had been seen with Amander, either in the yurt or before... *Could* she be mistaken? Was it possible? She thought not, with every fiber of her being, but suppose...

Rennie almost jumped over into the passenger seat as a sharp tap came on the window beside her. Looking out, she saw that it was Caskie Lawson. And he looked pretty pissed off at something, or someone. Probably her.

She rolled down the window. "Am I illegally parked, Sheriff? Or do you need a lift?"

Lawson snorted a laugh, which he tried unsuccessfully to pass off as a sneeze. "Sorry. Hay allergies."

"I'm sure. How sadly inconvenient for you, living smack dab in the middle of forty billion acres of hayfields. Please, get in, out of the deadly rain of allergen particles."

He gave her a look, but went around, opened the Mustang door and disposed himself on the front seat beside her. "Nice car."

"It's not so bad," she said agreeably. "For a rental. Okay, what do you want to yell at me about?"

"What gives you the idea I want to yell at you?"

"Besides that peevish-hen expression you've got pasted on your honest country kisser? That's a real giveaway, you know. Cops are always yelling at me for some damn thing or other; why should you be any different? Go ahead, let me have it, I can take it. I'm used to it by now..."

"At the risk of being blasphemous, come down off the

cross, Miss Stride, we need the wood."

He pretended not to notice her shout of laughter, but Rennie saw him smile a little to himself, with the knowledge that he'd gotten off a good line. And why not? It *was* a good line. But her nerves were just about gnawed through by worry and the incredible stupidity of pretty much everybody, and she desperately needed the laugh. Which had, indeed, something of the desperate about it.

Lawson went on all the same, well aware that he'd succeeded in his intent of disarming her, at least insofar as she could be disarmed. "I thought I had made it real clear that you were not to speak with anyone connected with the case."

Oh, that. Rennie, still smiling, tuned out as he geared up and got into it—yeah, he was pissed off, all right. But as he went on and on about how she had no business pushing her nose for news under the tent flap like some kind of journalistic camel, when she'd been specifically told not to, Rennie gradually sensed that there was something else going on, something that made her sit up and prick her ears to find out exactly what. Besides, she'd heard this same old rant before, from every policeperson she'd ever interacted with, from Marcus Dorner to Detective Chief Inspector Gordon Dakers of New Scotland Yard. She could rant along with them by now, practically word for word, and she very much doubted if some upstate speed-trap jockey was going to break any new and inventive ground in Rennie-scolding, so she tuned out some more and thought about Ned.

She was under no illusions about William Edmund Raven's character; she had known him for years, they had had their tiny brief fling long ago and now were good friends, much better as friends than they had ever been as flingers. They'd never been a couple, even; it had all been much too casual and ad hoc for that, and the whole thing had lasted only a few weekends anyway, whenever Ned had been in town with the band. She had been delighted when he married the stunning model Melza Rhys-Jones, and the three of them had remained close, with Ned's old London blues-club comrade Turk Wayland now added to the mix. So why on earth he would ever risk that happy marriage, and access to the sturdy, bright one-year-old son he adored, was a total mystery. Sure, it could be as simple as boys will be boys, and she would not put that kind of male stupidity beyond Neddy: he'd always been led around by his dick, the way so many men were when you came down to it, right up until he met Melza and had been instantly knocked out of his socks with love. And perhaps it really was as simple as he'd said: Amander had come on to him, he'd been flattered despite his protests, and that had been that. Just a quickie, or a few weeks of quickies, on the road, and if Mel hadn't walked in on them she'd never have known about it.

But she had; and Melza being Melza, she had not dealt forbearingly with it, and so here they all were. In the midst of the Raven-induced angst, Rennie's thought was unerringly led to Turk. He was a star even bigger than Ned: more famous than Ned, more talented than Ned, more gorgeous than Ned—scoring him would be the Groupie Medal of Honor. She'd seen for herself how Amander had appraised him, at the motel party, and the Kiwi vulture was far, far from the first. Before Rennie'd been with him, and for some months into their early relationship, she'd also seen how persistently the groupies stalked him, and how he courteously but firmly turned them down, every single time. One enterprising young tramp had even had herself delivered naked in a steamer trunk to his hotel room in Houston: Rennie, whom the groupie had not known about and had *not* been expecting to meet, had opened the door to receive delivery, and had promptly returned it to sender, slamming the trunk closed with its contents inside and moving it along down the hotel corridor, end over end, with instructive and well-placed kicks—much to Turk's amusement.

The point was, it would have been beyond easy for him to have racked up an impressive body count among those who were themselves beyond easy. Yet he'd never sullied himself with a groupie chick of any stripe, unless you counted Tansy and Sunny and several other rock queens as groupies, which certainly Rennie did not. Like her own occasional previous dalliances in the male end of the talent pool, Turk's past rock amours, just as occasional as hers, were simply dating in the workplace, casual office affairs of brevity and lightness and all-round pleasantness for all concerned, and nobody was uncomfortable with any of it.

And then they had gotten together, a year and a half ago now, and that had been that, for both of them. They'd never even *looked* at anyone else again. Yes, they'd had fights, yes, they'd had a spectacular and highly publicized breakup—more than enough cause for any rock star worth the name to go off the rails and stock his bed with copulation explosions of one groupie after another.

But Turk never had, and Rennie knew he never would. That wasn't the way he did things, as he'd told her. His word really was his bond and his choices did not come unchosen. He was the wall against which she could set her back, and for her that was something tremendous. Not to mention practically unique in the rockerverse...

After a while, as Lawson seemed to be running out of steam—he had nowhere *near* the wind that DCI Dakers or Detective Audie Devlin of Monterey had, obviously this guy was a sprinter, not a stayer—Rennie let her attention wander back to him, and she smiled charmingly and apologetically, as befitted the suitably chastised.

"I know. You're quite right. I'm sorry. Won't happen again."

Lawson looked at her, the tiniest grin beginning to steal across his face. "I don't mean to sound offensive, Miss Stride, but were you even *listening* to me? No, don't answer that... Because if you had been, you would have heard me say that your poking around under rocks has turned up one or two new and interesting creepy-crawlies and we're rightly glad of it."

Not for worlds was she going to let him know that he had scored. "Well," she said modestly, "it's just what I do. And I was *too* listening. You're quite right, I just now said so. Didn't I?"

He had leaned back in his chair, the grin now overspreading his features. "You did. But you weren't. And that's fine. No, it really is. Now, what else can you tell me about Mr. Raven that I will actually want to hear? And after that, I think we'll discuss Mr. Wayland again. No, he's not a suspect. But I do want to clear things up for the record so I don't have go down to New York and bother him there, as I've said before. Yes? Right, then."

When Sheriff Lawson was finished with his questions, none of which broke any new inquisitorial ground but did clarify several things he'd apparently been pondering, he sat on for a bit in the passenger seat, while another shower passed overhead and the sun sparkled with brief watery brightness through the rags of clouds. It was comfortable and pleasant in the Mustang, and Rennie was content to let him sit there, if that was what he wanted. It seemed that he had something else to say, and so she waited, half drowsing in the warmth of the sunlight through the windshield, and presently he turned to her again.

"There was a burglary at the festival command center Wednesday night," he said, apropos of apparently nothing, and Rennie woke up again from her dozy state.

"So I heard. Quite a few thousand dollars went missing. They were keeping it on hand for bands who insisted on being paid in cash before going on. Hardly an Aquarian mindset, to be so concerned about filthy lucre, but you can't blame them, really."

"Why is that?"

"The Monterey Pop Festival, two summers ago, like this one was supposed to be, was a pay-to-get-in event; minimal ticket charge, three bucks or something for each matinee and evening show, if I recall correctly. And like this festival, that one too ended up as a gratis free-admission concert. But no artists who played there received a fee: everybody donated time and labor, and they had all agreed to that up front. Except of course for Mr. Ravi Shankar, who insisted on being paid, at both festivals—how very material-world of him... Anyway, after Monterey, when people who were *not* the artists started to make money from the festival movie and other things, quite naturally the bands felt ripped off. After all, without them there would have been nothing to begin with, right? So. Woodstock was intended to be a money proposition from the start: tickets were to be paid for—more expensive than Monterey, eighteen dollars in advance and twenty-four at the gate, for all three days, which is a lot but still a hell of a bargain, considering the acts on the bill and free camping and parking thrown in—and the bands were all always meant to be recompensed."

"That's what we've been told."

"And were you also told that some acts are being recompensed far more handsomely than others? Oh yes! For all the lip service given to equality in the counterculture, it is widely known in the music trade that some are far, far more equal than others. For example, I believe Jimi Hendrix takes home eighteen grand for Woodstock, as do Lionheart and Thistlefit, highest-paid bands on the bill. But those acts are also getting an extra ten or twelve thou to appear in the movie, so say about thirty apiece. The Who are taking home eleven-two and the Airplane twelve-five—double their usual rates, I'm told, though that seems oddly low-ball, to say the least. Creedence, probably the hottest band in America at the moment, is getting ten, and Blood, Sweat & Tears, the most boring band in America, is getting fifteen. I haven't heard what the movie cut will be for any of those acts, but you have to figure minimum five grand each. Which all adds up. But the real unknowns like Sha Na Na and Quill and Honest Mollusk are getting three or four measly hundred—for the whole band, not even per head—but for them it's really all about the exposure and the experience, and no one is complaining too much. Or, if they are, they're doing it where nobody can hear them."

"Diplomatic."

"Quite. Then, since this did turn out to be a free festival, in the sense of no tickets being required or collected, mostly on account of all the fences were torn down and nobody had really figured out to collect tickets in the first place, there was renewed concern about payroll, and that's when some of the bands started to require cash on the barrelhead before they set foot onstage. Not exactly a peace-and-love attitude, but you can see their point."

Lawson nodded. "So when the burglary happened, they couldn't be paid as they demanded. Again, this fits with what the organizers told us. Now, we don't have access to cash money at all hours up here; the local banks, who could cover out-of-town checks, aren't open at off times like late at night or on the weekend, when the money was needed, and the vaults are set to timers, so nobody could get in when the need arose. There were no emergency cash reserves, apart from what had been on hand. Which was what had been stolen."

Rennie looked speculatively out at the foot traffic, which had only increased as lunchtime drew near. "I wonder if the burglary didn't actually *precipitate* the cash demand, rather than merely *result* in one? The acts hear there might not be enough bread to go around, so they start demanding to be paid in advance, therefore setting off a run on the bank. As it were. Only, the piggy bank is already empty, and maybe they're already aware of that before they start asking."

"That's a little complicated, don't you think?" He considered it for a moment or two, his own gaze drifting down the little main street to the closed and shuttered doors of the actual bank—a handsome pillared building of peach-colored stone, built in the late nineteenth century. "What would the managers have done, told the bands not to go on unless they had cash in hand? Would the groups have really done that?"

"If their managers told them to? Probably. I can think

of at least a few bands who would have gone right along with it, I'm sorry to say, though more likely most wouldn't have wanted to embarrass themselves in front of their friends. I name no names, to spare their eternal blushes. But yeah, the consequences could have been dire. This festival has already been declared an official state disaster area; if bands started refusing to play because of money, it could have turned into an official riot too. As yet it might."

"Hmm. Well, what we did was, we started looking into it when the shortfall was reported—one of the reasons we invited your Agent Dorner to come in on it. He'd been recommended," he added candidly, in response to the raised eyebrows. "By other people who'd dealt with him. Then it turned out that our bank president was able to cover the deficit himself, with cashier's checks he'd suddenly found in a drawer that hadn't been locked up like everything else. A little surprising, but whatever. Along with a private individual who guaranteed the whole thing out of his own pocket. And who insisted on remaining anonymous. Then the stolen money was mysteriously put back anyway, and it was all okay."

Ah, here came along one of those creepy-crawlies the good sheriff had spoken of, and Rennie thought she knew exactly how creepy and how crawly it was...

"How very civic-minded. There couldn't have been anything in it for either of them, the bank president or the mysterious benefactor. No, I was thinking more along the very suspicious lines that maybe someone thought that if the rather limited police resources of the area were suddenly being shared with a big burglary investigation, said resources would be more strained and stretched to cover two murders in addition. So if someone could *fix* the burglary, maybe those resources could be freed up to go more where they were really needed, to work on the murders."

"Interesting thinking."

"See? Civic-minded. This is what I'm saying. And precisely the same thinking could be applied to the attacks on Turk and Sunny Silver, though those don't look too likely of being sorted out just yet, or maybe ever; while Ned Raven's initial encounter with a live wire could probably be put down to accident."

"And his subsequent encounter? Though I wouldn't like to call Miss Evans a live wire, especially now she's dead."

"No... Well, I couldn't say about that. It's pretty solidly established that they *are* both murders now?"

"I don't see where we can make them into anything else," said Lawson, frustrated. "But again, I have no proof. Could still be accidental ingestion on Rivkin's part, though I can't imagine the means, and as for Miss Evans, still don't know. And as to why, and who, and even how...how can you murder someone with an allergy as the weapon? We're still working on that."

"You do know that Ned and Melza Raven had nothing to do with it, right?"

A sigh and a brief silence. "I reckon they didn't."

"He didn't rape Amander, and neither of them killed her, right?"

"No on both counts."

"Good. Then they can go. I say again, they can go?"

"Yes, yes, they can go. I'll give the duty officer the word. Do you want to go fetch them and take them back to the motel? No? Who could blame you, you've done quite enough. I'll have one of my men drive them."

"That would be best. And probably wisest too. Because you might end up with two more dead bodies. Or at least two majorly smacked-around ones. No, just kidding. Sort of... Well, this has been a most enlightening little chat we've had."

He grinned, and opened the car door. "To say the least, Miss Stride. To say the very least."

So the missing money is all taken care of, is it? Huh. I think I can put my finger on exactly *which civic-minded individual did the taking-care...* Rennie turned everything Lawson had said over and over in her thoughts, as she had lunch in an old-fashioned little ice-cream parlor on the main drag, all original tiled floors and marble soda fountain and dark wood display cases and red-leatherette booths, before she headed back to the motel. She'd indulged herself with a pot roast sandwich, a bit heavy for late summer, perhaps, but it was very good and she was very hungry, and she even ordered some apple pie to follow, thinking of Turk and how sad it was that he couldn't be sharing the very excellent pie though of course that did mean more for her. After that, she sat in her booth by the Victorian bay windows and cooled out for a while, watching the street traffic and trying to keep her mind off the murders, even if only briefly.

Well, *except* for the murders, things were pretty much under control. Turk was home and safe. Prax had successfully played her set. Ned and Melza were sorted out. Her stories had been rapturously received by her bosses. The festival sucked, but she wasn't sorry to be there. She was putting more mileage on the rental than she'd thought, but it was all expense-accounted and nobody would give her a hard time. She was more concerned about making sure she had enough gas in the tank at any given moment; she had no intention of ending up stranded on the side of the road like so many thousands of others…

She aimlessly drifted through a pleasant assortment of other vague thoughts, snorkeling her way through a straw at the further pig-out extravagance of a black-and-white ice cream soda; and then her luck, which had held firm and fast through so many scenes since her arrival at Bethel, suddenly and definitively ran out.

"Rennie, dahling!" The sharp, slightly nasal voice cut through her preoccupation, and she looked up, startled, to see Loya Tessman looking down at her, smiling like a shark. To Rennie's utter astonishment, the newcomer slid into the booth without waiting for an invitation and started babbling away across the table as if they were the best of friends. *Oh, no, this cannot,* must *not, be, we hate each other, Tessman and I, how creepy is this…*

"I'll just join you for a nice long chat, shall I, yes, Ted is out roaming around the town looking for some, I don't know, fishing tackle or bait or maybe those cute little waders the fishermen wear, he loves to go fishing up around here, we're thinking of buying some property along this trout stream in the next county over, the Beaverkill I think it's called, though why would people want to kill beavers, those cute little things, and 'kill', well of course *you'd* know all about *that…*"

" 'Kill' is the Dutch word for 'stream' ", said Rennie evenly, gritting her teeth as invisibly as she could manage, and watching Loya arrange herself comfortably on the red-vinyl banquette. "On account of how the Dutch, you know, first settled this area?"

Loya's well-rehearsed trill of laughter, known to peel paint off walls from coast to coast, pierced the comfortable low murmur of the place like nails on a blackboard, Oh *what* a silly thing she was for not knowing that, Rennie must think her *such* a stupid little ditzy person... Well, she'd get no argument there. Rennie firmly repressed a longing to apply the English meaning of the word...perhaps she could rename some local stream the Loyakill, once she'd drowned the relevant party in it. And if the Tessmans bought property in the next county over, the Waylands would have to make sure to buy their own weekend place as far away as they could. Like Canada.

Loya Mailing Tessman and Rennie Stride did *not* get on. At all. It was some kind of instinctive, deep-seated and ancient antipathy, inborn, like cobra vs. mongoose, hyena vs. lion, Coyote vs. Roadrunner. They had hated each other at first sight, much as Rennie and Devin Sweetzer, Loya's late unlamented bosom crony, had done, or, on a marginally lesser scale, as Rennie and Niles Clay still did. Maybe it was genetic, or a carryover from a past incarnation; it certainly was mutual. Up till this moment, she'd been able to avoid Loya at Woodstock; as she had noted, it was a big, *big* field. But it had just grown suddenly and intolerably small.

Unfortunately for Rennie and just about everyone else on the scene, Ted and Loya Tessman, former college sweethearts, were a genuine music-business power couple, what with Ted being the influential head of the giant agency Tontine, which serviced some of the biggest groups around, and Loya being the likewise influential publisher of her own teenybopper fan mag, Teen Angels. Which you would have thought might result in serious conflicts of interest, and you would have been correct to think so, even in the notably free-and-easy music biz. But to watch the Tessmans in action was to see made manifest a whole new definition of shameless and unblushing log-rolling: Ted booked acts, Loya pimped them in her rag's pages, demand was created for more bookings, which resulted in still more coverage and of course attendant ad revenue from record companies—a marriage made in rock-and-roll purgatory. Well, it worked great for them. Just not so much for everybody else.

Though in general Rennie was on excellent terms with almost the entire population of the rockerverse, and it with her, these two creatures she flat-out loathed, and Loya reciprocated the feeling; her no-neck husband generally communicated in grunts, so it was a little hard to tell. Things between the two women were kept short of outright warfare by a kind of unspoken nonaggression pact, very Cold War: Rennie knew perfectly well that her sterling reputation as a real journalist and her solid-gold connections—Turk, Prax, Fitz, the Sonnets, the Ravens, Elk Bannerman, just for starters—had a lot to do with that.

Nonetheless, even Oliver Fitzroy's pet and protégée and fair-haired girl couldn't afford to flout Loya unduly. And Ted was more powerful still; everybody hated them, but no one dared to piss them off, or kiss them off. Even Lionheart, itself a Tontine client, required Tessman's goodwill to a certain extent, much as Turk resented the thought, and he was planning to do something about it...

By now Loya had settled in, like the flu on a grizzling winter evening, and was chirping about the festival in an uncharacteristically and actually quite creepy little fashion. For her part, Rennie was trying to figure out what the hell was really going on, so that she could then figure out how to put a stop to it. So she nodded and smiled and watched

Loya's vulpine visage for the merest clue. The creature was up to something, and until Rennie knew what it was, she needed to keep her guard raised and her sword handy.

Loya seemed not to notice, but ordered iced tea and, after a little debate with herself, monologue really, about low-calorie options, a fruit cobbler to go with it, hold the whipped cream. Rennie's heart almost failed her—*oh God, she's going to stick around and* TALK TO ME, *I'm trapped, I'll* never *get out of here*... Because talk Loya did: now she was prattling on about how *groovy* the festival had been so far, and how *faaaabulous* it was to see everybody up here from the city, out of the usual boring old concert/club/press-party circuit. Rennie let her babble brookishly, tossing in an occasional murmured word to show that she was still there and still awake. After a while, she noticed that her own friends' names were starting to appear in the stream of endless piffle, sparkling pebbles tumbling in a gossip flood, and she started paying closer attention, sensing that Loya, like the shark her smile belonged on, was circling round and round her objective before she struck. It didn't take long.

"And how *is* that dear beautiful *dah-ling* Turk of yours, then? We were *so* upset, Ted and I, when we heard what *happened* to him, oh yes, it's all over the *festival* by now, you must have been *terrified*...and then having to play Friday night without *dear* Niles, what a *tragedy*."

Rennie drew a breath to respond, but the triangular dorsal fin had sunk beneath the surface and was coming up fast from below.

"And of *course* Ned and Melza, how positively *dreadful*, we've all heard, I'm sure you've been helping them, you're *such* a good friend. And Amander and Cory, so *totally* tragic—not to mention Sunny's little *accident*... It does seem as if Annadawn was right after all, and the festival is *cursed*, don't you think?"

And now came the snapping jaws and pointy teeth, the dead eyes rolling back for the bite. "I saw you talking to that sheriff in your car just now; did he have anything to say? What have they found out?"

Ah. She should have guessed: ordinarily Loya couldn't have cared less how Turk or anybody else was, not if they were lying bleeding at her feet, unless it was somehow to her benefit that she should know. So all this, then, was indeed a fishing expedition, the kind you didn't need to buy waders for. Or maybe you did, to protect yourself from the heaving flood of manure that Loya was deploying. What *was* she up to? Maybe no more than trying to land a nice big fat wodge of information to take home to Ted in her little Gucci creel, or to put in her magazine, like a trophy trout displayed on the wall of the den; but all the same, Rennie was annoyed. Well, this was one little fishie Tessman wasn't about to hook. Because Rennie was going to get one into mean sharky Loya first.

So she commanded a whole pitcher of iced tea for them both, sat back and began to spin a breathtaking tissue of lies, a tapestry of pure mendacity, laced with Loya's own trademark verbal italics. Oh, yes indeed, Turk was *absolutely* going to fire Niles Clay as soon as the current tour was over, because of how Niles had insulted her the other night, which *everyone* had seen, and because of his subsequent drugged-out failure to show up onstage; oh, no, wait a minute, what *had* her darling Lord Richard said to her in bed the other night? So *hard* to keep her mind on an idle comment, what with his...right there...well. No, yes, he *was* going to fire

Niles, but *before* the tour started, and ask Diego Hidalgo to join Lionheart to sing lead vocals instead, yes, *that* was it. Though now that Cory Rivkin was dead, so very sad, and Owl Tuesday was disbanding, that's *right*, they *are*, yes, you mean you hadn't *heard*? Turk was considering asking Terry Janoff to come on board, he could sing really really well, *much* better than Niles, don't you think, plus he'd come a lot cheaper than Diego, though of *course* you didn't hear any of this from *me*, you understand, all *strictly* off the record, you understand, my name totally out of it, because we're *friends*, aren't we, oh yes we are, and I *so* trust you...

Loya, agog with all this unprecedented gossipy largesse, simply gaped with astonishment and delight, her mouth wide open for the lure, more like a trout now than a shark, and the swift foaming current of the Renniekill swept it right in. Faithfully swearing anonymity, Loya kept on gobbling it up, and Rennie went on and on handing it out, playing her fish like a pro, disgracefully dragging all her friends into it. No one was sacred: everyone she knew, many ones she didn't know, anyone she could think of. She tried to keep a straight face as she reeled Loya in without a fight, but it was a struggle to preserve her deadpan as she watched the bugged-out gooseberry eyes get bigger and bigger with each delectable morsel, until they looked like those British sweets rather unpleasantly called gobstoppers. Well, this was one gabby gob Rennie would really enjoy stopping...

And was it ever going to be big fun to watch all these baby cock-and-bull stories go toddling off to make their debut in the pages of Teen Angels, that outhouse rag! The parties concerned could then have all the fun of virtuous outraged denial, as they rolled on the floor screaming with laughter while calling up to complain in the highest of dudgeon: What, has Loya Tessman gone stark raving *mad*? Fire Niles Clay? Certainly not! Diego *Hidalgo*? In *Lionheart*? Are you completely *insane*? We demand an immediate retraction and apology! And other variations along those highly entertaining lines. Something to look forward to.

Sure, it was evil, but it served the bitch right for trying to pump Rennie like that. There was simply far too much on the other side of the ledger for revenge not to be the pen and ink in which accounts were balanced out: all the insults and put-downs and condescending snubs that she'd endured in the past from Loya, because she'd refused to play Loya's game and suck up to her as the queen of the scene, and because Rennie had Turk and all Loya had was Ted and she was sick with envy. This was merely a bit of karmic payback. If the woman was a gullible sap, that was her problem. It might make things a little tense for Turk, with Ted, but still it was no big deal. Tessman was influential, sure, but he wasn't the only big important booker in town, nor was Tontine the agency most favorable to bands, and Turk *had* been looking for an excuse to make a change. If Tessman took it out on the band, there were plenty of other agencies who would be thrilled to pieces to have Lionheart on their roster, and who would fall all over themselves to do their best to get them and keep them.

But she doubted it would come to that, and in any case Turk had plans for expedient exits from all his business commitments, should abrupt flight ever prove necessary—that was the kind of careful planner he was, and he'd learned it at his grandfather's knee. Even if Loya did finally realize what Rennie had done, and complained of her to the mister, Ted was far too savvy and pragmatic to let feuds precipitated by his wife dictate his business dealings. Lionheart and Turk would likely not suffer in the least for Rennie's little spot of sniping—Ted was used to that sort of thing. If he let every little hissyfit Loya had with the rockerverse affect his work, he'd be out of business in a week.

After about fifteen minutes, when Rennie could see that Loya was about ready to explode like a water balloon if she couldn't get to her notebook and write down all this manna from heaven before she forgot half of it, she smiled graciously, left a big tip on the table and stood up to leave.

"Must get back to the festival. And I'm sure you need to go find Ted and get all that trouty stuff you were talking about. I hear there's a good place up the road a bit. On the banks of the Beaverkill, funnily enough. Bye-bye just now."

As she turned away, grinning to herself, Sovereign Records publicist Dian Cazadora, another of her unfavorite people, bumped into her on her way to join them in the booth. Rennie noticed that Dian looked visibly disappointed to see her leaving. Probably hoping to hear some hot gossip, like her dear friend Loya: really, did all these bottom-feeders have nothing better to do? Rennie grinned some more and practically pushed Dian into the booth, then thrust some money at the cashier and was out the door and tearing down the street as if hounds of hell were pursuing her. And perhaps they were.

Safe in the Mustang and heading back to the motel to change—she'd gotten caught in the rain on her way to the car, and was very damp indeed—Rennie was laughing so hard she almost drove off the road. Yes, yes, that had been a very mean-spirited thing to do, she was a horrible evil person, her friends were going to kill her. But nobody on

God's good green earth had it coming more than did Loya Tessman. Well, everybody needs a little life lesson once in a while. Which was something she herself might want to remember.

~18~

SHE PARKED OUTSIDE in the rear lot as usual, and went in through the side door to her room to change her rained-on clothing. Then she headed to the main lobby to see what was up. Observing Elk Bannerman sitting alone over by the fireplace— well, alone except for Mr. Bullneck, two more equally ominous-looking colleagues and a contemplative glass of twenty-five-year-old Scotch—on impulse she swerved aside. He received her as affectionately as he always did, even when she accused him right there of setting his dubious minions to sorting out the festival cash problem, freelance, in his own particular little way. He looked amused and not at all surprised that she'd figured it out, and said so.

"It was nothing, kiddo, no big deal. No deal at all. I had a couple of my guys talk to that cop from L.A., or private detective, or whatever the hell he is—"

"Marcus Dorner? I'm sorry, you had 'a couple of your guys' talk to MARCUS DORNER? Dear God in heaven! He's *federales*, you know. At least I think he is. Aren't you the tiniest bit worried he might pull an Eliot Ness on you? Or at the very least a Sergeant Joe Friday? For playing the Money Mitzvah Fairy?"

He laughed and put an arm around her shoulder. "No problem. He was happy for us to lend a hand. As for the dough situation, I have some, oh, let's say some good friends in the neighborhood up here, and I stopped by to see them. They were very eager to help me out, I can tell you. We laid the cash down so the bands could get paid, then we asked around a bit, about the money and where it had gotten to, and what do you know, there it all was, back where it belonged. Everything hunky-dory. No worries. No questions asked. Okay, maybe a few asked, with the answers filed away for future reference. It's all taken care of, so I don't want you troubling your brainy pretty little head about it. It was important for the festival to go on, right? We only made sure it would. I was glad I was here to help."

After Rennie had finished alternately thanking him and scolding him, even though it was no business of hers, or indeed any duty of his, he patted her hand and eyed her shrewdly.

"So, is it going to help us in tracking down who killed Amander, or that Cory kid?"

She shook her head morosely. "I have no idea. Though it should free up a copper or two. But I'm beginning to think it will be teatime in hell before I solve this one. Oh, while I think of it—why did you insist that Amander open for Bluesnroyals on the last leg of their tour? Because I heard you did, and that seems kind of an odd pairing, as they don't really cross over audience-wise."

Elk looked surprised. "No reason, really, except that Jack Holland owed me a favor and I thought the girl would pick up some good exposure with Ned Raven."

"Yeah, I guess you could call it that...and she certainly got some, all right."

"Meaning?"

"Oh, nothing really. But as to possible perps, there's just too many damn *people*..."

"Then concentrate on the ones who had access. I don't need to tell you how it goes, you're a pro by now: motive, means, opportunity."

"I *have* no motive. Not the smallest scrap of one."

"That's okay, that's fine. So concentrate on one of the other two. You told me it was peanut allergies that killed the drummer kid? Well, that's means right there."

"It's opportunity I fall down on. Everybody swears he wouldn't so much as look at a peanut through binoculars, so why all of a sudden would he eat one?" She looked up, suddenly hopeful. "Could Amander have been allergic too? Not necessarily peanuts, but maybe something else?"

"*Ketzeleh,* if she was she never told me. Sorry. I suppose it's possible. Does it matter?"

"It might. It might matter more than anything. But I won't know until I know. If you know what I mean."

Elk nodded, smiling faintly. "I do. And you will. I have no doubt. For a *shiksa,* you've got one good *yiddishe kop*."

She smiled back. "What a lovely compliment."

"I know how you hate it when I use a couple of words when a hundred would do, but they're *good* words."

Marcus sighed. "I'm sure they are. Go ahead, go on, use them."

"There's only one, really. Slaydar. Oh, come on, you know you want to hear it! Amander—even if she did mess around with Ned she didn't deserve *that*... And Cory Rivkin... Not to mention Turk being poisoned." Rennie shivered once, convulsively, thinking of how close it had come to Turk's name joining the other two on the front pages and in the obituary columns.

"You think they're all connected."

They were sitting in the main lounge of the motel, which at the moment was conveniently deserted. Pretty much everyone else had trekked out to the festival, where the music was reportedly getting started, though the sky was beginning to ominously cloud over. Elk had departed accompanied by his hulking goons, er, colleagues, to have lunch over at the nearby Concord resort with the management, who were, apparently, more good friends of his, or perhaps seeking to become better ones. As all his acts had performed, he would probably not even bother returning to the festival, but would leave the cops to do their job and make himself available back in the city, on the matter of Amander, should it be necessary. So he had bidden her a warm farewell and made her promise to eat skirt steak with him at Sammy's Roumanian on the Lower East Side, and to bring Turk along so Elk could meet him.

That left Rennie and Marcus uncomfortably alone. There was always Sheriff Lawson to keep them company, of course; but he wasn't around just now, so the professional and the amateur were left to their own devices, and probably also to a certain amount of disagreement as to which one of them was which.

Displaying considerable delicacy of feeling, Rennie had been reluctant to have this conversation in the room she'd been sharing with Turk. Not because of any vestigial Marcus-shaped temptation, of course, God no! Those days were long gone, and in any case Turk's possessions still strewn around the room, like a stag's antler blazes on trees deep in the forest, spelled out no uncertain message—his territory, his female—and it totally turned her on that it did. And not that she in her conceit thought that Marcus still had the hots for her; in fact, she had fixed him up a few months back with one of her acquaintances in L.A., a high-powered brunette investment banker she'd met through a reporting job, and they seemed to be enjoying themselves. No, she just wanted to keep both herself and Agent Dorner focused on the matter at hand, and with the motel at full capacity and then some, there was really no other place to conduct a discussion, even though it was public and anyone could have listened in. But people, though outwardly curious, nevertheless gave them a wide berth.

Marcus leaned back and studied her and repeated, more loudly and deliberately, "I say again, you think that somehow, despite all evidence that nobody can find even with a big enormous magnifying glass and a becoming deerstalker hat, the murders and the attack on Turk are all somehow connected."

"I heard you the first time! I was thinking! And no, I don't *think* they're connected, I *know* they're connected. Okay, not with any knowledge that would stand up in a court of law—yet—but yeah, I do believe they are. Because it is simply beyond the powers of my suspension of disbelief to think that Amander and Cory were not both felled by the lethal might of the lowly legume. Because nothing else seems to make any damn sense. True, it's weird and unlikely, on the face of it, that two rocknrollers here at Woodstock would be so violently allergic to peanuts as to keel over dead from it, but it's not an uncommon allergy and there are after all half a million people here so the odds are not extraordinarily against it. What *is* extraordinary is that someone, or someones, knew about it and took advantage of it."

Marcus sighed and shifted in the big armchair. He hadn't had anything to eat all morning, and he was longing to hit the dining room to grab some lunch before hungry rockers stripped the motel larders clean, like plaguey locusts—or at least get back into Monticello and score something there. Had Rennie known he was so cranky only because he was so famished, she would have offered some of her sandwich stash, at least to take the edge off until he could get to some real food. But he didn't say, and she didn't ask, and they both continued to labor under the delusion that both of them were ticked off at each other. It wasn't the first time, and it almost certainly wouldn't be the last.

"So, what do you think the deal is?"

Rennie looked at him for a while. "As I said. I think that they were both murdered by people who knew about their peanut bane, that's what I think the deal is. But I can't prove it. I can't prove that Amander even had an allergy. Yet."

"Leave Amander for a minute. What's the latest on the Ravens?"

"Oh—Sheriff Lawson told me he told them they could go. I wouldn't be surprised if they're already heading back to the city to hop on the next plane for their homeland. Very anticlimactic: all that storm and drama, and in the end it just made a noise like a hoop and rolled away. Though I'm sure they'll have plenty to say to each other on the plane home. I'll discuss it with them next time I see them, the little varmints; if they think they can pull something as stupid as that and inflict it on me, and not suffer any repercussions, they are very much mistaken. I just came from the village myself, actually," she added, "where I had that chat with stalwart Lawman Lawson. Didn't I *tell* both you and any member of the local fuzz within hailing distance that the Ravens had nothing to do with it? Why yes, I do believe I did. What the hell is *wrong* with all you people, you listen but you never hear..."

"Don't you ever hate being right all the time?"

"Of course. But the alternative would be far worse, so I've learned to live with it." She peered more closely at him. "You look hungry. Go and feed yourself before they run out of anything to serve and have to go out in the woods and shoot the daily possum special. Or I have some nice sandwiches from Kaplan's in our room fridge that Turk and I didn't get around to eating, you could have those if you like. Or there're some great little restaurants back in town, and a nice old-school diner up in Roscoe, should be open on a Sunday. We were supposed to have breakfast there yesterday, but events prevented."

"Yes, so I heard. And I appreciate your concern. But I want to talk to you first. Not about this. We haven't had a chance to talk, just us, since your, ah, accident last year."

Rennie laughed shortly. "Accident! I was shot, twice, deliberately, by a lunatic who you and your flatfoot brethren of the LAPD knew all about and did nothing to stop. A lunatic who killed five people and who tried to kill me and Turk, also twice. Each. Wasn't much accidental about *that*. She knew *exactly* what she was doing."

"And so did you," Marcus offered handsomely. "Your aptitude for unarmed combat, combined with Mr. Ares Sakura's intervention, probably saved your life and Turk's besides."

"There's no 'probably' about it!" she said with a certain amount of indignation. "And it was a whole hell of a lot more than you and the Los Angeles clown cops could manage. If memory serves, and it always does, you guys were the ones who thought Turk was doing the murders himself. How incredibly wrong you all were." She gave him a look that could have boiled away a glacier. "No, fathead, it was Turk who all by his hero self, going up unarmed against that crazy bitch to talk her down, saved everybody's lives. Only then did Ares shoot the gun out of her hand. All I did was break her arm and buy some time."

"A costly purchase, some might say."

Rennie stretched out her own arm and rather complacently admired the thin silvery line between wristbone and elbow crease—all that was left of the bullet graze. There was a smaller scar across her ribs, where the second bullet had plowed right through.

"A stone bargain, *I'd* say. It kept her away from Turk. That was all I cared about. Plus I got a dozen very nice diamond bracelets out of it. Not that I intend to ever be repeating it, mind you, not even for a truckload of tiaras."

"I hear you're going to be coming into those anyway. But that's not what I want to discuss."

"It isn't? Then what, pray?"

He sighed and didn't look at her. "I hate to ask, but—is there anyone, in your vast circle of acquaintance and knowledge, who *you* think could possibly be responsible for the deaths and the accidents? And any motives you could possibly ascribe to them? Because I'm plumb out of ideas, and I humbly admit it to Murder Chick."

Rennie had the grace not to gloat, at least not right out there on her face where he could see it. That had been a big admission for him, and she didn't want to jeopardize the fragile entente.

"Well, much as I'd love to think it's really Niles Clay,

purely because I loathe him so, and he *was* allegedly crashed senseless at the motel when I was attacked in the woods, and he *did* rather suspiciously stay out of sight all the next day and we never got to see if he was limping—" she began, and then caught herself.

Hellfire! Now where had *that* come from? And she hadn't been kidding, either, as she usually was when wishfully thinking of Niles and murder in conjunction. Interesting that Niles' name had leaped so instantly to her mind, though, when it hadn't before. She leaned back, thinking. Could Niles have merely feigned stoned incapability, in order that he could get out of performing Friday night and instead sneak into Amander's party and poison Turk? And if he had, was it to get back at Turk or to get back at Rennie? Or both? But why would he want to kill Cory and Amander? No, that was crazy talk. Or…was it?

"Could you pick a possibility and stick to it, do you think?" asked Marcus after a decent interval, and waited, patient as a hawk above a cornfield, for her answer.

The mice among the stalks weren't slow to show themselves, even though talons were waiting to pounce. "It's weird," she said slowly. "But I keep coming back to it. Before the festival, two friends of mine, astrologers, made predictions about the weekend. One said it was going to be glorious, the other one predicted doom and gloom and accidents. They both predicted rain, in case you were wondering," she added. "And see how very damp the whole thing has been… But I can't get rid of the feeling that, bizarre as it sounds, somehow the stars and planetary aspects are involved in all this. I know you don't believe in any of that stuff, but maybe you should give it a thought."

Marcus looked as if he were doing exactly that. "You

don't think that these two persons, or other astrology fans, could be involved in all this themselves?"

A scoff of laughter. "You wouldn't ask that if you knew them. Which of course *is* why you're asking me, yes, I *get* that. Well, one of them is way too cheerful, the other is way too dour. And while I am quite aware that that alone hardly excuses them as suspects, they're both far too incompetent to have organized anything as complicated as this. Besides, as far as I know, neither of them has anything in common with any of the victims."

"Apart from the rain, were their predictions for the festival consistent with their track records?"

Rennie considered, frowning slightly. "No, they weren't, now you come to mention it. In fact, the predictions were quite contrary to their usual slant on things. I'd have expected exactly the reverse: the reliably gloomy person to make the doomy prophecy, the cheery one to go for sweetness and light. Instead, it was as if they switched bodies, or at least charts. It made no sense, really. Though I suppose none of this makes any sense."

"I'm sure you're right," he said easily. "Okay, what about people who might profit by harming Amander or Cory? Or Turk, for that matter, as he's the one who was wounded most seriously in descending order of injury; Ned and Sunny's accidents seem too inconsequential to consider. Though of course they *are* being considered."

"We've been *over* this... Amander was basically, apart from screwing anything that moved, a slutty but inoffensive Kiwi nonentity who had played, what, three U.S. gigs counting this one; she hadn't been around long enough to make enemies. And if you're going to suggest yet again that she certainly made enemies out of Melza and Ned, put a sock in it."

"Sock, yes, *ma'am*!" He snapped off a mocking little salute, and she rolled her eyes. "Refresh my mind about Cory Rivkin."

She shrugged. "Again, inoffensive and not in any position to do anybody any harm. A much bigger star than Amander, of course, though not in any way a superstar, so comparatively little publicity value in offing him, which goes double and triple for Amander. Though not for Turk, of course. I hate to say it, but I think we might be looking for a mere common-or-garden psycho, just another killer of opportunity. The deaths, and though I hate to say this even more, the attack on Turk, seem random and motiveless. Which means we'll probably never catch whoever did it. And that makes me very sad, and very, very angry."

"You were thinking that Turk had been put out of action specifically to put *you* out of action, so you would be too wrapped up in what happened to him and you wouldn't have any attention to spare to investigate the deaths."

"I still think that, but I thought you thought that was just me being vainglorious and self-important."

"I *do* think that," said Marcus, and grinned when she looked outraged. "But no more than usual, and no more than you have a right to. I also think you may be on to something. Let's go back a little. Do you think it's possible that Sunny and Ned were, well, failed targets of the murderer? If that amp had landed on her the wrong way, she could have been killed, or at least much more seriously injured. Same with Ned: sure, there were puddles on the stage, but that mike might easily have been tampered with. And he's the one who got fried, not a stagehand or someone hanging out onstage. If the voltage had been high enough, we'd be looking at ex-Ned. No way of finding out now, of course. It's possible those two *were* only targets of opportunity, not necessarily singled out because they happen to be close personal friends of yours."

"Or they might have been both. Either way, what statement was the perp trying to make? Or was he merely trying to cast a shadow on the festival and was starting small, before working his way up to murder?"

"Almost as if it had been predicted." Marcus dropped the words into a thoughtful silence.

She stared at him. "Is that what you're getting at? Someone making predictions come true? But—why?"

"Not why but who. Who was making predictions of disaster for the festival?"

Rennie wouldn't meet his eyes. "I don't—"

"Oh yes you do. You even said you had a strange feeling that astrological forces were at work here."

"Sure, but only in the sense that Saturn was screwing us over and the Eighth House was afflicted! Not that anyone was deliberately trying to bring about destruction, to *kill* people and blame it on the planets!"

Marcus was gazing at her as intently as a gun dog holding point. "Who was it who predicted the bad things, Rennie? You know I'll find out sooner or later."

"Maybe. Maybe not. How's this: I tell you who if it starts looking as if the, ah, individual is responsible?"

"How's *this*: I tell Caskie Lawson you're withholding evidence?"

She glared at him. "I'm not, you know. I don't have a scrap of anything that could remotely be evidentially construed. If I did, I would certainly pass it along. And loads of people were predicting disaster; anyone with half a brain, who thought about the ridiculous premise of this festival for more than a blithering nanosecond, could see the possibilities for epic catastrophe."

"If I find out you do have something and are holding out on me—"

"Not a bit of it," said Rennie with some heat. "I do not *know,* as I've said; nor do I think, plan, consider, execute, contrive or channel the wisdom of the ancestors."

"Just because you say you don't know *anything* doesn't mean you don't know *something.*"

In spite of herself, she laughed. "And I'm contact-high stoned enough that that made perfect sense; what's your excuse? Okay, I'm not saying I do know something? But if I did—it all, well, just happened."

"As it so often does with you." Marcus looked exasperated, and also defeated. "Right. Well, you know the drill by now. If something turns up—"

"Bring it to you first," Rennie finished, giving him a little salute of her own. "Sorry, I already promised first dibs to Sheriff Lawson. But I know how to share my toys."

"Glad to hear it."

Many minutes after Marcus had gone, Rennie was still sitting there in the lobby, blank and unmoving, when Sheriff Lawson himself came out of the motel manager's office. Seeing her there, he came over and sat down in the opposite chair to the one Marcus had occupied; though their eyes met briefly, neither of them spoke.

Then Lawson, unnecessarily: "I've been talking to the manager."

"Yes, I can see that. On account of how you just came out of his private office. You headed here straight from our own little car confab, did you? Well, what have you and said manager been talking about? I'm pretty sure it wasn't the state of the housekeeping."

"Oh, a little of this, a little of that. In case you hadn't noticed, this is a huge crime scene, in several locations, and it's getting harder minute by minute to keep anything remotely resembling a handle on it all." He gave her an aggrieved look. "And a whole lot more so, considering *your* morning's work managed to remove the only suspect I so far had."

Rennie looked pleased. "Did it? But you're much too good a cop to have liked the wrong person for this, which Ned and Melza most certainly were." She shook her head, irritated. "I keep wanting to say 'Med and Nelza'; they're so interchangeable in their idiocy. Understandable that they'd each lie to protect the other; they *are* married, after all."

"And you'd think that by now they'd have learned that you don't do that when talking to the police during a murder investigation. They *are* friends of yours, after all."

"And therefore more likely to be aware of such niceties? Beg to differ. It isn't like that, really."

"Then how *is* it, Miss Stride? *More* people lying to protect their nearest and dearest? Perhaps you can tell me? Because I've got very little to go on here. So if you in your secret, or not so secret, identity as Murder Chick can help me out, I'd be much obliged. Yes, yes, I've read all about it, and I've talked to Agent Dorner and a couple other law enforcement officials who've encountered you in the course of doing their jobs, and all I can say is, they have my genuine sympathy. Perhaps we'll form a little club and have dinner when this case is done. Would you like to take a moment to get into your superhero costume before you think about answering?"

For the first time, Lawson's voice was tinged with impatience and annoyance. Not for the first time, Rennie felt genuinely sorry for him: his beautiful bucolic county invaded by a rolling tsunami of bizarre creatures, some of whom were famous enough to command worldwide attention, others of whom were vexing him out of his usual rural rut, er, calm predictable course, still further others of whom were killing people off with apparent impunity and he couldn't do a damn thing about it. She'd be cross too: in fact, she was. And that was due in no small part to Neddy and Mel. She shook her head, staring down at the carpeting. When this was over, she'd slap them silly. But first...

"How is it?" she repeated. "I don't know, and that's the best I can say. But if I die not knowing, my spirit will never be at peace, so by all means let's find out."

He stared at her, then his taut expression dissolved into lines of laughter. "I can't decide if I more pity Mr. Wayland or more admire him or more envy him. You're a lot of *some*thing, all right, Miss Stride, and I have to say I've never seen anything like it. When all this is over and it so happens that you're up this way again, I'd be pleased if you and Mr. Wayland will come have Sunday dinner with me and my wife on our farm."

Rennie smiled, unexpectedly touched, but even so, she still maintained a cool inner distance. *Stay sharp, don't fall for blinding country charm, he's working some kind of con here, pretending to be the absolute clodhopper I absolutely know he's absolutely not, so I think he needs a bit of a short sharp shock, like an anchovy in the sorbet...*

"We'd like that very much, Sheriff. We've actually discussed buying a weekend place in the area, you know.

Just giving you fair warning, so you can get into a new line of work before we move in. And the next time you and the Mrs. are down in the big city, we'll have you to dinner at our house. Perhaps you'd like to see Lionheart in concert; they're playing Madison Square Garden in December. Manhattan's great in the holiday season. But. Before we get to the social niceties, I have a small bone to pick with you."

"Oh? What's that?"

"What's all this bullshit I hear about kids heading to the festival being arrested and tossed in jail for petty traffic violations, and being held on bails that could buy any house in Sullivan County?"

Rennie had used the b-word quite deliberately, though otherwise it never sullied her speech—she thought it far too crude and unimaginative. She was gratified to see Lawson's face go red, as she had intended, and pressed her point.

"Come on! We've all heard about it. It's been happening all weekend through four counties, from Broome to Orange, in squalid little dump towns along 17—kids being busted and slammerized for broken headlights, dented fenders, jaywalking without any shoes on, whistling at cows, stupid made-up invented offenses, ordinances a hundred and fifty years old—what *is* this crap! It's redneck harassment, is what it is. You people ought to be ashamed of yourselves, hassling innocent kids like that. Not to mention violating all sorts of Constitutionally protected rights from here to eternity. Illegal searches and seizures, busts for having two joints among a carful of kids, disgusting pat-downs of cute braless chicks. What pigs you all really are."

Lawson's face was expressionless now. "Are you trying to get me angry, Miss Stride? Because it isn't working. I might not be on your side about a lot of things, but that kind of police behavior gets me standing right next to you in the protest lines. Because it's not right, and when we find out who's responsible for it, be they county cops or state troopers, they'll be punished."

"Oh please! They will not! You know it and I know it. You're only doing it out of spite. You can't arrest the people at the festival, however much they offend you, and they do, because where are you going to lock up half a million stoned lawbreakers, and you're really, *really* bent out of shape that you can't. Unless you're going to bring in the National Guard and have them encircle the whole field with bayonets fixed, which thought I'm quite sure has already occurred to the powers that be, and aren't they just longing to make it so. But it's easy-peasy to bust individual cars full of longhairs and pot, and get your frustrated law-enforcement rocks off that way. And here I always thought the worst you upstate fuzz did was set speed traps as a source of local income. Instead, you're officially the Sheriff of Pottingham this weekend, aren't you, and you just *hate* it, don't you."

"Are you finished, ma'am? Because I know you only meant to blow off some steam at what you see as the unfairness of it all. And I have to say I agree. To a certain extent. Don't forget that drugs *are* against the law, and so are those driving violations, and so is indecent exposure. But those kids will be out of jail tomorrow, and the only thing that will have happened is that they missed the show. Maybe that will teach them not to drive around topless with broken headlights and missing bumpers and cars reeking of pot. And that won't be such a bad little life lesson, I'm thinking. Discretion hardly ever is."

They glared at each other, knowing they came from

opposite sides and yet had common ground and a shared purpose after all, neither wanting to make an enemy of the other. After a few moments, Rennie sighed resignedly.

"No, you're right. I'm sorry. I just wish you could have found another way to demonstrate the weight of the law than coming down hard on poor harmless kids who only wanted to come to your turf and hear some music."

Lawson sighed too, but with relief. He really didn't want to provoke her, and thus distance the one solid help source he had in solving the murders; besides, he liked her.

"I'm sorry too, ma'am, and I promise that once we've worked out what we really need to work out, I will certainly look into what has you so upset. In the meantime, I do have to ask you a few more things."

She sighed and shook her head. "Ask away, Sheriff. Ask away."

But once given the green light, Lawson paused for several moments, as if he found the asking a little indelicate—whatever the questions might be, or the answers he thought he might receive—and didn't want to alienate Rennie even further.

"We found out something we hadn't thought to," he said, a reined-in carefulness apparent now in his voice. "And we found it right here in the motel. Do you have a friend called Lexie Kagan?"

Rennie's glance drifted thoughtfully to where Marcus had been sitting. "Lexie? Sure. She's more an acquaintance, not a friend, but I do know her."

"Did you know she had been having an affair with Amander Evans? And that Miss Evans dumped her two weeks ago?"

"No. No, I did not know that at all." Rennie was silent

for a few moments. "So. Do you have any hard evidence linking her to Amander's death? Since clearly that is what you're implying."

"Not such as what you might call 'hard'. When we spoke to Miss Kagan upstairs a little while ago, we noticed some bruises on her arms; those could mean anything, of course, but very similar bruises were also found on Miss Evans. Suggesting, perhaps, a physical struggle. Or bruises sustained in the course of intimate contact."

"Or moving furniture. Walking into a wall. Falling over a dog. Too many aspirins."

"All possibilities. But there's more. We found some letters from Miss Kagan in a suitcase in Miss Evans' room. A suitcase positively identified as belonging to Miss Evans. With both names and addresses on the letters. Love letters." He looked acutely uncomfortable saying so, though he tried hard to hide it.

Rennie, much more successfully, concealed the nasty shock this information had given her. "Circumstantial."

"That may well be so," allowed Lawson. "But for the most part, circumstantial evidence can be a pretty good indicator."

"Such as when you find a trout in the milk?" said Rennie irresistibly, and was amused to see Lawson's start of surprise. "No, I'm not a country girl, Sheriff. I just read a lot." A distant memory passed over her face like a quick shadow. "But I do know watered milk when it spills across my path. Even on a six-hundred-acre dairy farm."

"Again, that's as may be. But what can you tell me about Miss Evans and Miss Kagan? Separately or together."

"As I've been telling you all damn weekend, I know pretty much *nothing* about Amander Evans. Singer. From

New Zealand. Signed to Rainshadow Records by Elk Bannerman. I didn't even know about her and Ned Raven until this morning, and I've been friends with Ned for years. I met her once two weeks ago, or it might be three, in the city, backstage at the Fillmore East the night some friends played there. Turk was with me. And the other night, Friday night, or Saturday morning as I guess it was, when Turk and I went to the party in Elk Bannerman's room. That's it. Oh, and speaking of Mr. Elkanah Bannerman—"

He waved it away impatiently. "We know all about the money. Doesn't matter. But I need you to tell me something I need to hear. Miss Kagan, then?"

Rennie sighed, though she was privately astonished to hear that Lawson was aware of Elk's good deed. "Not best friends, not even particularly close friends. Lexie and I just know each other from around, in New York and L.A., and we like each other. We share a certain disdain for certain individuals who figure largely on the music scene, and it amuses us to mock them without mercy whenever the occasion presents itself, which is pretty much always. We've had lunch. Maybe dinner. And again I say, that's it. Oh, and I like to read her astrology columns. You do know she's an astrologer? Yes, a quite good one too, and I plan on hiring her to help Turk and me pick our wedding date. Now that's *really* it."

Lawson brooded over this for a few moments. "So any romantic relationship she may have had with Miss Evans—"

"News to me, as I just now said. And probably news to most people I know, if not almost all of them. But it's no big deal. Janis Joplin herself has boyfriends *and* girlfriends, though it's not common knowledge yet among the fans. So does my best friend Prax McKenna. And being as Amander

Evans was no Janis, or even a Prax, this is even less of a deal. Does it bother you, then?" asked Rennie, observing a certain renewed discomfort on his part. "That two young, attractive women were together like that?"

"Well…not bothered so much as a bit surprised, I'll admit." He shifted a little in his chair. "We're not such bigoted bumpkins up here in the hills as you seem to think, Miss Stride. Such—situations have been known to occur in our midst, and we most generally tactfully ignore them. None of our business, we figure, and it really isn't. Live and let live, though yes, I admit, some people *have* been known to make a big unpleasant deal of it, especially within their families or their churches, where you'd think they'd know better. If it makes me uncomfortable, it's nothing to do with her choice of romantic partner—I just don't like having to find out such very private things about people, especially in circumstances like these."

He smiled at Rennie's surprised expression. "So why am I a cop, you're wondering? Long story; maybe you'll hear it sometime. But not today. No—it's only that I wasn't expecting to come across that particular personal fact, and I very much dislike having to treat it as a possible motive for murder. And that's why we have brought Miss Kagan in to headquarters to answer a few more questions."

"Really? *Really*? First you torture my friends the Ravens, now you're going after my friend Lexie. Or Annadawn, as her professional name is."

Lawson looked amused. "You just now said she was only an acquaintance. And contrary to what you might think, we're not doing this simply to aggravate you and your friends. Or even your acquaintances."

"Oh, I know." Rennie studied her fingernails, a little

embarrassed. "Does she need a lawyer, do you think? I've already put one on notice for the Ravens, I'm sure I can get her to switch over to Lexie's defense if necessary."

But Lawson shook his head. "Not yet. Not anywhere near that yet. I'll let you know when, or if, it comes time to call in the city slickers."

Rennie laughed. "I appreciate it. But I don't suppose you're going to let me sit in while you question Lexie, are you, Sheriff?"

"Uh, no. You're right about that. We let you do that with the Ravens because we thought we'd get more out of them that way—which we did, except it wasn't the least bit useful—but not this time. Procedure."

"That's okay. No problem." Rennie looked more cheerful than she had all morning. "No problem at all. I'll just get her to tell me later. And you *know* she will."

"Unfortunately, I do."

Sunday August 17 - Monday August 18

Thistlefit
Joe Cocker
[The storm]
Country Joe & The Fish
Owl Tuesday (canceled)
Ten Years After
The Band
Johnny and Edgar Winter
Blood Sweat & Tears
Crosby Stills & Nash (and Young)
Paul Butterfield Blues Band
Sha-Na-Na
Jimi Hendrix (9am Monday; official end of Woodstock)

~19~

WELL, THAT CERTAINLY put a whole new slant on things, didn't it, damn it all...

When Rennie finally left the lobby, she was confronted by the spectacle of an absolute blockbuster of a downpour. So much so that she paused, awestruck, to admire it properly. Upstate New York was notorious for wild weather: blizzards that could pop up anywhere from fall to spring, blasting summertime heatwaves that parched crops, and people, to crinkly paper, even the occasional tornado. But its specialty was rainstorms, and this one was a doozy: curtains of rain being driven by battering winds, huge black clouds churning overhead and towering halfway to space, blanketing mist lowering right down into the valleys. The storm front had finally arrived: it had been racing toward them all morning, and now it was upon them. There had been a sprinkle or two earlier from its forerunning clouds, while Rennie was in town dealing with the Ravens and then having her nice lunch—until it was spoiled by Loya Tessman—but there had been no indication that something like this was in store.

She stood in the motel entrance for a while, watching along with numerous others who didn't care to brave the onslaught yet. When after a reasonable interval the storm did not appear to be letting up, Rennie went back to her room and changed into her emergency rain gear: the olive-drab rubberized Army-surplus raincoat she'd worn in college, one of Turk's summer sweaters, bought to cope with the *English* summer, old jeans, worn sneakers for the puddles and mud, a colorful Ukrainian scarf tied over the front of her pinned-up hair.

Congratulating herself for having come prepared, she turned up the cuffs of her jeans, put up the raincoat hood and dashed out of the motel, gasping as the thirty-degree temperature drop hit her and the rain slammed down on her with the force of a water cannon. God, those poor kids in the festival field, who had nothing to keep this off them… it would be like water torture, billions of tiny aqueous fists hammering them into the mud. She managed to get to her car, though not without getting soaked from the knees down, then sat there for awhile as the deluge bounced off the Mustang's roof. It seemed as if all the water in the world had decided to land on Sullivan County at once; the air was so saturated with moisture that it was actually hard to breathe without inhaling a faceful of rain, the vicious little drops so close together it was like being under a waterfall, pelting like stones and turning into mist when they hit the ground. The rain might raineth every day, but this was getting ridiculous…

Trying not to hydroplane, Rennie drove slowly and carefully through the sheets of water shimmering across the road, and arrived at Yasgur's farm not long thereafter. The crowd was huddled down right in place—there was nowhere else they could go, though some had retreated to the woods or into any tent that offered cover, and a few techs had even taken refuge under the stage and the footbridge and any other structure they could find. But the main mass of the crowd looked like a giant carpet of bright, soggy confetti spreading outward from the stage—though at least the enforced shower was rinsing off the mud—and Rennie's heart went out to them. This would go down in history as not a mere downpour but an epic affliction, on the order of the Ten Plagues of Egypt—first famine, now flood and storm. Hopefully there wouldn't be a rain of frogs as an encore.

As usual, her parking luck was in, and she managed to score a space in the performers' area—though that distinction was long since vanished, and now anyone parked anywhere they could find themselves a space—right at the intersection of Hurd and West Shore Roads, then ventured out of the car. Tearing as fast as she could through red mud already ankle-deep, and praying she didn't fall into it, she arrived, breathless, at the pavilion, where pretty much everyone who could cram under the canvas roof was already there, sheltering from the storm. She found a chair in a corner and huddled with some hot tea for a while, wishing the meditation yurt wasn't still off-limits behind its scene-of-crime tape so she could go and have a look, or maybe even meditate. Not that it could have told her anything, but still, you never knew—though it was probably under water or collapsed by now. So she drank her tea, and thought about what she had just now learned.

Well, well. She hadn't had a *clue* about Lexie and Amander, that was for sure; nobody had, or she'd have heard about it before now and not have looked like an idiot in front of Sheriff Lawson. They had obviously been incredibly careful and discreet, and good for them that they'd managed to pull it off. Far from being the golden drug-infused heaven of utter grooviness fans fondly imagined it, the rockerverse could show itself as an incestuous, backstabbing, gossip-ridden place, and pretty much nobody was able to keep anything of a secret personal nature away from its claws for very long. Truth be told, though, not many members of the rock scene ever wished to: she and Turk were almost unique in that.

For a moment Rennie's soul was buffeted by the hot winds of envy: how nice it would have been if she and Turk had been able to do as much as Amander and Lexie apparently had been able to do, and have kept their own relationship away from prying eyes. True, back in L.A., they had been spared gossip and public notice—for the whole first month of their idyll. Too bad that little groupie had turned up dead in their bed and blown their privacy all to hell forever…though of course it had been far worse for the groupie than for them, her being dead and all, and *really* forever. Poor Citrine. Or was it Amethyst? She couldn't remember, and was briefly troubled to realize that she couldn't. Really, she should be able to, it was only a year and a half ago…

With an effort, she grabbed the reins of her runaway self and pulled it over before she lost her stirrups and came out of the saddle. Getting back to Lexie and Amander: as she had said to Lawson, it was no big deal. Yet, in some respects, it really was. If not, then Janis and her girlfriend Peggy, and Prax and her occasional belles, and all those stories floating around about Jagger or Lennon or other big stars being gay, or bi, or at least experimental—if it really *were* no big deal, then everybody in rock who was so inclined would be a whole lot more open and up front about it than they were.

As it was, nobody knew for sure except people who were really clued in or actually personally involved, though denizens of the rockerverse got to see a lot more of what was going on than the average fan did. Would it make a difference? It might make some, Rennie conceded, refilling her cup from the thermos she'd been foresighted enough to have brought, though probably not enough to turn off the millions of worshippers, most of whom would either think it was cool or else wouldn't give a damn one way or another. It might freak some people out, yeah, maybe; might make the labels nervous, definitely; might provide still more ammunition for the haters and bigots and Republicans and other people who were already down on rock and rockers, absolutely.

Still, Amander's personal life seemed largely irrelevant; at least nobody had found any connection so far. And basically, as Sheriff Lawson had also said, it was no one's damn business, unless of course it had something to do with her death. Which they still had no motive for, or even any cause. She pursued it a little farther in her poor aching head. So: Amander had messed around with Ned, apparently merely for the hell of it, or the thrill of it. Melza had found out and had been furious, and rightly so. Ned had found Amander's body in the meditation tent, and Melza had claimed she'd killed her, and then Ned had claimed *he'd* killed her. Which obviously, unless they were both spectacularly good liars and the bluffiest bluffers who had ever bluffed, meant that neither of them had killed her, and the police apparently agreed, however reluctantly.

On the other side of the equation, Amander and Lexie had been having a quiet romance, and Lexie had sent love letters to her, which Amander had still had in her possession when she died. All according to Sheriff Lawson, who'd seen the letters and had brought Lexie in for questioning on the strength of them. Letters that maybe Lexie wouldn't like being made public? The ex-couple were both present at Woodstock, and had been at pains to ignore each other's presence—at least no one had actually seen them together. They were certainly not sharing a bed, or even a room, and Elk Bannerman his own self hadn't known about the relationship. Correction, Rennie reminded herself: Elk hadn't *said* he knew anything about the relationship, at least to her. And he did have goons at his disposal. And there had been bruises on both women.

But nothing seemed to indicate that either the label president or the astrologer would have had any reason to kill the singer. Elk might be vaguely embarrassed, being a gentleman of the old school, for whom such things as lesbian affairs simply didn't exist, but he would never have killed off an investment—at least not before it had paid out—and he would never have killed a woman, or ordered her killed. That wasn't code. As for Lexie: she might be hurt, she might be angry, she might feel betrayed—they didn't know enough yet to theorize—but murder? No. Lexie was too gentle and too smart for that. And yeah, yeah, Murder Chick knew that even smart and gentle people could be driven to homicide; she'd certainly seen enough of it personally. She just didn't happen to think that it was the case here. Still...

She looked up as someone paused beside the table, and lifted her thermos cup in salute. "Well, Kaiser, seems like Annadawn's predictions about this little carnival are more on the money than yours are. Disaster, doom, gloom. Though you were both right on the mark about the rain. What do you have to say about that?"

Kaiser Frizelle smiled, apparently untroubled by her gibe. "Even a blind chicken finds the occasional tasty corn kernel, Rennie. But I still stand by my own charts."

"You seem uncharacteristically charitable about Lexie scoring big with the astrological accuracy." Rennie looked narrowly upon him. There was certainly no love lost between Kaiser and Lexie, but this was a little strange, for him to be so calm about it all.

"I would have thought you'd be more concerned that your own prophecies be proved right, after all," she continued, watching him with perhaps more attention than the subject warranted.

He waved an indifferent hand. "That is, if you'll forgive me saying so, a very typical and short-sighted view, common to mundanes who are too blind to see what the planets reveal. I would have thought better of you. But I'm not one for cheap triumphs. In the end, you'll see."

He began to turn away, smiling rather maliciously down upon her. "After all, you're the one who should be concerned the most, yes? Murder Chick, I mean. I understand you haven't been able to come up with any solutions to the deaths...perhaps you'll find them among the Houses. I'd be happy to advise." He halted and turned back. "Oh, my manners. How's Turk? I heard about what happened."

Rennie continued to gaze up at him, her face severely neutral. "He's fine," she said after a while. "Completely recovered and safe at home. No problems."

"Good to hear. Good to hear. Do give him my best."

"I'll do that," she said, but only to his retreating back.

After Kaiser had left, Belinda Melbourne came ambling over to sit down at the table. She listened as Rennie recounted what had transpired that day and the night before, competently and dispassionately laying it out, one journalist to another, and then she somberly agreed.

"It probably *wouldn't* have made any difference to Amander if people had known she was bi—and why should it, it certainly hasn't to Prax or Janis or anybody else. But maybe it would have made a big difference to Lexie."

"You think? Would it have affected her work?" Again Rennie considered. "Probably not. Her so-called reputation? Possibly, but apart from her, who would really care? She wouldn't lose work because of it, not even with those glossy women's magazines who carry her column; they'd probably think it was groovy. Looking at it from the Amander side, Elk wouldn't care one way or another, so he's right out as a suspect, despite his mobbiness—why would he or his goons, and *yes*, I *admit* it, he has goons, rub out a brand-new signing and take the loss? He was trying to replace Tansy, and Amander hadn't done anything yet to put her in that kind of position. So, what then? If her thing with Lexie was the only motive for Elk's having her murdered, if it *was* murder—wouldn't it make more sense to rub out Lexie instead?"

"It would," agreed Belinda. "So, not Elk. Right. As that rather hunky sheriff told you, there were letters, which is physical proof, and they might have gone public. Young Amander did seem to enjoy flexing her fangs in people. You said she was actually threatening to publicly accuse Ned Raven of raping her, when *she* was the one who came on to *him* for sexytimes. And she was only amused when Melza wanted to scratch her eyes out, as indeed Mel should have. So our Kiwi songbird was a player and a tease and a mean little bitch, basically. Maybe she was pulling the same crap with Lexie, only Lexie reacted a bit differently from Ned and killed her to keep their secret."

"It could have happened like that," said Rennie, nodding. "Nobody likes to have their personal life out there for everybody else to judge and lie about and look at and paw over, especially if said personal life is a bit out of the ordinary, and I speak from weary experience when I say that. I don't think Lexie did it. But if she *did* kill her, *how* did she kill her? I do not know, and neither does anyone else. Except of course the actual killer."

Belinda shrugged. "What do you plan on doing to try and find out?"

"Talk to Lexie, certainly, when the fuzz are finished with her, and if they don't arrest her. But it would be really nice if I could come up with something big, and shut off an investigation before yet another friend of mine is arrested. A really solid, socked-in, locked-in motive would be great. But this isn't the one I was hoping for—oh, look who's here."

Rennie brightened as several more of their friends, drenched as baby ducklings, came into the pavilion and over to join them: Gerry and JoAnn Langhans, Liz Williams, Theo Lintern. She would have been happy to talk about the festival, the weather, even Turk, simply to get her mind off everything else, but they were all in the midst of a heated biz discussion, so she sat back and listened.

"Toby Secora from Stoneburner," said Gerry, filling Rennie in on their topic of debate. "The rest of them aren't here, but he came on his own for fun—he just told me that they sold the rights to 'Puddintane' for a chocolate-pudding commercial. He seemed very pleased about it."

"Son of Jor-El!" Rennie swore, explosively and creatively. "That's a *nice* little song, and it doesn't deserve being sold to push pudding. Not that I don't love chocolate pudding as well as the next person, and probably even more. But really!

You'd think the whole band would have died of disgrace on the spot. Especially Owen Danes."

"Owen's idea to begin with, Toby said," remarked JoAnn. "But they're one of those bands that share and share alike, so all of them had to agree to it. Which according to Toby they were all delighted to do. Really big bucks, he says. Which is great for them, of course. But it's a shame, really. That *was* a very nice little song."

"Owney ought to be ashamed. In fact, he ought to be put in the stocks for it, so we could all throw rotten tomatoes at him. I'd be the first one winding up for the pitch." Rennie was really steamed. "Okay, 'Puddintane' isn't any 'Ruby Tuesday' or 'Strawberry Fields' or 'The Banks of the Lethe', but something like this marks the thin edge of the wedge. If a band isn't ashamed to sell a good song, then they won't be ashamed to sell a great one."

"Pray, then, that we don't live to see 'Strawberry Fields' sold to flog jam, or 'Tuesday' put to work pushing, oh, let's say, precious gemstones," said Theo. "Though perhaps Strider wouldn't mind that last quite so much."

Rennie grinned. "Perhaps she wouldn't. But really no. It's a great and perfect song and I'd hate to see it suffer such a fate. Though it would be big fun to trash Mick and Keith for it if they did."

"Stoneburner clearly has no honor and no shame at all," said Liz gloomily. "I have no idea how they make the art they do and yet can still commit something as crass as that."

"Other bands manage not to sell out," Belinda agreed. "You won't catch the Dead shilling for corporate products. The British bands don't, at least not ones like the Budgies or Lionheart or the Beatles or Cream or the Kinks. And Janis would only do it for Southern Comfort—in fact, she already has, informally, purely by virtue of the fact that she drinks it so publicly, and the company gave her a lovely fur coat for it by way of reward, along with their eternal thanks for all the fine free promotional work. Though I guess that to her it wasn't work at all. It would have cost them a bundle more if they'd actually hired her to pitch it."

Rennie laughed. "Well, Janis is Janis, and she was really selling herself, not a song, so what does that make her? As for our friends across the pond, the Budgies would sooner be thrown in the Tower than hawk one of their songs for commercial use, as would all those others you mention, and if they ever do, that's the day they officially forfeit rock-legend status. Can you imagine Donovan or Dandiprat licensing their songs to peddle fish and chips? The Who haven't sold out, ha, like their album title says, not yet anyway, but I've heard Pete say that he doesn't give a damn what people do with his songs, as long as he gets paid for it. He doesn't consider the songs icons or shibboleths or anything like that; they're just, I don't know, like particularly valuable potatoes that he can sell for any and all purposes. Kinda sad and creepy."

Theo nodded. "Still, I have a terrible feeling we'll be seeing a lot more of it, which is much sadder and far creepier. Though even the Airplane did some radio spots for Levi's jeans, if you recall, before they hit it really big."

"That's true," said Gerry, "but at least they didn't prostitute an actual song of theirs to do it, it was only some weird thing they made up for the spots. And they hit it big in spite of the pimping, not because of it. And look at the Doors turning down Buick using 'Light My Fire.' The three musicians had signed off on it, but when Morrison found out he had a fit and threatened to take a sledgehammer to a

Buick onstage. Which would have been a nice little piece of performance art, come to think of it."

"Didn't Turk once threaten to do the same, Rennie?" asked JoAnn, all of them laughing at the image.

"He did," said Rennie with a reminiscent grin, "a few years back, before we met, when he was in a similar situation with 'Home Before Dark' and some other damn car company. He told me all about it: he informed the car people that if they didn't let him out of the deal—which he and Rardi as songwriters had *not* approved, only Francher, as manager—he was going to drive one of their cars onto the field at Lionheart's next stadium gig and fire a machine gun into the gas tank, until the hunk of junk exploded in flames. Or perhaps he said a rocket launcher. Anyway, neither commercial happened. And neither act of automotive mayhem, either. A good thing, probably."

"They do own the songs, though," Liz pointed out, quite correctly, after everyone had drunk to Turk's and Jim's excellent threats. "They wrote them, after all. They should be able to do what they want with them, or at least to keep other people from doing things they *don't* want them to do with them. Even if, much as I hate to say it, that means using them as hymns at the shrine of Mammon."

Rennie sighed. "Oh, I know. But those songs are the soundtrack of our lives. People listen to them, work to them, cool out to them, party to them, get stoned to them, make love to them, give birth to them, for all I know even die to them. It seems to me that selling them to push diapers or orange juice is…ignoble. It's not as if Stoneburner needs either the money or the exposure, and they're only going to garner a lot of bad feeling and loss of cred because of it. Fans don't like bands doing that sort of thing."

"Well," said Gerry, "we probably had better steel our souls and gird our loins and grit our teeth to hear 'Blowin' in the Wind' used to peddle air freshener. It's bound to happen sooner or later."

"It's the beginning of the end," said Liz disconsolately. "Or the end of the beginning. Is there no respect left for *anything*?"

~20~

After everyone had dispersed yet again, whooshing off excitedly in all directions, like jets peeling off from formation or billiard balls hit by the cue, Rennie sat on alone again, thinking some more. Liz had kindly given her some copies of Queen Anne's Fan, the British magazine she wrote for, but she was disinclined at the moment to read them, and had stuffed them into her shoulderbag for later. The discussion about selling rock songs for cheap commercial gain had put her in a cranky temper—not to mention she was still ticked off about her encounters with Sheriff Lawson and Agent Dorner—and she didn't want to inflict herself on anybody else at the moment. Especially she didn't want to encounter any artists just now, for fear she'd slap them senseless for faults as yet uncommitted—a little spot of pre-emptive criticism.

But it was an iffy situation, the one she and her friends had been discussing. On the one hand, she could perfectly well see that the people who wrote the songs had the inalienable right to do whatever they pleased with them, and if they were handsomely paid for it, so much the better—artists deserved every penny they could score, and then some. On the other hand...she and millions of other rock fans loved those songs, and it cheapened both the love and the music itself to hear the songs employed for tacky exploitative purposes.

The corporations were already cynically milking the counterculture for what they thought they could get out of it: co-opting the music that was its driving force seemed like a smart marketing move to those weasels. And for them, it probably was: they couldn't care less about the music or the feelings behind it or the artists who created it. For them it was only, always, about the money, and if ever it reached the point where it was only about the money for the bands too, that would be the point where Rennie Stride and rock and roll parted company for good and aye.

But what if, just f'rinstance, politicians likewise decided to try to climb on the bands' wagons? What crimes and aberrations might lie down *that* road, what sins against the Holy Ghost? Oh, the horror, the horror. Democratic pols might be marginally acceptable, at least some of them, but, say, worst case scenario, Richard Nixon tried to glom onto one of Turk's or Praxie's songs, to curry favor and sham hipness with the under-30 set? No. Just...no. True, it was a nightmare most unlikely to happen, given the parties involved, but you never knew what scum like that might try, in their desperation for youth votes. Though actually, on further consideration, Rennie would pay good money to watch *that* little scenario unfold: any politician of whatever stripe who presumed to try using rock to pimp himself and his policies would be taken apart, into teeny tiny pieces, as if at the fangs of a swarm of piranhas, by every hip newspaper and magazine and radio station in the land, and she would be right there in the forefront of the disassembly crew, wrench in hand. Some things could simply not be allowed to exist in a just world.

She shifted in the wooden chair, struck by the thought. What if that *were* a possible motive, though? For murder. How would that play out? Not as motive for Amander's murder, as she was a solo act and didn't yet have any hits anyway, but maybe there had been dissension in the ranks of Owl Tuesday over selling a song? She tried to recall what their hits had been. They'd never had a huge chart-topper, but a handful of their songs had made into the Top 20 and even one or two into the Top 10. They were a catchy band, not poppy but decidedly hook-oriented; she could easily hear their biggest singles put to commercial use, no question. Perhaps Cory Rivkin had planned to sell one, or not sell one, and the rest of the band had disagreed with him and so had, well, remixed him right out of the picture, as the easiest solution to the problem. Plus his three bandmates were among the few who knew about his peanut problem. She would have to find out how the Owls had shared their music publishing: if, like Lionheart, the songwriters alone got the money, that wouldn't make for much of a motive, necessarily, unless someone was simply jealous or angry and had killed Cory accordingly, out of pure spite, or even mere disapproval.

But if, like some other groups, especially the hippier ones, they went equal shares no matter who wrote the songs, crediting all published work to the band rather than to the individual songwriter, then that might very well bring murder into the mix. If someone wanted to sell a song they all had rights in, and the rest didn't want to see it sold, or if the situation were reversed and they all were hot to sell save for one lone noble principled holdout…who's to say what might not have been done in the name of music, which is really to say in the name of property rights? Which is what most crime was all about, when you got right down to it.

She shivered suddenly. The downpour had let up a bit from deluge status, but it was still cold and wet and windy—the white tablecloths were flapping like flags of surrender, and plastic cups and plates were flying off the tables onto the ground—and she found herself wishing for drier feet and warmer socks. Alas, the auxiliary footwear supply was back at the motel. Or was it? No, she'd flung a few things, including spare shoes and socks, into the back seat of the Mustang before leaving yesterday. How downright foresighted of her! She could easily slog over to fetch them and bring them back here to the pavilion to change—her feet could hardly get any wetter than they already were, on the walk to the car, and then she'd have nice comfortable unsoaked ones.

Getting up from the table, Rennie saw Lexie Kagan standing uncertainly in the pavilion entrance, where she had apparently just been denied admittance by the hippie guards on duty. Hey, *that* wasn't right: it looked as if orders had been issued to keep her out, how mean was that. Also the buzz of conversation among the tables fell off noticeably as heads turned round and stares grew hostile or judgmental: obviously the gossip about her and Amander had already made the rounds, and, from the look of the looks she was getting, the news about the police questioning too.

Clearly rattled, and unsure what to do next, Lexie stepped back hesitantly, her face reflecting her hurt and dismay to be suddenly persona non grata when her guest pass had worked perfectly fine before. Seeing this, Rennie immediately dashed across and pulled her inside, ignoring the guards' protests and glaring at anyone whose gaze crossed hers in a way she didn't care for. Thankfully, hippies were easy to intimidate. All you had to do was be more forceful on your trip than they were on theirs, which was laughably effortless of achievement, since most of them didn't even know what their trip was to begin with, or if they were even on it. Or alive at all. Clueless weeds.

Refilling the tea thermos from the big urn on the buffet table, she led the still very shaken Lexie over to the little dressing-room trailer that Prax had commandeered the night before, beyond the pavilion itself but within the wire security fence, where many such trailers and tents dotted the slope. Sitting her friend down on the steps, Rennie enfolded her in a shawl someone had left behind and thrust the warm thermos into her cold hands, sharply reminded as she did so of a time when Prax had done the same for her a few years ago. But back then she had just been almost hurled over a cliff to her death in the Pacific Ocean, so this present situation was a tad bit different.

"So," she said then, and Lexie raised startled guilty eyes, as if she were a scolded puppy, though Rennie's tone had been light. "You might have let me know about it, really. You and Amander, I mean. I'm not Annadawn, I don't get these things delivered to me daily through the power of the zodiac. I need to be told."

"I know," said Lexie humbly. "And I *should* have told you. Of all people. Once things started—happening. I knew you were working on the murders, and maybe I could have helped. But..."

"But?"

Lexie shrugged helplessly. "The night before the festival started, we were both in the motel, Amander and me, though obviously we weren't staying together, since she'd told me two weeks ago she didn't want to be with me anymore. Anyway, she saw me in the hallway, and she came to my room and told me about her and Ned Raven. I was really upset, and very surprised. There was no reason for her to throw it in my face like that, except only to hurt me. And then she said we—us—that what we'd had wasn't any more romantic or real than it had been for her with Ned. That she'd screwed him just to get attention and make trouble and hurt him and his wife, that she got off on it; and that she had hooked up with me for pretty much the same reasons. She said that was why she'd insisted we keep it a secret, so that now she could tell everyone she'd broken up with me because I was such a loser. She actually laughed about it, as if I'd been so stupid to take it seriously. She was the first woman I'd ever been with. I was crazy about her," added Lexie simply, looking at Rennie. "But she wasn't a very nice person after all, was she. It was as if I'd never really known her. And then—"

"And then she was dead," finished Rennie gently, when Lexie seemed unable to continue. She unwillingly called to mind the vibe she'd gotten off Amander, there at Elk's party—the sense of coldness, the cynical appraisingness, the way she'd dismissed Rennie and flaunted herself at Turk. Yeah. Not very nice at all. Still... "Doesn't matter how nice or not nice she was, she didn't deserve to die."

"No! Of course she didn't! But that sheriff found some of my letters to her in her suitcase, and that's when they picked me up and brought me to town to talk. Interrogate. I just got out, and I came straight here, I don't know why... the way everybody looked at me, and wouldn't let me into the pavilion... I didn't even know she had those letters with her; I mean, why would she?"

Why indeed. The girl certainly didn't seem the sentimental type, not like Lexie herself. And Rennie had noticed that there was no mention of reciprocal letters from Amander to Lexie; perhaps there had been none, which lack hardly surprised her.

"Were you trying to get back with her or anything? Is that maybe why she brought the letters?" *Or maybe was she trying to frame you for something, like murder, when it was really suicide?* For an instant, Rennie felt as if she were on the verge of some great Eureka! moment; then it vanished like a soap bubble as Lexie shook her head.

"No, not at all. I'd given up. She knew that. It was all just to hurt me. And it makes no sense. When we talked, she was cold and nasty and as mean as a snake. That's when she told me it hadn't meant anything." She looked defiantly at Rennie. "I'm not stupid, Strider, I know how it looks for me. Especially since there don't seem to be any other suspects. Thanks to you!"

"You mean Ned and Melza Raven?" asked Rennie calmly. "You wouldn't want them to be accused if they're innocent, would you? No, I can't believe that."

"No, of course I wouldn't." All of a sudden Lexie looked exhausted and defeated and in pain, and Rennie's heart went out to her. "She's dead, Rennie, and I loved her. At least I thought I did. Or that I could. Or might. And that she loved me back. And nobody seems to care that she's dead, or cares that *I* care."

"Now that's not true." Rennie gently pulled the shawl closer about Lexie's shaking shoulders. "People do care. About her, and about you too. But nobody knew that you and Amander were together, and now that they do, well, you'll see. The sheriff didn't give you a hard time, did he?" she added, with sudden sharpness. "Because if he did—"

"Oh, no, no, he was really polite and very nice. Considering he was asking me, basically, if I'd murdered my ex-girlfriend. Though he did wonder why we both had bruises on our arms."

"Why did you?" asked Rennie promptly.

"I don't know why Amander did, unless it's from whoever did, you know, hurt her, but I got mine when I tripped over my cat, at home, and fell into the coffee table." Lexie burrowed deeper into the warmth of the shawl, and then into the comforting circle of Rennie's arms, and then she started to cry. "He really thinks *I* killed her—I would *never…*"

"Oh, sweetie, I know you wouldn't! And everybody else knows too. And even Sheriff Lawson knows. Don't cry….no, on second thought, you cry as much as you like, you'll feel better for it. I'm right here."

When Lexie was finished with weeping, for the moment at least, she sat up and shrugged off Rennie's comforting arm, and gave her comforter a quivery smile.

"Thank you," she said. "You were right. I do feel better. I don't know why I should, but I do."

Rennie smiled back at her and passed some tissues from a nearby box. "It nearly always works. Something about brain chemicals." Well, it had worked with Melza, hadn't it? She'd give Lexie a Valium, as she'd done for Mel, but Lex would probably collapse right there if she dropped one now. At least Rennie hadn't had to sing this time. Still, eyeing Lexie as she worked at composing herself, Rennie thought she was strong enough for a bit of a tease.

"So, the planets didn't give Annadawn the Great and Powerful any kind of warning about this? Some fair-weather friends they are!"

Lexie managed a laugh, as shaky as the smile had been but a real one nonetheless. "You remember what I told you at the Sovereign brunch? Interpretation is everything. I saw some bad things, as I said, but I certainly wasn't seeing anything like *this*. There's a very good reason astrologers don't read their personal charts."

"Huh." Rennie unscrewed the top of the thermos, which Lexie had set aside while she wept, and poured out the steaming-hot beverage into two clean cups Prax had left on a shelf inside the trailer door. "The way doctors don't treat family or friends, I guess. Or why the shoemaker's kids always go barefoot... Here, drink this, it will make you feel better some more. Much more betterer, as Turk claims he used to say as a little boy, though personally I doubt he was ever ungrammatical in his life. The English and their everlasting godforsaken tea..."

The glimmer of a real smile then. "That's what you get for taking up with English nobility."

Rennie grinned in return. "Hey! I only took up with *one* noble English! And really he took up with *me*, you know. He was the one who made the first move."

"Which, the way I heard it, you didn't exactly rebuff with scorn."

"And why should I have?" observed Rennie, still smiling. "We were both grownups, perfectly capable of making our own decisions based on our own reasons and parameters. And we did. Like any other couple who made epic world-shaking endless love the night they met and moved in together the next morning. It's purely extra that he's going to be a duke one day and I'm going to be his duchess."

Color was coming back into Lexie's white little face, and also normal human curiosity. "And you're down with that now, are you? I seem to remember hearing some complaining and bewailing, a while back."

"You might have thought you did," said Rennie, mock-bridling, seeing that Lexie had drunk off her cup, and pouring her some more—tea was better for her than Valium, and so was prattle about other people's problems, even if it did have to be about Turk. "I was actually complaining and bewailing more about how he was a rock star and how *that* was going to adversely affect our life together, much more so than his eventual dukeliness. But we sorted it all out. And now we're fine. But we're not you and Amander, are we. It doesn't really matter if people know all about us, though certainly we would both prefer it otherwise."

"And Turk's not dead," said Lexie unthinkingly, and didn't see Rennie try to cover up a flinch the size of the moon. "But I don't know what to do now. I don't want to go back to my room, but that sheriff said I should stick around for a day or two after the festival, in case."

"Not a problem. Lionheart's motel rooms are empty; they all left on Saturday, but the rooms are paid up until Tuesday. If you need a place to crash, you're more than welcome to use one of them. I gave some away yesterday afternoon to other people who needed them, they'd been sleeping on any couch or floor they could find, even in their cars. There's still two or three left; we had eight altogether, arrogant entitled space hogs that we are. You'd be in a nice cozy little isolated corner of the motel, among friends, and you wouldn't have to see anybody else if you didn't feel like it. I'm staying on myself at least until tomorrow afternoon; it all depends on—" She put the verbal brakes on, but Lexie had been caught in the crosswalk.

"On whether the murders are solved. It's okay, you can say it. I want to see the murderer caught as much as you do. More. And yes, I *would* like to move down there, please, if you're sure it's okay. I don't want to have to sleep where Amander said those things to me and now she's gone."

Rennie put her hand on Lexie's arm and squeezed it gently. "Then you don't have to."

Having sent Lexie back to the motel to switch rooms—driven by the imperturbable Car Darch, who had private instructions not to let his newest charge out of his sight—Rennie seized the opportunity to splash her way down to the security trailer and make a phone call to Turk. Strictly speaking, she had no business tying up one of the festival lines with a personal call, but the people in the trailer had seen her with Sheriff Lawson and with Marcus, and they probably thought she was conferring on some hot new clue or piece of evidence.

Well, she wasn't about to inform them otherwise. But no; she was merely seeking refuge in hearing Turk's voice, the first time they'd talked since she'd left him in their bedroom on Saturday morning, mostly asleep. Which spoke impressively for his recuperative powers, as now he sounded much more like his usual, and lordly, self.

"When are you coming home? I need you here to soothe and comfort my fevered brow."

"You have a fever?" she asked sharply. "Since when? How high? Are you taking aspirin for it? Alcohol rubs? Drinking enough fluids? Did you call the doctor? Where the hell are Francher and Ares and Christabel, damn their eyes, they're supposed to be taking care of you, they're probably out carousing in Chinatown—"

He finally got a word in across her torrent of concern. "No fever, no. And I'm being looked after like an ailing emperor, so don't worry yourself on that score. I didn't mean to alarm you. I was just speaking figuratively. Well, just whingeing and feeling sorry for myself. I'm perfectly okay—though, honestly, completely knackered. And I bet you are too."

"Oh, I'm getting little naps here and there. I'm doing fine, really. I hope to be home by tomorrow night, and then we'll be together until the tour starts up. The festival looks to be running over into Monday morning, and I really want to stay to hear Jimi. But I don't think most of the crowd will stay along with me—people are leaving already, though more people are arriving for the last night. More outgo than inflow, so yeah, the audience is draining steadily away. People are tired of being cold and wet and hungry, and frankly, there's not much compelling left to stay for but CSNY and, as I said, Jimi. Most of the bands themselves are lighting out for the territories, once their sets are done with: the Dead couldn't leave fast enough—came off the stage and jumped into their getaway cars and never looked back."

"Following our fine example, no doubt."

"You guys were smart to scarper, let me tell you. Praxie left, too; I told her to go, they have that gig next week up at Tanglewood to get ready for. She drove down to the city with Juha and Bardo; she should be turning up there momentarily, if she hasn't already, which will make Ares happy. If the guys need a place to crash for a couple of nights, they can stay there too, right? You won't mind? Good… More than anything, though, I need to get this murder thing worked out before the circus leaves town. And Ned and Melza both confessing to a murder they didn't do did *not* help."

"They really should know better than that, the prats," Turk sympathized. "After all this time observing you in action on two separate continents, or I should say one continent and one island nation off the coast of another continent, you'd think they'd have more sense. And speaking of having sense—before this conversation proceeds any further, madam, know that I know exactly what you're doing up there. And I want it to stop."

"Why, whatever do you mean, my lord?"

"You're messing about with up-close and personal danger again. Don't try to deny it, we both know you are. Which is bad enough, even though I'm used to it by now, or should be. But I hear from impeccable sources that you're actually trying to hunt down the person who slipped me the downers, and—how did you put it? Oh yes, I believe it went thusly: 'I'm going to slit their throat with a boathook and then bathe in a tubful of their hot steaming blood'."

Rennie smiled proudly; she couldn't help it. "Well, I don't deny I said that. But how on earth did you come to hear it? Are you a wizard or something? To the best of my knowledge, you were upstairs in bed asleep when those words were spoken; did you astral-project down into the kitchen? Or had you snuck out of bed to lurk on the stairs? And my, what a good word-for-word memory you have there, Goldilocks."

"Intercom," said Turk briefly. "The workmen left it switched on when they knocked off work for their little holiday. After we came home and you got me safely tucked up, I awoke all alone in my bed of unconsciousness to hear a most interesting discussion going on, seemingly in the air. It was almost like a dream. A very fierce dream. Then I drifted off again. Listen. I love that you're so protective of me; it makes me feel all warm and gratified that you come right out and threaten for the sake of my well-being, but really, you shouldn't. Really. You shouldn't."

"In some parts of the world I could legally kill whoever was responsible."

"In some parts of the world I could legally trade you for goats. So knock it off, or I just might do that; they'd probably be a lot less trouble. If anyone is going to be doing any finding and punishing, let it be the plod. I always seem to be saying that to you, and yet somehow it still always seems to need saying."

"And just how the hell are you going to stop me if I don't? You're there, I'm here. Lotsa luck on *that* one, fella. But before I forget, you said you worked with Cory Rivkin and Owl Tuesday; did you ever hear anything about any peanut allergy he had? I spoke to the band, and they knew about it, but they didn't seem to make very much of it. Which seemed kind of weird, it being, you know, a possibly fatal condition which in fact did become fatal. Not something to be so casual about."

"No, I never heard anything along that line. And I should think I would have done; as you know, we played a month with them at the Troub, and we shared meals with a fair degree of frequency and even crashed at their house on the beach. But as well as the band being so off-hand about it, it doesn't make sense for Cory himself to have kept something as important as that as secret as he apparently and effectively did."

"Maybe he was just being a furtive little freak, then.

And look where it got him. Oh, and speaking of little freaks, how does it stand with Niles, O Man of Wrath?"

Turk's voice altered. "Ah. That. Well, at the moment we seem to be pretending that nothing ever happened, but I'm not sure how long I can keep on behaving as though he didn't unforgivably insult you, to your face, in public, in my presence, in front of friends. And I have a feeling that that wasn't the only time he's ever done so, but no, you're keeping the private insultings to yourself, aren't you. Yes, of course you are. I know you put up with it because you love me and you don't want to upset me or bring down the group unity. Thank you profoundly for that, and I love *you* for it, and we'll discuss it when you get home. As for Niles—I think he's probably perfectly willing to go on indefinitely as if it never happened, but I can't do that, and I think he knows that too. We'll sort it out between us. No pistols at dawn on the Sheep Meadow or anything along those traditional lines, I promise."

"I leave it to you, then. But fair warning: he says anything like that to me again and I get to beat him to a bleeding pulp right where he stands."

"I'll hold your coat," promised her mate. "You really aren't a gentle peace-and-love person at all, are you."

"No, I'm not, and I thank God for it. And so should you. Because you aren't either, and neither is anyone we know, actually."

"Wouldn't have it any other way. Still, peace and love—whatever happened to them, eh?"

Rennie laughed shortly. "Love will get you killed more and faster than anything else in the world. Peace too, quite a lot of the time, now I think of it. If Gandhi had tried to pull that passive-resistance crap with the Nazis instead of with you good old fair-playing Brits, he'd have been a snowball under a blowtorch."

"Thereby proving his point, however posthumously. But isn't that what we're always saying? Know your audience."

Rennie felt the words crackle through her, jolting her awareness, though she didn't know why. After twenty minutes more on the phone, hating to hang up, knowing she must, she'd extracted grudging promises from Turk to stay the hell in bed until she got home and he'd extracted nice descriptive promises from her about what she was going to do to make his time in bed worth his while, once she did get home and could join him there.

But after they'd finally and lovingly rung off, she was still thinking about what he'd said. Know your audience… good advice, but *whose* audience, and who was it who should be doing the knowing?

~21~

"ARE YOU RENNIE Stride?" came a little-girl voice from somewhere to Rennie's left rear flank.

"That depends on who's asking..."

Shutting the Mustang door, where she'd finally gone to change her damp footwear, as she'd been delayed from doing by her conversations with Lexie and Turk, she turned to see a bedraggled Woodstock waif. The child appeared to be about fourteen but was probably four years older, though not much more than that, and very pretty under the grime of the field: long dark-brown hair, damp and straggly from the downpour, flowed out from under the scarf tied across her forehead like an Apache headband. Muddy jeans and peasant shirt, bare feet and big hoop earrings, a sodden backpack dangling from one grubby paw, and of course the damn Woodstock Smile, all completed the look. What the well-dressed festival civilian will wear.

Oh, you poor sad little bun-faced thing... Rennie felt sharp sympathy, and at the same time deep thankfulness that she had connections and clout and had not had to sleep in the mire and ooze herself. Also shame for feeling so, though that part didn't last long.

"Yes, I am," Rennie swiftly self-corrected. "How can I

help you?"

The waif still seemed uncertain. "Oh, you know, I'm not really sure, but I've read about you in the papers where you solve things, and, well, you know, murders? I saw you onstage and walking around with Turk Wayland the other day, and someone told me who you were, and I thought maybe you could help—there's something that happened, so trippy, and I think the police should hear it, but I'm too scared to go tell them…I thought if maybe you could…"

"Of course I could," said Rennie in her most soothing tones, putting an arm around the girl, who was shivering a little by now, and not only with the windy chill. Her role at this festival seemed destined to be that of comforter rather than critic, but if she could maybe get something out of it, and do some helping while she was at it…

She opened the car door again. "Why don't you tell me everything? Come sit in here where it's warm and tell me all about it."

"Let's start with something simple. What is your name, please, miss?"

"Rainbow Galadriel Silverwindmistdancer," said the now de-grubbified child, with an air of great pride.

Marcus Dorner kept his eyes riveted to his notepad, so as not to have to notice Rennie struggling to control a snicker, though the snicker was aimed more at his attempt at decorum than at the grandiosely self-nomenclatured ragamuffin perched uneasily on the couch.

"Your *real* name, I mean. The one you were born with?"

"Oh…Sydell Radenberg." Sydell blew her nose on a tissue Rennie helpfully offered. "I live in Binghamton. My parents do, I mean. I hitchhiked here with some people I met. All on the back roads. The state fuzz wouldn't let us get onto Route 17, so we had to come the long way around, down into Pennsylvania and back up again."

The three of them were sitting in Rennie and Turk's motel room. After she'd heard an abbreviated version of the waif's tale, sitting in the car at the festival, Rennie had left urgent, detailed word at the security trailer for someone to tell Marcus to meet them at the motel, and had driven herself and the stray straight here. Full marks for Agent Dorner: he'd shown up quickly and unquestioningly. Yes, yes, she knew she'd promised Sheriff Lawson first crack at any information she turned up, but this kid would turn to dandelion fluff and blow away at first sight of an official lawman, however atypical and unthreatening he might be—which the calm and courteous Caskie really was, but still. So she'd summoned Marcus instead. At least she was familiar with his interrogation style, and could count on him to make it as easy as possible on everyone involved.

Awaiting his arrival, Rennie had thrust Rainbow Galadriel into a hot shower, and had the motel housekeeping staff wash and dry the mud-caked garments while she found something for the girl to wear in the meantime. Likewise, she had loaned her a hairdryer and comb, and given her a shawl and a spare pair of sturdy sandals when she shyly admitted she was cold and had nothing to put on her feet, and insisted that she have something to eat from the fridge stash. And all the while she'd been trying to push away uneasy memories of another such waif two summers ago, firmly resolving that no such similar fate would befall *this* one. She hadn't been able to save Adam Santa Monica, but by God she was going to make sure Rainbow Galadriel would be okay, no matter what...

So when Marcus arrived forty minutes later, he found a cleaned-up young Sydell in her own nice fresh dry clothes again, looking much more human than she had, and Rennie looking even more triumphant than *she* had. And he knew that look, oh yes, he knew it of old…

Rennie had quietly reassured her guest that everything was okay, that the new arrival wasn't the local fuzz and was on her side, then Marcus took over the questioning for himself, sitting on the sofa facing the girl while Rennie lounged on the bed listening carefully, still with that annoying smug air of accomplishment about her.

Okay, fair enough, she was probably entitled to it, thought Marcus, and began to put his first questions to his subject, using a warm, friendly voice carefully pitched not to intimidate or alarm.

"Miss Stride tells me you might know something about the death of Cory Rivkin the other day, Miss Radenberg. Is that true? Can you share it with us? And what made you decide to tell us?"

Sydell/Rainbow—not entirely sure at all about being addressed as 'Miss Radenberg'—glanced nervously at Rennie, who smiled and nodded encouragement. "Well—I *think* I might know *some*thing. I'm not sure. But I saw her, Rennie, with Turk Wayland, and I knew who she was, and I'd heard that she was really smart about this kind of stuff"—Rennie pridefully swelled like a puffer fish, and Marcus scowled at her until she deflated—"and anyway, there was this guy, and he gave me a peanut butter sandwich, and I ate it because I was so hungry, then I met Cory, and we started making out, and then he just—collapsed. And when everyone came over to help, I got scared and ran away. I didn't want to be blamed for anything. After that, I stayed with some other people I met, who'd come all the way from Minnesota; they have a big comfortable camping tent over by the woods, it has *three* rooms, and a screened porch and spare sleeping bags and stuff. They were expecting friends who never showed up, so they had extra things and space and they were nice enough to share. I've been crashing in the tent with them ever since. Hiding. Since it happened, I mean. I was so afraid. But I could hear the music just fine from the tent, so that was okay."

"It's all going to be all right," said Marcus quietly, though both he and Rennie had gone quite taut with excitement. "Nobody's blaming you, it's not your fault, don't worry. You're not in trouble, I promise. Okay, let's go back a bit, shall we? Who was this guy who gave you the sandwich? A friend of yours?"

Floods of tears. "No! I'd never seen him before!"

"Would you recognize him if you saw him again?"

"I don't know, he was just a guy. I wasn't really paying attention to him. He wasn't cute or anything. I think I might. Yeah, probably. Yeah, I would."

"When did this happen?" Though he knew already, from Rennie's terse outline of the situation, imparted to him outside in the hallway before he'd entered the room, Marcus naturally needed to hear the story straight from the filly's mouth; it only made sense, now that they seemed to have found the origin point of Means, Motive and Opportunity. So he was unobtrusively taking notes, and much as he hated to admit it, he had a feeling that Murder Chick was right again. As usual.

"Oh…let me think a minute, yeah, Thursday morning. The day before the festival started. We came early, to make sure we got good places to sit, but there were tons of people here ahead of us. We had to walk in all the way from Callicoon after our car overheated and died, that was where my shoes fell apart, and we had hardly any money for food, but when we got here—the people I was with, in the car—we heard that the Hog Farm was feeding anyone who needed something to eat. They're this commune from out West, really nice people. So we went over there to get some vegetable stew and brown rice and stuff, and I got separated from my friends, and then I met the guy."

"What did he look like?"

"I *told* you. Just a regular guy. Not cute or hunky. He was tall. Taller than me, anyway."

"Do you remember what he was wearing?"

"No...everybody is wearing the same kind of thing, you know, work shirts and jeans and tie-dye. He looked like that."

"How did he approach you?"

Sydell was coming more to the fore now, and Rainbow Galadriel was receding. "He was very nice and polite. He wasn't trying to hit on me or anything, if that's what you're thinking. He was walking around by the woods, over near where the Hog Farm people were, and I thought he was one of them. He started talking to me, and I told him I was still really hungry and didn't like to ask the Hog Farmers for more food when other people hadn't had any at all yet, so he gave me three whole peanut butter sandwiches. I ate one right there, and kept the others for later, just in case."

Her eyes widened with the wonder of it all, and Marcus' narrowed; Rennie looked smugger than ever. "And then he brought me to the *performers' pavilion*, so he must have been somebody, don't you think? He had on one of those badges, like the ones you're wearing, but I don't remember what his said, or what his name was. He gave me champagne and more food, fancy expensive stuff, shrimp and strawberries, I don't even know the names of some of the rest of it. It was all a lot nicer than peanut butter. And then Cory came over. They seemed to know each other, and the guy introduced me to him. I was so excited to meet a real rock star, I even have Owl Tuesday's albums at home, so when Cory started making out with me I just...and then he...he..."

More tears, and sobs, and some snorts and snuffles that were apparently meant to be words; it seemed clear that they weren't going to get anything more out of Rainbow Galadriel, or out of Sydell either, at least for a few minutes. Unless...

Rennie reached out and put a hand on the girl's arm, gently. "It really is better if you talk about it. Believe me, I know. If you don't—if you don't, it will eat you up inside. Better to get it out."

"Oh please, I can't, it's so hard to say!"

"I know it is. I know. But it's okay, I promise. It'll be easier once you get started. Just say it. It's okay. We're right here with you." Rennie took Rainbow's hand in both of hers, and the girl clung to her like a limpet with separation anxiety.

"It was horrible...you have no idea. He looked like he had a fever, all hot and flushed, and then his eyes, the whites of his eyes, oh God, it was awful, they turned bright red. And his skin got all funny-looking, sort of blotched. His lips turned blue and he couldn't breathe. Then he just... just fell over down on the ground and didn't move."

"He never said anything? Not a name or—"

"No, nothing. I don't think he could have, he was gasping so hard, trying to get air. It only took a few seconds.

Nobody realized what was happening. Then when he fell on the ground everybody came running. By then you could see that something was really, really wrong with him. When they did, I figured they could take care of him, and I kind of slipped away in the crowd." She looked at both of them, defiantly and guiltily. "Why *shouldn't* I? I didn't know him! I barely met him...we were going to go find someplace to get it on, maybe a tent or the woods. And then he was...oh God..." She dissolved again, and they let her cry herself out.

So she'd consoled three weeping chicks in twelve hours, Rennie thought—Melza, Lexie, and now Rainbow. She couldn't speak for the other two; they were grown women and they knew how to cope. But yeah, it was better that this young one didn't have to carry that around with her any longer than she had to. Truly, none of them should.

"Okay, it's pretty clear then, isn't it?" Rennie leaned forward to address Marcus as privately as she could. "I mean, this cat couldn't have gone around passing out you-know-whats on the off chance that—you know where this is going as well as I do. He had a plan, and he knew who to hit with it, and how to make it happen."

Marcus gave her a look: not in front of the child, she obviously hasn't grasped the significance of this yet. "I do know, and yes, he did, and also yes, it's no less than I've come to expect with you." He sighed and glanced at their guest, who was hiccuping now but sobbing less; even with her freshly washed hair and newly clean clothes, she looked utterly, blobbily wretched, scrubbing away tears with the back of her hand. "Miss Radenberg, again, it was absolutely not your fault, and we're very glad and grateful you came forward. Do you have someone to stay with?"

She looked at him, surprised. "Back there? At the

festival? Sure! Everyone!"

Of course. But not good enough, it turned out, to her even greater surprise. "We need a better way of staying in touch with you," said Marcus gently. "Out there, we'd never find you, and we might need to talk with you some more."

Certainly Sheriff Lawson would, and with her kindly Minnesotan hosts as well, but best not to scare her too much by mentioning *that*; she might bolt, maybe all the way back to Binghamton, if that was even where she really lived, and for sure they would never see her again. Plus there was that tiny detail that Marcus and Rennie had carefully not mentioned aloud: whoever had murdered Cory Rivkin with a peanut-butter sandwich knew that Rainbow Galadriel Silverwindmistdancer could probably identify him, and he might very well be looking to murder her in turn, with something a lot nastier, if equally final. They were all just extremely lucky that he hadn't already tried, or, indeed, succeeded: the fact that she'd been hiding in some strangers' tent since Thursday had probably saved her life.

Now Rennie leaned back on the bed again and sailed right in, with an air of having it all under control, which in many ways she did. "How would you feel about staying here, Rainbow? Not in this room, of course, but there are a couple of spare ones. My fiancé's band left yesterday, but the rooms are paid for until Tuesday checkout, you wouldn't have to pay anything yourself. I have all the keys. You could sleep in Niles Clay's room if you like. It's very comfortable, and you'd be out of the wet and the mud. The band and their girlfriends left all their passes too, so I can give you one to go on the helicopters back to the festival, and one for the pavilion, so you won't miss anything and you'd be able to get something to eat." *And not have to rely on murderous peanut-butter sarnies*... "At least then we'd know you were safe and where to find you. What do you say?"

It seemed Rainbow could find very few things to say other than Oh my God thank you so much, that would be so great, helicopters really?, the *pavilion*?, really Niles Clay's room?, *really*?, NILES CLAY???, ohmyGodohmyGodohmy*God*thankyousomuch. After a bit of this, she made a further shy request, clearly not wanting to seem greedy—did Rennie *possibly* think that Turk could please send her an autographed photo, she would have *loved* to meet him, but it was so groovy to have met Rennie, and staying in *Niles Clay's own room* oh my God how groovy was *that*. Rennie assured her that Turk would be delighted and a personally signed photo would be forthcoming, and took down the child's address. Hell, it was the least they could do to show gratitude—she'd ask Turk to sign and send a couple of albums, too.

After Rainbow Galadriel had twinkled off to her new accommodations down the hall, floating on air and clutching the key to Niles' vacated chamber, Marcus and Rennie sat in a kind of shared stupor, processing parallel thoughts. Rennie was the first to stir.

"That was a bit...unexpected. Do you think—"

"No. No, of course not. There's no reason she would have done it on purpose, or even known to do it. Peanut allergy might not have shown up right away anyway, and volunteer medical techs might not know to recognize the signs."

"Oh, I don't know. Blood-red eyeballs, blue lips, gasping for air—sounds pretty unmistakable to me."

"Nevertheless. Anaphylaxis isn't always the easiest

thing to diagnose. But he was carrying the medical alert card, which the ER people at the hospital saw, and you say that the other members of his band vouch for the allergy's virulence. A stroke of luck for us, because it'll take days, if not weeks, for the autopsy results to confirm it officially—I don't suppose the lab facilities up here in Brigadoon are exactly state of the art. And his family will want to come and claim him as soon as possible. I'd better call Lawson and see that he hears all this. He'll want to talk to the girl, and he'll need to get hold of her quick before she gets lost in the festival again, whether she means to or not. Or worse, and you know what I mean by that. Those hospitable Minnesotan campers with the nice big three-roomed tent with a porch will need to be talked to as well; shouldn't be too hard to find, if they haven't already upped stakes and headed home. In which case Lawson can notify the state police here and down in Pennsylvania to keep their eyes open for them on all highways going west. Don't worry, I'll tell him it was all your doing, so you get the credit... But you knew the victim: was his reaction to peanuts common knowledge in the rockerverse?"

"I knew *of* him," Rennie corrected. "And I don't give a rat's about the 'credit'... I met him and his band a few times and saw them play and met them a few more times, and I wrote a little piece on them once, and a couple of reviews. Turk knew him from a club in L.A. a couple of years ago, and *he* hadn't been aware of it; I asked him when we spoke a while ago. I myself never heard of any allergy, peanut or otherwise. Even the littlest bands have groupies and followers who know every single tiniest trivial thing about them; but on a more mainstream level, Cory Rivkin wasn't the kind of musician about whom such things would be widely known."

"Not like your own legendary close personal friends, you mean?"

Rennie ignored the dig. "I only mean he didn't figure largely in teenybopper fan mags, where they swoon and scream and write godawful groupie poetry and dissect every last personal detail about the object of their obsessions. I'm sure there are squealy Owl Tuesday fan stories existing somewhere in the literature of the rockerverse; I just don't happen to have seen any myself. It's bad enough I have to endure the sort of illiterate besotted gibber they write about Turk. Anyway, Cory wasn't exactly obscure: he was the drummer for a respected band that could hold their own with any act. Hey, they opened for Lionheart and didn't get booed off the stage; Turk even wanted them to open on the upcoming tour. That's nothing to be ashamed of. But you have to admit it's still a bit—"

"Convenient? Fortuitous? Coincidental?"

"All those things." Rennie fidgeted with a bit of bedspread she'd grabbed, twisting it between her fingers. "Sometimes accidents really are accidents. Even around me."

"So you say."

"I do say. But now we have a big old piece of information. And a big old clue to help with Amander."

"We do? How do you figure?"

Rennie sighed with exasperation. "Do I have to spell *everything* out? A p.b. sarnie killed Cory. What are the odds another one did the same for Amander? Not eaten, but dealt out by the very same person, who had come prepared with at least three of them at hand. As I've been thinking all along."

She saw with tremendous satisfaction that Marcus had

gone very, very still. As well he should! He really ought to have picked up on that as soon as she did, the instant Rainbow had mentioned the extra sandwiches that her benefactor had kept for himself.

"I called someone at the paper and asked them to check," she said then. "Apparently you can indeed die of peanut poisoning without even eating them or touching them yourself. You can die if peanuts were in the same box as your lunch. You can die if your favorite cookies were produced in a facility that also produces peanut snacks. You can die if a knife that has been used to spread peanut butter then slices you a piece of cake. And—wait for it, yes—if someone kisses you who has eaten peanuts or peanut products and your allergy is sufficiently potent, you could be pushing up the daisies before you even knew what hit you. Fatal kiss indeed. So now we know how Cory met his fate. I mean, we *knew* 'how'; but now we know for sure how that fate was administered."

As Marcus remained unmoving: "And I humbly submit that that is exactly what happened with Amander. She was kissed to death. Kissed to death with peanuts, just like Cory. Only we don't know if she was also allergic, and we have to find out. *Can* we find out?"

Marcus looked deeply unhappy. "I guess. But I don't know if we can find out in time. This whole shebang shuts down tonight, or more likely tomorrow morning. People have already started to go home. Let's hope our murderer hasn't split."

"He won't," said Rennie with conviction. "He—or she—will want to stick around to get the credit, out of necessity anonymously, of course. To see his cleverness rewarded by admiring, if totally negative, attention when all this goes public. That's what he's in it for. Didn't I *say* it would turn out to be a psycho? Yes, I do believe I did."

He nodded, then laughed. "At least we won't have to worry about finding young Rainbow again to make a statement. She'll spend the next day and a half in Niles's bed, kissing the sheets which I have no doubt whatsoever she will absolutely refuse to let the maid change, retrieving long black strands of hair from the pillows, weaving them into a loveknot and pressing them to her heart. She'll probably steal the Niles-employed linens and towels, too, and take them home with her."

"Whatever makes her happy, the poor little rabbit. What do you think is going to happen when she finds out she's the one who actually killed Cory Rivkin? She didn't mean to, of course, but really she did. If giving her Niles' room can help make her feel a little better before *that* comes down on her…and if it can make her a little safer as well… and make me a little less worried about her…"

Marcus gave her an odd look, which she chose to ignore. "That was very generous of you, in any case."

"Not a bit. Niles had been all 'Do Not Disturb' since early Friday evening, after he'd dropped every abusable drug known to medicine and probably a bunch that aren't, and on Saturday he was out of here like the proverbial hellish bat, zoom zoosh, as soon as he could stand up again, or so I'm told. He couldn't even stay to face Turk and Rardi, who were, and are, and will doubtless long remain, incandescently furious with him. Little skunk. I was *so* hoping that he would have turned out to be the murderer… Anyway, the rest of Lionheart decamped soon thereafter, and the roadies schlepped everybody's equipment out, and luggage too, except Turk's which is right here and I'll take that home myself, of course. Maybe Niles left behind a t-shirt or pair of silk briefs to gladden Rainbow's little fannish heart. And as I said, the rooms are all paid for, for a couple of days yet—we weren't sure how much of a rush we'd be in to get out of here, and Turk and I, and the Greens too, thought we might stay on for a few days, hanging out in the dear peaceful countryside, and then drive back to the city at leisure. Just a few quiet days before the tour gears up and we have to leave for L.A."

"And we see how well *that* plan worked out."

"Yeah... Anyway, since yesterday I've been parceling out the other empty Lionheart rooms to friends who'd been sleeping rough—Belinda Melbourne, Jay Rosevalley, couple more people. Also Lexie Kagan, who didn't care to stay in her old room, where she'd had the encounter with Amander, and who could blame her? Besides, though I certainly didn't mention it to her, she might be in danger every bit as much as Rainbow is—whoever killed Amander might think that Lexie knows something more, and decide to act on it. Same as with Rainbow. The rooms were going to waste in any case, and they might as well be comfortable, even if it's only for a night or two. I think there's still a couple left—do you need one yourself? No? Okay, only asking."

"Too kind, Mrs. Lacing." He saw her eyes flash at the ill-considered joke; he was tired, and it had just slipped out. "Sorry... It was good thinking to offer the kid one, though. I'll get Lawson to send a man here to keep an eye on her. I myself can't officially detain her, obviously, so maybe this will keep her around and—safe. As you say, accidents do happen."

"Yeah...yeah, they do."

&

Still, Rennie thought, after Marcus had taken his leave, that was surely no accident, and equally surely it was the biggest break they had had yet, and equally equally surely they both knew it. It had to mean *something*, that someone had known of Cory Rivkin's deadly allergy and had gone to all the trouble of chatting up cute young Miss Silverwindmistdancer—though the specific choice of her personally seemed a random one—and feeding her a potentially lethal weapon. Then he'd taken her to the pavilion and introduced her to one of the few people at the festival who could be harmed by peanuts to so fatal an extent—a choice anything *but* random—and had stood back to let events take their course. It was pretty much a foregone conclusion that the two chosen victims would get together: no rocker anywhere, and certainly not one of such humble status as Cory Rivkin, was going to decline a chance with a chick as pretty as Sydell Radenberg, and she was clearly a starstruck little thing, so the fact that the two had started making out pretty much on the spot and had immediate plans to get down came as no surprise.

The surprise, of course, came later. "Lips that touch peanuts shall never touch mine" had probably been Cory's mantra his whole life; but how could he have known Sydell had recently, and innocently, scoffed down a sandwich that was about to kill him stone cold dead? He probably hadn't even tasted it on her mouth; she'd said her unknown benefactor had offered her shrimp and strawberries once they got to the pavilion, and those would have taken the peanut taste away. Though not the lethal residue, obviously. Still, if you had a violent peanut sensitivity, you were often equally sensitive to other things too, and shellfish and strawberries were also right up there on the allergy hit parade...

Let's not complicate things... The unknown sandwich pusher had given Sydell a peanut bullet and then fired her at someone he knew would be affected, even killed—a potential full anaphylactic. So, murder by allergy. Plainly, Cory had been the known and intended target, and she had to admit that it was a fiendishly clever plan. But what possible reason could there be? Something personal, presumably. And how had the murderer known? She'd give a lot to know if Amander had fallen prey to the same fatal reaction; that seemed only too likely, now that they knew how it had been done. What had the researcher told her, there were millions of people with the allergy, though not that many among them who would have reacted as violently. One in a thousand, maybe. But surely Amander wouldn't have kissed Rainbow Galadriel—though she had done as much, and more, for Lexie Kagan...

Which reminded her. Now that Lexie had moved down here, and young Sydell was staying here too, she'd best get Rhino to assign a guard to the entry to the wing, and not wait on Lawson to post a cop. There was a convenient set of swinging doors that sealed the short hallway, with its eight rooms, off from the main corridor, and an Argus brute posted there could keep away anyone who didn't belong in the newly repopulated Lionheart chambers. Maybe she should check with the motel manager first...no, screw it, she'd just go ahead and do it herself. Right now.

Because she felt a definite need to protect them. Two people, both associated with the murders: who knew if they might be targets themselves? If the killer thought they could pick him out of a lineup… No, a bit of extra defense was definitely in order. She would ask Rhino as soon as she got back to the field; it wouldn't be a problem, he had enough spare muscle floating about and Ares could put it on Lionheart's standing account. They were damn lucky that Rainbow had come to them at all…they might never have known otherwise…

Weary from the day's events, knowing they were far from over, Rennie stretched out on the bed, clutching the pillow Turk's head had lain on, to consider all the possibilities so recently and so infinitely expanded…

She woke an hour later, startled and groggy, to a windy twilight and the phone shrilling on the nightstand beside her. For a confused and panicked moment, headachey, heart pounding, she was back in the morning before, when the phone had rung and she couldn't wake Turk up. Then she picked up the receiver and it *was* Turk, again and unexpected, speaking all low and sexy in her ear. Clearly he was feeling much better, and rather friskier, delighted to have caught her in the room; and he was wondering yet again when she would be coming home.

"I have to stick it out to the oh so bitter end," she said presently, and reluctantly, having given him a thorough account of recent events and receiving his repeated assurances that he had never heard one syllable about Cory Rivkin's allergy. *Oh God, I want to be home in bed with him right now soooo much, last night was the first night we've spent apart since the move to Manhattan, how in God's name am I going to manage being separated from him for this damn tour, last year's was bad enough, and this one is twice as long…* "I told Marcus this could be the big thing we needed to break the case."

She heard him laugh. "Oh, I'd give *anything* to have seen Marcus' face when you said that to him! I bet he thought he was rid of Murder Chick for good and all when we moved to New York. And now here you are again, and the poor chap has to suffer seeing you up close and personal all over again."

"Why would *he* be suffering? We were never together, not like a real couple anyway."

"And what do you suppose he now regrets about *that*? I thought he made it pretty bloody clear to us in L.A., how he feels about you. Or felt. But let's not go into it now. Anyway, I didn't mean that: I was simply referring to your apparently unending propensity to find yourself adjacent to murder. And driving Marcus nuts with it. As it were."

"It's not my fault if I—"

"I'm not saying it's your fault, my love, far from it! I simply find it endlessly droll that Marcus should repeatedly be made to realize he can't take a step without running slap into you already there, waiting for him like a spider."

"Really! I'd rather it were *you* running slap into me... with intent..."

When they finally hung up, Rennie went into the bathroom to throw cold water on herself and change for the festival's last acts. Last gasps, more likely. What she'd said earlier was true: people *were* already leaving; the crowd had noticeably thinned. There was still a very full house in Max Yasgur's pasture, though, as people had continued to arrive, even on the closing day, drawn by the TV and newspaper coverage; and since the roads were more or less clear for the first time since Thursday they had no problem getting there, though some of them had still had to walk in from miles out.

There was nothing on the Sunday bill that she herself wanted to see except Crosby Stills & Nash, making their big debut with Neil Young, and Jimi of course, who was the festival closer, as he had insisted. But given the long delays, which showed no signs of speeding up, it was now a certainty that he wouldn't get on until breakfast time on Monday morning, so he was probably kicking himself, or kicking his manager, that they had held out for closing-act status as befitted the headliner he now was. In fairness, the festival organizers, knowing that the audience was trickling away, had offered to let him go on earlier, to give him the big showcase he and his art deserved. But *everybody* here was a headliner, or most of them anyway, and as official headliner of headliners, Jimi had stubbornly refused to switch; by the time he took his fought-for place onstage, most of the fans would have left for home, so that seemed a bit self-defeating, to say the least… Still, that was his problem and his choice. No doubt he'd make the most of whatever audience he had left, whenever the hell he finally ended up performing.

As she was dressing, she suddenly wondered again about the money Ares had told her had been stolen, the money Marcus had supposedly been hired and flown in from L.A. to investigate—the money that Elk Bannerman had pretty much admitted to her his goons had tracked down and repossessed for the festival brass. Could it have been somehow connected to the murders after all?

"We don't think so," said Sheriff Lawson, when she encountered him at the security trailer and immediately put the question to him. "It seems to be an entirely separate crime, but really, the case is closed. The money was returned, and unless we get a solid lead, we're not pursuing it. There's too much else we have to deal with, and we're stretched mighty thin as it is. Did you have any more information?"

"Oh no, I was just wondering. Obviously the murders take priority, as they should. As they must."

"And the attempted murders," he added after a moment. "The 'accidents' suffered by Miss Silver and Mr. Raven, and certainly the attack on your fiancé."

Rennie stared. "I thought— The things with Ned and Sunny did seem like accidents. And Turk— You really think those were all *failed murder attempts*?"

"We didn't think that before. We do now. And Agent Dorner told us all about Miss Radenberg, and Miss Kagan too. We'll make sure they're protected. Good to know you're keeping an eye on them, though," he added, with no trace of sarcasm.

'Agent' Dorner, eh? Well, all righty then! "I hired one of Ares Sakura's guys to look out for Rainbow and Lexie. It seemed prudent. And I didn't think it was possible to prove anything about Turk's poisoning. I told you, Turk has no idea who gave him the wine; it could have been any of fifty different people, he said, none of whom he remembers. It might not have been meant for him at all."

He watched her carefully, and not without compassion. "Do you believe that? That it wasn't really meant for him? That it wasn't meant as a murder attempt?"

"...No. No, I don't believe that. I haven't believed that for a minute."

"And neither do I."

~22~

ONCE AGAIN IN the pavilion, and now it was the homestretch. The day that had begun at dawn with showers, though thankfully not until after the Airplane had flown, had finally cleared a bit around lunchtime, enough to get the stage swept free of water and a group or two on. But rain had been the motif du jour.

In the afternoon, of course, had come the real deluge, the frightening freak of atmospheric nature: the Catskill toad-strangler that went on and on and on, the one that was destined to be remembered forever after by anyone who was there, and by many more who weren't and who had only read about it in the papers and magazines, or had seen it on TV. Rain like bullets, wind like whips, the temperature free-falling thirty degrees in as many minutes—a black, dangerous, powerful storm, like something out of Tolkien.

It had ended, after what seemed like days but was only several hours. Then it had been, well, you couldn't call it *dry*, exactly, but unraining, then, for a while, and now it was pouring again. Despite Turk's nice warm sweater, Rennie was shivering in the shelter of the dressing-room trailer that she and Prax had earlier commandeered, out behind the pavilion. She listened to the rain, cold snare drums on the metal of the roof, and felt sorry yet again for the unprotected hordes out there in the field, many of whom had thrown in the towel, if only they'd had one, on Woodstock, and over the past few hours had started heading home in a steady, soggy exodus. The further dose of rain had been the last straw, and they just couldn't take any more—for them, Woodstock was over.

. At least they had only seen rain and wind, however apocalyptic... Just let there be no lightning, please God. One Zeus-sized bolt in the middle of that pasture could still take out ten thousand people—and those sound and lighting towers were all too convenient conductors.

Still, she'd earlier overheard the stage crews discussing the worsening situation. The power had had to be turned off, because the thick electrical cables hadn't been buried deep enough and the rain was washing the dirt away, so half the audience was sitting on or near live wires. The tarps that roofed the stage and the pavilion were filling up with water, like a tall ship's sails in the tropics—hundreds and hundreds of gallons that could do serious damage if they burst free at the wrong time. So stagehands were sent swarming aloft, topmast men on a frigate, to lance the sagging canvas and let the water drain through.

A dangerous feat in itself; more dangerous still, they also went up the towers to secure things there, and to shoo off the audience members who had climbed the structures hoping for a better view, or to escape the mud. Yeah, and making a really good target of themselves for those lightning bolts while they were at it...

The perils hadn't stopped there. The stage itself, waterlogged, was moving. Like a landslip, it was perceptibly shifting, slipping a little on its footings, sliding downhill.

Toward the audience. Oh great, just what they needed: the Woodstock Mining Disaster of 1969.

But the afternoon had come and gone without catastrophe. Occupied with murder business as she had been, she hadn't seen much music. Then again, there hadn't been much to see. She'd missed Gray and Prue and Thistlefit, which she did regret, and Owl Tuesday had of course canceled, which was sad; Country Joe and the Fish put her to sleep and Joe Cocker annoyed the hell out of her, so she hadn't at all minded missing them. And then had come the big rain. After it, Max Yasgur himself, dairyman now legend, stood shyly at center stage and spoke warmly to the multitudes, telling them how proud he was of them, how well they had all done, and they cheered him to the rafters, if rafters there had been. And then, like rainbow angels, a flight of helicopters came by overhead, and they were dropping daisies on the crowd, thousands and thousands of flowers out of machines that were otherwise more accustomed to dropping bombs and death.

Wrapped up with wrapping up her detectiving at the police station and motel both, Rennie had missed all that. But she was there now, and would remain until the last note sounded. By eight, when Alvin Lee finally went on with Ten Years After, the rain had started and stopped several times, though thankfully it was only intermittent drizzles now, no more epic drenchers. At least the stage was cleared and swabbed dry, and the evening's roster was proceeding, though Rennie, still preoccupied with murder considerations, was not paying much attention. Ten Years After was fine, and she liked Alvin, but the Band and the Winter brothers weren't her thing, and Blood Sweat & Tears was the weekend's one glaringly false programming note, too brassy and slick and poppy. The crowd was bored stupid by David Clayton-Thomas' poser-iffic Vegas strutting and bogus vocal stylings, as unimpressed as the Monterey fans had been with Hugh Masekela. Ah well, one dud out of the bunch wasn't bad. And of course they had all heard giants. Giants not at the top of their giantly form, true, but giants all the same.

Someone had rustled up some fresh coffee for the big urns, and Rennie had managed to get her thermos filled up with the hot, steaming beverage, black and loaded with sugar. She wrapped her hands around the steel cylinder and drank eagerly, feeling the caffeine rush waking her up. Crosby, Stills & Nash had just gone on, publicly augmented for the first time ever onstage by Neil Young. God, those boys could sing…

She was feeling rather lonely at the moment. As she'd told Turk when they spoke on the phone, Prax and the rest of Evenor had decided to head down to New York earlier that day; though Prax had nobly offered to stay and keep Rennie company in Woodstock's waning hours, Rennie had even more nobly urged her friend to go back to the city and crash at the prow house, keep Turk and Ares company instead—traffic permitting, she should have arrived long ago. On the Lionheart side, the Greens were flying back to L.A. tomorrow to sort out last-minute tour details, along with Shane and Jay-Jay. Rardi, Niles and Mick had taken advantage of the hiatus to nip home to England for a few days, and would head to California straight from there. Depending on how Turk was feeling, he and Rennie would be joining them all in L.A. for a week's worth of rehearsals prior to the tour's kick-off dates, beginning with the big Labor Day stadium show in San Diego. Presumably the matter of Niles would be addressed by the band at some point; but that was their concern, not Rennie's.

She and Turk, of course, would enjoy a brief stay in their Nichols Canyon house before the tour commenced; after the San Diego opener, Lionheart was scheduled for two shows at the Los Angeles Forum, and Turk was plotting a hit-and-run surprise appearance at the Whisky, or possibly some other Sunset Strip venue. Rennie's own plans after that were dictated by the work on the prow house and her own work: as things looked now, she'd probably follow the band to Honolulu and San Francisco, and then come home to dig in for the duration, except for those weekends when she'd fly out to join Turk wherever they could manage it.

But for now she remained here in the chilly country night. And so did a number of other friends—she hadn't been entirely abandoned. Belinda Melbourne was still here, and Rennie brightened at the prospect of more company—Marishka Erzog and her beau Bill, Sledger Cairns, Francie Nolting, plenty of others. As she looked around the pavilion, she saw numerous familiar faces, many of them artists who had performed earlier that evening. Of course Marcus was still present...and Sheriff Lawson. She stretched prodigiously, every single muscle in her body, one at a time. This had been the longest damn day in the whole entire history of days; there must have been some astrological reason for it, or maybe a few extra hours had gotten added with no one noticing.

The final countdown was on, anyway, and it wouldn't be too long before Jimi would wrap things up. And then she could slope off the back way, the county road to Liberty that she knew so well by now and that so few other festivalgoers had discovered, and pack up all her and Turk's things and then crash till the afternoon, or even evening. By then the highways should be clear, or at least clearer, and she could cruise the Quickway right down to the city; or, if that was still clogged, she could take 17B south along the Delaware, past Port Jervis and across New Jersey, which might be even better, as hardly anyone but locals knew that road was even there. Belinda could come with if she needed a ride home—for company, and also to help Rennie stay awake.

Well, provided they had found the killer by then, of course. If not... She had faith in Sheriff Lawson, but if his entire half-million-person suspect pool was vanished into the ether, then unless they caught some spectacular break she didn't see that there was much that could be done. Which was, no doubt, exactly what the murderer was counting on. Though she was still betting on him to stick around for the credits—and the glory.

Rennie saw Marcus crossing the pavilion, clearly looking for someone. Probably her. She stood up and waved her arm to attract his attention, and he altered course to arrive at the little trailer. She made room for him on the step, drawing her feet up and moving inside, and he sat down out of the drizzly mist.

He didn't speak for a few moments, listening to the ethereal harmonies floating from the stage. Then: "What is it?" she asked, seeing his face.

"Your little protégée Miss Silverwindmistdancer was attacked in the motel. She was coming out of her room—the room you gave her, the room we both thought was such a good idea for her to stay in for her own safety—and someone grabbed her from behind and started dragging her down the hall toward the door to the parking lot. With no good intent, I have no doubt."

"My God! Is she okay?"

He nodded, distracted again by the music. "Yeah…yeah, she's fine. Thankfully, one of Ares Sakura's little elf helpers who was hanging around—six-seven and two-eighty-five, some elf, another of your good ideas?, yes, I thought so—saw what was going down and chased the dude away. Didn't get the chance to tackle him, unfortunately."

"Is she very upset? Oh, God, Lexie Kagan, I gave her the room right next door—"

"Lexie's fine too. And oddly, young Rainbow doesn't seem upset. They're both under police protection now, anyway. I'm starting to think Rainbow's too stupid to live. Or rather"—he caught himself—"too stupid to know a damn thing. But clearly I would be wrong in thinking that."

Rennie nodded in her turn. "Because equally clearly someone thinks she knows something she shouldn't."

"Do *you* think that?"

"No, I think she knows *exactly* what she knows, and what she *should* know. And what she knows is the face of the guy who gave her that damned sandwich. So if she can identify him for the cops, or at least if he thinks she can…"

"Then it's worth him taking the risk to take her out. And if she can identify him as sandwich man, maybe Ned Raven can identify him as the guy who was walking past the yurt, right before he went in and found Amander dead. The guy who told him it was the meditation tent." Marcus looked suddenly nervous. "Are they still here, the Ravens? Or did they head back to New York?"

"As far as I know, still here. They had planned to leave earlier, but they were too tired and upset. They left a message for me at the motel. They're probably back there now, asleep. Shall I try to get hold of them and tell them to stick around?"

"No. I'll have one of the cops call the motel and let them know. Or maybe Lawson can send someone in person. In fact, I think that's a better idea. If this guy *is* out trying to get rid of people who can ID him..."

"...then I put Rainbow right where he could find her, no muss, no fuss. And Lexie too." She looked deeply annoyed with herself. "At least I thought far enough ahead to put a guard on them. And Rhino set Car Darch to bodyguard the Ravens, so they're probably okay too. But to go after a witness right there in the motel! This cat must be getting desperate."

"So are we."

Marcus departed to look for Caskie Lawson, and Rennie remained where she was, giving herself over to the music while she still could. CSNY were starting their second-half electric set, having done an acoustic one first. This gig was only their second public performance ever, and in front of half a million people—less, by now—and as they'd told her earlier when she'd been chatting with them in the pavilion, they were scared to death. You could hear it: they were positively twangling with second-night nerves, but it didn't matter. A few songs in and they had started to forget themselves, and nothing could detract from those soaring voices.

To take her mind off a possible murderer looking for Ned and Lexie and returning to have another go at Rainbow, she started to write her summary story in her head. The music story, anyway. The crime one would, obviously, be very different—though hopefully just as conclusive. And, of course, about more of a success. Overall, the festival had been overrated, sloppy and even mangy: though somehow the staff had managed to keep it just this side of pure chaos, a miracle in itself, few of the performances had done justice to what these groups could really do. On the other hand, in its sheer scope and size, its quality of performer, its jury-rigged muddling through and the dogged professionalism of the stage crew and the appreciativeness and temper of the audience, the thing had been epic.

Sure, it had dragged and been disorganized, and there was the rain, and the lack of food and shelter and sanitation for the masses, but in all fairness, nobody had expected a crowd this size, ten times bigger than the biggest estimates. And the crowd had risen to the occasion: no violence, no rapes, no racial incidents, no hate speech, no reported crimes. Well, *crimes*… Two murders, and three other episodes, and some stolen money. Which had been returned. Not good, but not bad either.

So no, there had never been anything like it, and there wouldn't be ever again. There would be more big music festivals, sure, but they wouldn't be like this. Turk, of all people, had suggested that this might become the benchmark by which all rock festivals would be judged hereafter; she must remember to tell him that he had been quite right.

The energy was beginning to wind down, though; you could sense it. It wasn't the diminishing audience size, though that was part of it; it was more that people, hungry and wet and cold and exhausted, were finally running out of enthusiasm and endurance, and even interest. Which was sad, though probably inevitable: the Sunday- slate acts weren't what anyone would call high-energy, and were not likely to help people stay awake and up for things. Except of course for the very last act of all.

Everybody knew that Jimi Hendrix was the festival star, if the festival could be said to even *have* a star—the participants were almost all of them stars, and those who weren't soon would be. Two years ago, at Monterey, Jimi had been an unknown, an exotic, entirely unexpected. Now he was a rock prince, perhaps the most influential guitarist now playing, some would say the most influential one who had ever played. Not for the intricacy of his sound, like Turk, or for the strength of it, like Juha, or its sweetness, like George Harrison, or the innovation, like Clapton; but for a quality different than all of those. Rennie could put no name to it, though she knew it when she heard it, but she had never surrendered herself to what it did, and she knew that she never would.

Because Jimi's was not the kind of music that she would listen to, for joy or for pleasure or even for choice; for that she had her beloved favorites—the Airplane and the Beatles and the Stones and the Doors and the Dead and Cream and Janis and Big Brother and Quicksilver; and, at least when Turk wasn't home, Lionheart. Not forgetting the Byrds, the Who, Dylan, Baez, Donovan, the Kinks, Buffy Sainte-Marie, Buffalo Springfield, Creedence, the Hollies, the Fariñas, Steeleye Span, Judy Collins, so many more she couldn't even remember, rock and folk, and classical, and the great 50's music of her childhood and teen years. And the bands of other friends besides: Evenor, Bluesnroyals, Cold Fire, Sunny Silver, Dandiprat, the Budgies, Thistlefit.

For her, what Jimi played was not what she would characterize as music; which sounded totally weird, because of *course* it was music, it was riffs and songs and notes and solos like everybody else's. But it was true, in a strange sort of way, a way totally *un*like everybody else's. It wasn't merely music but musical evolution—change, not just changes, played on the strings and the fretboard, something new. She didn't find it beautiful, particularly, or charming or exalting or tuneful or any of the other qualities she required in what she listened to; she didn't really understand or enjoy it, it didn't speak to her heart or her soul. But it *was* amazing—and so she would endure the festival windup to hear it, for as long as it took. Change needed to be honored as well as merely acknowledged and observed.

Gerry Langhans had come to sit next to her, with JoAnn on her other side, both of them as flat-out beat as she was and all of them leaning against each other like tired horses. After a while, she remarked dreamily, "I would so love to be able to time travel. Wouldn't you? I bet you anything that people from the future are going to want to come back to this, to Woodstock. They'd be here already, right this minute, and we wouldn't even know it, would we. How trippy is that?"

"And are you among them, these bold voyagers from tomorrow? Could be a little freaky if you run into yourself."

Rennie laughed. "Not I, by God! I'm here now, that's more than enough for me. But how could you *not* want to go back to something like this? This is not someplace I personally would choose to revisit, because of course I'm already here and I have not the smallest wish to return, but other times? You bet! To see a herd of grazing brontosaurs in midtown Manhattan, or sit in a garden that's been buried under a shopping center and read a book you lost in a move when you were nine, or help put up Stonehenge..."

JoAnn patted her arm. "We like you just fine in the here

and now, Strider. I can't imagine the havoc you'd wreak in the past, setting things right. Or the way *you* think is right, anyway, out there along the space-time continuum or the chrono-synclastic infundibulum, or whatever the hell."

"There's that," she admitted, laughing. "With the benefit of hindsight, of course."

"Or the help of the zodiac," said Gerry. "Can't do anything these days without the aid of the planetary powers."

"So it seems, my friend. So it would darn well seem."

They sat on in companionable silence, listening to the last of CSN&Y's golden sun harmonies floating over the field and the trees and out up into the hills. To Rennie, that was just about it. There was nothing of note left now except Jimi. Up next was the Paul Butterfield Band, who, no matter how many times people told her were terrific and bluesy and fabulous as hell, she just didn't get. Maybe it was like that whistle only dogs could hear; her musical ear simply wasn't tuned to it, and to her they seemed boring and blah. She liked *other* blues, both traditional and rocked-up, so it wasn't that. Maybe it was the Emperor's New Blues. Whatever. She couldn't stand Frank Sinatra either.

And after Butterfield, immediately preceding Jimi, and the dizziest of contrasts, was slotted a sort of novelty band from New York, Sha Na Na, a dozen pompadoured doo-wop 50's re-creationists, college boys costumed in gold lamé and greaser leather. They seemed as bizarre a miscast on this bill as Blood, Sweat & Tears, but who knew, they might prove a lot more fun than they looked on paper. If Butterfield was as much of a stage hog as he had been at Monterey, though, Sha Na Na, who had taken their name from the catchy hook of that great old Silhouettes song "Get

A Job", might not have a chance to actually *get* a job here; at least not if the organizers wanted to put Jimi onstage before lunchtime. But Rennie figured that by this point everyone was simply so tired and so battered and so blank that they would just let the thing spool out as planned, the course of least resistance, however long it might take. Not that anyone had much resistance left at all.

Past sunrise, and she was trying desperately to stay awake for Hendrix's set, which was imminent. She'd quit the trailer, and had gone down to the command center, where, since journalism knows no timeclock, she was now waiting to call Ken Karper at the Sun-Tribune, to update him on the most recent developments and have him pass it along to Burke Kinney at the Clarion—their usual process. There wasn't a lot new to report, though her earlier communication that Ned and Melza Raven were in the clear regarding Amander Evans' murder had not come amiss. Hopefully she would soon be able to offer up the identity of the real killer, and she and Ken could then do their reportorial double act, as they had for years now, journalizing in tandem on yet more rocknroll murders. And murderers.

She didn't have Elk Bannerman's amazing Bat-phone available this time, and the phones in the command trailer were being used at even this ungodly hour, so rather than truck herself out to the banks of pay phones to try to find an available one, she decided to wait until one was free here, and nobody minded—in fact, they didn't even seem to notice that she was there at all. So she'd curled up on a ratty old sofa in the corner, with two cheese Danishes from the pavilion buffet table and yet another thermos full of coffee. She wasn't worried about missing Jimi: when he came on, she'd hear him.

She looked irritably around. No one to talk to, everybody gone or busy, bored bored bored, nothing even to read...oh, wait! She still had those back issues of Queen Anne's Fan that Liz Williams had given her on Saturday, what a lifesaver. Liz had left around four in the morning, getting a ride down to New York with the Sonnets, Theo Lintern and some other Britfriends, to catch an afternoon plane home out of JFK—hopefully the traffic wouldn't hold them up too much and they'd be able to make their flight. They'd all taken their departure with mutual promises to meet up in England next time Turk and Rennie were over, and Liz had given her a few more magazines; she'd put the previous lot into her shoulderbag and had been toting them around for the past couple of days, forgetting to leave them in her room. But now she was glad of them all, and she pulled them out and began to riffle through the pages as she ate.

For an underground rag, the Fan was a very handsome publication. Not quite a slick, but printed on high-quality paper, it had explosive, and expensive, color graphics, wild typography and nicely done layouts. And some very solid content: as she read, Rennie was amused to encounter names she knew. Liz herself—literate and funny. Belinda Melbourne, with a warmly appreciative story on the Kinks. Loya Tessman with her smarmy, smirky little syndicated column, pimping her husband's acts as she always did, boasting of lunch or dinner with this star or that. San Francisco groupie queen Kaleidah Scopes with her own regular feature, Rock Cocks, discussing what she knew best...well, she *would* know best, wouldn't she.

After ten or fifteen minutes, Rennie was done with the

first couple of issues, and picked up another, with a nice photo of the Who on the front, dated several months back. She idly scanned the table of contents. Oh look, someone else she knew writing a column, how had she missed this in the other issues…

And as she read, and reread, and reread yet again, she sat bolt upright on the couch, and her eyes widened and all the blood went out of her face. All of a sudden, getting a phone to call her editor seemed of staggering insignificance: because at last, at long freaking bloody goddamn LAST, she had someone to hunt down and destroy like the rabid animal it was.

~23~

Monday morning, August 18

SHE HAD SCOURED the pavilion, the dressing-room trailer area, the security area, even the medical tents, with no luck. It was full light out now, and she could see that practically the entire audience had magically melted away in the night. It was really eerie: the field now was almost empty, as if those who had been there had evaporated, or been beamed up into space. They had stolen away like a great caravan moving on, back to their homes or the next hippie oasis, who could say, and the field where they had huddled for three days was a sodden morass of mud and rags and litter.

But a resolute tenth of the hordes had remained to the bitterest of ends, a decimation in reverse, waiting to hear Jimi Hendrix close the festival out. And empty as the field now was, it was still by headcount alone a bigger audience than Madison Square Garden, five Fillmore Easts and all the rock clubs in Manhattan put together. It paled only in comparison to what it had been a few hours before.

Where the hell is *everybody? Marcus, Lawson…him?* She scanned her immediate environs with a burst of irritation that was surpassed only by the panic she felt. Now that she knew how and who, it all seemed so obvious. But *why*, now *that* was the big remaining question… She made one final desperate sweep through the pavilion and headed back toward the stage.

And found herself not twenty yards away from her quarry. He was lurking under the bridge to the stage, like a troll waiting for the Billygoats Gruff to trot across; he was not looking in her direction, but out over the field, and the look on his face was pure malevolent satisfaction. No one was around in that secure area but Jimi's roadies and the festival crew, working to set up for the last shout of Woodstock. Sha-Na-Na had gone over surprisingly well, energizing the crowd—paltry by comparison to what the numbers had been—and had just clattered offstage, babbling excitedly amongst themselves, delighted to have performed so creditably, even more delighted to have been the lead-in group to the emperor of the festival himself. In the destroyed field full of musical ghosts, the remnant audience members were bundled together bleary-eyed; some were even still asleep in the dawn chill.

But the one she sought was awake and aware, and most importantly, he was *there*. As she had known he would be. She came at him stiff-legged and silent and intent, like a leopard stalking prey on the savannah, approaching him from behind, from upwind; if she'd had fur, her hackles would have been standing straight up.

As if he sensed her presence, Kaiser Frizelle turned and smiled. "Ah. Rennie. I knew it would be you. That Aries sun and Virgo ascendant of yours. I knew you'd be the one to figure it out."

She was shaking so hard she could barely speak. "And so I should be, you evil, evil son of a bitch. You killed Cory Rivkin and Amander Evans. You tried to kill *Turk*."

"It was nothing personal. You must see that."

"Nothing PERSONAL? *I'll* make it personal! I'll make it so goddamn personal that between the fist I'll jam down your throat and the telephone pole I'll ram up your ass, you won't be able to *breathe*. And the amp that fell on Sunny Silver and the wet wires in Ned Raven's vocal set-up? Framing Lexie Kagan? Going after that little groupie kid? Your work too, I presume?"

"Of course."

Rennie was finding it harder and harder to keep the tide of rage at bay, and finding fewer and fewer reasons why she should. "But *why*? What had any of them ever done to you? Or are you just a total lunatic?"

" 'Lunatic'. Yes. Under the control of the moon. I had predicted peace and love, deliberately, because of course I knew it wasn't going to be," said Kaiser dreamily. "I could read it all as clearly as Annadawn did. But she—our little Lexie—made the mistake of saying so. So when I heard that she had predicted difficulties and even death, I knew I could make her be a suspect, to take any suspicion away from me. And it worked. You saw how it worked. The cops thought she killed Amander on account of being dumped. It was perfect."

By now, Rennie was possessed of such fury that she had been rendered momentarily speechless, but Kaiser didn't appear to notice, and blithely continued on, in the same dreamy underwater voice.

"I planned on killing Amander last night, Sunday night, not Friday. Then Thursday afternoon, I saw you were here, and the next night Turk came to the room party. I emptied some downers into a cup of wine and passed it to him. He never even looked to see where it came from. That was to keep *you* out of my hair," he added venomously. "I figured unless he was extremely unlucky, Turk wouldn't actually die. If he did, all the more cred to my predictions... But you'd be so busy taking care of him you wouldn't have any time or attention for solving the murder, and would probably leave the festival to go home with him. Then I'd be able to claim credit for predicting Amander's death. And avoid the blame, of course."

Rennie had recovered her powers of speech. "I saw. In that magazine Liz Williams gave me. You said in your column that in summer, a star would fall in the sight of thousands. You very carefully did not say which one, though the little hint that it could be someone from Down Under was a nice touch. I presume to leave your options open, according as to what target presented itself. You did for Cory Rivkin first, I suppose."

He nodded, still smiling vaguely. "Yes, that was a test to see if it worked, which I was pleased to see it did. I knew about his allergy, you see; I had once done his chart, and when I wondered why his House of Health looked so afflicted, he told me all about it. So I did some research, and I found out that even a trace of peanut oil can kill an allergic person. I knew he would never accept a few actual peanuts, of course, and I certainly wasn't about to kiss him myself. So when that little groupie said she was hungry I gave her some peanut butter sandwiches that I'd scored from the Hog Farm. I made sure she ate at least one right there, and then I invited her into the performers' pavilion—I had a pass, of course, and she was thrilled. I set her up with Cory when he came over and gave her the eye. It was ridiculously simple. She was so pretty I knew he'd be taken with her. Obviously, they did some making out."

"And never had time to do any more than that."

"No," he said, with something oddly like sadness. "Peanut allergies can be fatal almost immediately. It would show up on lab tests, I'm told, but not right away. And by then Woodstock would be long over."

"And Amander?"

"I knew about *her* allergy, too. Oh yes, she had one as well. You suspected as much, didn't you? Well, you were quite right." He walked a few steps over to sit down on the stairs leading from the stage, and Rennie noticed, as she hadn't before, that he was limping on his right leg, and she smiled with satisfaction—score one for her, then!

Now he looked up at her comfortably, as if settling in for a nice chat. "Lexie and I aren't always at daggers drawn, you know. She came to consult me when she and Amander first got together, to get a chart done to see if they had a future, and that's how I found out about the peanut thing. She didn't tell you she knew about it? No—probably she thought it would throw suspicion on her. I thought if I killed Amander and could get Lexie blamed for it, or even just suspected, that would get rid of her and do wonders for my career, especially if she was thrown in jail."

"I can't believe I'm actually asking this, but how did you bring it off? Killing her, I mean."

"That was easy too. I managed to get Amander off by herself at the party. I told her I had cast a horoscope for her now that she wasn't with Lexie anymore, with wonderful aspects in it, but we needed to talk about it privately, and she fell for it. Like you, I have a car up here, so we left the party and I drove her from the motel back here to the field. There was nobody around out by this little pond over in the trees, down by that cottage some of the stars were using, and after I read her this bogus chart we made out for a while. It didn't need much persuasion."

"You needn't gloat, you cockroach."

Kaiser smiled at her, and the smile flickered with luminous insanity. "Why not? Surely you don't grudge me my moment of triumph."

"I grudge you *oxygen*! I grudge you your *pulse*! I grudge you your continuing ability to move your vile carcass across the protesting land! And by God I would like nothing better than to put a *stop* to all those things, right here and right now."

He wasn't listening. "I knew about her and Ned as well—for someone who liked chicks, she sure was into guys, too. She really was a little tramp. But she would never have become a real star, you know; her planets were inauspicious, and she didn't deserve to be one. Anyway, I'd already eaten another peanut butter sandwich, back at the party. She never knew what was happening to her. It was over pretty quickly; then I carried her up to the meditation tent. Anybody who saw us probably figured she was stoned and I was being a good and caring hippie friend, helping her through her bad trip. Anyway, there was no one in the tent, thankfully, and I dumped her there, propped up on pillows. She looked as if she was Zenned out meditating. Again, nobody noticed."

Unexpectedly, Rennie found herself feeling sorry for Amander; however nasty a piece of work the girl might have been, she hadn't deserved to die like that. Nor had Cory, who'd been a far worthier person.

"Ned Raven noticed. He could ID you."

Kaiser handwaved it away. "He saw me outside the tent, but I very much doubt he could recognize me. And he didn't see me actually *leaving* the tent. Amazing, really, that no one did. You would think that with half a million people around, somebody would have, but no. Then I went back to the pavilion and the motel, to make sure people saw me in both places. It worked like a charm."

Rennie was hanging on to her temper with both hands by now, but her grip was slipping fast. "But why? I don't mean why her or Cory, or Sunny or Ned or even Turk, but why at all?"

"I wanted to go and fight. You know. In Vietnam. I'd been in ROTC at college. I would have been an officer. But they didn't want me. Something about 'pronounced mental instability', can you believe that? So I went off to New York to be a hippie instead. I would have much rather gone to Nam. I started writing for the Khaos, casting charts, but then Annadawn came along and got all the good gigs with the magazines that I was trying to get into..." Kaiser spread his hands and smiled, shrugging. "So I had to out-predict her. It was the only thing I could do."

"You killed Amander and Cory, you tried to kill Turk and Ned and Sunny, you did all this because you *got rejected by your draft board*? You're INSANE!"

"Am I? You could be right. But that wasn't the only reason. No, I really wanted to prove to people that my astrological predictions were bang on the money, and what I knew made it easy. Now nobody will ever doubt me again. Stars died, and I foretold it. I'll be in big slick monthlies, not crappy little underground rags. I'll have superstar clients begging me to cast their horoscopes."

"Not from prison, you won't!"

Again he waved it away. "That will never happen. It is not in my chart, and the planets do not speak so."

"Yeah, well, we'll just see what they have to say, the little pieces of solar-system garbage, when the cops get here. But you didn't quit there, did you? You went after that kid you tricked into kissing Cory. You tried to kill her when you saw her in the motel, only you didn't figure on the Argus bodyguard being right on the spot. They'll both identify you with no difficulty whatsoever. And Ned as well."

"Perhaps. A chance I took."

"Seems a fairly pointless one." Rennie took a deep breath. "So. You went on record predicting the death of a star. And then you made it happen. That was your big plan."

"Brilliant, wasn't it? Yes, it took me months to put it all together. Now that British rag will have all the cachet of a perfect Kaiser Frizelle prediction. But of course it won't if you tell people I killed her. And you're the only one who's figured it out. You really are good at putting stuff together, aren't you..."

"In all modesty, yes, I am. But—all anybody has to do is read that prophecy and figure out *you* were the one who caused it, not the blameless planets. Kind of a pretty big flaw in your plan there, Zodiactionable. Because it's not a prediction if you *actually make it happen*! And if you tell people about it...can you really be that stupid?"

He didn't seem to hear her. "Too bad I didn't think to predict Murder Chick's death while I was at it."

In spite of herself, Rennie laughed. God, was there no originality left among homicidal madmen anymore? "Like you tried to bring off in the woods the other night? Yes, we see how successful *that* was. What makes you think it would go any better now? How's your leg, by the way? I notice you're limping... What did the medics have to say? Or did you just patch it up yourself with some first-aid cream and a butterfly band-aid? Must have hurt like hell."

He looked at her in silence, his eyes affectless and dull as a rattlesnake's coiling for the strike, but she was unconcerned. The day she couldn't take down a weed like Kaiser Frizelle was the day she'd hang up her spurs for good—she'd never so shame Ares' training. And it was extremely unlikely he had a gun, the way a few other deranged killers she'd recently confronted had had. So she would probably do best just to keep him talking. Surely the cops would notice, sooner or later, they had to be around here somewhere, the lazy bastards, did she have to do *everything* herself...

"How did you manage Ned and Sunny?"

Kaiser seemed delighted that she was so interested in how he'd made everything happen. "I was helping those roadies carry the amp stacks past Sunny backstage. Nobody even noticed how I unbalanced the one that fell on her, and while they were all fussing over her I just disappeared myself into the crowd. Electrocuting Ned, that was simply Mother Nature helping me out with some timely rain, though I did loosen the mike stand connections. I had no idea who'd be unlucky enough to eventually stand in the puddle and close the circuit; happily, it turned out to be someone as high-profile as Ned, and not some nonentity roadie."

Rennie tensed up every single muscle in her body for the answer to the ultimate question. "And—Turk?"

"Downers in the wine, but you knew that. If he'd died, of course, it would have been endless kudos to me. I did predict the death of a star in summer, you know, and Turk's a tremendously bigger star than either Cory or Amander. But, hey, can't have everything."

Rennie heard that last through a screaming white silence. *That's it, that's enough and more than enough...* Without benefit of anything that could remotely be called a thought, she pulled the hunting knife from the sheath on her belt where she still carried it, drew back her arm and let it fly like a javelin, all in one smooth motion. Her aim was true: the razor-sharp point hit Kaiser squarely in the left thigh and stuck there, as if he'd been a big evil dartboard and she'd thrown the winning flight. He made no sound or cry of pain, but merely looked down at the protruding knife handle, and the upwelling blood, with an expression of vague and academic interest.

"Now you'll have holes in *both* your legs, you fucking gargoyle!" she snapped. "And a great big bloody matching one in your *THROAT*!" And went for him like the dogs of war let slip.

"*That's* for Turk!" She suited actions to words, fetching him a right cross that connected with his jaw and could have felled a bison. "And that, and that, and oh *especially* that, and *this* one's for Cory, and Amander, and this, *this* is for Ned, and for Melza, and Lexie, and Sunny, and Rainbow Galadriel, and Turk, and me, and for Turk and Turk and Turk and Turk and Turk..."

He didn't even attempt to defend himself, just sat there placidly on the steps as she rained blows down on him with each name she snarled, bone-crunching clouts that would have flattened any sane human, leaving him bleeding from split lips and broken nose. Then, just as she was seriously getting her fingers into his throat, she found herself pulled off by the scruff of her neck like a misbehaving puppy.

"Leave it," said Marcus Dorner, with the weight of the law in his voice and the weight of six feet of trained cop muscle behind his arm.

"I will *not* leave it! Did you *hear* him? He poisoned Turk and he killed Cory and Amander and he—"

"I said leave it, Rennie. We heard everything. We were coming for him anyway. They'll take care of it now. Look."

He nodded to where four county police officers of roughly the size and tonnage of combine harvesters were stolidly standing, Sheriff Caskie Lawson off to one side. Lawson touched his hat brim to Rennie, in a respectful, almost military salute, then nodded to his men, and they moved in. Surrounding Kaiser, who was smiling up at them like a happy child, his face already swelling and purpling, bloody where Rennie's fists had smeared his nose across it, they talked to him soothingly, removing the knife from his thigh and wrapping the wound with a clean handkerchief. Then they led him away, across the ruined acres that had been so green and lushly perfect only four days before, to the row of cop cars that awaited.

Rennie and Marcus watched them go. "Why didn't you let me kill him?" she raged, still restrained by his iron grip on her upper arms and still breathing fire and slaughter. "I don't often want to kill people, you know. Well, not *that* often. I'm an easygoing sort of person. I don't ask for much. But he really deserves it. In fact, he deserves to be tied to four horses and torn apart. I saw some in a paddock right down the road—"

Marcus pulled her backwards into his arms to calm her, because clearly she was on the verge of total freakout, and after an instant's stiff resistance she allowed herself to be held, though her body remained as tight and tense as a wound-up crossbow.

"You're right. You're right. He absolutely does. But I can't let you do that. As it is, I'll have to do some fancy footwork to talk them out of busting you for battery, assault and knife-throwing to the detriment of the public, though I have a feeling that Lawson will just look at me and say 'Knife? What knife? Bruises? Oh, he must have tripped over something.' And based on what I saw just now, I'd say Frizelle won't even remember you beat the snot out of him. Besides, I think our good Sheriff feels he owes you, as so many of us end up feeling, and indeed owing…take the amnesty and be grateful, you wretched girl. What would I tell Turk, not to mention Prax and Stephen, if I let you get arrested for homicide?"

She pulled away from him to stand alone, trembling with the fury that was still pounding through her, like magma zooming up a volcano vent. "You would tell them that it was totally justifiable and then Turk would hire me King Bryant as my lawyer. Our rock and roll Clarence Darrow of record. And no jury on earth would convict me."

He gave a snort of exasperated amusement. "God, you never change, do you? You're still such a—"

"Such a what? Come on, let's hear it."

"Such an easygoing sort of person," he said, smiling.

"I am just that very thing."

"Never mind. You did great. Turk's safe. Ned and Melza are in the clear. So's Lexie, though I think some official words will be had for not telling us about Amander's allergy when we spoke to her. Not serious words; she was obviously scared she'd somehow be blamed. Understandable. Sunny's okay. Even little Rainbow Galadriel is okay. We've got him.

After you and I had our little chat about astrologers and their Woodstock predictions, Lawson and I looked into it. We knew he was the only other astrologer besides Lexie that you had any kind of acquaintance with. So we read all those columns of his and searched his apartment and hotel room and found all his research and notes and plans. It was as good as a confession. And then he did confess, right here, to you, and we heard it. He won't be doing this to anyone again."

"So you say."

"I do say."

They stood staring at the stage in the growing light, angry, sad, exhausted—but just now exalted also, as they listened to the swan song of Woodstock ringing out. As Lionheart had played "God Save The Queen" at midnight, the anthem now was "The Star-Spangled Banner" by the dawn's early light, as it had never been played before and would never be played again.

Standing at the center of the weatherbeaten and perhaps antimagic wooden stage, Jimi Hendrix was no dying swan but a rock phoenix, glowing in colors that reflected the dawn behind the mountains, burning himself to life and glory out of the ashes of the festival, the gypsy sun and his attendant rainbows. It made no difference that only about fifty thousand weary people were left to hear him, out of ten times that number that had been present the night before—he played for whoever could hear him. He played for the whole round world, and he played for and with his band, and he played for no one but himself. He was here, and they were here, and the music was here, and nothing else mattered.

~24~

"SO. YOU READY for the road, Ampman?"

"Think so. Hope so. Well, I rather have to be, don't I."

"Couldn't you push it back a week? Or even two? Or a month? Or cancel it altogether?"

Turk sipped at the cocoa in the pottery mug, and smiled at his anxious mate. "I'm the lead guitarist in a touring band, sweetheart. I don't *get* to be sick or tired. Just shoot me up like a racehorse and shove me out onstage. No, no, don't look like that, I promise I'm feeling fine. Or I will be, by the time it all starts, with all those herbs and vitamins and tisanes you're stuffing into me. I have the rest of the week to recuperate, lying here in this supremely comfortable bed and being waited on hand and foot. I should get poisoned more often. No, just kidding. And also no, we can't cancel the dates, and I wouldn't even if I could. Since the album is basically dead on its feet, we need the tour more than ever. Though I don't think it's going to make much difference. Not after our little Bethel adventure. Bethel means 'house of God' in Hebrew, did you know that?" he added.

"Actually, I did know. Hardly lived up to its name, did it. Wasn't quite the three days of peace and music that we were promised, either. And I hear Yasgur's fields will take a year to recover. But at least we got out of there alive."

"More than some did."

"Yes. Well. Maybe you boys will score a bit of a sympathy vibe out of it all."

"Perhaps we shall. And I'm not proud: I'd take it in a heartbeat."

It was the week after Woodstock, and already the papers had gotten bored with the festival story. It had all been remarkably schizoid. After the initial editor-perverted accounts of Nightmare in the Catskills, which had only made all parties to the "nightmare" roar with laughter, the media had succumbed to the Woodstock spirit, or the power of autohype, exactly as Juha and Bardo had predicted, and were endlessly repeating the party-line mantra of super-duper extra-groovy peace, love and music, like enthusiastic, if brainwashed, parrots. It hadn't been a nightmare, not quite; but it also hadn't been all the rest of it either.

For her part, Rennie was willing to split the difference: sure, there had been some magic moments, and the peacefulness had been something of a miracle, though really not all that much of one since everybody had been too high to move, much less fight, but mostly it had been—well, not to put too fine a point on it, now that she had had leisure to reflect, she had mostly hated it. She would have felt that way even without all the murders and accidents and Turk being poisoned, and she was pretty well fed up with hearing about how grooooovy it had all been, and deeply bored with all the preening self-congratulatory hype. The music hadn't been the greatest, and the participants had been annoying, and the milieu had been wearisome, and the whole exhausting thing had just gotten right up her nose and stayed there. It had been very different from Monterey, that was for sure: but Monterey was two years ago now, and times had changed.

Still, the media had by no means gotten bored with what continued to bubble up from the festival grounds like toxic tar from polluted sands: Amander's murder, and Cory's, and the attempts on Sunny and Ned, and the apprehending of Kaiser Frizelle as the crazed maniac behind it all. Not to mention Turk's poisoning, which had finally come to light—thanks to Rennie herself, who vengefully thirsted for Kaiser to get nailed to the wall for everything he possibly could, and who had dropped the hammer on him to editor Ken Karper with clarity, point and extreme prejudice. She'd even have pinned the Woodstock mud and rain and bad brown acid on him if she'd thought she could make it stick.

Fitz had of course presented the bill for Turk's air rescue, in the form of a first-person feature story from his star reporter and an exclusive interview with Mr. Wayland—a modest and indeed agreeable bill, and neither Rennie nor Turk had minded paying it one bit. Reluctantly playing down her physical assault on Kaiser—of which, naturally, she was burstingly proud, and who could blame her—she had written up a terrific feature, and Fitz had greeted it with joy, as he always did when she scored big for his side. Their bargain, as always, was that the pure-news version of the story, handled by Karper, would be free, as far as possible, of Murder Chick stuff, and Fitz had agreed with what seemed to Rennie slightly indecent haste.

But her color piece was a thoughtful and a good one, one of her best ever, and Ken too, who was by now comfortably used to mirroring her, and genuinely glad of the opportunities she sent his way, had outdone himself.

Rennie had demurred at handling the Turk interview herself, though, considering, with a certain brand-new reportorial refinement of feeling, that, since she was now officially and publicly engaged to Turk, the time had finally come for her to step away from Lionheart stories, and Fitz had agreed, though with no great enthusiasm.

So he had sent in Belinda Melbourne instead, like an eager bench player going in for the injured star quarterback, and Belinda had been delighted to suit up, only making sure first that her good friend Strider was okay with it. But for once it hadn't been up to Rennie: Fitz was their mutual boss and team owner, and he called the plays. So Belinda had made the game-winning throw, doing a bang-up job with the interview—Turk had given her some brilliant quotes—and Rennie was delighted and only a tiny bit professionally jealous of the journalistic score. Even Caskie Lawson had proved himself a superstar in print, though Marcus Dorner, for reasons of his own, had kept out of the public mix, which went ditto for Elk Bannerman, twice over.

And now it all seemed to be dying down, at least to Rennie's weary, wary eye, and things were more or less back to normal. Except, of course, for the bitterness fiesta already building against the festival organizers from some of the bands who were feeling, perhaps with justification, majorly ripped off, exactly as they had in Monterey's aftermath. Some things never change, some lessons are never learned; doubtless it would all sort itself out down the road. But Lionheart, at this point, didn't particularly care: they had ten weeks of hard touring ahead of them, and they were due to hit the trail in a fortnight.

The Wayland-Strides were in their bedroom at the moment, Turk tucked up in the fourposter, Rennie lounging backwards atop the coverlet, facing him. Her knuckles were all bruised and banged up from where she'd whaled on Kaiser, though that hadn't stopped Turk from giving her, or her from sporting, a Kashmir sapphire ring as a thanks-for-saving-my-life present combined with a sorry-sweetheart-I'm-off-on-tour-leaving-you-alone-to-deal-with-the-construction-mess bribe; the velvety blueness of the stone went rather nicely with the equally blue bruises on her hands. But bribe or no, she had insisted that Turk remain abed until the weekend, and as he was still feeling a bit understrength, he hadn't argued with her. Not that it would have done any good.

From a distance, they could faintly hear the workmen on the job, but otherwise it was quiet. Since there was still work to be done, the room was functional but bare—the bed, a mirrored dresser, a bookshelf, a tall armoire—but Rennie was eagerly anticipating the day a few months hence when she'd finally be the mistress of a clean and fabulous house. The main contractors were already gone, taking the noise and dust with them, and that had been the worst of it—the structural combining of the three brownstones, now successfully and tastefully one.

Neither she nor Turk had wanted to lose any funky original nineteenth-century detail that could be spared or restored—the medallioned or tin ceilings, the marble fireplaces, the pocket doors, the stained glass, the fabulous old woodwork—and now the painters and paperhangers and tilers and floor finishers were coming to the end of their own labors too. Soon it would remain only to get in cleaners to wash and mop and sweep up, and then Rennie could get down to the decorating—her favorite part. Everything major was already bought and in storage, waiting for her to give the go-ahead, and she was looking forward to a happy time playing with furniture and heavily patronizing East Village antique shops, once Turk and the boys were out on the road.

"Anyway, you don't start the tour till Labor Day," she said consolingly, laying her head atop his knee. "We're off to L.A. next week. Ares will have the house ready for us; that was a great idea of yours to make him resident house-sitter and give him the downstairs guest suite. Prax will help him out. Belinda will keep an eye on this place till I get back and can hire a live-in assistant; she says she knows somebody who'd be perfect, and who has an artist-handyman husband too. And I've already told Francher he's not to even *think* about rehearsals till we're all in L.A. He said fine."

Turk laughed. "Yes, the one thing you don't want to do before a big road trip is over-rehearse."

"Well, no," she said, laughing too, "but Francher knows what will happen to him if he disobeys me, and by my reckoning he still owes me for doubting you last year when you got busted for Tansy's murder. In fact, I'd say he'll owe me for that until the end of time."

"I don't see why," said Turk, trying to reach behind him to rearrange his stack of pillows. "*I* forgave him for it. Why can't you?"

"Because you're a better man than I am, Gunga Din. As I've said many times before." She adjusted the pillows and cast a critical eye over him. "You look pretty good for someone who almost got murdered by a crazy person."

"Yes, I should think I do," he said complacently. "And you're wondering right about now why I'm not angrier about almost having been murdered."

"The thought has crossed my mind. Why else did I practically pulverize Kaiser Frizelle, not to mention sticking a knife into him, twice, if not to make up a little for your peril and discomfort?"

Turk grinned. "I'm sure you did so purely for unselfish reasons of your own, which undoubtedly made sense to you both then and now. Noble reasons, I hasten to add. Honorable reasons, as they always are. Still, I'm glad you got to enjoy yourself a bit. As for my own rage and fury, I can take secondhand vengeance through you, and that's quite as good, really. Or even very slightly better, as I don't have to lift a finger."

"Pleased I could help out."

He shook his head wonderingly. "So, was he evil? Or just plain barking mad? Either way, he had pretty much released the last remaining fingertip of his grasp on reality, hadn't he. That should teach us all not to mess about with occult powers we do not understand."

"Occult doesn't enter into it. The guy *was* barking mad, and had been for some time. If he'd been in any other line of work but rock and roll, people would have noticed it long ago. You didn't see, but he was so completely crackers at the end that he didn't even feel it when I beat the crap out of him and threw a knife into his leg. And if he *isn't* insane but is just faking the whole trip, then yes, he's totally evil, and should be put away forever. Or put down. But as for evil, what do people expect me to do when it gets up right in my face and hurts people I love? Discuss its motivations with social-worker understanding and then take it out for ice cream? No. That will never happen."

They were comfortably silent for a while. Then Turk: "What's the story from upstate? Everybody gone home who was free to?"

"By now, yes. Gray and Prue went back to London about four in the morning on Monday, escorted by their Argus guardians; ditto Ned and Melza, only on Monday afternoon. Elk Bannerman is no doubt already looking for his next singer-songwriter act—though what with Baz, Tansy and Amander all ending up deceased, you'd think he might reconsider, and try to sign a Bach choir or a singing nun or something, just to break the jinx. If jinx there be. Belinda says Lexie Kagan's gone to Tuscany, to get away from everything for a bit, which who could blame her. Even young Rainbow Galadriel Silverwindmistdancer is back home with her folks, sadder but wiser. Pretty much covers everybody, I think."

"Not quite everybody: I had a phone call from Alec Faldo of Owl Tuesday. There's going to be a wake over the weekend for Cory Rivkin at the Troubadour; we ought to send flowers, and Lionheart should too—tribute to a onetime colleague. I'm sure Francher will remember, but we should remind him anyway, as we won't be in L.A. yet when it happens."

"Yeah, flowers, for sure. I'll do it, before I forget; we should have it down by now, sending floral memorials, we seem to do it so often..." Rennie sighed and stretched. "Rock and roll as usual. Though I really didn't see all that much rock and roll to write about for Fitz, being rather busier with other things. Belinda and the rest of the gang got to see a lot more. Still, doesn't seem like much of a loss. No offense meant."

"And none whatsoever taken, believe me. Though Alec did mention a curious little story in Loya Tessman's column in the Pillar yesterday all about how I'm going to sack Niles and hire Terry Janoff as lead singer; we both had a good laugh about that. I'd wonder where it could *possibly* have come from, but I recognize your fine Shakespearean hand. Nice diversionary work there, my lady. Maybe Niles will even believe it, and clean up his act. I have no objection to reigning by terror if I must, even bogus and vicarious terror. But if I know Fitz, which I think by now I can say with a fair degree of certainty that I do, I expect he's much more pleased with what you *did* get to write about."

"Yes, I suppose he is." She looked sorrowful for a moment, and he reached down to tug gently on her hair, and she smiled.

"How's our Marcus, then?"

"Okay, I guess. He stayed on to help tie up loose ends with the sheriff's department and the state troopers. He told me he was going back to L.A. after that," she added more cheerfully. "He should be there by now. And I really do think he's a Fed, even if he isn't admitting it."

Turk took another careful swallow of cocoa—iced, as his throat was still recovering from its soreness and he didn't want to stress it right before a tour. Even if he didn't use his voice much in concert, he'd still have to talk in interviews.

"You're probably right. No matter. And you're square with the law, then, madam, are you? I don't fancy finding the house invaded in the middle of the night by rozzers intent on dragging you off to face assorted charges."

Rennie brightened. "All cool on that front. Sheriff Caskie Lawson, isn't that the perfect name for a country copper, even said rather handsomely that Sullivan County owes me bigtime for my assistance. I modestly suggested right back that Sullivan County could just as handsomely settle said debt by handing over that gorgeous old Arts and

Crafts table from the interrogation room, since they never use it. He said they'd consider it. I bet it's already on a truck on its way down from Monticello. We can put it in the foyer."

"Never miss an antique trick, do you."

"Plus I did say I'd replace the table with two fine new ones more suited to the purpose… Nice of him to give us all those fresh tomatoes and peaches and corn and stuff from his own farm, as a token of appreciation."

"And very tasty it was, too."

"We'll have to schlep back up there to testify at the trial, but we're used to that by now and let's not worry about it just yet. And there might not even be a trial, if that wacko cops a plea. Though when we do, we can accept Sheriff and Mrs. Lawson's kind Sunday dinner invitation. Perhaps by then it will be apple cider time. And there might be pie."

"That would be very pleasant. Well, as you say, we're used to it. In fact, we've been down these roads so often that I don't even need a map anymore. Perhaps I *should* be more exercised about an attempt on my life, as you seem to feel I ought, but quite honestly, it's all getting a bit old. With you, it comes with the territory, as I've said before."

He struggled with the pillows again, and Rennie took them away from him and plumped them up to his liking. "I don't say I'm entirely at peace with it, mind you," he added. "Just used to it. And I suppose you're worth it."

"Of course I am. Now drink up your nice cocoa, and I will read to you."

"Really? No one's read to me since I was a very little boy." He settled down into the pillows and looked at her expectantly, setting his empty mug aside on the nightstand. "What shall you read me?"

"I was thinking I'd start you on *The Lord of the Rings*?

You keep promising you'll read it, and you never do. And if you ever hope to truly understand me, you really must."

"It might be a bit too sensational. In my weakened condition, I mean. Having been poisoned and all."

He looked rather pleased with himself for having been so: perhaps it wasn't as cool as Rennie having been shot on his behalf, but it was still right up there.

Rennie laughed and reached for the huge thick leather-bound book on the nightstand on her side of the bed, and opened it at the first chapter head, where an old silver bookmark stood in the pages. 'A Long-Expected Party', indeed…

"You're a rock and roller, my lord. A guitarist in a working band. You just now said so. I have a feeling—just a feeling, I say—that you can take it."

Epilogue

When the phone rang one dark rainy autumn night some weeks later, Rennie turned over on the pillows and grabbed for it. She had gone to bed early, alone on Turk's side of the fourposter, where she invariably slept when he was on the road—it made him seem closer. Their huge and newly adopted mahogany sable collie, Macduff the Thane of Gondor, was asleep on the other side, strictly against house regulations. Rennie was glad to have him there, though—he was company, and he made her feel safe when she was alone, even with the newly hired live-in assistant and her husband, Hudson and Daniel Link, over in their own flat on the other side of the house—and he came alert with the first ring.

Which Rennie did also. Turk and Lionheart were in Denver, heading into the last leg of their long, long tour: they had another break coming up, and she was scheduled to join him for five days in New Orleans. Only he would call her this late—as a rule he phoned at least three times a day, when he was on the road—and as she set the receiver to her ear she felt a touch of foreboding.

Which was justified, and not entirely unexpected: Turk's grandfather the Duke, who had been ill on and off since early summer, had taken an abrupt turn for the worse, and was not expected to last much longer.

"He won't go to hospital," said Turk on the other end of the phone, his voice a mixture of pride and vexation. "He says he's damn well going to die in the same damn bed ten other damn Tarrant dukes have died in."

"How long will it take us to get there?"

Fending off Macduff, who had sensed her sudden change in mood and was both inquisitive and concerned—also ecstatic, because now of course Pack Leader's Mate was awake, and would play with him and scruffle his tummy and entertain him until morning, saving him from a long, boring night of sleep—Rennie made an emergency call to Eric Lacing in San Francisco, who was delighted to help out his technically still-sister-in-law and condolence-ful when he heard the reason. A private Lacing jet with transatlantic capability was, by happy circumstance, parked and idle and available in New York at the moment, and after a few phone calls back and forth, a new flight plan was quickly filed.

Turk, in the meantime, was winging eastward on the last flight out of Denver; he'd called from the airport right before boarding. Rennie arranged things for her absence with the quietly capable Hudson, threw some stuff into a couple of suitcases, said goodbye to a disappointed Macduff and met Turk when he got to JFK at dawn, where they went on board the luxurious Lacing plane.

Another commercial flight would have been a bit faster, but they appreciated the comfort and security the private jet gave them, and were very grateful to Eric, as they had been to Fitz—good to have friends with a private air fleet. In any case, the New York weather had cleared, so there was no delay in taking off, and they arrived in England after sunset, at Manchester airport, where a helicopter was waiting to take them to Locksley Hall, the Tarrant family seat in Yorkshire. Landing on the broad lawn on the south side, they hurried through the gateway into the ancient, enormous castle, which had lights blazing all over, even on the mighty ramparts, as if for a great ball or party.

"Ravenna," said the Duke in a surprisingly strong voice. "Come sit by me, girl. Want to talk to you. Privately. Richard, kindly leave us; we'll talk again later. I won't keep her long. You too, Valeria my dear."

Turk, with an encouraging nod and glance for Rennie, offered his arm to his grandmother, and they went out, the footman on station in the hall closing the doors behind them. It was mid-afternoon on the day after their arrival, and the Duke hadn't felt up to seeing them until now. So they'd slept in, and had some lunch, and taken two horses out for a couple of hours on the vast estate despite the chilly weather, and fifteen minutes ago they had been ushered into the ducal chamber for a brief audience.

Rennie sat beside the huge tapestried bed and looked at her grandfather-in-law. *Which now he'll only be in retrospect—I'll never really get to know him, and that's so sad. I think we could have been good friends, in spite of everything—and I bet he'd have gotten along* great *with Grandma Vinnie...*

He was faintly smiling, but she could sense that he was ready to roll, and not in the least unhappy or reluctant to do so. On the contrary—he had his lunch packed and his skates on and his ticket in hand. And why not? He had achieved a more than biblical fourscore and fourteen, and he'd lived a full and much-honored life, having passed it almost entirely on his own terms. Not a bad deal, all in all. She smiled back at him.

"If you're worried about the succession, sir, please don't be. Turk—Richard and I will take care of it. We'll have six. Just as I promised. You kept your side of the bargain and went to a Lionheart gig, and I intend to keep mine and give you the heir and sufficient spares."

The Duke chuckled. "And some girls, hopefully, to fill out the tally."

"Three boys and three girls, just as Richard wants. We'll keep going till we have them all. Maybe we'll marry off one of them into the Mountbatten-Windsors."

"Parvenu Huns."

"Or not."

The old man waved his fingers dismissively. "Doesn't matter. As long as you make my grandson happy. He's very special, Richard is. I always knew that. Never really told him so until you came along and made me. You were quite right to make me go to see him in concert; I only wish I'd gone sooner. Too late now. But you're special too."

He was silent for a while, and Rennie respected his silence. "Our kind of show is just about over," he said then. "By the time you two come to the job, very few people will be living like this." He gestured around him. "Maybe that's the way it's supposed to be, and all for the best. Still, this has been going a long time, and I should be sorry to see it end. But then I won't have to."

Rennie smiled and patted his hand. "Well, Duke, rock stars, at least, will still be living like this. So he's got it covered either way. And we *will* keep it going. For as long as it needs to. I promise that too."

ꙮ

Hilary Oliver Richard Arthur Tarrant, fifteenth Duke of Locksley, nineteenth Marquess of Raxton, thirty-second Earl of Saltire, Viscount Estover, Baron Cheriton, Baron Kelder, Baron Wedmore, VC, KG, GCB, DSO, died peacefully two days later, his family by his bedside. The next day, Rennie took the early train to London to pick up her mourning outfit. Turk's mother had suggested Chanel, but Rennie, who'd had quite enough of that sort of thing with Marjorie Lacing, had other ideas, and as soon as she had arrived at Locksley Hall, she had phoned her good friend Punkins Parker and thrown herself on her mercy.

Good thing Punks had her measurements on file. The designer had instantly risen to the occasion and worked day and night, putting her entire studio on the job, to whip up appropriate mourning threads for the future marchioness. Now, half an hour before the funeral, Rennie stared at herself in the tall gilt-framed bedroom mirror. *God, how grownup I look—kind of scary...* But Punks had outdone herself: Rennie was wearing a superbly cut black crèpe A-line dress that Jackie Kennedy would not have scorned to wear to her husband's obsequies; sheer black stockings and black leather court shoes completed the ensemble. A bouclé wool coat collared with fox lay on the chest at the foot of the bed, with a matching fur muff and long leather gloves, all of it unrelievedly funereal in coloration.

Sitting in the window seat, staring out at the autumnal landscape while she dressed, Turk too was somberly clad: it was only the third time Rennie'd ever seen him in *any* kind of a suit, let alone traditional English morning dress, as was correct for a funeral. He looked quite smashingly sexy—though she probably shouldn't have been thinking that at the moment—but he'd drawn the line at the requisite top hat, and his father hadn't insisted. Catching her eye, he turned abruptly and went out, muttering something about seeing to something, but she knew he just required a moment or two alone. Missing the tour was the least of his worries; the band had been scheduled for a break, and nobody had a problem with postponing a few gigs—they could always fit them in somewhere.

Herself garbed for the service, Agatha, Duchess of Locksley, came in a few minutes later and held out a long black chiffon veil, nodding approvingly at Rennie's attire. "Most suitable. If you'd also wear this, my dear? It's the tradition. Just for the chapel and up to the mausoleum. The Dowager, the new Duchess and the wife of the new Marquess all wear them."

I like you a lot, Your brand-new Grace and future Mum-in-law, but dear God, how Jane Austen is this going to GET?

"But I'm not—"

"But you will be. You're wearing the ring, and that's what matters. So, if you wouldn't mind terribly? It's for Richard, really. Later, he'll be glad you did. And so will you."

And she could not refuse.

So it was, on an overcast Yorkshire morning, that Rennie entered the ancient Locksley Hall chapel at Turk's side, her hair pinned up under the flat crèpe pillbox that held the veil in place. Apart from her ring, her only jewels were her great-aunt's double strand of pearls and a large antique diamond brooch borrowed from Turk's grandmother. White jewelry—diamonds and pearls, modernly acceptable mourning ornaments. If the Queen wore it, which she did—as Rennie could perfectly well see, since Her Majesty was sitting RIGHT OVER THERE—it was okay. All these new things to learn, all these feet to put wrong. Like a centipede worried about which one comes next. But she had always been a quick study; and as with the centipede, the trick was to just not think too much about it. And she could certainly do that.

The procession of chief mourners was according to family protocol: Turk's father entered escorting the Dowager Duchess; the late Duke's casket already reposed before the altar, covered with a heavy gold-fringed pall bearing the family arms and his ducal coronet placed atop it. They were followed by Duchess Agatha on the arm of her husband's elder younger brother, Lord Rupert, and finally by Richard, Marquess of Raxton, and his affianced lady. Other family members and castle staff were already seated in the pews on the right, with honored guests and friends, including several major royals and the most major royal of all, longtime intimates of both the late Duke and the new one, on the left.

Looking stylistically contextual for the fourteenth-century chapel—seventeenth-century hair and beard, eighteenth-century caped topcoat, nineteenth-century cutaway coat, waistcoat and trousers—Turk was off somewhere within himself, almost oblivious to his surroundings, the way he got in performance. Rennie, her hand on his cashmere-coated sleeve, both to give comfort and to feel comforted in turn, was acutely conscious of the covert attention focused on the two of them, and with some relief, and shaking a little, she took her seat beside him in the high-backed family pew, grateful for the bit of privacy it gave them. And even more grateful for the unobtrusive electric space heater bar down by their feet: the royal pew enjoyed the same modest comfort, but everyone else had to shiver in the chapel's freezing chill, and had dressed accordingly.

The high-church service, conducted by the Dowager Duchess's younger brother the Bishop of Shropshire, was brief and satisfyingly gloomy, the music and hymns having been impeccably selected by Turk. Halfway through, the new Marquess reached for Rennie's gloved hand, and she raised his to her lips and kissed it, then drew it into the fox-fur muff—despite his own gloves and the heater, his fingers were icy. They held hands for the rest of the service, and all the way back up the aisle, following the casket outside to the row of black Daimlers that would convey the family and important mourners to the mausoleum.

When they emerged into splintered rays of sunlight piercing dramatic clouds, Rennie's hand tightened on Turk's arm, her eyes wide with surprise: a Victorian funeral coach stood there, its engraved-glass sides framing the casket placed within, a tall bunch of black ostrich feathers at each corner. It was drawn by six splendid Friesians, with black plumes on their bridles and black ribbons in their manes, a Dickensianly garbed driver in mourning bands on the box. As soon as everyone was settled in the cars, the coach set out on its slow journey out of the castle courtyard, to the ducal mausoleum that crowned the hill across a little valley from the Hall, about two miles away, and the cars crept after.

Wow! I see that ye olde Englishe tradition is alive and flourishing, even in death. Or maybe especially in death... Rennie, who after seeing the funeral coach had been half-expecting a row of sleek black broughams instead of sleek black limos, found herself seated in the lead car with Turk and the Dowager Duchess, who had asked that they both ride with her. There wasn't a whole lot of talk en route, but she got the feeling that the redoubtable old lady was comforted by her grandson's presence—by his youth and strength and the sense of continuity he brought her, and he'd always been her favorite grandchild. And by requesting Rennie's presence, she was giving a public blessing and stamp of approval, and Miss Stride was well aware of the honor.

The procession wound its way through crowds of locals standing silently to attention, lining both sides of the drive: the men baring their heads, the women making brief bobs and tossing single flowers as the funeral coach went by, and again as the Queen's car passed—for respect, not servility. Rennie found it surprisingly moving, and for Turk's sake, and the Dowager's, fought back tears that threatened on several occasions. At last they all came to the mausoleum, a severely classical monument that could be seen for many miles around, with an ancient family cemetery spreading out from the rear—only the dukes and their duchesses were entombed in the enormous domed edifice itself, all other Tarrants making do with slightly less grand monuments in the graveyard.

Rennie stood in the suddenly snow-flurried air beside a stone-faced Turk as his grandfather's coffin was carried past them into the mausoleum, by house and estate workers proud to do their duke one final service. She bent her face into the fur collar as the wind bit, and a flash of foresight came to her: this was where they themselves would one day end up, she and Turk, asleep together beneath the dome, among the bones of his ancestors going back hundreds and hundreds of years. It was a jarring thought, yet also an oddly comforting one.

"It was very strange," she said that night, lying in Turk's arms in the huge brocade-curtained bed. His rooms here at Locksley were even more over-the-top than those at Cleargrove or Tarrant House, but she had barely noticed, being concerned only with him. "To think I'll be with you someday forever in that vault, an ocean away from my family and friends."

He tightened his arms around her, kissed her hair. "You don't have to."

"But I want to. You're the one I want to sleep next to for the rest of time, alive or dead. That's the whole point. We'll be there together. And all the Tarrant dukes and duchesses before and after us. I like that idea. And that chapel we just buried your grandfather from is the one we'll be married in and the one our kids will be christened in and the one we'll be buried from ourselves one day. Continuity. I like that too. I like it a lot."

They spent the next four days at the Hall, helping his parents cope; the royals had left immediately after the lavish post-service luncheon for family and intimate friends, so at least that particular social complication had been removed. Turk had spent much time consulting with his father and the family solicitors, and Rennie had lent a helpful hand as needed to both duchesses, who had been very impressed with her. Now, bidding the senior Tarrants an affectionate farewell—they all desperately needed alone time of their own by now and they pretty much chased them away—Turk and Rennie were free to drive down to Cleargrove, and were there by suppertime, where they dined quietly in

Turk's rooms and went early to bed.

While overseeing the arrival of the luggage, the housemaid had amiably told her, "Breakfast is at nine, m'lady, in the yellow dining room, as you may remember from the last time you were here. But since you and his lordship are the only family members in residence, just you let the kitchen know if you don't feel like getting up early—and what with the funeral and all who could blame you, so sad, we had our own little gathering here in His late Grace's honor—and Chef will see that late breakfast is left out in the terrace room till eleven, or served up here if you'd rather, all quiet-like, or in bed if you find yourself too tired to come down. Whatever your ladyship likes."

'Your ladyship', forsooth! A bit premature for that, *I'm thinking, and I might have to put a stop to it. But maybe we all need to be getting used to the new reality…including me…* She had hastily put in a request for late breakfast for two in the terrace room, nothing elaborate please, and the girl smiled benevolently upon her and went away, leaving her to do some desultory unpacking and a lot more staring aimlessly around the room.

Next morning, keeping up the look in a black silk Zandra Rhodes poet shirt and black pants and black boots and a choker of huge black keshi pearls, Rennie came down to the terrace room at five to eleven, and saw with delight that the table was set with the same Staffordshire transferware her grandmother had given her. Turk, who had gotten up an hour before she did, was now finishing up his own meal and reading the morning papers, most of which had pictures of them both splashed luridly across the news pages.

Rennie glanced over at the headlines, the theme of

which was, in varying terms and unvaryingly colossal point sizes, "Rock & Roll Duke and Duchess to Be". With photos of both of them. Oh, hell. Well, it couldn't be helped, and they should have expected that tabloid photographers would sneak into the crowd of locals outside the castle. At least Fitz's papers were decently subdued about it, because Fitz knew she would slaughter him like a hog if they weren't. She gave Turk an assessing glance: he looked a little tired, but apart from that he seemed unstressed and even cheerful. He had rebelled against the mourning color scheme, or lack of color scheme, and was dressed in faded cords and a white shirt, with a nice moss-green sweater she'd seen him wear before but at the moment couldn't remember where.

She chose to ignore the papers—he'd almost certainly scanned all the relevant stories, and probably felt like discussing them even less than she did—and raised her teacup to him instead.

"Look at this, Flash, it's the same china we have at home, the stuff I got from my grandma."

"Half the grannies in Great Britain have it. I always loved it as a little boy, because it has pictures of historic British castles and Locksley is on the soup plates. That's how I knew we were meant for each other," he added, "when I noticed you had it too."

"I see." She tucked into the plate of food she'd fetched from the row of silver chafing dishes on the sideboard: poached eggs, sausage, bacon, ham, potato cakes, grilled tomatoes, buttered toast. *'Nothing elaborate', indeed!* But she was really hungry.

"What are we doing today? *Can* we do anything? Do we have to hang around and reflect on mortality? Are you okay?"

Turk reached over and forked a fat sausage from her plate. "Whatever you like, and yes we can, and no not a bit, and yes I really am. Actually, I thought we might run over to Pacings and spend the day with the Sonnets—does that sound appealing? Gray rang up earlier, whilst you were still snoring like a sloth, and asked us. Condolences, of course," he added. "From him and Prue and Snapper and Sacharissa."

"Get your own damn food if you're still hungry, Your Marquessness, and keep your mitts off mine… Yeah, we could do that, that would be good. Very kind of Graham and Prunella to ask us. And I do *not* snore. Or, if I do, it is delicately and teensily adorable, the way a kitten snores. But I don't."

"Like a piglet." Turk turned a page of the paper he was reading. "Like baby bears."

Rennie grinned. "Fine, *whatever*, let's go to Pacers. It occurs to me how very pleasant it would be to have a nice day by ourselves. You and Gray can hang out and do guy stuff, and Prue and I can drive into Bath or Bristol or Salisbury and buy things. I know this antique jewelry shop…"

"You always know an antique jewelry shop."

When they finished breakfast, Rennie went upstairs to fetch her jacket and bag. Meeting Turk in the huge vaulted entry hall, they went out the front doors and down the sweep of steps, to where his car had been brought round and was standing on the manicured gravel drive, waiting for them.

Rennie stopped on the bottom step to stare. "Wow! I say again—wow."

"Glad you like it." Turk beheld his trusty steed with

affection and pride. It deserved both: a 1938 Bentley roadster, with big fenders and running boards, classic British racing green with a black leather interior.

"It's terrific," said Rennie, patting its nose as if it had been a pampered pony—she knew not to feed it a sugar lump—then climbing in and settling herself next to Turk. "I love the Porsche, of course, but this is really special. Where was it the last two times we were here?"

"In the carriage house, undergoing some restoration. My great-uncle the Bishop gave it to me when I went up to Oxford," he said, starting it up with a satisfactory roar and bone-shaking idle. "He knew I loved the car, and afterwards, when I was disowned and trying to get the band started, he paid for the petrol and insurance and road tax and upkeep because I was so poor. I must have been the only starving musician in England who drove a classic Bentley. Uncle Bish had bought it new, back in the day, and to hear my great-aunt tell it, he took better care of the car than he did of his children, or indeed his parishioners. But he is after all a bishop, a pretty senior one too by now, and Sniffy—that's the Archbishop of Canterbury—thought he shouldn't be zipping around in a sportscar that so loudly bespeaketh the world, if not the flesh and the devil also."

"What does he drive now?"

"A Roller."

"Of *course* he does!"

As they arrived in the Pacings courtyard, Gray came tearing out to greet the car, which he'd never met before. Turk got out to join him in enthusiastic discussion, and their women left them to it.

"Guys and their dick extenders," said Prue, hugging Rennie and shaking her head. "Gray's even worse. You should see what *he's* got out in the car barn."

"Oddly enough, even the guys who really don't *need* their dicks extended seem to go in for deeply phallic vehicles. Either that or cars a teenage girl in the Midwest would drive."

"I've noticed that too. Well, they'll be messing about with the bonnets up for hours. It'll divert Turk's fine mind from his grandfather, yes? Come on, let's get the Rover and go shopping in, let's see, Bath, I think. You look as if you need to get *your* fine mind diverted from your approaching marchionessity oh my GOD is that the *RING*? You could choke a Doberman with that! Let's have a look, then…"

"What did you and the She-Sonnet do today?" Turk asked as they were driving back to Cleargrove after tea. "Besides shop, I mean. Very pretty earrings, by the way. And thank you again for the shirts and the books."

Rennie cast a swift look sideways. "Oh…you're most welcome. Well, we, you know, talked. She had some things to say about your sad though inevitable ascension in the ranks of the British peerage. It's interesting, really," she continued, staring straight ahead at the country road unspooling under the Bentley's wheels, and putting a hand on Turk's thigh, sensing his sudden stillness. "You're the one and only rock star that the British high aristocracy has to date cast up on the beach. You'd think there would be more, or at least more musicians and writers and painters? Just going by sheer numbers. It seems strange that out of a gene pool of thousands, there should be so few artists. But you're the first pop idol to come out of Debrett's since Georgie Byron."

He laughed, relieved. "That sort of thing is rather

rigorously discouraged in families like mine, as no doubt you've noticed. We don't breed for art, we breed for breeding. I was lucky that my mother thought it was good for me to learn piano at a very young age, and when I proved not untalented, she made sure I continued, even in the face of my grandfather's displeasure. He pitched a fit about it—no grandson of his was going to do anything as poncy as play a musical instrument. Especially the heir to his title. And, being a duke, he was accustomed to getting his own way. Whilst Mummie, being an independently wealthy commoner with a will of tempered steel, was every bit as accustomed to getting *her* own way, and she pitched an even bigger fit. It was a conflict for the ages, a battle of the titans. Cleargrove and Locksley and Tarrant House and probably England itself shook with the reverberations of combat. Like the Irresistible Force meeting the Immovable Object. But in the end she triumphed."

"And then when you turned pro she pitched another fit. The biggest of all. Until you told her your marriage plans anyway."

"Well, encouraging artiness goes only so far."

"I see. And the world-spanning fame that came with it?"

"Oh, they're of at least two minds about that. On the one hand, they think it's quite deplorable for me to be out there being so publicly and familiarly known to the unwashed masses; on the other, they reason that since I insist on doing this, it's infinitely preferable that I should be top of the heap, since after all I *am* a Tarrant and that is where we belong by divine right. But we agreed from the start that I should keep my secret identity going for as long as I could. Suited us all, for our own differing little reasons."

"Until you got arrested for murder and blew it all

straight to hell."

"Yes, well, there's that."

"And got involved with an ink-stained wretch of a reporter who happens to be a murder magnet and, oh yeah, not yet de-wedded either."

"That too." He reached over and took her beringed left hand and kissed it. "Although I hear she's properly affianced at the moment."

"Yes, I've heard that myself… I phoned Stephen before we left Locksley, and told him to expedite the annulment proceedings," she said then.

She felt Turk's joyful start of surprise, but didn't look at him. "We've been lazy long enough, he and I; there was no excuse but sheer inertia. You and Ling have been angels of patience. Anyway, as I told your granddad, annulment is the way to go, rather than divorce. Since we only had that little justice of the peace elopement in Maryland, it'll be a piece of cake; most of the work has already been done over the course of the separation—we filed for annulment as soon as we lawfully parted company, and it's been three years, after all. Neither of us will contest it, and it's only a matter of signing off on the paperwork. Stephen made noises about a pile of alimony, but I'd rather not take anything at all from that lot. Getting legally pruned from the branches of the Lacing family tree will be reward enough. They can swing from branch to branch without me from now on, hooting and gibbering amongst themselves."

When he didn't answer immediately, she looked over; he was smiling. "You're in for it now, sweetheart," he said then, catching her glance, his smile widening. "Three hundred guests, the castle chapel at Locksley, the Raxton tiara—now that I'm Raxton and not Saltire anymore—not forgetting Auntie Lilibet and her dear little handbag…the whole package."

"I love any package of yours."

"So you keep telling me. And so I love to hear. And speaking of which—I remind you again that we'll be required to reproduce."

"Can't wait to start trying, Raxton. Your grandfather and I even discussed it."

Turk almost drove the Bentley into an adjacent hedgerow. "*WHAT?*"

Rennie was laughing, remembering. "When I was at Cleargrove that first exciting evening, back in February. Your mum had been creatively grilling me for an hour after dinner—and let me tell you, she's good, but she's nowhere *near* the same league as Marjorie Lacing, who is a 9.5 at least on the open-ended Torquemada Torture Scale for Daughters-in-law—when His Grace rescued, er, fetched me out, and dragged me off to the portrait gallery for a quiet chat about my fertility."

"Oh dear God, I am *so* sorry…"

"No, no, we had a nice little talk. Kind of sweet, really. He just wanted to make sure you were depositing the Tarrant DNA into the right maximum-yield account, and who could blame him. He reminded me about it when we had our little private convo at Locksley, before he died. Oh, and he also made me promise never to let any child of ours marry a royal."

"No fear!" said Turk fervently. "But we have to have them first. Which means we have to get married first."

Rennie pretended to consult an imaginary datebook. "We've already missed one October, so how does October 1970 sound? Nice and cool, lovely autumn colors… Stephen and the General will make sure the annulment activates at lightspeed, now that Ling is pregnant—oh yes, she is! Eric told me when I asked to borrow the plane, and in the midst of everything else going on I forgot to tell you. Another incentive for speedy action, as they want to have a quick San Francisco ceremony, to get the sprog safely born in lawful wedlock, and then a big fat Hong Kong wedding next summer. So say Thanksgiving for the annulment to kick in; then at New Year's, like the Queen's Honours List, our formal engagement announcement appears in all three Timeses—London, New York and L.A. The rest of the time goes for wedding prep. Then, as your people so strangely put it, Bob's your uncle. Though Bob's certainly not going to be my husband. It seems like a long time, but it's really nowhere near as long as it sounds."

"Time enough for the solicitors to work up their whacking great settlements and jointures and dowers and portions and entails. Be warned—you'll be signing papers for a week."

"Not to mention time enough for Her Godmotherly Majesty to write it into her schedule."

"She'll be ready to leave Balmoral by then; she can pop in at Locksley on her way back to London." He swung the car off the motorway and onto the familiar B-road that led through several preposterously charming villages to the gates of Cleargrove. "October at the Hall is incredibly beautiful. Your ladies can wear velvet, and I can wear manly suede and leather with the rest of my blokes. Gray and Ares, of course. Rardi. My cousin Oliver."

"A fine studly group!"

"Punkins to design our wedding garb, of course."

"Damn straight! I categorically refuse to get myself up in

dreary bourgeois white satin, like those dull little suburban chicks I went to school with. And you are *not* wearing a morning suit."

"Indeed I am not. We have far better taste, you and I."

"Indeed we do. Punks can do the clothes for the whole wedding party, she'll have a blast."

"Any ideas for your brideswomen?"

"Prax and Prue, no question. Berry Rosenbaum. Belinda Melbourne. If I ask one sister the other will be upset, and six attendants is too many, so no sibs. And I love that Brit custom of adorable little kids as mini-bridesmaids and pageboys."

"Plenty of tinies to choose from."

"And the Raxton tiara, you said? Of course, it's not as if I've never worn a tiara, after all…in fact, I once wore a tiara that belonged to the whore who founded the Lacing family fortunes. No, really, she was an actual, working hooker; she ran a very successful and classy bordello, even. And she was, with the exception of my lovely gay brother-in-law, the only Lacing I remotely enjoyed being related to. Let me tell you about her."

They spent a quiet evening, Turk playing Bach fugues on the piano in their sitting room while Rennie packed their bags for their return to the States the next day—an evening flight to JFK out of Heathrow, overnight in the city, then on to Des Moines for Turk, meeting up with the band. She could have had a maid take care of the packing, of course, but she had resolved to put off that sort of thing for as long as possible. She was perfectly capable of stuffing four pieces of luggage on her own; besides, they were leaving most of the clothes here anyway, for their next visit.

Turk was anxious to get back to the tour, as much to take his mind off his grandfather as to satisfy his Lionheart obligations, though thanks to some inspired schedule juggling by Francher the band had to make up only three concerts; and Rennie herself was looking forward to being back in New York—already the prow house was home. After they'd finally gone to bed, he lay stretched out beside her, unmoving, and she looked over at him, thinking she knew the cause of his apparent disinclination, and touched his cheek, putting just the right amount of sympathy into her tone.

"A hell of a way for us to get a week off in the middle of the tour."

He smiled, as she had intended, but she could see the effort it cost him. "New Orleans would have been preferable."

She trailed her hand down his chest. "Not tonight? To take your mind off things? I'll even do all the work... Or would you like to just cuddle, then, or talk about your grandfather, or anything at all?"

"Actually, I think I *would* like that, all those." He stared up at the pleated gold silk underside of the bed canopy, way up by the ceiling some twenty feet above their heads. "It's something I've known was coming my whole life. And now that it's finally happened...apart from the Guv'nor being gone, I really oughtn't to feel so upset, or however it is I do feel. I wasn't expecting to feel like *this*, though I suppose I should have been. I was *born* the Earl of Saltire, so I never had to deal with this before."

Rennie heard the changing mood in his voice, moved to grab the reins before it got out of control. "Honey, why on earth *shouldn't* you be upset? Just because you knew this would happen one day doesn't mean you can't be sad and scared and unhappy now that it has. There's a lot more to it, though, isn't there?"

He was silent for a moment or two, aware of what she was doing, undecided if he was going to let it happen. Then: "You know how I feel about history, and my family's place in it, and my place in the family. But all the other peers of this kingdom, how are *they* going to feel when an unregenerate rock and roller enters their sacred velvet-and-ermine'd ranks? Because you know I'm never giving up my music, no matter what. And I'm never giving up my title, either. *Our* title... At least as a courtesy earl Richard was still under their radar, especially using Turk's name. Ever since we got here, though, I've had the sense that I've kind of lost that protection now, and will only lose it all the more as we go on."

She twisted onto her stomach and propped herself up on her forearms. "Why should you care the teeniest tiniest toss how the hell they feel? They should be more concerned with how *you* feel. Yes, Turk, they should! This has been coming to you down the centuries for over a thousand years, if my math is correct. It doesn't *get* any more destined and descentful than that. And you deserve it as much as any of them. More. Because you've never been anything but humble and gracious and modest about it. Because you've actually worked with your hands for a living and earned your keep and gone hungry and homeless sometimes even, the way real, regular people do. Because you don't act like an arrogant condescending dickhead. Because, unlike them, you have so much more going for you than a title. Let *them* learn how to deal with *you*, and if they can't, then let them just put a sock in it. What can they do to you anyway, kick you out of the duke club?"

He was still uncertain. "You make me sound like Little Lord Fauntleroy."

"Hey, nothing wrong with that! Young Ceddie gets an undeserved bad rap. He was quite the decent bloke, and no pantywaist either. Not unlike Fauntleroy, you too have been challenging your class's sensibilities ever since you were a lad—they should be used to it by now, the walking fossils. I know you have great respect for your ancient family and class traditions, and so you should, but you have to have respect for your own new personal traditions as well. And so must they. You're going to be a *duke*, for God's sake; *you're* going to be the one who sets the pattern for *them*. Rank really doth hath its privileges. You should look forward to demonstrating that. Besides, isn't there a fine British tradition of eccentric peers down the ages? You'll fit right in."

"You seem to have it all sussed. Well, no surprise there."

She studied his face, put a gentle hand over his heart. "But that's still not the bottom line, is it. You're thinking about your dad and you. When the time comes—and God willing it's a long, *long* way away."

Turk gave her a haunted look. "I *am* thinking about that. It's a horrible system, isn't it, that requires you to lose a parent before you can assume your supposedly rightful place."

"Quite horrible, yes, how typical of you Brits to have dreamt it up. But you've *already* assumed your rightful place, my love. Yes, you have. And you earned it yourself. It didn't need anyone to die, or anyone to bestow it upon you in suitable ceremony. It's yours. It's always been yours. And I've been with you for some of it. As for the rest of it—

not to worry. I'll be with you for that too. For all of it. Slider and Strider."

He smiled at last. "Duke Richard and Duchess Ravenna."

"Yeah—but it doesn't matter anymore. I wouldn't be wearing this"—she flicked the ring—"if it did. Being consort to a rock star is one thing. Being consort to a duke—quite another. But." She kissed his throat beneath the beard and put her arm across his bare chest. "My lord Earl...my lord Marquess...Your Grace the Duke...Mr. Guitar God...it's all still you."

Turk shivered once, head to foot, and laid his head on her breast as she pulled him to her. "It's one step the nearer now, though."

"It is." She tightened her grip. "It is. But never you mind. Never you mind. We're bringing rock and roll right along with us. Whether rock and roll likes it or not."

Home Before Dark

I was crying in the sunlight on the floor
Broken toys around me
I was running in the sea so far from shore
Then you came and found me

I was freezing in the snowy winter chill
I was cold and lonely
I was standing in the wind upon the hill
Seeing you only

But now the night is falling fast
Sunset clouded, blue dusk dim
Darkness coming like a wave
Still one star on heaven's rim

Home before dark
I don't want to be out here
alone in the night
Home before dark
Take me to where it's warm
and safe and bright

[bridge]

I can sing myself a planet
I can write myself a home
I can weave myself an ocean
I can build myself a poem

But I can't get home before dark
I need your light to help me make it
It's no walk in the park
Please promise me you won't forsake it

Don't let it get so dark
that I can't see your face
I need to find my way
In this lost and lonely place

Don't stray so far from me
that I can't touch your hand
Head homeward with me now
through this wild and empty land

[bridge]

Home before dark
I don't know if I have the strength to get there
Home before dark
I can see that the two of us aren't yet there

Home before dark
And I need for you to be coming with me
Home before dark
'Cause I never want you to stop running with me

A long time back you left your loving mark
Now help me get my heart home before dark

~Turk Wayland

From the forthcoming Rennie Stride Mystery,

Scareway to Heaven: Murder at the Fillmore East,

sixth in the series and scheduled for release in

early 2013…

Prologue

December, 1969, New York City

*I*N THE LIGHTLY *falling snow, the Art Deco-styled theater marquee looms bright as an ocean liner. Beneath its shelter, masses of young people, in Navy peacoats and Army-surplus jackets and long Victorian cloaks and embroidered sheepskin Afghan coats, mill and shuffle in the cold like steerage passengers on the Titanic, all steaming breath and stamping feet, waiting for the doors to open for the night's final show.*

The place has had several lives: first it was a Yiddish theater, then it became the Village Theater, and now it is the Fillmore East, best and hippest rock venue on the Eastern Seaboard; some would say best in the world.

The heavy bronze doors, sculptural and polished, finally swing open, and the crowd begins to file inside, hooting and laughing, handing their tickets to the heads in green jerseys who stand smiling to collect them; clouds of pot smoke hang in the air. Just past the ticket-takers there is a bright mirrored lobby, and past that, the auditorium itself. Much of its original ornateness, now a trifle shabby, has been faithfully maintained: everywhere marble and plush and velvet, a huge central crystal chandelier, a heavy crimson curtain, gilt and fancy molding on the fronts of the mezzanine and balcony and boxes.

From the lobby, a sweeping staircase with brass banisters leads up to a fancy second-floor foyer, now the refreshment area, behind the mezzanine level. Two small stage boxes, gilded and curtained, flank the fancy proscenium arch: sound equipment in one, lighting paraphernalia in the other. The sound booth on the right-hand side has a dual purpose: it serves as a VIP hideaway for visiting notables, rock and otherwise, to watch the show in private, concealed from the audience by a semicircle of velvet curtain.

A utilitarian flight of stairs leads up from backstage to two floors of even more utilitarian dressing rooms—the kind of décor that would not look out of place in a politburo meeting hall in a drab city in Bulgaria. The most impressive thing about the dressing rooms is the people who use them: rock royalty, various ranks of lower rock peerage, and those who aspire to serve, or ascend to, either or both.

Down on the stage, the blue-lit work area is narrow, but it runs the full width of the house, with turntables to hold the heavy and bulky band equipment, tiers for the light show built like rabbit cages against the back wall, and tall loading doors that open right onto East Sixth Street.

Bill Graham, owner, promoter and master of ceremonies, scuttles around like Groucho Marx on speed, swearing at people, hugging people, running down people who don't leap aside fast enough. He wears two wristwatches, the one on his left wrist showing West

Coast time, the other set to Eastern; he claims it saves endless mental arithmetic, sparing him from always adding or subtracting three hours. Ever since he began dividing his time between two coasts and two Fillmores, West and East, he has worn the twin timepieces.

Blond, bespectacled Kip Cohen walks by on his way to the tiny cluttered office just off the lobby, smiling serenely; Graham's second in command, the managing director for the venue, he looks like a scholar of troubadour poetry in the original Provençal, not a power in the rockerverse. Large and imposing Kim Yarbrough, chief of security, watches as the excited crowd streams past, and confers with his house-t-shirted lieutenants.

After twenty minutes of scurry and scrum, the lights dim, the curtain goes up, the crowd settles down. Bill comes out onstage to greet the audience and announce the lineup, then introduces the opening act, who nervously troop out to grab their axes. Then the first real note of music rings out, beginning the continuous buzzing build all the way through to the headliner. Showtime!

Outside at two in the morning; both shows are over and the neighborhood has settled down for the night. Second Avenue is strangely quiet in the snow that has been falling steadily since before midnight. The streetlamps are fat fuzzy spheres of yellow light, fleets of snowflakes driving silently past. There is not a single vehicle moving on the avenue: no headlights as far as the eye can see, just the jewelled Christmasy flicker of traffic signals and the blowing snow like diamond dust in the road.

On the narrow, uneven sidewalks around Sixth Street, no one has lingered outside in the cold. The musicians have long since split for parties and hotel rooms and bars and beds, their own or someone else's; the fans have dispersed, happy, sated and stoned; the Fillmore stage and cleanup and front office crews are still busy inside wrapping up the night's business.

Some of the audience and performers alike have hit one of the nearby all-night Ukrainian restaurants; they can be seen through the steamed-up plate-glass windows, tucking into big bowls of soup, borscht or mushroom barley or chicken noodle, plates of pierogis, burgers, omelets and home fries. Two blocks up on the corner of St. Mark's Place, people are hanging around Gem's Spa, drinking egg creams or coffee, eating pretzels, unwilling or unable to go home, or just waiting for the next interesting thing to come along.

A few blocks south, on East Second Street, erratic wavering footprints lead in from the avenue, marring the smooth whiteness. Sudden noise and laughter as three stoned people stagger up to the gates of the old cemetery, a surprisingly large expanse of trees and shrubs, the ornate tombs now mantled by snow. They consult briefly, then heave themselves clumsily up and over the high wrought-iron fence and gates: two young men, and a young woman whom they both pull up after them, one hauling on each arm. They are all still laughing as they run and stumble through the quiet graveyard, coming to rest at last in the lee of one of the largest and most dramatic monuments, their backs set against the cold, cold stone.

After a while, it grows quiet. One figure leaves; another enters, and leaves again shortly after. Then everything is very, very *quiet.*

Chapter One

Three weeks earlier

GOD, SHE LOVED NEW YORK. It was so nice being back. L.A. had been, well, L.A., there had certainly been moments; and San Francisco had of course been wonderful. But this was home, this was *her* home: clever, vital, grimy, sublimely uncaring of anything beyond its rivers.

"I never actually lived in New York before," Turk observed, mirroring his mate's thought as the pair of them so often did, and Rennie glanced up at him as they walked. "Just stayed for a month or so at a time on several occasions, at assorted rock dive hotels like the Albert and the Henry Hudson, back when we were getting started and playing clubs in the West Village or uptown. It's a real city, like London. All the little villages running together. I love the energy, too. Like Rome must have been, back in the day."

"Oh, we're better than Rome. We're the mightiest city that

ever was. And I think you know what a very lucky boy you are to be living here."

Turk Wayland and Rennie Stride were heading down East Tenth Street from the Second Avenue Deli, half a block to their brownstone across from St. Mark's Church, laden down with shopping bags full of containers of chicken soup and barbecued chicken and grilled hot dogs and fried potatoes and corned-beef sandwiches in wodges so massive that you had to unhinge your jaw like a python to take a bite. Recent snow lay in streaky patches on the ground: it was much, much colder than usual for mid-November. For the tiny distance they had to cover, they were dressed very warmly, and they were walking fast even for New Yorkers.

Back in February, when they had first become engaged, they had decided to keep their Hollywood Hills house but move their base of operations to Manhattan. It was three thousand miles closer to England, for one thing, and Turk now had new obligations in his native land for which New York would be a lot more convenient. After seven years, he was weary of his band Lionheart's endless touring, and he wanted to go off the road for a year while he figured out the group's next direction and worked on the music to take them there. After that, he intended that he and Rennie should live like grownups: six months a year in New York, split the rest of their time between L.A. and England, schedule subject to change without notice. So Rennie had gone up to San Francisco, closed down her flat in the Haight, arranged to have everything shipped east and come ahead on her own to look for a place for them.

She was a New York girl, and she was absolutely thrilled to be moving back home again after four years in West Coast exile. She'd been born in Park Slope and had grown up there and in Forest Hills and Riverdale; after graduating from Cornell she had attended journalism school at Columbia, and she'd never imagined living anywhere but Manhattan for the rest of her life. The only borough she hadn't lived in was Staten Island, because, you know, *why*? Then she'd met and eloped with young corporate lawyer Stephen Lacing, and he'd made her drop out of grad school and dragged her out west to his hometown by the Golden Gate. It hadn't taken long for her to cut herself loose, though: she'd walked out on him and his super-wealthy society family after less than a year of unhappy wedlock—'lock' being the operative syllable—and once she'd gotten into the San Francisco rock scene she so badly wanted to be in, she'd stayed on.

Then she'd moved to L.A., where she and Turk had crossed fated paths, and they'd fallen in love, and she'd been living with him in his Nichols Canyon house ever since. Still, she'd never thought of herself as anything but a New Yorker.

And she knew her way around her island. But she dutifully checked out all possible neighborhoods when Turk had said go look for a house we can buy, just so she could tell him with a clear conscience that she had done so when they ended up living where she had planned on them living all along.

It had been great fun imperiously ruling out vast tracts of Manhattan real estate. Upper West Side: too uptown. Upper East Side: too uptight. West Village: possible, but only with care—Near West Village, smug; Far West Village, thugs. Gramercy Park: gorgeous houses, but however much Turk and Rennie might protest that they were quiet and well-behaved—which they really were, just a girl from the boroughs and a boy from an English castle or two, or six—the gas-lit Gramercians would never cotton to a notorious rock and roll couple in their midst. Especially not with that superstar thing of Turk's attracting fannish hordes; not to mention that pesky murder trip Rennie had going. Oh well, their loss. The Gramercians', not Turk's and Rennie's. There was a new area called SoHo, *So*uth of *Ho*uston: huge loft spaces in former factories now coming available for people to live in, but it was like opening up the frontier—you had to walk miles to forage for food and the only laundry option was to go down to the river and smack it on a couple of stones. And despite her Columbia sojourn, in an enormous apartment across the street from the cathedral of St. John the Divine, anything above the top latitudes of Central Park, East Side or West, was strictly Here Be Dragons territory.

Which left the East Village. Not as pretty as its western counterpart, but cool and historic and edgy, the perfect neighborhood: part young hippie and artist and student incomers, part elderly Ukrainians who'd supplanted Germans who'd supplanted Irish, part old Yiddish New York. All of which resulted in pleasingly ethnic restaurants and craft shops and boutiques and old theaters and clubs and, yes, food stores and laundries, all up and down the avenues and the side streets and over to Tompkins Square Park—much east of that few people ventured, as it was still a little too hardcore. But in 1969, from Third Avenue to Avenue A, Houston to Fourteenth Street, was really the hippest possible place for a hip rock and roll couple to hiply live.

But *where* could they live? They had a lot of desires, needs and requirements, especially Turk, so it wouldn't be easy to find somewhere suitable and they'd have to extensively, and expensively, buy and renovate it when they did—renting was right out. She'd inspected brownstones on St. Mark's Place and the tree-lined blocks facing the park, a mini-Plaza-Hotel-looking building on the corner of Third Avenue and Seventh Street, even deconsecrated churches and synagogues and a small terra-cotta office building on Astor Place.

Then she'd seen this: the prow house, as she immediately dubbed it, sitting like the front end of a ship right on the acute angle made by Tenth and Stuyvesant Streets as they converged in front of the eighteenth-century St. Mark's Church-in-the-Bouwerie. It was a beautiful old Victorian brownstone, with bay windows on the point like a ship's bridge, at the end of a terraced double row of equally beautiful houses. Prettiest house on the prettiest block in the whole East Village. She fell in love on the spot, and so did Turk, who when he came east to look at it was instantly reminded of London, of Edinburgh.

They bought the whole building, which cost a lot less than you'd think and was a lot smaller than it looked. Then Turk decided it wasn't going to be big enough, and bought the two adjoining buildings as well, one on Stuyvesant and the other on Tenth—you can do that when you're one of the most famous rock stars in the world and your father is the second-richest duke in England. And Rennie had at last made peace with those unalterable facts; she still insisted on chipping in her fair share—Turk realized it meant a lot to her to be able to do so—but someone's pride had had to be sacrificed to the relationship. She had known from the first, in her heart of hearts, that it would have to be hers, and she had worked her way to being okay with it.

At any rate, in a mere six months, at staggering expense and with consummate taste, and adding in colossal bribes to relocate tenants, the three smallish brownstones had been reconfigured into one largish V-shaped mansion: hangout space and a music room for Turk on the top story, newly skylighted and roof-gardened; a writing den for Rennie behind the fourth-floor bay window; and their duplex bedroom-sitting room behind the second- and third-floor ones. Eight guest suites—well, you need that many when your friends are always coming to town and your band is always wanting to crash; besides, a few would be required for nursery duty down the road.

Plus living room, dining room, morning room, breakfast room, two parlors and a library; big slate-floored ground-level kitchen down four wide, shallow steps from the dining room; a climate-controlled guitar vault and a seriously soundproofed recording studio down in the acres of cellars. Add a few unfinished rooms saved for future unspecified purposes, a house office, a private flat for Hudson Link, their newly hired live-in assistant, and her artist husband who doubled as handyman, a bunch of bathrooms, a tiny yard surrounding the street frontage and an equally tiny sliver of garden out back, and that was it. A lovely home for them and an absolutely brilliant investment for the Duchy of Locksley.

Friends had suggested that there might be problems with importunate fans if they didn't dwell in a giant doormanned uptown fortress like the Dakota, but Rennie wasn't worried. This was her native heath, and she knew her people: New Yorkers wouldn't cross the street for the Second Coming, bless their pointed little hearts, and it was considered incredibly uncool to annoy famous neighbors in their actual lives, like at the newsstand or the dry cleaners or the butcher's. Besides, in a building like the Dakota, they would never have the space, freedom or configuration they required. Not to mention the on-site studio.

Even if fans figured out who was living in the prow house, it wouldn't really matter. Oh, they might get a few Lionheart diehards hanging around for autographs, but Turk wasn't a Beatle, he didn't attract that ridiculous level of attention—and they'd take precautions against anything more serious, having learned their stalker lessons in L.A., the hard way. Apart from that, no true New Yorker ever even *looked* at any other New Yorker, and that was the way New Yorkers liked it.

The house was set well back from the sidewalk like all the others on the block, behind the wrought-iron-fenced garden area and a code-locked gate; they'd put in an alarm system, cameras and one-way glass, and once they added some more shrubbery and maybe a bit of casbah-style grillework, they'd be fine. This was the way they wanted to live, not shut up in some pretentious Park Avenue apartment building infested with Social-Register Republicans. Besides, Bob and Sara Dylan had recently moved themselves and their tots into a townhouse over on Macdougal Street, living there pretty much the way Turk and Rennie would be living here, and they hadn't had any problems. Well, except for that wack job who kept 'researching' their garbage.

Mental note to self: put bear traps in trashcans…

Speaking of bears, they had the dog now, a huge, Victorian-looking mahogany sable collie of ursine proportions—Macduff the Thane of Gondor, as they had frivolously named him when they rescued him from the ASPCA. But he was by no means as frivolous as they were, being as dignified and smart and cuddly and devoted as the best of his hyper-protective breed, beautifully behaved and always on the alert for trouble—to him, everybody was a possibly dangerous predator threatening his little flock.

And they'd left Turk's black Porsche and Rennie's burgundy Corvette back in L.A.: those wheels were too identifiable, and also too tempting to car thieves. Cars in Manhattan were a hassle anyway: you couldn't drive around on a daily basis without making yourself nuts. If they wanted to get away for weekends, they'd rent. Otherwise, they'd take subways and buses and taxis and limos and choppers and private jets like everybody else.

Turk had gotten into it immediately, the anonymity and ease. Realizing that he could go out on the street and no one would bug him, he'd quickly developed a routine of a morning walk with the dog to Tompkins Square Park and breakfast at one of the funky little Polish or Ukrainian coffee shops—Veselka on Second Avenue, Leshko's and Odessa over on A—where he would run into local artists or fellow musicians or Allan Ginsberg over the eggs and home fries.

As for location, location, location, it couldn't have been better for their needs and purposes: the Fillmore East a few short blocks south, hip little boutiques all over, the second-hand paradise of Fourth Avenue's Bookshop Row a brief stroll to the west, friends both old and new living in the neighborhood. It was perfect—a quiet, old-fashioned street lined with oaks, maples and flowering pear trees, with the sound of Westminster chimes from the bell tower of St. Mark's across the street. You wouldn't ordinarily think to find rock figures living in such staid surroundings; but both Turk and Rennie were far from ordinary rock figures.

"Doesn't he get hassled by fans all the time, walking around down there?" Prax McKenna, Rennie's best friend and a superstar herself, once asked. "He is, as you know, fairly recognizable."

Rennie had shaken her head. "Nope. First off, anyone tries to mess with him on the street, the dog rips their throat out. Plus he's this tall, strong guy, and he's been trained by your own adorably lethal boyfriend in unarmed combat—he could take anybody's head off with one deadly whack, no problem. But it's *not* a problem. Below Fourteenth and east of Third every cat looks like a rock star. Long hair, beard, boots—he blends right in. He just decides he's going to be anonymous—he turns off the Turkness, I've watched him do it, it's amazing—and so he is. He loves it. He even takes the subway."

"Oh, he's such a stud! And nobody ever recognizes him?"

"Couple of times, but only in context. Once outside the Fillmore when we went to see the Airplane; one time when he went up to Manny's Music to buy another damn guitar, how many freakin' axes do you people *need*, and someone rumbled him coming out of the store. Anyone else just thinks they're really, really stoned and it can't possibly be Turk Wayland sitting next to them at the movies eating popcorn. Besides, this is New York: don't look, don't ask, don't tell, don't care. It's not just a good idea, it's the *law*!"

Turk was home just now after the Miami gig, for a week's r&r: Lionheart was taking a well-deserved break from the killer tour schedule that had had them more or less continuously on the road since Woodstock, back in August. Now they were resting up, gathering their strength before the last few East

Coast dates and the big huge grand finale at Madison Square Garden the first Saturday in December. While the other guys had promptly fled Miami for the Bahamas and tropical beachy goodness, Turk had caught the first plane up to New York to join Rennie for *his* idea of a break, helping her put the final touches on the new place before their first houseguests started arriving. And she was glad and grateful, both for his presence and his assistance. But sometimes she looked at him and sighed and wondered why the hell they couldn't be on a beach in the Bahamas themselves…

Printed in Great Britain
by Amazon

65257022R00244